PRAISE FOR KENDRA ELLIOT

"Every family has skeletons. Kendra Elliot's tale of the Mills family's dark secrets is first-rate suspense. Dark and gripping, *The Last Sister* crescendos to knock-out, edge-of-your seat tension."

—Robert Dugoni, bestselling author of *My Sister's Grave*

"*The Last Sister* is exciting and suspenseful! Engaging characters and a complex plot kept me on the edge of my seat until the very last page."

—T.R. Ragan, bestselling author of the Jessie Cole series

"Kendra Elliot is a great suspense writer. Her characters are always solid. Her plots are always well thought out. Her pace is always just right."

—*Harlequin Junkie*

"Elliot delivers a fast-paced, tense thriller that plays up the small-town atmosphere and survivalist mentality, contrasting it against an increasingly connected world."

—*Publishers Weekly*

"Kendra Elliot goes from strength to strength in her Mercy Kilpatrick stories, and this fourth installment is a gripping, twisty, and complex narrative that will have fans rapt . . . Easily the most daring and successful book in this impressive series."

—*RT Book Reviews*

THE LAST SISTER

ALSO BY KENDRA ELLIOT

MERCY KILPATRICK NOVELS

A Merciful Death

A Merciful Truth

A Merciful Secret

A Merciful Silence

A Merciful Fate

A Merciful Promise

BONE SECRETS NOVELS

Hidden

Chilled

Buried

Alone

Known

BONE SECRETS NOVELLAS

Veiled

CALLAHAN & MCLANE NOVELS

PART OF THE BONE SECRETS WORLD

Vanished

Bridged

Spiraled

Targeted

ROGUE RIVER NOVELLAS

On Her Father's Grave (Rogue River)

Her Grave Secrets (Rogue River)

Dead in Her Tracks (Rogue Winter)

Death and Her Devotion (Rogue Vows)

Truth Be Told (Rogue Justice)

WIDOW'S ISLAND NOVELLAS

Close to the Bone

Bred in the Bone

THE LAST SISTER

KENDRA ELLIOT

Published by Montlake, Seattle

www.apub.com

ISBN-13: 9781542006729 (hardcover)
ISBN-10: 1542006724 (hardcover)

ISBN-13: 9781542006705 (paperback)
ISBN-10: 1542006708 (paperback)

Cover design by Caroline Teagle Johnson

Printed in the United States of America

First edition

For my girls

Memory is inherently unreliable. With time, it degrades. With trauma, it fragments. In isolation, it festers.

—Ellen Kirschman, PhD

1

She wrapped her shaking fingers in the hem of her sweater to avoid damaging any fingerprints as she slid open the rear patio door, following the trail of blood. Outside it was dark, daybreak still a few hours away, and the air was cold with the coast's salty mist.

The smeared blood went across the small porch and down the wood stairs. She followed, her heartbeat pounding in her head as she ignored the heavy smell of smoke in the air. The blood trail vanished in the grass and poor light, but she instinctively knew to check the woods at the back of the yard.

Something swayed in a tree. She couldn't breathe.

Please. Not again.

2

"Who disturbed the scene?"

FBI special agent Zander Wells tamped down a rare rise of temper as he stood behind the small home in Bartonville and stared at the surrounding tall firs. The blatant disregard for standard procedure—standard procedure *everywhere*—made him want to punch someone.

An unusual urge for him.

"My deputy is a rookie. He's young," said the gaunt Clatsop County sheriff, brushing rain from his cheek. "I think shock took over. Haven't had a violent death in this town in four years, and it didn't help that he knew the victims." Sheriff Greer shook his head, pity in his gaze. "He sincerely thought he was helping."

Zander exchanged a glance with FBI special agent Ava McLane. She rolled her eyes.

Fewer than a thousand people called Bartonville home. The tiny coastal town sat on the banks of the massive Columbia River, not far from where it emptied into the Pacific Ocean. The city was remote, separated from Oregon's heavily populated Willamette Valley by the hills of the Coast Range and thousands of acres of timber. Zander's drive from Portland had taken a little less than two hours.

At their feet one of the victims was zipped up in a body bag. Zander and Ava had silently viewed the young man inside before she'd gestured for the tech to close the bag. Ava's face had been blank, but a spark of rage had shown in her eyes. The man's face would be permanently imprinted on Zander's brain.

Along with the condition of the man's dead wife inside the home.

There had been a rocky start to the investigation. The first responding deputy had cut the rope when he saw Sean Fitch hanging from the backyard tree. Three other deputies had tramped through the scene and moved both bodies during their response. An initial declaration of a murder-suicide by the sheriff had wasted precious hours before the medical examiner showed up and disagreed.

The ME wasn't the only person who had questioned the sheriff's declaration. The witness who had reported the murders had later called the Portland FBI office to report that the hanged black man had a hate symbol sliced into his forehead. An upside-down triangle inside a larger triangle.

Sean Fitch's Caucasian wife had been stabbed over and over in their bedroom. It appeared Sean had been stabbed in the same room and then dragged out of the house and hanged.

"It doesn't reflect well on your department that a civilian had to report this as a possible hate crime." Zander stared at Greer as water dripped from the brim of the sheriff's hat. It wasn't raining; it was drizzling mist. The type of northern Oregon coastal weather that fooled you into believing it was safe to step outside, while in reality the dense mist clung to every inch of clothing and skin, drenching a person rapidly.

Greer grimaced and looked down at his boots. "We don't get racist shit like this in our county—and blood had obscured the cuts. I'm still not convinced that's what those marks represent."

Zander understood. The triangles weren't a commonly known Klan symbol. But the sheriff had been in law enforcement a long time.

He should have known something wasn't right.

"Even so, the noose and the victim's skin color were clear," said Ava. "If that's not a red flag, I don't know what is."

Greer shook his head. "That kind of crime doesn't happen here. Suicide is much more prevalent."

The small sheriff's office employed three detectives. Two were out of state, testifying in a trial, and the third was home with the flu. Sheriff Greer had started the initial investigation himself, without asking for help except from the state police crime lab, to process the scene.

Was the man rusty, Zander wondered, or just overconfident?

Either way, Zander and Ava now had a mess to unravel.

Zander stared at the mud under the tree. A dozen yellow numbered crime scene markers dotted the ground along with dozens of prints. A long depression where the body must have lain at one point. A length of rope. He looked up. Another piece of rope dangled from the branch. The bare deciduous tree stood out among the towering green firs; its pale, thick trunk and knotted branches alluded to a long, rough life.

The branch wasn't that high, but it'd been high enough.

"Two killers. At least," Ava muttered under her breath, and Zander silently agreed. Sean Fitch wasn't small. Hanging the man had taken effort.

Persons motivated to make a point.

Zander turned and walked back to the home, taking care not to walk through the obvious body drag trail where the killers had pulled the man out of the house—although several boot prints had already stomped through it. He paused and took a look at the burned brush against the back of the house, where the smell of gasoline permeated the air.

Someone had tried to burn the house and failed miserably. The siding was scorched, and a few bushes wouldn't survive.

"Not a lot of intelligence in that maneuver," Ava commented. "Maybe the fire was an afterthought?"

"They brought gasoline," said Zander.

"We're in a rural area. I bet plenty of people carry a gasoline can in the back of their truck."

"True. Possibly one of them panicked and thought they could cover up some evidence by burning down the house."

"They underestimated Oregon rain."

Zander stared at the darkened siding for a long moment, disturbed that it felt unconnected with the rest of the scene.

He moved up the concrete steps to the back door and slipped booties over his wet shoes. Ava joined him and covered her shoes too. They still wore gloves from their first quick pass through the house.

They stepped into the immaculate but aged yellow kitchen. He'd already looked for an indication that a knife was missing but hadn't been able to tell. The Fitches had a drawer full of mismatched utensils. No knife set. Black fingerprint powder coated the cupboard and drawer handles.

A dried trail of smeared blood passed through the kitchen and out the back door.

More black powder. More evidence markers.

Moving down the narrow hallway, he balanced carefully, keeping his feet on the few bare inches of carpet close to the wall, avoiding the wide bloody track.

Zander and Ava paused in the doorway of the largest bedroom. Signs of brutal violence covered the room. A large dark stain indicated where Lindsay Fitch had bled out on the carpet next to the bed. Lindsay's body had been loaded into a vehicle to be delivered to the morgue, but he and Ava had viewed the woman before entering the scene. He was accustomed to coming late to crime scenes where the bodies were usually long gone.

Squares of the carpet had been cut out and removed by the state crime lab's evidence team. Torn, tiny chunks of discolored carpet pad dotted the exposed plywood. Arcs of blood swept up the walls, splattered on the ceiling, coated the headboard, and left streaks on the lampshades. More blood covered the sheets. The metallic odor filled Zander's nose as he snapped a few photos with his phone.

Why does our body's liquid essence smell like metal? A nonliving substance.

Sean's blood had been tracked from the far side of the bed and into the hall, the swath dotted with occasional yellow markers.

Again Zander agreed that at least two people must have been involved. It appeared both victims had been surprised and quickly subdued. Each had only a few defensive wounds on their hands or arms. A mishmash of bloody tread marks crossed the bedroom's carpet. Zander believed he saw two distinct treads, but he knew the boot prints of the responding deputies had to be eliminated.

He exhaled. How was Sheriff Greer not raging about his department's response?

"The bodies need to go to the main Portland medical examiner's office," Ava stated as she scanned the room. "Not a satellite examiner's office. Dr. Rutledge should oversee this."

Zander nodded. The rest of the case needed to be handled without flaws. The state's top medical examiner needed to step in. There was no room for more errors.

Racial overtones. Scene contamination.

From here on out, the deaths would get the proper investigation they deserved.

Zander heard the sheriff stop in the hall behind them.

"Has Bartonville ever had its own police department?" Zander asked. He and Ava had reviewed the logistics of response coverage in the rural area before they had left the FBI office in Portland. A few fluid layers of outside law enforcement extended over the tiny town where the murders had occurred.

"No. The city of Astoria responds occasionally, but our county department in Warrenton is closer to Bartonville, so usually we do." Sheriff Greer cleared his throat. "State police step in when we need technical support or more manpower. Usually pretty quiet around here.

Picks up during tourist season. State would help us out if I gave them a call."

Zander caught the subtext. *The FBI isn't needed.*

"What kind of suspect first came to mind when you saw this scene, Sheriff?" Ava asked politely. Zander recognized the tone. She was angry. He'd worked with Ava for more than five years and knew her every mood. He admired her; she was relentless and sharp.

The sheriff pulled at the skin under his chin as he thought. "Dunno. We have our share of idiots and drunks and meth heads, but I can't imagine this kind of violence from any of them. Probably wasn't a local."

"You said the Fitches had only lived here a year?" Zander asked, hoping the protectiveness the sheriff showed for his residents and deputies wasn't affecting his ability to conduct the investigation. His reluctance to consider that the murders were homegrown was the equivalent of viewing the case through a peephole.

"About that long. I believe they moved here because Sean got a position teaching history at the high school. Lindsay's a waitress."

"I'd like to talk to your responding deputy," Ava stated.

Zander instantly pitied the deputy. Ava's good looks and dark-blue eyes didn't reveal that she was a ferocious interrogator. The man wouldn't see it coming.

"After I questioned him," said the sheriff, "I sent him back to the department to get started on his paperwork while the events were fresh in his head. He knows he screwed up. Feels bad about it. I suspect he's gone home by now."

"Where can I find Emily Mills for an interview?" Zander asked. He and Ava had already decided to split up the interviews to cover ground quickly. Ms. Mills had discovered the murder scene when she arrived at the house early that morning because Lindsay Fitch was late for her waitressing shift and hadn't answered her phone.

Ms. Mills was the resident who had personally called the Portland FBI after Sheriff Greer had brushed aside her concerns that the crime could be racially motivated. She had refused to hang up until Zander's supervisor gave her his word that he'd send an investigator to the coast that day.

Zander doubted Ms. Mills was the sheriff's favorite person at the moment. A flicker of annoyance in the sheriff's eyes confirmed his thought.

"Emily works at Barton's Diner in Bartonville," he said with a dull tone. "Big place that looks like a log cabin. It's on the main road. Can't miss it." The sheriff frowned and looked past Zander and Ava into the bedroom. "I was a deputy when Emily's father was murdered a couple of decades ago." Sheriff Greer glanced back to the agents, his eyes wary. "We haven't had a hanging in this county since his."

Tiny hairs stood up on the back of Zander's neck.

"Wait!" Ava exclaimed. "You've had hangings here before? And you just mention this now?"

The sheriff's mouth flattened into a thin, pale line. "Did you hear me say 'decades ago'? His killer has probably died in prison. Can't be relevant."

"But the person who found Sean Fitch hanged in a tree is the daughter of a man who was hanged?" said Zander. "You don't find that the slightest bit unlikely?"

Exasperation crossed the gaunt face. "This is a tiny community. Everyone knows everybody. You can't kick someone without finding out their sister or uncle went to school with you or married your cousin. When I heard Emily found the bodies, I felt bad for her but wasn't surprised by the coincidence."

Ava and Zander looked at each other, each easily reading the other's thoughts.

Neither of them believed in coincidences.

3

Emily Mills's hands shook as she snapped photos of her outfit and stared into the ancient full-length mirror in her bedroom. She zoomed in on her shoes and took another picture. She slipped them off and dropped the tennis shoes in the paper grocery bag on the floor, wincing as she saw a dark-red smear on the side of one.

Lindsay's blood. Or was it Sean's?

She stripped off her jeans and sweater and added them to the bag, her stomach in knots.

She'd never get the sight of the brutalized young couple out of her mind.

The amount of blood in the bedroom.

Her brain knew the human body held around five quarts of blood, but the sight of it spread throughout that bedroom had made her drop to her knees, clutching at the doorframe to stay upright.

She'd known instantly that Lindsay was dead. No one could survive that.

Her shaking fingers had touched the woman's cheek. Lindsay was cold, her eyes sightless.

Shuddering at the memory, Emily slipped on a faded University of Oregon sweatshirt and a clean pair of jeans.

Emily had spent several hours waiting and watching outside Lindsay's home as deputies came and went. Her interview with the sheriff had felt short, too short, but he had asked her to stick around for the state police evidence technicians to arrive. Two techs had finally arrived, unpacked their equipment, and photographed everything out front before they moved into the house.

Eventually one had returned and taken prints of the soles of her work shoes.

She'd been surprised they hadn't requested her clothes or taken her shoes, but she knew someone later might want to examine every shred of evidence, including the clothing and shoes of the person who had discovered the bodies in the double murder.

Emily had known Sheriff Greer's initial suggestion that Sean and Lindsay had died in a murder-suicide was wrong and had bluntly told him so. He'd taken a step back, his gaze startled at her insistence, but had tried to mollify her by stating he'd take a look at the evidence when the crime scene team was finished. Sheriff Greer was a fossil—a kind fossil, but he was a bit behind the times. He had his job because he was solid and dependable—sort of like the ancient refrigerators that never break down. Unlike the cheap ones manufactured today.

The call from the FBI had stunned the sheriff. He'd marched out to her car, where she patiently waited, to ask if she'd actually gone behind his back. Emily had nodded, looking directly into his shocked eyes. He didn't intimidate her. Few people did. She would always say and do what she thought was right.

Sean didn't hang himself.

Sean didn't carve the Klan symbol into his own forehead.

The sheriff was dense if he couldn't see those facts.

She rubbed a hand across her eyes as the cold numbed her fingers, and her vision slightly tunneled.

Not now.

The sensation wasn't a surprise. As soon as she'd seen Sean, she'd known she'd be haunted by dreams and panic attacks as she had been in her teen years.

Emily tore out of her house, knowing something was very, very wrong. Outside she looked up and shivered. It was dark and cold, and the heavy winds whipped her nightgown around her bare legs. Behind her the flames crackled and grew, and the smoke burned her eyes. She strained to see the shape in the dark. A flash from the fire lit up her father's face as he dangled from the tree branch.

Breathing deeply through her nose to fight the panic, Emily shoved the dream away as she dug in her minuscule closet for clean boots. The images had tormented her dreams for nearly two decades, growing less frequent year after year. She'd thought she'd conquered it for good. Rattled, she shoved her feet into the boots. The old nightmare about her father would invade her nights—and days—for weeks. Maybe months.

Without another glance at the paper bag, Emily left her bedroom and jogged down the ancient stairs, the old varnished wood creaking in protest, and headed for the kitchen. The timeworn Queen Anne mansion was from a different era, built by her great-great-grandfather in the late 1800s. Emily and her two sisters had been raised in the mansion after the death of their parents, and Emily had returned when her marriage disintegrated.

"Emily, you're not going back to work, are you?"

Emily slowly turned around, her breath stuck in her throat.

I don't want to talk about it.

Aunt Vina stood in the hall, her hands on her hips. Her great-aunt was tall and sturdily built, with white hair and piercing blue eyes that could see into her nieces' brains and instantly spot a lie. Aunt Vina's two sisters had the same skill and also lived in the mansion with Emily and Madison.

The trio of interfering great-aunts had good intentions but often exasperated Emily. Vina, Thea, and Dory. The three older women were social leaders in the tiny town, a role they took very seriously since the town carried their last name: Barton.

"Yes, I'm headed back to the restaurant. I'm sure they need me."

Vina raised a brow. "Can you tell me what happened at Lindsay's home?" Her eyes softened. "Such a lovely young couple. I'm so sorry, my dear."

Clearly her aunt had heard about the deaths.

Emily exhaled.

Avoiding the aunts, she had sneaked into the mansion to change her clothes after the sheriff said she could leave. She hadn't wanted to talk about the horror she'd discovered that morning. But the high-speed gossip chain must have already swept through Bartonville. Aunts Thea and Dory were noticeably missing at the moment—usually they were present in the kitchen at this hour. No doubt the two women were out gathering intel and keeping Aunt Vina in the loop.

"Lindsay and Sean are both dead, but it's unclear what happened." Emily choked out the words.

Blue eyes bored into her skull. "And Greer is in charge? He's a good man. But he is getting up there in age," Vina said, watching Emily closely.

Emily nodded and blindly reached for the back door handle, her eyes wet.

"You were married to a police officer," said Vina. "I bet you spotted more details about the deaths than Greer did."

Emily's sorrow turned off like a faucet at the mention of her ex-husband. He would have been furious that she had gone behind the sheriff's back, insisting it wasn't her place to call the FBI.

He had a lot of opinions about what wasn't Emily's place.

Emily had never held back her thoughts about his opinions.

It was part of the reason they were divorced.

Emily turned back to Vina, for once biting her tongue. She was too tired for a discussion and didn't want to add to the gossip chain. The news that the FBI was investigating would spread soon enough. "I'm sure we'll hear what happened," she said noncommittally. "I need to get to work."

Vina nodded, sympathy in her gaze. "Your staff is going to be crushed about Lindsay."

Emily's stomach twisted.

She nodded at Vina and left.

I can't tell them about the horror that was done to Lindsay. Or Sean.

4

The sheriff had been right; the Barton Diner resembled a gigantic cabin. Zander paused before he opened the door, examining the huge logs that formed the outer walls. Just like a kid, he ran his hand over the timber. The round wood appeared too symmetrical to be real, but his fingers told him it was authentic. He was in logging country. He'd passed three log trucks with full loads as he'd driven to the diner, bringing back memories of when he was a kid and would see the big trucks on the highway towing one huge tree trunk that filled the entire trailer.

Inside the diner a bald cook with a long goatee and a white apron appeared to be both waiting tables and filling the orders in the nearly empty restaurant. The older man paused midstride when Zander asked for Emily Mills. Pain flashed in the cook's eyes, and he said she was probably at home.

He'd heard.

"Do you know the address?" Zander asked the burly man as he deftly delivered two burgers and two salads to an elderly couple and then topped off their coffee. His name tag said LEO.

"Google Barton Mansion. Can't miss it." Leo walked away without glancing back.

Mansion? Zander entered the words into his phone and saw the home was minutes away. Everything was close in Bartonville.

His GPS directed him uphill. Bartonville was built on a slope, and many of the homes had an amazing view of where the Pacific Ocean met the wide Columbia River, which separated Oregon and Washington. The town's businesses were at the bottom of the hills where the land was flat, adjacent to the docks and beaches. The streets led up and across the hills in a basic grid on which homes with steep peaked roofs and roomy porches sat on close lots. Most of the homes needed attention. Missing paint, crumbling stairs, bare lawns.

The sky was gray, and the clouds were low, obscuring part of the river and the coastline of Washington on its other side. On a day with blue skies, the views had to be stunning. The northern Oregon coast was known for its rugged beauty, but living in the small coastal towns was often depressing in the fall, winter, and spring.

Gray skies. Frequent drizzle. Howling wind. Few people.

Most of the coast and river towns squeaked by on a tourist-based economy that slowed to a crawl during the cooler months. Fishing and logging were the other local economy cornerstones, but they waxed and waned with the unpredictable whims of weather and politics.

Zander parked, stared at a house, and then double-checked the address. Sure enough, the gigantic home that nearly filled the city block was his destination.

Mansion indeed.

The massive three-level house had a turret that extended up another two levels, no doubt giving a marvelous view of the water. A huge wraparound porch, tons of big windows, multiple gables, and elaborate finishes added to the grandeur. Steep stairs led up to the porch and large double doors. A few towering firs were in odd spots on the large lot, looking like sentinels guarding the house.

He stepped out of his vehicle and looked closer. As with several of the smaller homes he'd passed, the paint was faded and flaking. A few of the porch rail's spindles were missing. The lawn was lumpy and spotted, and many bushes had grown wild.

He couldn't imagine the cost of the upkeep for the home. *Mansion.* A plaque on a metal stand next to the sidewalk caught his eye.

Barton Mansion

Built in 1895 by George Barton, owner and founder of Barton Logging and Lumber.

Zander climbed the stairs to the wide porch and knocked on the door. The oval window in the huge double doors gave a rippled view of the interior. Old glass. Everything on the outside of the mansion looked old, and he wondered how much was original. He tried not to stare through the glass as a woman approached and opened the door.

He estimated she was well into her seventies. She stood stiffly with her chin up, and her pale-blue eyes scanned him from shoes to hair. "The mansion isn't open for tours today," she announced. "Only the second Tuesday of each month."

Zander held out his ID. "I'm looking for Emily Mills."

The woman's eyes cleared in understanding. "This is about the Fitch couple?"

He nodded.

"You just missed her. She's headed to the Barton Diner."

Zander grimaced. "I just came from there. They sent me here."

"Well, fiddlesticks. You must have crossed paths." She pressed her lips together. "She's pretty shook up."

"Are you her . . . mother?" Zander felt unprepared, a rare sensation. He hadn't taken the time to research his first witness. He knew she was gutsy enough to go behind the sheriff's back and contact the FBI, and that her father had also been hanged. Not just anyone would hold his boss hostage on the phone until he agreed to send an agent. Especially not after discovering two dead friends.

That was the extent of his facts on Emily Mills.

"You flatter me. I'm her great-aunt." The woman paused, and her nostrils flared several times. "Do you smell something?"

He sniffed, smelling nothing but sea air and the faint odor of wood polish that had emerged when she opened the door. "I don't."

"Blood. And worse." The woman stepped out, forcing Zander to back out of her way.

"Ah . . ." He glanced at his pants and shoes, wondering if she could smell the crime scene from his clothing. Certain bad scents clung to clothes and hair no matter what protective equipment was used.

She had followed the wide porch to the corner of the house before he determined there was no visible blood on his shoes. She turned the corner and recoiled, her hands covering her mouth as she gasped.

Zander was instantly at her side and spotted the mangled, bloody animal on the porch in front of a side door. The tail indicated it had been a raccoon.

"If you'll tell me where to find a shovel and bag, I'll take care of that," he offered.

The woman continued to stare at the corpse, anger flashing in her eyes. "Crud bucket."

If the sight wasn't so disconcerting, her remark would have made him smile. "A dog must have left it—unless you have other predators around here." He suspected bears or cougars lived in the hilly forests adjacent to Bartonville. The animals even wandered into the Portland area.

"I'll call my nephew Rod to clean it up," she answered. She looked away, not meeting his gaze. "It happens occasionally—like you said—predators." Her fingers fluttered as she lowered her hands, and her face had paled several shades.

"I'll handle it," Zander said firmly. She directed him to a small shed at the back of the home, where he found a shovel and black plastic garbage bags. He suggested she make some coffee, and then he went to clean up the mess.

Breathing through his mouth, he noticed the raccoon's head was barely attached to the rest of its body. He pushed the fur out of the way with his shovel, bending over to take a closer look. The cut looked nearly precise to him. Not like the mangled damage from an animal's bite. He awkwardly maneuvered the corpse into the bag and stopped.

A small hole in its shoulder.

He prodded the injury with the shovel, wishing he'd kept an extra pair of gloves from earlier.

The animal had definitely been shot.

He tied the bag and grabbed a nearby hose to clean off the porch. Uncertain where to take the remains, he left the black bag at the corner of the house.

After scrubbing his hands, he was seated at a table in a run-down kitchen with a cup of coffee at his fingertips. He'd expected a large, modern kitchen with all the bells and whistles to match the outside splendor of the mansion. Instead the room was small and the appliances were old. Again he wondered about the cost of maintaining the gigantic home.

His hostess's name was Vina, and she sat across from him drinking tea. Her color was better, and her hands had been confident as she passed him his cup, but she appeared distracted.

After a few moments of polite small talk, her countenance changed and her eyes narrowed. "Can I be honest with you, Agent Wells? I don't think an animal left that creature on our porch."

Zander waited. He had not mentioned the nearly severed head or bullet wound.

"It's happened a few times, and I've always suspected teenage punks. We have our share in Bartonville. There's not much in town to keep them occupied."

"So they kill animals for entertainment?"

"Something like that. I've reported it to the police, but I can understand how an old woman's complaints about occasional dead vermin is far down their priority list."

Zander suspected she hadn't shared all her speculations about the raccoon with him. "I thought most small-town teenagers liked to drive aimlessly up and down the main streets and steal their parents' beer to drink with their friends."

"We have that too. Lots of it."

He paused. "There was a bullet hole in the raccoon."

She sighed, a look of understanding on her face. "Idiots."

"Do you suspect some particular teens?"

"No."

Her answer felt a little too quick.

"Are you being harassed in any other way?" he asked quietly. "I know you don't have a local police department, but the county sheriff should hear if you've had trouble."

"I'm sure it's nothing. Some people see the house and assume we're rich." Disappointment filled her eyes. "But truthfully this house is a burden. The cost of maintenance is insane, and outside of Social Security and what we bring in from the diner—which isn't a gold mine—we have no other source of income. Five people live here. We have no other place to go."

"I'm sorry." Having his suspicions confirmed turned his mouth sour.

"At one time, the Barton family sat at the top of everything. We helped build the school, the city hall, and we employed a large part of the population at the mill. When the town needed something, they came to us."

"What happened?"

She shrugged. "Politics, the economy, competition, ego. A little of each."

"You mentioned a nephew. Does he live in the home?"

"No. Rod lives on the other side of town. We call him when we need a bit of muscle around the house. He keeps the mansion mostly shipshape."

"Who lives here with you?"

"Two of my sisters, Emily, and her younger sister, Madison. My third sister was their grandmother, but she passed years ago. Those girls have always been like grandchildren to all of us."

Zander couldn't help but like Vina Barton. She was direct, confident, and polite.

He set down his cup and leaned forward, holding her gaze. "Vina, this morning Sheriff Greer mentioned Emily's father had been hanged."

She blanched. "Why on earth would Merrill bring that up?" Anger flashed. "I don't know why he has to stir up painful memories."

She doesn't know.

"Vina." Zander paused, debating the necessity of telling her. "Sean Fitch was hanged."

Her teacup clattered as she lowered it to its saucer. She thrust both hands into her lap, her face pale again. "What?"

He waited. Vina had heard him; she just needed a moment to process. He studied her facial reactions.

Shock. Disbelief. Then acceptance. She looked nauseated.

"What happened to Emily's father?" Zander asked quietly. "I don't even know his name."

"Lincoln Mills."

Vina stared out the window past Zander, her thoughts in the past, her eyes sad. She was quiet for a long moment. "Lincoln was dragged out of his house and hanged about twenty years ago."

"They caught his killer," Zander stated.

She turned a questioning look on him. "Yes. It sounds like you already know the story."

"That's the extent of what I've heard."

"Then you know most of it."

"Why did the killer do it?"

"Who knows? Chet Carlson was his name."

A chill raced through Zander's nerves.

"But they had the evidence to convict," Vina said. "We're all positive it was him."

"Did you know the man who was murdered this morning?"

"I knew who Sean was. I know he taught at the high school and that his wife worked at the restaurant. Can't say I ever had a conversation with him."

"Any idea why someone would want to hurt either of them?"

"Only the obvious. He's black. And he married a white woman," she stated matter-of-factly.

Zander couldn't speak.

Her gaze softened. "Shocked, are you? Every community big or small harbors some sort of hate and ugliness in its underbelly. Oregon has a very racist history. I'm not proud of it, and I don't support it, but I won't pretend it doesn't exist. Hopefully that isn't the reason that nice young couple was murdered."

"He was hanged," Zander forced out. "That's a pretty clear message."

"Or someone wanted the shock value. Or to put investigators on the wrong path." She tilted her head a degree, her gaze narrowing. "Why am I doing your job?"

"You're not." But Zander was grateful for the reminder; he knew better than to let his focus narrow. Vina was correct to consider alternatives. "Was Lincoln Mills black?"

"No." Her expression closed off. "He was a good father, and his death was a tragedy. His girls have suffered horribly since he died."

5

It was midafternoon when Emily arrived at the diner and tried not to stare at Madison's long, pink tulle skirt and black T-shirt as her sister waited tables. Old Converse tennis shoes and a small tiara rounded out the outfit. The clothes would be understandable on a thirteen-year-old. Or a six-year-old. But her sister was thirty-one.

Emily sneaked to her tiny office without being seen and collapsed into a chair, her brain scrambling over how to talk with her staff about Lindsay's death.

Her employees were her second family. Along with Madison, Leo, her line cook, and Isaac were currently working. Isaac did everything besides cook and wait tables. Dishes. Cleanup. Prep work. The sullen teen wasn't a talker, but he was a good worker. With Lindsay and herself—and sometimes the aunts—the five of them kept the restaurant running through the quiet months. Lindsay's absence would leave a gaping hole.

This wouldn't be easy.

Emily procrastinated, balancing the books for the previous day, the numbers soothing her overstimulated mind. It took only a few minutes; business was slow. She sucked in a breath and forced herself to leave the office.

Madison spotted her, and Emily gestured for her sister to follow as she headed toward the kitchen. Only two tables were occupied. Emily shoved open the swinging door and stepped into the kitchen, feeling the tension in her shoulders reduce a bit. It always happened. Behind the kitchen doors she was no longer on display to the diners. Back here it was just her and her employees. A place to relax before putting her hostess face back on.

But today was different.

From his position behind the prep area, Leo caught her eye and immediately laid down his knife and wiped his hands on his apron, his expression guarded.

Emily's throat closed. She couldn't speak.

Behind her, Madison stopped just inside the swinging door. Leo read Emily's face. Her cook had worked in the restaurant since before Emily was born and was like an uncle to her. He turned his head toward the out-of-sight dishwashing alcove and shouted, "Isaac. Can you come out here?"

The teen emerged, his apron soaked and hesitation in his step.

The three employees stared at her, waiting.

Madison spoke first, her voice cracking in a show of emotion unusual for her. "What happened to Lindsay? Was she really murdered? Her husband too? Rumors are flying, and I don't know what to believe. They say their house is crawling with police."

Leo and Isaac were silent, their gazes on Emily. She looked directly at Leo and saw he was expecting the worst. She gave it to him.

"Lindsay was killed. Sean too," Emily finally forced out, her mouth bone-dry. "They don't know what happened yet, but they're investigating."

Madison sucked in a rapid breath with a sob. "No. That can't be true. I talked to her last night."

"Holy shit," Isaac muttered, thrusting his hands in his back pockets. He wouldn't look at Emily, staring anywhere else in the kitchen, his eyes growing red as he rapidly blinked.

Leo was silent, but waves of shock and sorrow rolled off him. He didn't have any relatives and had adopted the diner's employees as his family. Emily knew Lindsay had been a favorite. He abruptly turned and marched off. Emily heard the rear delivery door open and slam shut.

"This isn't happening," Madison muttered, her lips white. "You're mistaken." She grabbed the counter near the coffee machine.

Emily shook her head, unable to speak.

Sean's hanged body flashed in her mind. A bloody Lindsay on the floor of her bedroom.

No one needed those details right now.

"How?" Madison spit out. *"How?"*

"That's for the police to determine."

Fury and sorrow alternated in Madison's eyes.

"Do we need to close the restaurant?" Isaac asked. "You know . . . because . . ."

The idea had crossed Emily's mind more than once. She looked from Isaac to Madison. "Your thoughts?" The two stared miserably at each other.

"I'd rather stay busy," Isaac mumbled. "I don't want to sit around at home and think about it." He wiped a hand across his face.

The bell on the front entrance sounded. Customers. Madison's distraught expression vanished. "I've got it." She spun and hit the swinging door hard with her palm to open it.

Emily froze and then went after her, concerned with Madison's emotions at the moment.

"Madison!" A child's shout sounded from the front lobby. A small girl dashed over and stopped in front of Emily's sister, admiring the tulle skirt and crown. "You're so pretty today," the child sighed, her rapturous gaze studying Madison from head to toe.

Madison bent over and smiled, meeting the child's eyes. "Bethany. I *love* your boots." The girl grinned and squirmed in pleasure, lifting a pink-rubber-booted foot into the air.

Emily held her breath. The upset Madison from the kitchen had been abruptly replaced with a caring waitress.

Emily glanced at Bethany's mother and father. He held the door open for his wife, gesturing her ahead of him. She didn't recognize the attractive couple. Or the little girl. Not locals.

Clearly Madison had made a new friend.

Madison took Bethany's hand and tipped her head at the mother. "I've got a great table ready for you." She and Bethany led the way, talking nonstop, the mother following.

Bethany's father didn't trail after his family. Instead he turned his serious gaze on Emily.

"I swear Madison isn't crazy," Emily told him, her mouth still dry from the bleak minutes in the kitchen. "She just has an odd sense of style."

He glanced after the trio but made no move to join his wife. "I like the tiara. You don't see that every day." He turned his attention to Emily. "I'm looking for Emily Mills."

Emily looked at the mother and girl, now deep in discussion with Madison at a table near the toasty fireplace.

The corners of his lips lifted in a small smile. "Not my family. I just held the door."

"You looked like a family," Emily stated, sizing him up. The three of them could have graced the cover of a parenting magazine. "She could easily pass as your daughter." They had the same shade of light-brown hair and gray eyes.

An odd expression flashed over his face, and he pressed his lips together.

Emily felt as if she'd made a faux pas. "What do you need with Emily?" she quickly asked, unwilling to announce her identity to a stranger.

He pulled identification out of his coat's inner pocket and opened it for her. "I have some questions for her about this morning."

Special Agent Zander Wells. The FBI had arrived.

Her call had been taken seriously. She offered her hand. "Emily Mills. I'm glad you're here."

◆◆◆

The FBI agent sat across from Emily in her tiny office. She'd started to lead him to a table in the diner and then realized they needed absolute privacy. Her office was cramped—and that was describing it nicely. Her tiny desk was pushed into a corner, barely leaving room for two chairs and a filing cabinet. Her walls were covered with shelves, packed with three-ring binders of paperwork for the restaurant and a few framed old photographs. Agent Wells focused on one. She followed his gaze.

"That's my sisters and me. I was about ten years old, so that means Madison was seven and Tara fifteen." The three girls were posed in front of the big Barton Diner sign with pots of colorful flowers at their feet. They all wore shorts and squinted in the sunlight.

A good day.

"The restaurant has always been in your family?" Agent Wells asked.

"Yes. My grandfather opened it in 1978." She wondered how long the agent would engage in small talk. His eyes were sharp as he took in the rest of the office, giving her a few moments to silently take his measure. She estimated he was around forty. When he'd first entered with the woman and girl, she would have guessed closer to her own age of thirty-four. But now, close up, she could see there were lines at the corners of his eyes and the faint start of silver at his temples. His calm gaze returned to her, and she searched his face for a hint of his thoughts. He was unreadable.

She didn't like it.

"Do you mind if I record this?" he asked.

"Go ahead." She frowned. "When Sheriff Greer talked to me, he didn't even write anything down. Of course, it only took two minutes."

Agent Wells started to record. "Some people have good memories. Now . . . you were here at the restaurant when Lindsay was supposed to start her shift?"

"Yes. She was to be here at seven. Leo stuck his head in the office at five minutes after to tell me she was late. That's when I first called her. She didn't answer her cell phone, and I left a message."

"Leo is your cook? Has he worked here long?"

"Leo is an original employee. He was a busboy when the place first opened." She smiled, imagining the large cook as a teen. "I don't think he was older than thirteen. My grandfather paid him under the table for years."

"What did you do when Lindsay didn't answer her phone?"

"I waited a few minutes, called again, waited a little more, and called a third time. That's when I dug out her employment application and looked up Sean's number. No answer on his phone either."

Agent Wells nodded, his calm eyes locked on hers.

"I decided to drive over. It's only a few minutes. I told Leo I was leaving—there were only four people eating in the diner at that time, so I knew he could handle everything for a few minutes." She took a breath. "I fully expected that Lindsay had overslept."

"And when you got to her home?"

"I noticed two vehicles were parked in the driveway and rang the doorbell. I waited and then rang again, very surprised that no one was answering. I called her cell from the front door, and I heard it ring inside. That's when I tried the door handle." She looked down at her hands, her fingers digging into her thighs. She folded them in her lap, feeling as if she were in church.

"The door was unlocked?"

"Yes. I pushed it open and called out for both of them—I didn't want to startle anyone. As soon as I stepped inside, I knew something was wrong."

"What do you mean?"

"I could feel it. The air felt thick inside—I don't know how to explain it. It felt . . . wrong." She looked up and spotted a brief flash of recognition in the agent's eyes.

He knows what I mean.

"And I could smell it. The blood. I could smell the blood." The words stuck to her tongue as she remembered *how much* blood she had seen in the bedroom and how hard her heart had pounded, making her entire body vibrate.

"I saw a dark trail that led from the bedroom and down the hall toward the kitchen."

"You'd been in her home before?" he asked.

"Yes. A few times. Even though she was my employee, we were friends. We often watched *Game of Thrones* together, and I'd help her on the nights she fed the football team."

"The football team?"

"Sean coached the high school's football team along with teaching history. He'd have everyone over for dinner a couple times a month."

"All of them?"

"It's not a big school," Emily pointed out. "Maybe twenty or twenty-five kids would come. Lindsay loved it. She'd plan all week to make burgers or pizza or spaghetti. Those players can eat a lot."

"I imagine." The agent looked slightly stunned.

"She and Sean really loved those kids," Emily said quietly, remembering how happy the little home had felt when it overflowed with hungry teenage bodies. A contrast to how still and stagnant it had been that morning.

"This couple was popular." It wasn't a question.

"They were," Emily said. "They both put out a lot of positive energy that made people feel good. Everyone liked them."

The two seconds of silence that followed her words seemed to stretch forever.

Someone didn't like them.

Emily Mills was a good witness, Zander admitted.

She was calm and seemed to have clear memories of the morning. Not only had she painted a consistent picture of the crime scene; she'd also given insight into the victims' lives.

After she'd determined that Lindsay was dead, she'd followed the blood trail out of the house and spotted Sean. That's when she called 911. A single deputy arrived first, and she waited out front as he cleared the home.

"I couldn't believe it when I realized the deputy had cut the rope." Emily briefly closed her eyes. "He'd taken so long inside the house, I went to check on him and found him in the backyard, essentially having a panic attack. That's when more officers showed up. It was a bit of a mess after that. No one seemed to know what to do."

"You sound like you were very calm about a horrific situation."

"Trust me, I was screaming inside. But during emergencies my brain focuses on what needs to be done next. I guess I compartmentalize to get through them."

"The sheriff told me it'd been four years since he'd had a murder in his county."

Scorn shone from her eyes. "That's no excuse. They should have known how—" She clamped her mouth shut.

"How what?"

"How to secure the scene. Police work 101." She glanced away. "I was married to a cop for five years. That is basic stuff. It should have been second nature to them."

"What about when the sheriff arrived?"

"One of the older deputies had things organized by then. Sheriff Greer walked the scene and then talked to me, asking what I'd seen. When he said it looked like a murder-suicide, my jaw nearly hit the ground. I asked if he'd seen the bloody drag marks from the bedroom to the outside. He said it could be from Sean walking outside, or maybe he moved Lindsay around."

"You noticed the symbol on Sean's forehead, correct?"

"Yes. When I asked the sheriff about it, he said Sean may have cut himself while killing Lindsay. He told me I was jumping to conclusions by suggesting it was a hate crime." Emily's eyes were hard, anger lurking behind them. "That's when I called the Portland FBI office."

"I'm glad you did," Zander told her. "We might not have been notified for another day or two."

"Did you already talk to the first deputy?"

"My partner is currently interviewing deputies at the sheriff's office." He mentally ran through his list of questions for Emily. "Do you know of anyone who would want to hurt the Fitches?"

"No," she said firmly. "They haven't been here that long, but our community immediately embraced them. They brought a spark to the town. They were such a cute couple, and Lindsay loved it here."

"Where did they move from?"

"Portland. I'm not sure where exactly. I think Sean's family still lives there. I don't know about Lindsay's family." Her forehead wrinkled as she thought. "I can't remember her talking about them. I didn't pry."

"Were you her closest friend in town?"

She frowned. "She considered my sister Madison to be her closest friend."

He glanced at the old photo of the three sisters. Emily stood out as the brunette between her two blonde sisters. The smallest girl had her arms spread wide and her chin tipped up as if she wanted the photo all for herself. He had no problem believing that she'd grown up to be a tiara-wearing waitress. Emily's hands were on her hips, her legs long and thin, giving a hint of the tall woman she'd grow up to be. The oldest sister's smile was coy, her gaze locked on the photographer. "Where's your other sister?"

Emily turned her head to look at the picture. Zander had the feeling she'd done it to avoid eye contact, not to refresh her thoughts about her sister.

"I don't know."

Curiosity lit up his brain. Her tone had been flat, removed, and a distance formed between the two of them in the tiny office. He said nothing, waiting.

Emily finally looked away from the picture after a long silent moment. "Tara left town around twenty years ago. We haven't heard from her since."

Twenty years? No contact?

Zander looked back at the photo, and Tara's coy gaze now felt directed at him.

Someone knocked on the door.

Without getting out of her chair, Emily stretched for the doorknob and easily opened the door. A teenage boy peered around the door, and his hair fell across his eyes. He shoved it out of the way and turned his attention to Emily.

"Hey, Em. Something's happened to your car out back."

She straightened. "Like what?" Concern in her tone.

The teenager grimaced. "Looks like they got your tires again."

Again?

"Dammit!" Emily jumped to her feet and grabbed her purse. "We'll have to finish this later, Agent Wells. I think we got through most of what happened this morning."

"Call me Zander." He stood. "I'll come with you."

He wasn't done with Emily Mills.

6

Fury rocked through Emily as she stared at the two flat tires on her Honda. She pulled up the hood of her coat to avoid the rain and to hide her anger from Zander.

Two weeks ago it'd been four flat tires. And before that a broken passenger window.

What else will happen today?

She ached to go home and shut down her brain. It had experienced enough trauma.

Sucking in a breath, she focused on the issue in front of her. If her mind wandered to Lindsay and Sean, she'd crack.

"I've got to install cameras," she muttered. She'd considered it after the first incident and then again after the second. Now she was kicking herself for letting it slide.

Isaac stood beside her, mist collecting in his hair. "I'm really sorry, Em. People are shit."

"You didn't see anyone?" Zander asked Isaac.

Isaac ran a hand through his long hair, and concern shone in his eyes. "No. I was taking a bag to the dumpster. I didn't notice until I was walking back. I looked around then, but no one was here."

"Is this where it happened before?" Zander asked her. He turned in a circle, scanning the small employee parking area behind the restaurant. "No cameras?"

"No cameras, and yes. Last time it was all four tires." Emily swore under her breath. Buying four new tires had hurt. Now she had to find the money for two more. "I should have put up cameras. Would be cheaper than new tires."

"You'd still have to buy new tires," Isaac pointed out. "But at least we'd know who did it."

She noticed Zander's gaze lingering on Isaac. She understood. Isaac didn't present the best first impression. His stringy hair was always in his eyes. He slouched. And his jeans always looked a half second away from falling to the ground. But he was a good kid. Emily trusted him.

"Did you report the last incident to the police?" Zander asked.

"No." Emily felt her face flush. "I didn't consider it worth their time."

Zander's silence felt judgmental.

"Do it this time," he said quietly. He pointed at the back wall of the restaurant. "For decent coverage, you need a camera there, there, and over there. A couple out front would be a good idea too."

Five cameras?

"I need to pay for new tires first." *And pay off the other four.* "This is ridiculous," she muttered. "I didn't need this today."

"Can I give you a ride somewhere?" Zander offered.

"I hate to take up your time."

"Oh, don't worry. I'll still be working during that time. We weren't done."

He grinned, and she blinked at the transformation of his face. The solemn, serious agent looked ten years younger when he smiled.

"In that case, you can drive me home. I'll borrow one of my aunts' cars."

"Barton Mansion?"

Her head jerked toward him in surprise.

"I was there earlier today, looking for you. I met one of your aunts. Vina."

"Just one? You're lucky." Emily crossed her fingers that Vina hadn't talked his ear off. She looked at Isaac. "Will you tell Madison I'm headed home?"

Isaac gave her a casual salute and strolled toward the back door, hiking up his pants with one hand and stepping over a giant puddle.

"He's a good kid," she told Zander, who was watching Isaac with a frown on his face. "I gave him a chance when no one else would, and he's paid me back tenfold."

She tensed, waiting for him to contradict her. Instead he pointed at an SUV on the street. "I'm parked over there. Ready?"

Her tension evaporated, but now she was off-balance. She'd automatically expected pushback on her comment about helping Isaac, and it had never come. Her ex would have asserted that Isaac was a useless teen and not worth her time. She shook her head at herself as she followed Zander, suddenly exhausted.

The tires were nothing compared to her discovery that morning, but the incident had weakened the walls that were keeping her emotions in check.

I refuse to fall apart in front of him.

◆◆◆

Zander followed the same route to the mansion from earlier that day. Emily sat silently, but he swore he could hear the gears grinding in her head as she thought about everything that had happened. His own train of thought was going full speed.

"Emily, I know you haven't reported the damage to the police, but have you told your aunts?"

"No, I don't want to worry them with extra expenses."

"How many harassment incidents have you had at the mansion?"

"What?" Her shoulders twitched at his question. "What are you talking about?"

Uh-oh. "I cleaned up a slaughtered raccoon that had been left at your home today. Vina said it wasn't the first time."

He glanced at her. Her face was white, her dark-blue eyes locked on him.

"You have to consider that the damage to your car and the dead animals left at the mansion are related. They're both harassment. Chickenshit harassment. Who has it in for you or your family?"

Another glance showed him she was staring straight ahead now, her lips pressed together. He'd either surprised her or stated out loud what she was already thinking. He parked in front of the mansion, turned off his vehicle, and waited for her answer.

She finally met his gaze, her eyes uncertain. "I don't know." Her voice was low but not nervous.

"My statement didn't surprise you."

"No. It's crossed my mind."

"You haven't discussed it with your aunts?"

"No, like I said, I didn't want to worry them."

"I think they should know about these other incidents. Maybe they've seen things they didn't share with you." He raised a brow. "You might be surprised at what communication can reveal."

She tipped back against the headrest and briefly closed her eyes. "I know you're right."

He checked the time. "I'd like to talk with you and your aunts some more, but first I need to check in with my partner. I'll make a phone call and then knock, okay?"

"Sounds good." She got out of the SUV and marched up the stairs without looking back.

He watched her leave as he listened to Ava's phone ring.

"Hey, Zander," she answered.

"Anything out of the deputies?" he asked.

She sighed. "I know these kids went to the police academy, but I swear they forgot half of what they learned. I don't think there is much around here to keep them on their toes. Sounds like they deal with a lot of DUIs, drugs, and domestics."

"Doesn't surprise me. How many did you make cry?"

"Only one. The first responder. Nate Copeland. And honestly I'd barely started asking questions when he fell apart."

"Losing your touch?"

"Some of these guys are young. I feel I should hand them a video game controller and make them a sandwich."

Zander grinned.

"Anyway, Copeland was all apologetic about cutting Sean down. He lives in Bartonville, so he knew the victim. They'd had beers together. He said he'd panicked when he saw Sean, and he was overwhelmed with a need to quickly get him down so he could breathe—even though his brain knew it was too late."

"If he knew Sean, did he have an idea of who would do this?"

"Well, that's where it gets a little odd. He also said Sean and Lindsay were having marital problems."

"No shit." Zander was surprised. This was a different picture from the rosy one Emily had presented. Who was right?

"When I pressed the issue, he said he wasn't aware of anyone who would hurt the couple."

"What about the other deputies?"

"They didn't know Sean. They live east of Astoria. What did you get from the first witness—Emily Mills?"

"I got a slightly different picture of the Fitch couple. She says it was heavenly bliss in their home and can't think of anyone who would hurt the couple."

"Huh. What did she say about her father's death?"

"I haven't gotten to that. We were interrupted because someone had slashed her tires. Again."

"What?"

"It appears she and her aunts have been the target of some harassment lately. Dead animals left on doorsteps, car damage. Stuff like that."

Ava was silent.

"I'm about to talk to her and her aunts. I'll get more information on the father's death."

"It's so weird. Two of them hanged. But the father's case was solved."

"It's definitely odd."

"While we're waiting on forensics and the medical examiner," Ava said, "I'll get in touch with Sean's family in Portland and find Lindsay's family."

"I'll contact Sean's and Lindsay's friends here in town and dig into the old hanging a little bit."

"Keep in mind that's not the case we are here for," Ava pointed out.

"True, but since the first victim's daughter plays a role in this case, I want to eliminate any involvement on her part."

"She *is* involved," Ava stated. "She found the bodies."

"You know what I meant. Did you check in to our hotel yet?" Neither of them had paused since arriving in Bartonville. They'd jumped in with both feet.

"No. I'll contact them so they don't give away our reservations."

"Okay. Let me know what you find on the families." Zander ended the call and stepped out into the misting rain.

◆◆◆

Emily tried to see her aunts through Zander's eyes.

No doubt he had noticed that all three women wore the same shade of lime green. It was hard to miss. Dory wore a thick, green cardigan because she was always afraid of being cold, and the tip of the always-present facial tissue protruded from her cuff. Thea's snug-fitting zip jacket was for runners. One that guaranteed she'd be seen while power walking on the side of the road. Vina's green blouse was simply practical, just like Vina herself.

The three women were as different from one another as could be, but there was nothing they liked better than coordinating their clothing nearly every day. "It shows people we're united," Thea had told Emily one time. "When we're talking to the city council, they know we mean business."

Emily didn't think the matching colors were needed. Everyone in town knew the Barton sisters were a formidable trio.

Emily and Zander sat at the old table in the formal dining room, waiting for the aunts, who had dug out a formal tea set that had to be older than the mansion. Dory had been thrilled when Zander agreed to tea. Emily watched him out of the corner of her eye, convinced he was a coffee drinker but pleased he wanted to make her aunts happy. Dory had pulled Emily aside for a moment and with a wink and a whisper told her that Zander could park his shoes under her bed anytime.

Emily couldn't think of a response.

She knew the aunts were trying to cheer her up and distract her from thinking about that morning. Their efforts were appreciated and even working a little.

The three silver-haired women happily scurried in and out of the dining room, preparing the formal tea even though it was closer to dinnertime.

Zander leaned in to Emily. "Why aren't you wearing green?" he whispered.

She snorted. "That is *their* thing. They've been doing it since they were teens."

"Lime green every day?" His eyes were wide.

"No. Matching colors. They discuss it before bed every night. I'd say they match eighty percent of the time. They get a big kick out of it. Trust me, they're pleased you've met them on a coordinated day."

"Huh." Zander sat back in his seat. "They're charming."

"That's just one of their Jedi skills."

"What are their others?"

The three women bustled in with their hands full before she could answer.

"So nice to have unexpected company, even if it's because of a horrible tragedy," Thea said as she poured Zander's tea, her bright-red lipstick clashing with the lime green. "But I'll have to do an extra hour on the treadmill to combat all these cookies."

"I'm really sorry about the circumstances, but the cookies do look good," Zander told her, eyeing the large assortment of sweets. "I'll have to hit the treadmill too."

Her aunt smiled. "I can tell you don't need to. You're a man who takes care of himself. Have you ever tried Health—"

"Thea!" Emily and her other aunts spoke at the same time.

Thea blinked. "What?"

"Don't buy anything she tries to sell you," Dory told Zander earnestly, placing a hand on his sleeve. "They're all poppycock and scams."

"They are not," Thea huffed. "I've had excellent results from everything I sell. I wouldn't support a product if I didn't believe in it." She moved to pour Vina's tea but avoided eye contact with that sister. She enthusiastically embraced every sell-from-home product; she was a born saleswoman. Emily had a drawer full of crazy print leggings that she never wore and a bathroom counter full of expensive skin-care products that didn't make her skin look any better than the items she bought at Walgreens did.

It was hard to say no to Thea.

Emily's appetite vanished as she looked around the table at her smiling aunts. For several minutes she'd forgotten she'd discovered her murdered friends, but reality returned in an abrupt rush. She stared at her teacup. Lindsay would never have another chai latte. Emily would never step into the restaurant break room and be greeted by the rich fragrance of Lindsay's daily drink addiction.

She filled her lungs and slowly exhaled.

Glancing to her right, she caught Zander watching her, his brow wrinkled in concern, and the oddity of the situation caught up with her.

An FBI agent is having tea with us.

"Aunties," Emily began. The three women immediately gave her their attention. "I got two flat tires today." The three women started to talk at once, and Emily held up her hands to quiet them. "This isn't the first time. Clearly my vehicle has been targeted when I park behind the restaurant. No other employees have had a problem. Vina, Zander told me you found a dead raccoon on the porch today."

"I did."

Thea and Dory peppered Vina with questions, which she ignored.

"It's the third animal in the last six or eight weeks," Vina admitted.

Zander spoke up, looking from Dory to Thea. "Have either of you experienced any sort of harassment-type incidents?"

The two women exchanged a glance and then shook their heads. "Not that I can think of," Dory said. "What about Madison? Has anyone asked her?"

"No," said Emily, mentally shaking herself. She'd forgotten to mention the tires to her sister. "I'll ask when she gets home tonight. I know her car has been fine."

Dory peered at Zander. "I thought you were in town to solve those horrible murders, not worry about some flat tires."

"I am. I was interviewing Emily when the tires were noticed. That's when I wondered if her vehicle and your home have been targeted by the same person. I'll finish Emily's interview when we're done here."

Thea leaned an elbow on the table, rested her chin on her hand, and studied Zander intently. "What is the next step for you? Do you have any leads on the murders? Do we need to be locking our doors at night?"

"I hope you lock your doors every night," Zander murmured.

"We do when we think of it," Dory announced.

"Don't interrupt," Thea ordered. Dory rolled her eyes and dabbed at her nose with her tissue. "I heard the first responder screwed up the scene. Some of those young deputies are as sharp as a mashed potato sandwich," Thea continued, her blue eyes challenging. "Is that true? People around town are saying it was a drug deal gone bad. Really bad."

"No," said Vina. "I heard it was a domestic dispute."

"I heard it was someone passing through town." Dory wiped her nose again.

Emily bit her lip. Zander had given each woman his full attention as she spoke, but a hint of desperation lurked in his eyes. Her family was a lot to take at once. He was getting off easy with Madison still at work.

"Aunties! Leave him alone. You know he can't talk about an active case."

The three women looked apologetic.

"We don't know much yet," Zander told the chastised women. "You'll hear when we do."

Dissatisfaction filled their faces.

"I know this may seem awkward to ask, but what might help is if you tell me some more about Emily's father's death."

Emily froze, and a loud buzz filled her ears. *Why?*

The nightmare images of her hanged father returned and destroyed the walls keeping her emotions at bay.

I can't be here.

She stood, and her chair's legs squealed as it shot backward. "You'll have to excuse me for a moment," she choked out. She rushed from the room and up the stairs, her vision tunneling.

Who told him?

Guilt swamped Zander.

What was I thinking? He hadn't discussed Emily's father's death with her. The sheriff and Vina had talked with him about it, but Emily had not. He started to rise.

"Sit down," Thea ordered, her eyes sharp. "Give her a few minutes. She'll be fine."

Zander slowly sat, studying the three women. Thea appeared to be the thinnest of the three, but her tone would have stopped a platoon.

"Her father's death isn't a comfortable topic," Dory said. She turned to Vina. "My stomach hasn't felt right since breakfast this morning. Are you sure those eggs weren't past their expiration date?" She laid a hand on her stomach, and a frown pulled down her lips.

"They were fine. And you're fine too," Vina informed her.

"I'm sorry," Zander told the three women. "I shouldn't have brought it up in the middle of conversation."

The three women waved aside his apology. "I've been thinking about his death since you were here after lunch," Vina told him. "It's very upsetting that another man was hanged, and Emily found him."

"Did Emily see . . . her father?" asked Zander.

"Oh, no," announced Thea. "She was asleep, thank goodness. Both her and Madison."

"And the other sister?"

The women exchanged a look. "Tara had stayed at a friend's home that night," said Vina. "She was eighteen and a little wild. According to her mother, Brenda, the two of them had argued that evening, and Tara stormed off."

"Emily told me that Tara moved away," Zander stated. "Tara has been out of contact with your family?"

Each of the aunts' faces drooped. "That's correct," said Vina. "Every now and then we discuss hiring someone to find her, but Emily says to let her be. If Tara wanted to still be part of this family, she'd contact us."

"I've searched a bit with the Google and some dot-com things," Thea admitted. "I can't find her."

"I suspect she's changed her name in some way." Dory patted Thea's shoulder. "She was an independent sort, which I suspect is why she seemed so out of control. Her parents had tough rules about alcohol and curfew, and Tara wasn't fond of rules."

"Did the family live here with you when the girls were young?" Zander asked.

"No. Brenda and their father had a house a few miles from here," Dory told him.

"It was a sweet little home that backed up to the national forest. Lots of space where the kids could be outside and explore all day long," Thea said with a sigh and a faraway look. "It was horrible that everything went to hell after their father was killed."

"What do you mean?" Zander spoke carefully, wanting to hear the story, but fully aware that the women's perceptions would be colored by their relationship with the family. He took careful mental notes, wanting to compare them with the official case file.

Thea picked a crumb from the front of her green jacket. "The house had been set fire, and they lost everything that night. It was tough on Brenda."

"Understandable."

"The four of them moved in here," added Vina, "so we could help with the girls. Brenda . . ." Vina glanced at her sisters.

"Brenda wasn't a strong woman," Thea stated. "She had spells."

Zander was silent, wondering what the official medical term was for Brenda's "spells."

"She'd lock herself in her bedroom for days at a time when the girls were tiny," Dory said in a low voice. "After Lincoln died, she couldn't function."

Depression?

"She committed suicide a week after his death," Vina added.

Zander sat back. "That's horrible."

Those poor girls. First their father and then their mother.

"She always refused help. We begged her to go to the doctor each time, but she brushed it off, telling us she was just tired."

“Who found her?” He hated to ask the personal question as much as he feared the answer.

“I did,” said Vina. “Her bedroom. Upstairs here.” Her eyes were haunted. “She hadn’t been happy to return to this house where she grew up. She wanted her little home and her family back.”

“Not only did Chet Carlson murder Lincoln,” Dory said, her voice tight, “he destroyed their home and decimated their family.”

The scorched siding of the Fitch home flashed in Zander’s mind.

He kept his expression neutral, unwilling to mention it in front of the women.

Another coincidence?

“I’m so sorry,” Zander told the women. All the lively spirit had been chased out of the room. By him. First he’d upset Emily, and now the aunts. He looked down at his plate. He hadn’t touched the elaborate desserts. “I should go.” He stood, not allowing their weak protests to change his mind. “Tell Emily we can finish her interview tomorrow.”

He gently disengaged himself from their goodbyes and escaped outside, but not before Dory pressed a small bag of cookies into his hand. He stopped on the sidewalk, looking up at the grand home, seeing it in a different light. Now he understood what was behind the tired and neglected property. The decades had been tough on the inhabitants; the home reflected their hard times.

The plaque caught his eye again.

“Not the peaceful life you imagined for your heirs, was it, Mr. Barton?”

7

Emily sat on the edge of her bed, furious with herself.

She'd overreacted. Zander Wells was doing his job. Had she really believed her father's death wouldn't come up when she was the one who'd found a hanged man?

Even she couldn't deny the horrible coincidence.

But she wasn't ready to talk about it.

She stood and paced, knowing she wasn't in a position to discuss what had happened that night. She'd been thirteen back then. She'd been asleep and had seen nothing.

At least that was the story she told everyone.

She backed away from her father, feeling the heat of the fire grow hot against her bare legs. The strong wind made his body sway and the tree branches thrash in the dark, and shock froze her limbs. A movement far to her right yanked her attention from the horror before her. Two people dashed into the firs, their clothing catching flashes of light from the fire before they vanished. For a split second, the fire lit up the long, blonde hair of the second runner.

Tara.

Faraway sirens cut through the crackle of the flames.

Emily shuddered. The cold wind from that night penetrated her bones every time she remembered. She recalled going back in the house, coughing in the smoke, and waking Madison and her mother to get them out of the home. The three of them had gone out the front door and huddled in the front yard. She'd been too petrified to say what she'd seen behind the house.

She told the police she'd been asleep until the smoke woke her.

Tara didn't show up until midmorning. The police had gone to pick her up from her friend's home and break the news.

Emily had watched her older sister cry over their father, waiting for her to say she'd been in the yard that night. But Tara never mentioned being at the scene, and so Emily didn't bring it up. She figured that Tara must have had her reasons for the silence, and Emily knew she would also protect whatever her sister wanted to keep quiet.

The family was never the same.

Tara and her mother fought more, and five days after her father was killed, Tara announced she was moving to Portland to be with friends. More yelling, more arguments. She vanished the next day. No goodbyes.

Emily felt abandoned. Another hole shot through her heart. Tara had left before Emily found the courage to ask her about the night their father died. Tara's secret left with her. Was it incriminating? Would it implicate someone? Was that person Tara?

To protect her sister, Emily stayed silent too.

Brenda seemed to crawl inside herself. A few days later, their mother took her own life.

Emily was broken. The foundations of her family were gone.

Emily stepped up, shouldering responsibility for her younger sister, desperate to protect the last family member she had.

The two younger sisters were fortunate to have three loving great-aunts who were determined to give them the support their mother no longer could. The mansion became their home. A safe place.

Many years later, Emily escaped to the mansion again after her marriage disintegrated. Her heart was broken and her psyche desperate for a place to rest and recover. The huge house was the rock where she always felt secure.

After the deaths, Madison had never left the mansion. She flitted from job to job and man to man. The last two years at the diner had been the longest she'd ever held a job.

Emily never knew what was going on in Madison's head. Her sister wasn't one to share her feelings. As a kid, Madison had seemed to never stop talking, her nose in everyone's business, always bursting with crazy ideas. But she'd changed after her parents died. Madison pulled inside herself, the gregarious child suddenly silent. Now Emily saw the old Madison only in her outlandish sense of style: the hats, the heels, the tulle, the tiaras. But before the deaths, she'd been called her mother's mini-me, a reflection of her mother's personality and looks.

Their mother had been spontaneous. She'd keep the girls home from school so they could escape to the beach and study the tide pools and stuff themselves with saltwater taffy. They would have impromptu dance parties in the living room, her mother blasting the music of the Spice Girls and Chumbawamba.

She loved us.

Why did she leave us?

Anger and resentment flared. She and her sisters had been children, too young to understand their mother's inconsistent behavior. But the adults around her knew she struggled with manic depression and refused all help. After multiple rejections, no one did anything more. No one told her to see a doctor. No one interfered.

Would she still be here if she'd been treated?

Emily shoved away the moot question. Her mother was gone.

Emily stopped at the window. Zander Wells was striding toward his SUV. She watched, her mind numb. He turned back to look at the home, and Emily stumbled back from the window. It was doubtful he'd seen her spying on him, but her face heated anyway. From a safe distance she noticed him scowl at the house. Her fingers grew icy.

She had no doubt he'd discover who murdered Lindsay and Sean. She'd seen and felt the determination of Special Agent Zander Wells. He was sharp. Thorough. And seemed to genuinely care about the victims. She suspected he didn't have many unsolved cases.

But how much of her family's dirty laundry would be exposed along the way?

◆◆◆

It was after 1:00 a.m. when Emily heard the stairs creak under Madison's feet as she crept up to the second level. There was no silent place to step on most of the stairs. Emily had searched and experimented for years. Skipping five steps in a row wasn't an option, no matter how long her legs grew. Her bedroom was the closest to the stairs, and no one came or went without her knowing. There was a narrow servants' staircase from the kitchen, but it was even noisier and easily heard from their aunts' bedrooms.

The main stairs had always been the best choice.

Feeling like a mother, Emily got out of bed and opened her door, watching as Madison unsteadily took the last step and held hard to the newel post. Filtered light from the streetlamp backlit her sister, creating a clear silhouette. Madison's shoes were in one hand. She'd changed out of the tulle skirt and into jeans at some point.

Emily wondered at whose house. "Hey."

Madison unsuccessfully choked back a gasp. "Jeez. Don't do that," she said in a loud whisper, glaring at Emily in the dim light.

Emily stepped back into her room, holding the door open. Madison gave a grumbling sigh and followed. Emily closed the door behind her.

"What?" Madison clasped her shoes tight to her chest and looked down her nose at Emily. An admirable feat considering Emily was several inches taller. The scent of tequila filled the room, and Emily tamped down her temper. Her sister must have been at Patrick's Place. A local bar she often used for escape.

Emily wished Madison would open her heart to her instead of seeking comfort with strangers.

"You have to open the diner in the morning." Emily knew that was the wrong way to start this conversation.

"I know! I don't plan to be late."

"You've slept through entire shifts," Emily stated. "Did you plan those?"

"I don't need this." Madison turned to leave.

"Wait. That's not why—"

"I know," Madison said, glancing back at her. "It's about Lindsay. Why do you think I'm so late?" She sucked in a shuddering breath.

Empathy filled Emily. They all mourned Lindsay, but the loss of her friend had to be a deeper shock for Madison.

"Down at Patrick's Place, they're saying Sean was hanged," Madison whispered. She met Emily's gaze. "Is that true?" Her voice quivered, and even in the poor light Emily saw the terror in her sister's eyes.

This is why I didn't tell her any details.

"Yes, it's true, but he was stabbed first. That may have been what actually killed him."

"Oh God." Madison clasped a hand over her eyes, her shoulders slumping. "I can see it. It won't go away."

Emily touched her arm. "I understand. It's all I can see too."

"It's not Sean I see." Madison's whisper was nearly inaudible.

"I know." Her heart cracked. Emily would do anything to take away the sight in her sister's head.

And her own.

The sisters rarely talked about their parents' deaths. It was a taboo topic in their home. One best swept under the rug so they could pretend it had never happened. Because dwelling on it would take over their minds and hearts, keeping everything else out.

"I wish Mom was here." Emily strained to hear Madison's hushed words. "Or Tara."

Tara's face flashed in Emily's mind. Eternally eighteen.

She is nearly forty now.

The old sense of abandonment pushed on a door in Emily's mind, and she said nothing.

Madison lowered her hand, and her eyes glittered in the dark. "You don't care, do you? You don't miss them at all," she hissed.

"That's not fair—"

"You barely say a word about either one. Our sister is out there somewhere, and you won't talk to me about her."

Truth.

"I've looked for her," Madison said. "You change the topic every time I talk about her."

"She knows where to find us. We've never left this town. If she wanted to be part of this family, she'd be here. I'm not going to waste my time searching for someone who doesn't want to see us."

She deliberately threw out the last sentence, wanting to shock Madison into silence.

Emily pressed her lips shut. She'd said enough.

But flames still shot from Madison's eyes. Emily knew how to calm them.

"Remember when Dad would pile us in the car and just take off for a long weekend?" Emily said softly. "Just the four of us so Mom could have some kid-free time. We never knew where we were going, but Dad made friends everywhere. The Redwoods. Pendleton. Portland. That wild animal place in southern Oregon . . ."

"Wildlife Safari," Madison added wistfully. "I touched a giraffe's tongue. Dad wasn't supposed to put the car window down, but he did."

"The animals came right up to the car."

"Bears and tigers. Elephants."

A good day.

Silence filled the room as they were caught up in their own memories.

"Is that why you stayed up past one?" Madison asked. "To tell me not to be late for work?"

To see that you got home safely after a horrible day.

"Something like that."

"I'm not going to sleep tonight." Madison swayed on her feet. She turned away and put her hand on the doorknob.

"That makes two of us." Emily's mind had been racing from the moment she lay down. It showed no sign of slowing. The wilt in her sister's usually perfect posture struck a chord in Emily's chest. "I'm really sorry, Madison. I know how close you were to Lindsay."

Her sister paused. "Maybe we weren't as close as I thought," she said softly. She opened the door and walked away, one hand on the wall to keep her balance.

Emily listened to her steps. Madison's door opened and closed.

What does that mean?

8

"Weather report says there is a strong storm coming soon," Ava commented as she met up with Zander in the diner parking lot the next morning. Zander wasn't surprised. The wind had nearly whipped his SUV door into the car next to him as he stepped out. It wasn't raining, but the air was heavy with salty, cold moisture.

The morning was gray and depressing again. Miserable. But a dozen vehicles were parked in the lot of the Barton Diner. He judged them to be local vehicles. Heavy-duty trucks and small older sedans that had been weathered by wind and salt. Zander was starving for food and warmth. The log cabin diner gave off a welcoming vibe and a promise of good coffee and hearty food. No doubt the locals came for the same reasons.

Inside he automatically looked for Emily, but he didn't see her, and disappointment briefly flared. The restaurant was half-full, and the smell of bacon made his stomach rumble, returning his focus to food. Madison approached, a coffeepot in hand. Her black jeans were constructed of more holes than fabric, and her hot-pink satin top hurt his eyes. "Take a seat anywhere, and I'll be right with you." She handed them two menus and strode away in red spike heels.

Out of the corner of his eye, he saw Ava's brows shoot up. They took the closest booth, near a window, and opened their menus. Ava's gaze followed Madison. "That can't be the sister of our witness."

"It is."

"She looks nothing like her." Ava studied the waitress. "But I like her hair. And confidence."

Zander turned to look. He hadn't noticed Madison's hair, but now saw it was in a complex, messy knot at the nape of her neck. She poured coffee, cleared plates, and delivered an order without missing a stride in her heels.

"She's got control of the floor," Ava went on. "Misses nothing."

"You waited tables?"

"College. And a bit after. It's not an easy job."

Watching Madison efficiently work, he wondered what her relationship with Emily was like. He'd learned a bit about Tara and Emily at the mansion yesterday, but not Madison.

He needed to focus on the murders, not the three sisters. "Did you talk with Sean Fitch's relatives yesterday?" he asked Ava.

"The sheriff hadn't contacted his family yet, so I requested that an agent from the Portland office visit and inform them in person. He gave them my number and told them to call when they were ready to talk. His father called me within a few hours. As you can imagine, they're hurt and confused."

Madison appeared at their table. "Coffee?"

"Please," Zander and Ava answered in unison. Madison turned over the coffee cups on the table and poured.

"Do you know what you want?"

Zander ordered an egg-white omelet, and Ava asked for apple French toast with a side of eggs. He glanced at the menu and saw hers came with whipped cream and caramel sauce.

He immediately regretted his order.

Madison didn't write anything down but gave a smile as she took their menus.

"That's not breakfast," Zander said after she left. "You ordered dessert."

"That's why I added the eggs. Any place can make an omelet. I judge a restaurant by their French toast. There are hundreds of ways to do it, and I like to see if places are lazy or unique."

"I think you're expecting too much from a rural diner."

"We'll see." Her smile was smug.

"What did Sean's father have to say?" Zander steered them back to the case.

Ava's smile faded. "He was in shock, of course. Sean's mother wasn't ready to talk, but the father wanted answers."

"Which you didn't have."

"The family is doubly stunned by the possibility that this is a hate crime. Actually, his father fully believes it is—not because Sean had told him there were issues, but because of the scene."

"He knows how his son was found?"

"He does." Ava lowered her gaze to her coffee and wrapped her hands around her mug as if they were cold. "I've never had a case like this," she said softly.

"Me neither," Zander admitted.

"The father said he'd told Sean not to marry Lindsay."

"Christ. Because she was white?"

Ava nodded. "He liked Lindsay. He knew they were in love, but he didn't want his son to deal with the additional stress that can come from a mixed-race marriage. He said life is tough enough."

Zander swore under his breath.

They were both silent for a long second.

"He didn't know who might hurt his son," Ava went on. "Stated Sean was always an easygoing guy with a lot of friends. He hadn't heard from Sean in several weeks, but he said that was normal. I want to talk to him face-to-face at some point. He did give me a few names of Sean's friends, and I'll try to contact them today."

"What about Lindsay's family?"

Ava looked out the window, frustration forming a line between her brows. "I can't find much. Her mother died a few years ago, and she had divorced Lindsay's father when Lindsay was a toddler. She never remarried. No other kids. I'm trying to find the father, but he's been elusive."

"Friends?"

She grimaced. "I'll have to use her old work history and contact her previous employers to find any personal information. Sean's father wasn't a big help. He said she had a few friends attend the wedding, but no family."

"Maybe her father has passed."

"Sean's father was under the impression they were estranged in some way but wasn't positive he was alive. Claims Sean said she didn't like to talk about her family. It sounds like she didn't keep in contact with anyone. I don't know if we'll find a lead in her background."

Zander glanced at Madison, who was filling water glasses and chatting with a table of men in heavy work boots and coats. "Emily Mills says Madison was Lindsay's closest friend."

"Good to know. I'll put her at the top of my list. I'm sure she can tell me who else Lindsay socialized with. What about the autopsies? Have you heard from the medical examiner?"

"Dr. Rutledge called me at six this morning."

Ava's eyes widened. "Let me guess. He was already at work."

"Yep. Wanted to let me know he planned to perform both autopsies this morning." Zander sighed. "I think I answered coherently."

"And it's too early to expect any news from the state crime lab."

"Definitely. I did ask for priority processing on Sean's laptop that was sent to our computer forensics lab in Portland."

"Everybody wants priority," Ava commented.

"True. And the manager's big sigh when I asked for it didn't give me a lot of hope."

They both sipped their coffee. Forensic evidence took time. TV had taught the public that forensics could solve a crime in an hour, but more often it took months. Zander knew he could use the FBI lab back east if he needed a certain piece of evidence handled quickly, but he preferred to use it selectively instead of swamping it with every scrap of evidence from a scene. As the investigation went on, he'd narrow down which pieces of evidence took precedence.

Madison appeared with their order and efficiently set down their plates. Ava's smile widened as she studied her French toast. Zander's oversize omelet was stuffed with sautéed peppers and onions, and a parmesan cheese sauce oozed out the sides.

"Do you need anything else?" Madison asked.

"Looks perfect," said Ava. She already had a fluffy bite on her fork, headed for her mouth. Her blissful expression after her bite reminded Zander why he'd once been half in love with her. He'd told her his feelings last fall during his once-a-year depressive alcohol binge, but it hadn't affected their friendship or work relationship. The fact that her fiancé was a good guy and a close friend had smoothed the way once Zander had recovered from the acute embarrassment of sharing his deepest secrets at his lowest moment.

"Good?" he asked.

"Amazing. I don't know what coats it, but the fried crunch is spot-on." With a wink, she cut a slice in half and transferred it to his plate.

He tasted his omelet, and unexpected flavor exploded in his mouth. He took three rapid bites, no longer regretting his choice.

"How's your room?" Ava asked between mouthfuls.

He snorted, and she grinned in understanding.

His hotel room was bare bones and hadn't been updated since the 1980s.

He didn't mind; he could sleep anywhere. But he hadn't cared for the earthy scent of dampness. It permeated the carpet and curtains. The bedding and towels were fresh, but this morning his clothing seemed limp from the wet air.

The two of them made fast work of breakfast and were lingering over their coffee when Zander saw Emily emerge from the kitchen. She wore a jacket, so he assumed she'd just arrived. She stopped to talk to a table of four women, each one with a baby or toddler on her lap. Some sort of mom's group, he surmised. She admired each baby and then patted the shoulder of one mother. The woman's smiling little girl made him suck in a breath and focus on his coffee.

He looked up to catch Ava eyeing him, her gaze deliberately blank. She wisely didn't say a thing.

"Good morning." Emily stopped at their table. "How was your breakfast?"

"Amazing," Ava stated at the same time that Zander replied, "Great."

"I'm glad to hear it."

"Emily, I'd like to talk with Madison," Ava told her. "When is she off work?"

Emily frowned. "What for?"

Her reluctance caught Zander's attention. *Overprotective sister?*

"I've hit a bit of a wall on Lindsay's closest relatives. I was hoping she could help."

"Oh." Emily glanced over her shoulder at her sister. Madison had four breakfast plates balanced on her arms as she strode to the far end of the restaurant. "Once the breakfast rush is done, she'll have time."

Zander's phone rang, and Emily stepped away. Sheriff Greer's name was on the screen.

"Wells," Zander answered.

"Greer here. I got a call from a bar manager who says Sean Fitch got in a bar fight the night before he died."

"Where?" Zander's heart sped up.

"Patrick's Place. Local dive."

"They open this early? Who's the manager?"

"They're not open, but Paul Parish is the manager, and he's there now. He'll let us in."

Annoyance briefly flickered at the thought of the sheriff observing as Zander conducted an interview. Or maybe he expected Zander to observe him interview the manager.

"I'll be there in a few minutes," Zander told him before hanging up. "Sean Fitch supposedly got in a bar fight the night before," he told Ava.

Her eyes widened. "Interesting."

"The sheriff says he'll meet me at the bar."

She wrinkled her nose. "Enjoy. I'll talk to Madison as soon as this place clears out a little more."

He slid out of the booth and put on his coat. "Check in later?"

"Absolutely."

9

No sheriff's vehicle was present at Patrick's Place.

For two seconds Zander considered waiting for Sheriff Greer, and then he got out of his vehicle. Patrick's Place was on the oceanfront. In fact, most of the building stuck out over the ocean, balanced on a network of pilings and heavy beams. The squat one-story building didn't have any windows in front, and Zander hoped there were windows on the ocean side to take advantage of the view.

It might be prime real estate, but the parking lot was gravel with scattered broken glass. The surf swirled around the pilings as he drew closer, leaving dirty white foam stuck to the wood. It should have been a nice-looking bar in an ideal location. Instead it felt tired and run-down. The building creaked as the waves receded, and Zander wondered if he was taking his life in his hands by entering it. Orange neon light above the door sloppily formed the name, appearing to read **PATRICK'S LACE.**

Not a good name for a dive bar.

The front door swung open, and a thirtyish guy with a thick beard and a gray stocking hat stepped out, looking directly at Zander. "You Agent Wells?"

"I am. Paul?"

"Yep."

They shook hands. "Paul Parish at Patrick's Place," Zander said with a grin. "That's some alliteration."

Paul blinked at him. "Uh . . . yeah."

He doesn't get it.

"There isn't a Patrick anymore," Paul said, still viewing Zander with confusion. "He died about five years back."

"Who owns the bar now?" Zander asked to move the conversation farther away from his alliteration comment.

"I do."

"The sheriff told me you're the manager."

"I'm that too. I was manager when Patrick was still around, so people are used to calling me that."

"So what happened Thursday night?"

Paul shifted his feet and peered past Zander to the road. "Probably should wait for the sheriff since this is about . . . a murder. Can't believe Sean is gone."

Zander studied the discomfort on Paul's face. "How about you show me around your bar while we wait. This is a great location."

The owner's face brightened. "Can do." He tugged on the door's heavy wood handle, and the door moaned as it opened. Zander entered and was greeted by the odors of stale beer and fryer grease. The interior was well lit; every streak on the grimy floor tile and scuff on the tables was visible. No doubt the lighting was turned down in the evening. The actual bar with shelves of alcohol and stools was spread across the back of the building.

There were no windows.

Regular square tables filled most of the floor, their chairs upside down on their tabletops, leaving the floor available to mop. One corner of the bar was empty. A motionless disco ball hung above the clearing, and a jukebox sat nearby.

"Nice place," Zander said. "Business good?"

"Winter is slow. Summer's better."

"Get a lot of tourists during the summer?"

"Some. The Jiggy Bar down the street gets more. It has windows, and I think tourists like to be able to see inside a new place before they enter."

"Then you should put in some windows. Windows across the back too. Shame to miss the ocean view."

Paul gave a one-shouldered shrug. "Maybe someday."

Zander wondered if his disinterest was because of cost or if he didn't care for change.

The front door opened, and Sheriff Greer appeared. Out of the corner of his eye, Zander saw the relief on Paul's face.

Am I that uncomfortable to converse with?

"Hey, Paul. Good to see you. You too, Agent Wells." Greer nodded at Zander as he removed his hat. "Sorry I'm late. Can you recap what you've covered so far?" He looked from Zander to Paul.

"Nothing yet," said Paul.

Satisfaction crossed Greer's face. "Good. Walk us through it."

"Well, I was tending bar—I usually do on Thursday nights. There were probably twenty people inside. A basketball game was on the TV." Paul gestured at a small screen behind the bar. "Sean came in around—oh, it was probably eight or so."

"Do you have cameras?" Zander asked, scanning the ceiling and corners.

"No. What for?"

Zander stared at him. "In case of crimes. Fights. Robberies."

Paul waved a hand. "Not worth the investment to me. We've never been robbed—unless you count the time four college punks decided to help themselves to a half dozen vodka bottles. My customers stopped them from making it out the door," he said with a flourish.

"I remember that," agreed Greer. "Two had fake IDs. It was a pleasure contacting their parents."

"So, back to Sean. Eight o'clock. Thursday." Zander redirected the reminiscing.

Paul ran a hand down his beard. "Sean was sitting right there." He pointed at a barstool at the center of the bar. "His usual drink is Coors Light."

"He comes in a lot?" Zander asked.

"Not really. Maybe once a week."

That seemed frequent to Zander but maybe not to a bar owner.

"Did Lindsay ever come with him?" he asked.

"Nah. Haven't seen her in here."

"You know who she is?"

"I do. Seen her around town and in the diner."

Zander noticed Paul referred to Sean and Lindsay in the present tense. It was probably more comfortable for him. Their deaths hadn't sunk in yet. "I assume Sean talks to you if he's sitting at the bar?" Zander asked, mentioning the couple in the same tense. "What's he talk about?"

Paul frowned. "I don't know. Basketball? Sometimes he has funny stories about the kids at the high school. He never says their names, though," he added quickly. "Just tells me about the shit they pull."

"Who does he hang out with when he's here?"

The owner crossed his arms. "I thought you wanted to know what happened Thursday."

"I do. I'm also trying to get a better picture of the victim."

"These are pretty standard questions," Greer added.

Zander appreciated the backup, since so far the sheriff had been silent.

Paul twisted his mouth as he concentrated. "Sean doesn't single anyone out. He just talks with whoever is closest."

"How'd Sean seem on Thursday? Talkative? Was he watching the game?"

"He didn't say much on Thursday. I think he mainly watched the game, but he'd been here a solid hour before the Osburne brothers came at him."

Zander spoke to the sheriff. "Osburne brothers?"

Sheriff Greer grimaced. "Troublemakers. Not the brightest bulbs in the box. I've dealt with them at least a half dozen times for DUI, fighting, and speeding. They're usually mellow unless they're drinking."

Paul was nodding at the sheriff's words. "I've had to cut them off or ask them to leave a few times. Kyle is an obnoxious drunk. One of my bartenders has had a lot of trouble with him."

"And the other brother?" asked Zander.

"Billy," said Greer. "Follows his brother's lead. Both big guys, but Kyle probably has thirty pounds on Billy."

"The two of them together don't create a whole brain," Paul added.

Sheriff Greer snorted. "You got that right."

"Okay." Zander had a good picture of the men. "Who approached who?"

"Well, I didn't see when it started. I heard the crash and turned around. Sean was on the ground, and his stool was knocked over, with Billy swinging and kicking at him, so I think he approached Sean."

"What did you do?"

"Grabbed my bat." He walked around the bar and pulled a hidden bat off a low shelf. "I hollered at them to break it up, but I was on this side of the bar, and they ignored me. Well, Billy ignored me. Sean had gotten to his feet, but he was focused on avoiding Billy's fists and boots."

"What was Kyle doing?"

"Holding back the crowd," said Paul, resting the bat on his shoulder. "A couple people tried to get involved, but few will stand up to Kyle or Billy when they're pissed. I came round the bar and knocked my bat on a few hips to clear a path. When I got through the crowd, I pointed my bat at Kyle and told him to get Billy off Sean. Both were back on the floor by then. Kyle gave me a shitty grin, grabbed his brother's shirt, and hauled him off Sean. I ordered them out, and they left."

"You didn't call the police?" Zander asked.

Paul glanced at Sheriff Greer. "They got better things to do than bust up a fight. It was over, and Sean could stand upright. I gave him a beer on the house, picked up his stool, and he went back to watching the game. It was handled."

"Sean wasn't hurt?"

"Oh, he was hurting. I fixed up a bag of ice for his lip, and I noticed he moved stiffly when he finally did leave."

Zander made a mental note to ask the medical examiner about abrasions and bruises.

"Did anyone ask him how it started?"

"Dunno. I didn't. No one is surprised when the Osburne brothers act up."

"Do you think Sean's race had anything to do with it?"

Paul scowled. "Don't know. I didn't hear what was said between them." His face cleared. "But I told you one of my bartenders always has a problem with the Osburnes—he's Mexican. They give him shit about that."

Two strong guys. Possibly racist.

The Osburne brothers were checking some boxes.

"Did you notice when Sean left?"

Paul thought hard. "He left right after the game. I remember he was disappointed in who won. He tossed down some cash for the beer and left. I can't believe he'll never be back," Paul said in a stunned voice.

"Can you give us some names of other people who witnessed the fight?" suggested Zander.

Paul hesitated.

"We don't have to say it was you who gave us the names. There were plenty of people there who could have identified others."

Paul's face cleared, and he rattled off three names, which the sheriff wrote down.

Checking what time the game had finished would be easy enough. At least Zander knew Sean had still been alive at that point. He spoke to the sheriff. "Can we visit the Osburnes?"

"I'll show you where they live," Greer said as he turned to the door.

"Hey, Sheriff," Paul said. "You gonna make book club tomorrow?"

Zander gawked at Paul. *Book club?*

Greer paused. "Your wife making the nacho dip?" the sheriff asked hopefully.

"Yep."

"I haven't read the book yet."

"You should start it. It's a good one about a real plot to kill George Washington, but you know it doesn't matter if you read the book. Just show up."

"I'll be there." The sheriff continued toward the door.

Zander silently followed, reminding himself to never make assumptions.

10

Emily parked in the quiet clearing and hoped the ghosts would stay away.

The pile of rubble grew smaller every year as it decomposed—rain, sun, and time breaking down the components. Small grains blew away with the wind. Ferns and wild grasses sprouted. In its death, the old house had given life to small glimpses of nature.

After the fire her childhood home had been knocked down, but no one hauled anything away. She wondered what kind of chemicals had leached into the ground. What nonbiodegradables would still be present in a hundred years.

No one cared.

As she stepped out of her car—with new tires—she estimated it had been four years since she visited the spot where her father died and her home burned to the ground.

It still hurt.

Good memories flashed. Hide-and-seek with her sisters. The day her father put in a swing set. Lazy summer days making "homes" in the tall grass. Bug bites. Itchy poison ivy that made her cry. Her mother had tied mittens onto her hands, and Emily had torn at them with her teeth, desperate to scratch.

Not all good memories.

But memories of poison ivy were better than remembering the night her father was murdered.

Flashing police lights. Fire engine sirens. Their hoses and water.

Madison clung to their mother, her face buried in Mother's coat. The flames lit up their mother's face as she watched the fire grow higher and the house start to fall in on itself. Shock. Fear. This wasn't happening. This had to be a dream. Emily hung tight to her mother's arm. Her mother said nothing, dumbly staring at the flames, and Emily's gaze searched their surroundings. Firemen ran and shouted. Police did the same.

A policeman approached, his face grim. And Emily knew they'd found her father.

It wasn't a dream.

Tires crunched as a vehicle approached behind her. Emily turned and her heart sank.

Brett.

The Astoria Police Department SUV parked, and she saw that her ex-husband wasn't in uniform. It was Saturday. His day off. After five years she still remembered his schedule. Annoyance shot through her. Why did her brain retain minutiae of her ex-husband's life?

How does he know I'm here?

He had no reason to be on this property. That meant he'd followed her.

Rage simmered under her skin. But she displayed no emotion.

A habit. A protective habit around Brett.

His door slammed, and he strolled over to her, nonchalantly eyeing the rubble heap and the surrounding trees. His casualness was scripted; he did nothing indifferently. Especially when she was involved.

"Hey," he said. More indifference.

As if it weren't odd that they'd crossed paths a mile out of town at the edge of the woods.

Where *no one* went.

"Hey."

"Saw you drive past me in town. I waved, but you didn't see me." He stopped three feet in front of her, his brown eyes locked on hers.

Her stomach twisted. At one time she'd melted when those eyes were turned on her. She'd longed for him to notice her, and when he finally did, she'd believed her world was perfect. Now it meant he was analyzing her, searching for nuance, hunting for subtext in every move she made and every word she said. Studying her like a bug under a microscope.

She held very still.

"You're right. I didn't see you."

"I saw where you turned and knew there could only be one destination." Concern shone on his face. "Don't tell me you come up here a lot."

"I don't."

At one time he'd been everything she thought she wanted. Strength. Maturity. Love. He was six years older than she, and she'd adored him since she'd been ten. When she was eighteen, he'd finally looked her way, and he'd liked what he saw. He became the foundation of her life.

And then the ruler of her life.

They married two years later, and it started with small things. Questions about where she had been. Wanting immediate answers to every text. Warnings about her male friends: guys have only one thing on their minds. Asking her to stay in with him instead of attending her regular girls' night.

She'd done what he asked, flattered he craved her full attention, a result of his deep love for her.

But then the requests slowly tightened around her neck.

Why shouldn't he have her email password? What was she hiding?

Why did she talk to male friends? Wasn't he enough?

Why couldn't he tag along when she went out with her girlfriends? They were his friends too.

When she refused anything, he'd question and calmly engage her for hours, trying to convince her to see his side. He loved her, he treated her like a queen. Why shouldn't she do some little things to help him feel more secure in their relationship?

It became easier to do as he asked to avoid the emotionally draining, hours-long conversations. Over time she learned to walk on eggshells around him, trying to keep him happy and content.

The constant scrutiny drove up her stress levels and wore her down. She realized she could no longer live under the same roof with him and asked for a divorce.

He was insecure. It wasn't her responsibility to cater to it.

He moved to the debris pile and kicked at an old roofing tile. "I hate this place," he said. "I don't like what it represents. Your life turned upside down that day."

"It did." *As if I'm not fully aware.* An acidic taste of anger filled her mouth.

He looked back at her, his eyes dark. "I worry about you."

She controlled her shiver. "I'm fine. I like the quiet here."

"You can find quiet in a place where your dad was murdered and your house burned down?"

Jerk. He'd said it deliberately, wanting to twist the knife in her heart under the guise of concern.

"It's true." *Keep answers short.*

"Your whole life went down a new path. Your sister left and then your mom died."

He sank the knife to its hilt.

She silently counted as she inhaled and exhaled, pacing her breaths, keeping her calm.

"I assume you still haven't heard from Tara." He turned back to the house as he spoke.

"No. Have you looked for her?"

At the police station, Brett had access to search tools that the average citizen did not. But during their marriage, she'd never asked him to look. They'd rarely talked about Tara.

He and Tara had dated for several months during her senior year, breaking up only weeks before their father was murdered.

"No, I've never looked for her," he said. "It's none of my business. She broke up with me, remember? And she always talked about getting out of this shit town. She had her eyes on bigger things, so I'm not surprised she left us all behind." He shrugged.

Emily didn't believe that. Brett didn't like that Tara had left without a backward glance at him. His insecurity kept him from understanding how that could happen to him.

She suspected he'd searched for her and failed.

But his ego wouldn't allow him to admit it.

"Madison has researched extensively," Emily stated, watching him. She'd learned to read him as carefully as he read her. During the last months of their marriage, they'd tentatively circled each other, each constantly guessing what the other was thinking, their verbal communication in the toilet. All trust gone.

"Oh. Good for her. Nothing, though?"

He's too casual. He wants to know.

Does he still want her after all these years?

Emily was always second. Second sister. Second choice.

Deep down she'd known he didn't love her enough—she was just another infatuated woman to bolster his insecurity—but she had chosen to ignore it. Instead she'd naively hoped to replace Tara in Brett's heart.

Later she'd realized he didn't hold Tara in his heart; he just couldn't accept that she had dumped him. It turned into an obsession.

"Madison hasn't found her. She thinks Tara changed her name."

He nodded. "Makes sense." He turned back to her, his gaze probing. "Want to get a cup of coffee?"

She stiffened. Nothing would be more uncomfortable. "No, I need to get back to the diner."

"Okay. I'll follow you out."

Like hell you will. "Go ahead. I'm going to spend a few more minutes here. Memories, you know," she said, scrambling for a reason to make him leave.

He studied her for a moment.

He was still attractive. Her brain recognized it even if her heart screamed for her to get away.

"Emily . . . we weren't that bad together, were we?" He sounded apprehensive, but curious.

She couldn't speak. Had time erased everything she'd explained to him?

His insecurity had turned her into a shadow of the independent woman she'd been. It'd taken over a year for her to find her confidence again.

"It's been five years, Brett. I'm not going to start this discussion again. We said everything that needs to be said."

He frowned. "I know, but—"

"No buts. Why waste time examining something that is long over?"

"But when we're together—like now—it feels—"

"Wrong. It feels very, very wrong." She glared, her eyes begging him to stop.

The corners of his lips sagged, and his brows came together, sending mild panic up her spine. Emily knew the signs. He was preparing to argue his point until she simply gave in, exhausted.

But they weren't married anymore.

"Go home, Brett." She turned away and raised one hand in farewell, hoping he'd take the hint. Not waiting to find out, she headed toward the tree line, passing through what used to be the backyard of the home. She walked blindly, her hearing attuned to the sound of his car door.

Relief swamped her as his door finally opened and closed. A moment later the engine started.

Thank you, God.

She hadn't spoken to him in months. What on earth had prompted him to attempt a possible reconciliation today? Short-term memory loss?

Occasionally she'd see him drive through town—he still lived in Bartonville. She hated that her heart seized every time she saw an Astoria police SUV, and her head turned to see if it was him.

Their breakup had been ugly.

She slammed to a stop, and Brett vanished from her thoughts as she stared at the short tree trunk.

Years ago, after Chet Carlson was put away for her father's murder, someone had cut down *the* tree. She'd never known who. She'd never asked, and no one ever brought it up. The destruction felt justified, and no doubt it had been a healing moment for someone. She'd long suspected one of her great-aunts had cut down the tree.

But seeing the stump was always a shock.

She passed the stump and walked into the firs. Wind rustled through their branches, making the colossal trees gently sway. The ground was soaked. Weeks of continual rain had turned this entire tip of the state into a sodden site. She stopped and rested a hand on a trunk, feeling the vibrations in the bark as it swayed. Out of habit she scanned the ground around the trees, looking for cracks, signs the wind had loosened the root ball of one of the giant trees. It was rare for one of the trees to fall, but a strong windstorm after weeks of rain could cause a disaster.

She'd seen homes crushed by the immense trees. Her mother had always worried about falling firs when they lived in the little house. She'd often walked the woods, looking for cracks after heavy rains and wind.

Firs hadn't been the end of the home.

Her throat grew thick, and she couldn't swallow. Tears threatened, and she let them roll. No one was here to see her. No prying eyes or pointed questions to answer. She leaned against a fir and allowed herself to feel. Feel the pain and loss and rage at the destruction of her family. It erupted, swamping her, and she bent at the waist, wrapping her arms around her abdomen. She'd lost her father and her home, and then Tara, and then her mother. A domino effect that had started with her father's violent death.

Fifteen seconds later, the avalanche of emotions was gone, leaving her drained, with sweat at her temples and gasping for air. A headache threatened at the base of her skull, and her legs felt like weak twigs. This wasn't the first time she'd fallen apart in this place.

It was one of the reasons she stayed away.

She shuddered and looked about, spotting the stump through the firs.

The rest of the forest faded away as she stared at the blemish among the wild growth.

Something happened here, the stump said.

Something deadly. Something final. Something irrevocable.

Chet Carlson had received a life sentence for her father's murder, and the punishment was a small bandage on her damaged heart. It helped. But it didn't heal.

There was no one to punish for her mother's suicide. Emily blamed Chet Carlson, but she knew her mother and the adults who had claimed to love her mother shared a bit of the fault too. The passage of time had applied tentative protection around her pain. Sometimes the protection held fast; other times it let pain seep through.

Right now the pain seeped, inflamed by the sight of the home's pathetic remains.

And the resurgent memory of Tara's betrayal.

11

A phone call from Seth Rutledge, the medical examiner, delayed Zander's plans to pay a visit to the Osburne brothers.

Dr. Rutledge caught Zander in the parking lot of Patrick's Place. He said he had preliminary findings from the autopsies of Sean and Lindsay Fitch. Zander joined Sheriff Greer in his county SUV, squeezing under the computer and monitor that stuck out over half of the passenger seat—a typical annoyance for the front of a law enforcement vehicle—and put his phone on speaker.

"Go ahead, Seth. Sheriff Greer is here too."

"Morning, guys." Dr. Rutledge's voice filled the vehicle.

"Don't tell me you're done already," Greer said.

"I start early," answered Dr. Rutledge. "A typical autopsy takes me about two hours. Sometimes more, sometimes less."

"I trust you were extra thorough with this couple," said the sheriff.

"I'm thorough with each body."

Zander bit the inside of his cheek at Seth's pointed comeback. "We just found out that Sean was in a bar fight the night he was killed—or the night before he was killed, depending on your time of death," he told Seth. "The bartender witnessed kicks to his stomach and some blows to his face. I assume you found supporting evidence?"

"Definitely. And that answers a question of mine," answered Dr. Rutledge. "At first I'd assumed Sean's abrasions and scrapes were from fighting with his attackers. Then I got his preliminary blood results."

Zander and the sheriff exchanged a glance.

"Both Sean and Lindsay had large doses of GHB in their system. I doubt he was conscious enough to fight his attackers. It makes sense if he received the injuries in an earlier fight."

"What's GHB?" asked Zander.

"The type I found in the Fitches is basically homemade Ecstasy. There's a euphoric high and then a crash, making people sleep heavily—or die. The homemade stuff can vary in potency, especially when the makers get sloppy. It's flat-out dangerous."

"Holy shit," muttered the sheriff.

Zander was stunned. Had the couple taken the drug themselves? Or had they been drugged to facilitate the attack? "Did the forensics techs say they'd found drugs in the house?" he asked the sheriff. Greer slowly shook his head, his countenance grim.

"We'll notify forensics to watch for it in the evidence they took from the home," Zander told Dr. Rutledge. "What would they be looking for, Doc? Pills? Liquid?"

"Judging by their stomach contents and the drug levels in their blood, it was ingested in liquid form. So take special care with any used cups, bottles, or mugs. Check the liquids in their refrigerator. It's colorless and tasteless."

The sheriff scribbled a note. "We need to go back through the home. I know the refrigerator contents weren't taken for examination. Same with dirty dishes."

"Sean had drinks at the bar," Zander said quietly.

"That doesn't account for Lindsay being drugged," said the sheriff, still writing in his notebook. "But let's keep it in mind if nothing turns up in their house."

"Could it have been injected?" Zander asked, wondering if something could have been administered during Sean's bar scuffle.

"I didn't find any injection sites," answered Dr. Rutledge. "But Sean had abrasions on his knuckles, jaw, and cheekbone, and deep bruising on his abdomen and back. Consistent with fighting and being kicked."

"Any other injuries?" Zander asked.

"Not current. He had an old break in his radius and was well on his way to heart disease."

"He was only twenty-seven," the sheriff said, shock in his voice.

"Yep. I see it in younger people all the time. And also his heart was no longer beating by the time they hanged him. Livor was present in his lower extremities. He was hanged soon after being killed."

"They hanged a dead man," Zander said slowly. The killers had an agenda.

"They did. Maybe they thought he was still alive, but one of the stabbings cleanly sliced through his aorta. He bled out quickly. This was his cause of death." The doctor paused. "Nineteen stab wounds. Twenty-one on Lindsay."

Zander's head reeled. Someone had been angry. Very angry.

"And Zander." Dr. Rutledge's voice lowered. "Lindsay was pregnant. I'd say around two months." The doctor's tone was careful.

Zander's vision narrowed, focused on the cars speeding by on the road beyond the parking lot. He felt the sheriff's curious stare pointed his way. "That's horrible." His voice was even, flat, as he tried to ignore the sudden ringing in his ears.

"Think she knew?" muttered the sheriff.

"In my experience, most women know," said Dr. Rutledge. "But some go into labor with no idea that they were pregnant. I thought those were made-up stories until it happened to the daughter of a friend of mine." Wonder filled his voice. "They scrambled to buy diapers and a car seat. No one knew."

Zander briefly closed his eyes. Why were some people handed children while others agonized and suffered to create a family?

"Did she have defensive wounds, Doctor?" asked Greer.

"She had two cuts on her lower arms. With the amount of GHB in her system, I suspect this was a feeble attempt at defense. Livor mortis is consistent with the position she was found in, on her side. She wasn't moved."

Unlike Sean.

Had Sean been the target? Zander wondered. Or both? Was the pregnancy a factor?

Not knowing the motive bothered him.

"Time of death, Doc?" he asked.

"I estimate between midnight and three a.m."

"Both of them?"

"Yes."

"Anything else that would help us at the moment?"

"Not for now. You'll have my report this evening . . . well, except for the extended toxicology results. I requested additional testing, and sometimes it takes a while."

"Good call. I'd like to know if they had anything else in their systems."

Zander ended the call and sat silently for a moment. The sheriff respected the silence. Zander suspected his brain was also going at full speed. Dr. Rutledge had given them a lot to process.

"Do we want to go to the Osburnes' right away?" Zander asked.

Sheriff Greer's hands tightened and twisted on the steering wheel. "Maybe we first need to see if any Osburne fingerprints turned up in the Fitch household. From what I understand, the brothers wouldn't have visited Sean and Lindsay socially."

Zander understood. A visit might tip their hand. The presence of the brothers' fingerprints inside the home would most likely indicate they'd been there for the attack. "Let's drive by and see if anyone is home. You know what they drive?"

"An older Ford king cab and a Durango."

Zander was duly impressed by the prompt response. But the sheriff had known that the Osburnes had fought with Sean ahead of their visit to the bar. He might have checked.

"Sheriff," Zander asked, "how many race-based crimes do you see every year around here?"

Greer rubbed at the back of his neck as he thought. "Dunno. You never know if race is what started something. And honestly, ninety-nine percent of the population around here is white. That other one percent is Latino."

"Any reported race incidents involving the brothers?"

"I'll have to look. As far as I know, they pick fights with everyone." He shook his head. "Every time I cross paths with them, they're working somewhere new. Or not working at all."

Zander wasn't surprised. The entire coast of Oregon was slightly isolated. A low mountain range separated the cities from the rest of the state, and few extra jobs were available. Unemployment was high. This was no California coast with warm weather and perfect bodies. Living on the Oregon coast took dedication and a thick coat.

Greer turned the ignition. "The Osburne place isn't very far from here."

"I'll follow."

The sheriff's Ford Explorer abruptly pulled onto the shoulder of the narrow road and slammed to a stop. Zander sucked in a breath as he hit the brakes and pulled in behind him.

Zander had been distracted, studying the homes along the two-lane highway. Maybe it was the bleak weather, but the properties scattered among the tall trees and brush had depressed him. Many held broken-down vehicles, rusted swing sets, and barns with giant holes in their roofs.

Greer stepped out of his vehicle, and Zander did the same. As far as he could see, they weren't near a home or driveway. There were only trees.

The sheriff's face was grim as he strode toward him, and the hair on the back of Zander's neck rose.

"What happened?" Zander asked, his stomach sinking.

"Just got a call. One of my deputies shot himself this morning, so I need to go there first. The Osburnes will have to wait."

"What?" Shock jangled through Zander's nerves.

Greer crossed his arms and looked away. "It was Copeland," he said through white lips.

Zander instantly placed the name. "Your deputy from yesterday morning. The one who took down Sean's body."

"He's dead. My boys say he used his service weapon."

Zander couldn't speak. *Is this related to the Fitch murders?*

"I need to go." The sheriff turned away, his shoulders stooped.

"I'm coming with you."

Greer glanced back. "Thank you, but that's not necessary."

"Yesterday your deputy was the first officer at a crime scene that I'm investigating, and today he's dead?" Zander held the sheriff's gaze. "I'm coming."

Greer stared. He looked as if he'd aged ten years since they'd talked at the pub. "Suit yourself," he muttered.

He knows I have a point.

Zander climbed back in his vehicle and immediately called Ava.

Minutes later Zander parked behind the sheriff again. The Copeland home was in a small residential neighborhood full of cookie-cutter one-story homes on small lots with green grass. The street was crowded with law enforcement vehicles. Clatsop County, Astoria, City of Seaside, and even a state patrol vehicle. Officers stood in small groups in front of the home, and neighbors pressed against the caution tape, snapping pictures.

Ava's SUV caught his eye. She was on her phone, pacing beside it. She had still been in downtown Bartonville, so she'd beaten them to the scene, and because Ava had interviewed Copeland yesterday, she knew where he lived. She hung up as Zander and Greer approached, her blue eyes somber.

"I updated the boss," she told them. "And I was told the medical examiner went inside the home here a few moments ago."

"Copeland was such a young kid," muttered Greer.

"He was young. Do you think the murders got to him?" Ava asked. Her tone indicated she found it doubtful.

"How'd he seem when you talked to him yesterday?" Zander asked her.

"He was shook up and definitely upset, but I got the sense he wanted to see justice done for the couple." Her eyes narrowed. "I didn't see an officer not wanting to live because of what he'd experienced." She gestured at Greer. "But you knew him better."

"I never saw or heard of any suicidal tendencies on his part," said the sheriff. "But let's get the facts first."

Greer scanned the groups of waiting officers. They'd all stopped their conversations and were facing his way. Palpable pain radiated from them as they waited for their sheriff to do something, anything.

Zander knew the sheriff could do nothing to ease the grief.

"I want two officers to keep the civilians back from the tape," Greer ordered the closest group. "Tell them to put their phones away. Have some respect." He ducked under the tape and headed up the short walk. Zander and Ava followed. The three of them signed a log held by a deputy at the front door.

The deputy's eyes were red and swollen, but he stood ramrod straight as they wrote down their names. The sheriff removed his hat and rested a hand briefly on the deputy's shoulder. He gave a quick squeeze and nodded but didn't speak.

Gratitude flickered in the deputy's eyes.

The three of them passed through the front door, and Zander squared his shoulders to face another death scene.

The body was in the living room immediately to their right. Nate Copeland sat in a recliner, his feet on the raised footrest. The chair had been reclined back so far that it was almost flat. Copeland could have been taking a nap except for the blood caking his head and neck. A young Hispanic male bent over the body, doing something under Copeland's raised shirt. He looked up at the trio.

"Hey, Sheriff."

"Dr. Ruiz," said Greer. "This is Special Agent Wells and Special Agent—"

"McLane," said the young medical examiner, looking at Ava. "We met a while back. Or is it Special Agent Callahan now?"

"Not yet," Ava answered. "The wedding is this summer." She glanced at Zander. "Dr. Ruiz handled my DB on a case at the coast last fall."

Dead body.

The medical examiner straightened as he removed a thermometer from the slit he'd cut at Copeland's liver. He checked the reading and then gently bent the body's arm back and forth at the elbow. "No rigor," he stated as he also moved the officer's fingers. "Body temperature is only a few degrees below normal. What's the temperature in here?"

Zander stepped to the thermostat on the living room wall. "Seventy."

Dr. Ruiz tipped his head as he studied the body. "He's been dead about two or three hours."

The sheriff exhaled loudly. "Midmorning. Not long, then." He turned and motioned to a deputy near the door. "Start a canvass of the neighborhood. See if anyone heard anything." The man nodded and left, stepping around a crime scene tech with a camera.

Greer waved her in. "You got here fast."

"Hearing it's one of ours lights a fire under everyone," she said. She frowned at the medical examiner, clearly unhappy that he was working in the crime scene.

"I took my own pictures before I touched the body," Dr. Ruiz told her. "I'll get them to you, and I'll be out of your way in a minute."

Ruiz turned back to Copeland as the tech started to circle the edge of the room, snapping pictures nonstop. The medical examiner shone a flashlight in Copeland's mouth. "Entrance wound through the hard palate." He gently palpated the skull. "Good-size exit wound."

Based on the blood and brain matter splattered on the chair and wall, Zander had already assumed that. Copeland's weapon lay in his lap, his hand at his side. Zander stared hard at the gun and the position of Copeland's hands and arms. He didn't see anything that indicated Copeland hadn't shot himself.

But he was keeping an open mind.

Is someone tampering with this investigation?

Dr. Ruiz glanced at Greer. "We'll check his hands for GSR."

"Of course he'll have gunshot residue on his hands," Greer pointed out. "He handles guns every day. For all I know he took his weapon to the range yesterday."

"The particle count from the residue will tell us," Dr. Ruiz said. "It'll be very high if he fired the weapon right here." The doctor removed his gloves and set them near the gun. "I assume I'll be working on this one?" He glanced at Greer. "Or are you sending it to Portland like yesterday's deaths?"

Sheriff Greer looked to Zander and Ava.

"No offense, Doctor," said Ava, "but since Seth Rutledge has already seen two bodies from this case, I think he should see this one."

"You think it's related to yesterday?" Ruiz asked.

"We can't rule it out," answered Zander. He looked over the living room, noting the furniture and decor seemed a couple of decades old. "Do you know if Copeland lived here alone?" he asked the sheriff.

"Yesterday he told me he lived with his parents," answered Ava. "He also said they were in Mexico for several weeks."

"Who found him?"

"One of the other deputies—Daigle—was to pick him up this morning," said Sheriff Greer. "They had plans to go to Short Sands. A beach south of here," he clarified. "Daigle called it in after he found him."

"He still around?"

"I saw him out front." The sheriff strode to the door and looked out. "Daigle! In here," he shouted. "Please," he tacked on almost as an afterthought.

The deputy who appeared wore sagging jeans and a heavy coat. His round face was blotchy and his eyes swollen. He deliberately kept his gaze on the sheriff, avoiding the sight of the body.

Zander felt for him. Daigle looked barely out of high school. The same thing he'd observed about Copeland yesterday. To him all the deputies appeared very young, and he wondered if he was simply getting old.

He didn't feel old. Forty wasn't old.

Except maybe in the eyes of twentysomething-year-olds.

Ava frowned at the deputy, two lines forming between her brows, and Zander wondered if she was having the same thoughts.

The deputy shook hands with Zander and Ava as Greer introduced him. Polite. Exceedingly polite. Often what Zander had seen from fresh graduates of the state's police academy before they had much experience.

"When did you last talk to Copeland?" Ava asked.

"Last night, ma'am," Daigle said as he wiped his nose on his sleeve. "We agreed I'd drive and pick him up around noon."

"He sounded interested in the trip?" asked Zander.

"Yes, sir. We were both looking forward to getting out of town for the afternoon."

"It's cold, damp, and windy," Ava pointed out. "Why would you go to the beach?"

The sheriff snorted lightly as Daigle answered earnestly. "If we waited for perfect weather around here, we'd never leave home. We're used to it. Shorty's has some protected areas where you can build a fire and stay out of the wind."

"What do you do there?" It sounded miserable to Zander, protected or not.

Daigle shrugged, looking at his feet.

Drink. Smoke pot.

Zander exchanged a glance with Ava, whose lips twitched. He wondered if Daigle had drawn the short straw to be the driver.

"Nate needed to get away after his shitty morning yesterday," Daigle explained.

"How'd you get in the house?" Zander asked.

"Door was unlocked. I rang the bell, and no one answered. I could see—see him through the window, so I opened the door."

"Copeland ever say anything in the past that made you worry for him?" Zander continued.

"No, sir. I understand what you're asking. I never dreamed this would happen in a million years. I'd say I'm his closest friend, and I never saw this coming. If he had depression, he never told me about it."

"Many people won't discuss it," Ava said quietly. "Even with their closest friends or family. We'll check for some antidepressants."

"I can't believe he did this knowing I'd be the one to find him," mumbled Daigle. "Fucker." He wiped an eye.

Ava's eyes were gentle. "Maybe he trusted you."

"Still sucks. Never gonna get that out of my head." He glanced briefly at the body and shuddered.

The sheriff raised a brow at Zander and Ava. They nodded. "You can go, son," he told the deputy. "We'll talk later."

Daigle left without a word.

"Has anyone reached Copeland's parents?" Zander asked.

"I left a vague message for them to call me. Nothing yet," answered Greer. "Let's take a quick look around."

The three of them split up. Zander took the single bathroom, where he checked the medicine cabinet and under the sink. He found medication containers, but the names on them were John and Helen Copeland. Except for a blood pressure prescription, he wasn't familiar with the names of the drugs.

"Nothing in the bedrooms," stated the sheriff as he walked down the hall.

"No medication in the kitchen," Ava said from the rear of the house. "But come take a look at this."

Zander and Greer joined her in the kitchen, where she stood in front of the open refrigerator. "See that?" She pointed at a six-pack of Miller Lite on the top shelf. "It's right next to an unopened container of ranch dip." She gestured at the counter, where three bags of potato chips sat next to a small cooler. "Looks like he intended to go somewhere today."

"Like to hang with a buddy at the beach." Greer swore under his breath.

Zander opened the cabinet under the sink and pulled out the trash. He carefully dug through the top items with gloved hands and found what he was looking for. A receipt for beer, chips, dip, and a bag of ice. "Is there a new bag of ice in the freezer?"

Ava checked. "Yep."

The three of them exchanged a long look.

"By the way, the prescription containers I found have different names on them," Zander said. "John and Helen Copeland?"

"Those are his parents." The sheriff was grim. "I've known both of them for over twenty years. Telling them is going to be one of the hardest things I've ever done." His face sagged.

"We can—" Ava started.

Greer raised his hand to stop her. "I'll talk to his parents. It's best coming from someone they know." He paused. "Not that there's any good way to deliver this news."

Zander stepped closer to the others and lowered his voice. "There's a good possibility this isn't a suicide."

Emotions struggled on the sheriff's face, and he rubbed his temple. "I'm trying to keep an open mind, but I don't like what you're implying. I *know* this community."

"This crime could have come from outside your community," Zander said.

"But why?" Greer's voice cracked.

"If we knew that, we'd have our murderers," answered Ava. "Whether it's homegrown or not, something is rotten in this little town."

"And I don't think it's over," Zander said slowly. He had no basis for the statement; it was his gut speaking.

The look in Ava's eyes told him she agreed.

12

The handle to the Anita Haircut salon's door was in Emily's grip when someone behind her called her name. She turned away and clenched her teeth as she spotted who had spoken.

Leann Windfield.

Leann was a reporter for the county's online newspaper and liked to poke and pester Emily's family. Leann had used her job to write several articles about the Bartons, framing them as historical pieces while emphasizing that the Barton family had always been self-centered and money hungry. She presented the history in such a way that her opinions appeared based on fact. The problem was that Leann had cherry-picked her facts, leaving out anything good the Bartons had accomplished.

Leann had been in Emily's high school class, but they hadn't had the same circle of friends. They could have ignored each other all four years, but for a reason Emily never understood, Leann had singled out Madison for harassment.

Even in high school, Madison had continued to be quiet and keep to herself. To students who strove to meet the status quo, she was perceived as an oddity. They didn't understand her, so they picked on her. It was like when a pack of wolves attacks a pure white wolf for his difference. Mean girls ran in packs, and Leann was the head bully, bolstered by her group of followers.

Madison ignored them; they never physically touched her. She shrugged when Emily tried to talk to her about it, and Emily's heart broke over the treatment of her younger sibling. But the mean girls spread stories, passed from student to student, and many liked to repeat the words to Emily to see her reaction.

Leann had no bone to pick with Madison. And Madison's lack of response should have taken the joy out of Leann's harassment, but Emily responded. Fear of consequences didn't stop Emily when she had a little sister to protect.

The fuse of her temper was long. She rarely reacted out of anger. But the spark had traveled along the full length of her fuse when it came to Leann harassing Madison.

Madison was Emily's responsibility.

Emily strode down the school hallway, her gaze fixed on the blonde ponytail amid four other ponytails of different hues. Emily's utter preoccupation blurred the lockers, doors, and students she passed. She had one goal. "Leann!"

The ponies turned as one.

Emily stopped nearly nose-to-nose with Leann. Both of them were popular, both got good grades, and both had large circles of friends. The power balance was equal. Emily felt rather than saw other students stop and stare, their whispers white noise in her ears.

"Why did you spread that rumor about Madison?" Emily hissed. "I traced it back to you starting it at Bryan Sprig's party. You know it's not true."

Leann looked to her ponies for support. "I think it's true. Your sister is weird."

"She's a straight-A student."

Leann shrugged. "Lots of psychopaths are smart." A slow smile crossed her face. "You know, they say it can stem from a tragic event in childhood. Her brain probably cracked soon after your mother's did."

Emily couldn't speak as the head pony turned and led her herd away.

A deluge of emotions slammed into Emily, making sweat start under her armpits, Leann's sham smile filling her mind. They'd butted heads several times since high school. All of it instigated by Leann.

She wasn't worth Emily's time.

Emily turned back to the Anita Haircut door. *Ignore her.*

"I hear you found two dead bodies yesterday."

She stiffened. "Go away, Leann."

"I'm trying to get some facts for my article."

"Then talk to the police."

"I have. A statement from you would be helpful."

Emily looked back at her. "You've never said a kind word about my family in person or in the paper."

"I just report facts, Emily. That's my job. Did yesterday stir up some bad memories for you?" Fake sympathy shone in her eyes. "Must have been horrible seeing something like that . . . so similar to your father's death."

Every cell in Emily's body screamed for her to get inside the salon to put space between herself and the leech. But she didn't. Warning bells rang in her brain as she slowly pivoted. She wasn't angry, but she craved satisfaction.

And thinking before she spoke wasn't her strong suit.

"How is that *fact-reporting* job treating you? I heard they cut everyone's pay again."

"Tell me what happened yesterday. The public deserves to know." Ignoring Emily's comment and all business now, Leann tapped the screen of her phone, and Emily assumed she'd turned on a recorder.

"I've got nothing to say."

"I heard your tires were slashed later that day."

"What about it?"

"Seems odd to happen so soon after you discovered two murders."

"I also burned my fingers at work," Emily said in a mild tone. "Do you think that's odd so soon after the murders?"

Leann tapped her screen again and dropped the phone in her purse, giving Emily a side-eye. "Sarcasm isn't appropriate. Two people are dead. I understand the FBI is in town to give a hand in the investigation."

Emily said nothing, thinking of Zander Wells. She didn't need to tell Leann about the agent. It had taken less than one day for her to see that Zander was damned good at his job. And when her aunts swarmed, it hadn't intimidated him. Another plus in Emily's eyes.

"If you don't want to talk, I'm sure one of your aunts will." Leann edged closer, fake curiosity in her eyes. "I wonder how they feel about the second hanging in Bartonville's history."

Emily was finished with the conversation. And Leann. "If you hound my aunts with a single question, I *will* call your boss."

Emily spun back to the door and yanked it open, the bell on the inner handle clanging loudly. Inside three women stared at her, their mouths slightly open. They hovered at the window, where they'd enjoyed a view of the altercation. The door swung shut behind Emily, and she silently groaned as she met their eyes.

Anita was the first to recover, strolling back to her salon chair as she spoke. "I see that snippy reporter has you in her sights again." She waved her scissors so her client in the black nylon cape would sit back down. "Stay away from her, Emily. One time she wanted an interview about the shop, but it turned out she was fishing for information about one of my clients. I don't gossip," she said firmly as she combed and snipped at the wet head of her client, who nodded in affirmation.

Emily disagreed with her gossip claim.

"That girl has had it in for your family for years," Anita said, making eye contact with Emily in the mirror. "What's she after this time?"

"Just the usual." Unless Emily wanted her words spread across town, she knew to keep them to herself in the salon. She sucked in a breath and frowned as she studied the faces, remembering why she'd come. "I thought my aunt Dory had an appointment right now."

"She canceled. Not feeling well, the poor thing."

Just the usual.

One day Dory would acknowledge that she'd rarely been sick in her life—except for that time she had food poisoning. If her hypochondriac aunt would put the energy she burned worrying about her health into something else, she could change the world.

"Thanks, Anita. I'll catch her at home." Emily stepped back outside into the cool air, thankful to see that Leann had left. Remnants of irritation vibrated under her skin.

Why do I let Leann get to me?

Since yesterday morning, Emily had been off-balance, caught up in a whirlwind of fresh and old painful memories. She felt as bleak as the coastal weather. Gray. Unstable. Cold.

Abandoned.

Tara and her parents now haunted her thoughts in a way they hadn't for years. She'd experienced nearly thirty-six hours of distressing events. Emily pressed her fingers over her eyes, trying to erase the images of her father that kept attacking her brain.

Her life had veered down a difficult road since the night he'd died. She'd dreamed of leaving town for college, marrying the perfect man, having 2.5 kids, and enjoying a wonderful career. Instead her life was money issues. Family issues. Ex-husband issues. Madison issues.

Maybe she should have escaped, like Tara.

Does she know our mother committed suicide?

Would her mother be alive if Tara had stayed and told what she'd seen?

Zander wanted to send the sheriff home. The strain of the last two days showed in Greer's face, and his movements had slowed considerably. Instead the two of them were finally on their way to the Osburne brothers' house. The sheriff could offer valuable insight into the interview, and the brothers might be more open to a familiar face—even if the sheriff had arrested them a few times—than an unfamiliar FBI agent.

They left Ava behind at the Copeland home to keep an eye on the crime scene team. The Copeland parents had called the sheriff as he and Zander were getting ready to leave. Seeing Greer's face as he read the name on his phone screen had made Zander thankful that notifying the parents wasn't his job. The sheriff had stepped into the backyard to deliver the news.

His eyes and nose were red when he returned.

The sheriff's vehicle took a sharp turn off the highway. If he hadn't been following someone, Zander would never have spotted the driveway. A beat-up line of mailboxes was the only indicator that homes were somewhere down the rocky road. Water splashed against the undercarriage as his vehicle bounced through deep puddles. He passed a faded sign: **Roamer's Rest**. Up ahead he spotted several manufactured homes in an uneven row.

A bright-turquoise house made him wonder if the owner had gotten a good price on the paint or if, possibly, their cataracts had softened the true intensity of the shade.

Maybe they simply liked the color.

The other homes were browns and grays, blending into the landscape subdued by the mist. It was as if a cloud had nestled into the valley with the small manufactured home park. Zander scanned the tall firs surrounding the homes, wondering what quirk of nature concentrated the heavy mist in the area.

The sheriff parked and Zander pulled in alongside him. Stepping out of his vehicle, Greer pointed at the turquoise home, indicating their target. "Believe it or not, they're easygoing boys," the sheriff told him. "Not very quick to react. I don't expect any trouble."

Unless they've been drinking.

"We don't need backup?" Zander asked.

"We're just talking. They'll be fine."

Zander checked the far side of the home and then stood back on the gravel drive as the sheriff took the few steps to a small wooden porch along a long side of the home. "I don't see another door," Zander said quietly.

"Nope. They built an addition that eliminated the other exit."

"That can't be up to code."

"It's not." Greer looked at Zander and shrugged. "They're aware. Not much else I can do."

The sheriff slid his flashlight out of his utility belt, stepped to the side of the door, and rapped it on the wood frame.

"Billy? Kyle? You home? It's Sheriff Greer. I have some questions about the bar fight the other night."

Zander watched the windows and spotted a flutter of curtains at the closest one. He'd unzipped his jacket but left his weapon holstered, same as the sheriff, hoping Greer was right about the best way to approach the brothers.

The door opened. A man in his forties wearing faded jeans stepped out. A red flannel shirt with its sleeves rolled up revealed parts of several tattoos. His hair was a little too long, but he was clean shaven. He swaggered, the air of a brawler hovering around him. He spotted Zander and gave a hard stare, staking his territory.

Amused, Zander kept his gaze relaxed and nonchalant.

"Your brother home, Kyle?" asked Greer.

"He's workin'."

"Where's he working these days?"

"Auto parts store."

"In Warrenton?"

"Yep. Been there three months."

Zander pulled out his phone and sent a text to Ava, requesting one of the deputies at the Copeland scene go to the auto parts store to keep Billy Osburne in sight and to follow if Billy left the store. Ava responded with a thumbs-up.

"Good for him. How about yourself?"

"Still lookin'." Defensiveness rose in his tone.

"Something will turn up," the sheriff said. "You know the bar fight I'm talking about at Patrick's the night before last, right?"

"Yep." Kyle shoved his hands in his pockets. "Everyone walked away. No big deal."

"It was Billy, right? You watched and then pulled him off?"

"That's right. Wasn't more than fifteen seconds. The dude was back to drinking his beer at the bar before we left."

"That's what Paul told us too."

Kyle took in Zander again, looking him over from head to toe. "Who's he?"

"He's from Portland. Helping us with a case. How well do you know Sean Fitch?" Greer asked, pulling Kyle's attention back.

"Don't know him at all. Never talked to him, but I've seen him around. Not many black guys in town. He sticks out, you know?" Kyle grinned, apparently in the belief that he was amusing.

"What about Billy? How well does he know Sean?"

Kyle glanced over at Zander. "You'd have to ask Billy."

"He knew him well enough to start a fight," Greer said casually.

"Sean started it," Kyle firmly stated.

Zander watched the man's body language. Kyle was tightly strung, moving from having his hands in his pockets to crossing his arms across his chest and then back. Zander studied his knuckles and hands, searching for bruising or abrasions. He saw none. Kyle's eye contact with the sheriff was pretty good, but he was frequently distracted by Zander and kept glancing his way.

None of his movements were unusual for a man being questioned by the police. Guilty or not.

Kyle hadn't said a word about Sean's death.

Does he know?

"Why did Sean take a swing at Billy?" asked the sheriff. "He pissed about something?"

Kyle rubbed his chin. "He and Billy have an ongoing thing. You'll need to talk to Billy about that." His gaze narrowed on the sheriff, and his tone hardened. "What's Sean saying? That Billy started it? That's a bunch of bull."

Zander froze, scouring every subtle clue in Kyle's tone, face, and body language.

If Kyle was lying, he was damned good.

The sheriff didn't flinch. "I don't know. We'll talk to Billy next. What time's he done with work?"

"He's off at five."

Just another hour or so.

"Why don't you give me a heads-up on what this *thing* is between Billy and Sean."

Kyle twisted his lips to one side, his focus on his feet as he considered. He finally looked up. "You didn't hear it from me."

Greer nodded.

Zander tensed, shifting his weight to the balls of his feet, wanting to move closer to catch the revelation. Kyle surreptitiously glanced left and right, his eyes gleaming, and he lowered his voice.

"Billy was fucking Sean's wife, Lindsay."

13

"Do you believe Kyle doesn't know Sean was murdered that night?" Sheriff Greer's face was troubled. He posed the question to Zander as they stood in the parking lot behind the sheriff's department in Warrenton. They'd left the Osburne home without mentioning the deaths and were still stunned by Kyle's revelation about Billy and Lindsay.

Zander vacillated, unsure which news was more important to their case—that Kyle didn't know Sean and Lindsay were dead, or that Billy possibly had something going on with Lindsay.

"You'd think Kyle would have at least heard some gossip by now," Zander answered. "But I have to say, I didn't get the feeling Kyle was lying. He seemed sincere to me. But surely Billy has heard about the murders at work. I find it odd he hasn't told Kyle."

"The auto parts store is here in Warrenton, though. Could be the word hasn't spread this far from Bartonville yet."

"Two murders? It was even on the news last night."

"Do you think those two brothers watch the news?"

He had a point.

"If Kyle isn't working, he could be out of the loop too," Greer said.

"I struggle to believe that in a community this small, some people haven't heard."

The sheriff spread his hands, indicating the empty surrounding hills. "A lotta space between some of the homes. You'd be surprised how many people around there don't talk to another human for a week or more. It's very possible." He rubbed his eyes. "Dammit. For a few minutes, I actually forgot about Copeland's death. What a fucked-up day."

"We need to have Dr. Rutledge check the paternity of Lindsay's baby," Zander muttered.

"What difference will it make who the father is?" Greer said bitterly. "Both the mother and the baby are dead."

Dead. Mother. Baby.

Zander fought to hide the shudder that abruptly racked his limbs. "You know as well as I do that it could indicate motivation. Or at least part of the motivation," he said. "We should find out anyway. I'll shoot him an email."

"We'll need a sample from Billy."

"Let's first see if it's Sean's." Zander took a deep breath. This case was getting more twisted by the minute. "Has Kyle or Billy been in the prison system?"

The sheriff took off his hat and ran a hand through his hair. "I remember Kyle going away for a bit. Assault charge, I think. I want to say he was down in Salem at the state pen. I think Billy's only been held in the county lockup, but I can double-check." He replaced the hat and gave a firm tug on the brim. "Let's head inside and take a look. I need to check in with the crime scene unit back at Copeland's too."

Zander followed the sheriff toward a back door at the department. "Did you get a good look at Kyle's tattoos?" he asked. Clear, black, curved lines burned in Zander's memory. But the top of the tattoo had disappeared under Kyle's sleeve.

Greer frowned. "Didn't pay attention, I guess." His face cleared. "We have photos of his tattoos on file from his arrests. I'll find them. We started recording tattoos about five years ago. Sometimes the Portland Police Bureau's Gang Unit wants to see a tattoo on someone we arrested. They track gang tattoos."

"I'd like to see the rest of the tattoo on his right forearm. It went under his sleeve."

"What do you think it is?"

"Could be an indicator of how Kyle feels toward other races."

"Was it the same symbol as on Sean's forehead?"

"No."

Greer deflated a bit. "I'm not up to date on this shit. Wonder how many other things I'm oblivious to." He yanked open the back entrance and led Zander through a hallway lit by fluorescents. He unlocked a door with his name on it and motioned for Zander to enter.

Zander took a seat. The sheriff stepped behind his desk, woke up his computer, and turned the screen so Zander could watch. While he waited for the sheriff to find the files, Zander sent a quick email about Lindsay's baby to the medical examiner. There were two voice mails from Ava, and he read the transcriptions on his phone. The first said the county deputy was still watching Billy and keeping an eye on his vehicle as the man worked inside the store. The second asked if he knew about a community meeting tonight to address the Fitch murders.

First I've heard of it.

He wondered if the news of Nate Copeland's death had gotten out. He had doubts about it being a suicide, but the public didn't know that yet.

They shouldn't *know that yet.*

Zander was about to mention the community meeting to the sheriff when Kyle Osburne's mug shot appeared on the computer screen. Make that several mug shots of Kyle. The sheriff was correct that Kyle had been arrested a number of times. Greer clicked and scrolled and muttered under his breath until he found what he wanted. "Yep. Kyle was in the state pen for eight months. Got out two years ago." He clicked some more. "Here are the images I was looking for."

He opened a file of thirteen photographs. Zander leaned toward the screen. The pictures had been taken at different times. The progression showed that Kyle had actively acquired more ink. He had an eagle across his upper back and a tiger on his calf. The most recent photo showed the tiger had been enhanced with color when compared to an older one where it was simply an outline. Kyle's right arm had a tribal band around his bicep, and Zander eyed it, wondering if it was simply decorative or had a deeper meaning. The sheriff scrolled down the page, and a shot of Kyle's right forearm rolled into view. The tattoo was a simple shield with two letters inside.

Ice touched Zander's lungs.

"Is that the one you wanted to see?" the sheriff asked.

"Yes. Scroll back up to the right arm with the tribal band on the bicep, please."

The sheriff did, and Zander noted the date. "Now back to the forearm view." He checked its date, remembering Kyle had been in the prison system two years before.

The forearm tattoo had been added after his prison time.

Zander sat back in his chair. He'd been right but didn't feel victorious.

"Well?" Greer was impatient.

"The *E* and *K* in the shield stand for European Kindred," Zander said slowly. "I've come across it in a case before. It's a white supremacist gang that originated in the Oregon prison system about twenty years ago and spread to the streets."

"Never heard of it."

"It's real. On the streets it's more about the drugs, but racism is the primary tenet. Did you say Billy and Kyle had drug arrests?"

"Both do."

"Do you have tattoo photos for Billy?"

Greer nodded and started to search. A moment later he opened a file for Billy. In the photos, Billy had only one tattoo. A lion roaring on his right deltoid.

Zander was strangely disappointed.

"This photo is four years old. He could have more by now," Greer stated.

"We need to have a talk with Billy Osburne." Zander checked the time. "You want to meet him outside his work? I'm sure Kyle has let him know we paid a visit."

"We definitely need to do that."

"Ava left a voice mail asking if I'd heard about tonight's community meeting regarding the Fitch murders," Zander told him.

The sheriff jerked in his chair as his gaze flew up. "*What?* Tonight? We'll see about that. Who on earth—oh, I can guess who organized that." He glowered at Zander. "One of Emily Mills's aunts."

"Why do you think that?"

"Because they've got their wrinkled fingers in every pot in Bartonville."

Zander glanced at the sheriff's weathered hands. He must feel entitled to use that descriptor since he had wrinkled fingers too.

"Where would they hold the meeting?"

"Probably the Methodist church hall. It's the biggest place in town—every group rents it for their gabfests. It holds more sinners' meetings than saints'." The sheriff stood up. "Let's go find Billy first."

14

Madison burrowed her nose into the fuzzy collar of the thick coat and curled her cold hands inside her pockets. She was trespassing, but the dock supervisors wouldn't care if they spotted her. The deserted employee bench behind the warehouses at the dock was hard and cold, but one of the best places to watch the sunset.

A half hour ago she'd noticed the sky far to the west had cleared, promising to show off the first visible sunset in weeks, so she had headed for the docks. She'd crammed an old *Goonies* baseball cap on her head, determined to ignore the icy air.

The sky started to change, and she sighed, watching the blues and pinks move across as the ocean turned a glassy silver, mirroring the colors of the sky. The wind had taken a rest, and the water was calm.

She could almost forget that Lindsay was dead.

Her eyes closed, and her friend's warm smile took over her thoughts.

That FBI agent—McLane—had been gentle and tactful with her questions that morning, and Madison had respected the keen look in her eyes. The woman was determined to find out who'd killed Lindsay and Sean. Madison had answered her questions the best she could, letting the tears flow.

Tears were a good shield. They hid her eyes from exposing her thoughts and gave her time to consider each question. They also made other people tread carefully, not wanting to make the crying jag worse.

It'd been an effective tool for McLane's interview.

Madison had nothing to hide from the agent, but she didn't allow people to peek into her brain and explore what made her tick. The questions and answers were about Lindsay, but she knew the agent was studying and forming opinions about Madison as they talked.

She was a good actress. Skilled at deflecting and masking.

Keeping people away was her specialty.

McLane had asked when Madison saw Lindsay last. An easy question. They'd worked together the day before. Lindsay had been the opening solo waitress, sufficient for the off-season breakfast crowd. Madison came on for lunch, and the two of them had easily covered the mild rush.

The agent's questions about Lindsay's recent attitude and state of mind had been harder to answer. Madison had thought back, realizing that lately she'd barely spent time with Lindsay outside of work. That was unusual. But Lindsay had broken their plans a few times—meeting for drinks or heading to Astoria to shop. Even a trip to Portland.

Lindsay had been quiet. Less laughter, less lightheartedness. Fewer texts.

Madison hadn't seen it until McLane asked.

"Did she mention any problems with her husband?" Special Agent McLane had asked her. "Was she worried about anything at home?"

Madison had no answers. But in hindsight, she had subconsciously known something was wrong. Something else had been taking up Lindsay's time and depressing her.

Had she been a horrible friend to not see it?

Had Lindsay and Sean been having trouble?

She took a deep breath of the salty air, savoring the western sky as it grew pinker and more intense. The sun was close to setting—maybe another five minutes. Her cell phone stayed in her pocket. The colors could never be captured. Instead she simply enjoyed each sunset as it came, confident that there would always be another to see.

No more sunsets for Lindsay.

Her eyes burned.

Why Lindsay? Why Sean? And why was he hanged?

The last question disturbed her acutely because of the similarity to her father's death. But she refused to let others see the depth of her feelings.

Madison liked walls. Protective barriers around her thoughts and fears.

Walls kept her heart safe.

If she didn't feel anything for anyone, then she couldn't be hurt if they were taken away.

Lindsay had sneaked under her usual barriers. Madison had thought getting to know the outgoing young waitress was safe. Now Lindsay had been forcefully removed from Madison's life, leaving her insides in shreds.

She couldn't let anyone in again.

She pulled up her legs, braced her boot heels against the bench, and wrapped her arms around her legs, enjoying the show. The sky's colors now spread to the east, where they met the day's dark-gray clouds. Gentle waves rippled through the colors reflected by the ocean.

Flames of yellow and orange hovered near the sun as it seemed to touch the water. She set her chin on her knees, willing the sun to slow.

Flames. Madison woke as her bedroom window flashed with light, and she blinked at the odd glow. Emily's bed was empty, and patterns flickered across the bed and up their bedroom walls. Madison stood, balancing on the foot of her bed to see out the window. Fear froze her in place, her fingers gripping the windowsill. The bushes against the house were on fire. Through the smoke and flames, she spotted Emily in her nightgown, but she faced away from the house, looking toward the woods. Her sister took several steps, picked up something from the grass, and clutched it to her chest, her profile now clear to Madison. Emily stared across the yard, and Madison followed her gaze.

Her mother ran among the firs at the far edge of the yard, the light from the fire catching her long, blonde hair. Suddenly the flames flared below Madison's window, nearly reaching the roof. Madison lost her balance and fell backward onto her mattress, losing her breath. And then Emily was inside, tugging at her arm. "Wake up! Fire! We've got to get out of the house!"

The sky around the sinking sun turned the deep orange of hot coals.

Madison hated fire with a passion.

Emily had shoved Madison out of the house and then gone to find their mother. Tara was at a friend's. The three of them had clutched each other, watching the house burn.

Later she learned how her father had died, and her child's heart broke in half, crushed by the loss and cruelty.

And a few days later, Tara left, and Madison blamed herself, convinced she had driven her away with her sisterly inquisitiveness.

Her mother might as well have vanished that fateful day. She became a brittle shell, a whisper of the woman she'd been, a shadow of herself.

Then she too was gone.

A third blow to her ten-year-old psyche.

Madison pushed away the deluge of old hidden emotions that threatened as she sat at the ocean's edge.

She had learned she should never share her heart with another. People left. People died. It hurt. It was best not to become attached.

The aunts tried their best to fill the empty family-shaped holes around Madison, and she loved them for it. But their presence was not the same.

"Is that you, Madison?"

Madison lowered her legs and swung around to face the woman, her elbows and feet ready to strike. She'd instantly recognized the voice but couldn't stop her reaction.

The old woman in the long, padded coat stumbled backward. "I'm so sorry, I'm so sorry, I didn't want to scare you. I don't like to scare people." She covered her face with her hands.

Madison's spine relaxed, and her heartbeat slowed. "It's okay, Alice. I was just startled."

It was another Bartonville loner.

Over her thick knit scarf, Alice Penn gave a toothy smile—more of a grimace that flashed her teeth without projecting warmth. Alice was harmless.

Alice had wandered Bartonville for as long as Madison could remember, living in a tiny house near the abandoned seafood processing plant. Rumor had it that her lover had died in a fishing boat accident, and that she'd walked the docks since then, waiting for him to return. Madison knew the story was false. She'd talked frequently with Alice, and even though Alice wasn't mentally all there, she was fully aware he was dead.

The woman's mind skipped and jumped around between decades. Sometimes she believed she was in high school, her parents still living. Other times she believed she was late for her cleaning job at a hotel that had closed a decade ago. Some days she knew Madison's name; other days Alice called her a name from some shadow of her past.

Around Alice, Madison didn't feel compelled to hide.

She could be herself.

Alice's bent, shuffling form was a familiar sight on the streets of Bartonville and surrounding towns. Alice walked every day, no matter the weather, and often ended up on the bench that Madison loved. Sometimes Alice would talk the entire time they sat; other times she was silent.

Alice's family was gone, but the people of Bartonville looked after her. Madison brought her leftover food from the restaurant, and Leo, the diner's cook, made sure her house was stable and secure.

Tonight appeared to be a silent night instead of a talkative one. Alice sat quietly on the far end of the bench, with as much room as possible between herself and Madison. Alice mumbled about being late and missing the best part of the sunset, but her eyes locked on the vibrant slivers of its remains, barely blinking. Several minutes later the light was nearly gone, leaving a dark-lavender sky that steadily grew darker.

Alice sighed and pushed to her feet. "A good day. A very good day today. I hope your day was as blessed as mine, Madison."

She had the voice of a young woman.

"It wasn't too bad," Madison replied.

Alice tilted her head, her eyes nearly invisible in the dimming light. "I don't hear joy in your words, Madison. How can you watch the heavens outdo every sunset of their past and say your day wasn't too bad?"

Because my closest friend was murdered. And I think I may have let her down before she died. Why didn't Lindsay tell me what was going on with her?

Why didn't I ask?

"You're right. It was amazing."

"Good. Good. Good. That's better. Now. We had both best be going. I don't want to be late for the meeting at the church." She steadied herself with one hand on the back of the bench.

Madison jumped to her feet, ready to grab Alice if she toppled. "What's happening at the church tonight?"

Like a curious puppy, Alice tilted her head again. This time her gaze solidly collided with Madison's. "Why, there's a meeting about the murders, of course. We've got a killer in our town."

15

"He's gone?" Zander was fuming.

The deputy wouldn't look him or Sheriff Greer in the eye.

Billy Osburne had disappeared into the wind. His truck was still in the parking lot, having been watched carefully by a deputy, but when they stepped inside the store, they'd discovered Billy had left fifteen minutes before. The other auto parts employee was baffled by their interest in Billy and also surprised that his truck was still in the lot.

"Billy didn't act worried about anything," the employee told them. "He asked if I could cover the rest of the evening since things were slow." He shrugged. "Then he left. I assume he called a ride. What do you think is wrong with his truck?"

Zander didn't tell him that Billy had been under surveillance.

The deputy on Billy duty drooped. "I saw him through the store window not that long ago. I couldn't see him the whole time unless I went in the store. I figured I was good as long as I had his truck in sight."

Greer simply stared at his deputy, making the man wilt even more.

Zander could almost hear the lecture that had to be running through Greer's brain.

"Since you're so good at watching his truck," the sheriff finally said, "you can continue watching it for the rest of your shift after you call in his description. I want everyone keeping an eye out for Billy Osburne."

"What if I'm needed somewhere else?" the deputy asked, his focus on his shoes.

"If no one else is available, then go, dammit. Citizens come before an empty truck." Greer shook his head and turned to leave, gesturing for Zander to follow him.

"Back to Kyle's," stated Zander.

"Yep. I doubt Billy is there, but I want to put the fear of God into Kyle."

The sheriff had shown himself to be a man of few words and reminded Zander of a parent who could get his kids into line by giving them "the look." As they returned to their vehicles, he wondered exactly how Greer would instill the fear of God in Kyle.

◆◆◆

"You called him," Zander stated to Kyle as they stood on his porch again.

There was no repentance on Kyle's face. He stood calmly in his doorway, leaning casually against the frame, trying to avoid the deadly stare of the sheriff. Zander understood. Even he was slightly unnerved by the fire in Greer's eyes. Their temperature would scorch skin.

"Of course I did. You didn't say not to. You had to expect that I would call him—but I didn't tell him to get lost. That was his own idea. I told him he wasn't in trouble for the fight."

"Then why did he run?" Greer asked. "He didn't take his truck, so I assume he called someone to pick him up. There's no place to go on foot around there."

"He's not real fond of you, Sheriff." Kyle shrugged, finally daring to quickly glance at Greer. "Even I got twitchy seeing you at my door, even though I've stayed out of trouble. Can't help it."

"Who would he call?" Zander didn't care for Kyle's attempt to place the blame for Billy's disappearance on them. He was surprised the man had suggested it under the hot stare of the sheriff.

Kyle screwed up his face in thought. "You got me there. He really doesn't have any friends."

Greer snorted.

"Maybe another guy who works at the store?" Kyle added hastily.

Annoyance struck Zander as he realized they might have to go back to the auto parts store to get some names. Back and forth, back and forth.

Ridiculous.

"What about a girlfriend?" he asked.

Kyle's expression cleared. "That's possible. I wouldn't say girlfriend, but I know he hooked up earlier this week. Didn't come home for two nights. I don't know anything about her," he added, beating Zander to his next question.

"A hookup and Lindsay Fitch?" Zander asked.

Kyle grinned. "Is there ever enough?"

"No name?" Greer scowled.

"Nothin'. I don't give a shit where he sticks it." He pressed his lips together and took a swift gander at Greer as if worried he'd be berated for cussing.

Zander believed him. Frustrated, he pointed at the bottom half of Kyle's tattoo below his sleeve. "Where'd you get the European Kindred tattoo?"

Kyle pulled away from the doorframe and tugged at his sleeve, a frown in his eyes and on his mouth. "What's it to you?"

"I'm curious. Indulge me." Zander met his stare.

Greer shifted his feet and tucked his thumbs into his duty belt, and Kyle carefully considered the sheriff's hard expression. The silence stretched among the three of them.

"I was with them in prison," Kyle finally said, raising his chin. "You have to choose a side unless you want your ass kicked every day."

Zander eyed the tattoo's smooth edges and sharp color. "That's no prison tattoo. A professional did that."

Kyle's shoulders twitched. "Kinda hard to brush people off once you're out. They have expectations."

"They wanted you to deal for them?" asked Greer in a tone that sounded like Zander's father when he was in trouble.

"No one tells me what to do." Defiance flashed.

"Billy have the same tattoo?" Zander watched him. Kyle was struggling to hold still. His hands went into his back pockets and out again, and then he tried to resume his earlier casual, slouchy stance against the frame and failed, looking like a board leaning against a wall.

"Nope."

Zander glanced at the sheriff and lifted a brow. *Done?*

Greer scrutinized Kyle, making him twitch again. "Let me know if you hear from Billy. Immediately. Tell him we have questions."

"I already told him that," Kyle muttered. He stepped inside and closed the door.

Greer and Zander exchanged a look and headed toward their vehicles.

"You do a pretty good fear of God," Zander commented. "He was starting to look like a tweaker."

"I had kids."

Zander's lips curved slightly. "No calls or emails on the Copeland scene?"

The sheriff checked his phone and tapped the screen, perusing his email as they stopped at his vehicle. "Nothing." He shoved his phone in a pocket and looked back at the Osburne house. "I can't get Nate Copeland's face out of my mind."

He wasn't the only one.

"I'm struggling with the idea that it might be murder," Greer said slowly. "Who lets someone shoot them in the mouth? Nate didn't have any defensive wounds. No signs of a struggle at all."

"No forced entry," Zander added.

"That doesn't bother me much. Few people lock their doors here. He could have gone outside for something that morning and left it unlocked."

"Perhaps the autopsy will reveal he'd been incapacitated in some way. A blow to the head that hid under his hair or had been disguised by the exit wound. Maybe he was drugged."

Greer gave him a side-eye. "Like the Fitch couple."

Zander grimaced. "Depending on what the autopsy turns up, we should request testing of the food and beverages in his house."

"Shit." The sheriff threw up his hands and stalked away several steps. *"What is going on?"*

"We're jumping ahead," Zander pointed out, taken aback by Greer's visible frustration. He'd begun to believe the quiet man was part android. "Let's get that autopsy report first."

"I know." The sheriff pinched the bridge of his nose and exhaled heavily. "How in the fuck did I suddenly get three dead people in my county?"

Zander said nothing. Greer didn't need his encouragement. He was venting, something Zander understood too well.

"I think I should stop by that meeting at the church," the sheriff said. "My truck-duty deputy can ask at the auto parts store for employee names and find out about a possible girlfriend—or whoever—and get us the information."

"We'll both go to that meeting."

Madison drove Alice to the Methodist church and silently argued with herself about whether or not to attend the meeting. She didn't want to hear details of Lindsay's death and face nosy questions from busybodies. But she did want to know how the investigation was proceeding. Her need for answers overpowered everything else, so she parked, resigned to attend and avoid as many people as possible.

Alice thanked her for the ride and darted out of the car before Madison had turned off the engine. Surprised by her speed, Madison watched until Alice disappeared inside the church.

The parking lot was nearly full. Fear had brought people out of the woodwork. She slammed her car door and strode toward the building, wondering how her community would calmly discuss two murders. She wore the *Goonies* cap pulled low on her face and kept her coat collar high, preferring to not be noticed.

"Hey, Madison."

Knowing that voice, she turned and faced the tall man. So much for staying under the radar. "Uncle Rod. I'm a little surprised to see you here."

"A double murder in the city limits? You bet I'm curious." Her mother's brother had been the only male relative in Madison's life since her father's death. Even though he lived on the outskirts of Bartonville, he rarely mixed with the townspeople. Madison appreciated him. He was one of the few people who didn't eye her with sympathy, wondering why she kept to herself. He simply accepted her for who she was.

He followed her up the church stairs and then placed a hand on her shoulder, and she turned to find worry filling his face. "Here I've been concerned about you and your sister losing a close employee, but Lindsay was more to you than that, wasn't she?" His eyes studied hers.

Madison swallowed, tempted to brush off the personal question. But this was her uncle; she could talk to him. "Yes. Lindsay was my closest friend." Not that she had a lot of friends.

"I'm sorry, hon." He pulled her into a big hug, and she rested her head against his shoulder. He smelled of rain and coffee. Comforting scents. For a long second, she believed everything was going to be all right.

Nothing will ever be right again.

He let go and patted her on the back as he opened the door for her. "You'll get through this. You've done it before."

Before.

Fresh pain radiated from her heart to her toes, making her stumble as emotions from her parents' deaths ambushed her. He took her elbow, and they stepped into the crowded church foyer, where people tried to fit through the next narrow door into the sanctuary. She lifted the brim of her cap and looked for Alice but didn't see her. Once inside the big room, she took a place by Rod, leaning against a side wall since few seats on the hard pews remained.

The church was nearly fifty years old and smelled of dusty wood and candle wax. The four windows on each side of the sanctuary looked like custom stained glass, but Madison knew the original beautiful windows had been replaced with factory-made imitations. The effect wasn't quite the same. When a broken stained-glass window at the Barton mansion needed replacing, her aunts had engaged in a fierce debate about its fate. Eventually a custom window had been commissioned, instead of the cheaper option. Dory and Thea had grumbled about it for months, but Vina stood by her decision.

Near the small podium at the front of the sanctuary, her aunt Vina spoke with a tall, bald man. Wearing a hot-pink jacket, Vina glowered at Harlan Trapp, Bartonville's mayor, her hands on her hips. Considering Vina and Harlan always butted heads over town issues, Madison had no desire to hear their current discussion—or Vina's lecture. Nothing made Madison slip out of a scene faster than confrontations and arguments. She scanned the audience, knowing the evening's discussion could grow heated, and prepared her escape route.

Beside her, Rod folded his arms across his chest, his gaze also on Vina and Harlan. Madison took comfort in his large presence.

Maybe I can stick this out.

She owed it to Lindsay.

Two more hot-pink jackets caught her eye, and she spotted Dory and Thea in the audience. Thea was talking animatedly with two women in the pew behind them, and Dory was speaking with Simon Rhoads. Madison wrinkled her nose. Simon had been after Dory for years. He was pleasant but always smelled medicinal, as if he'd spread Vicks VapoRub in several places. Dory claimed she didn't smell anything, but her sisters agreed with Madison.

Madison knew Dory would never move out of the mansion, and the sisters would never let Simon Rhoads move in. Dory claimed she spent time with him to offer help with his arthritis and high cholesterol. Nothing made Dory happier than discussing medical symptoms. The aunts joked that Dory was robbing the cradle because Simon was in his sixties.

Other familiar faces jumped out of the crowd. Isaac and Leo from work. Leo said something to Isaac, and he immediately straightened from his slumped position.

Leaning against the opposite wall was Leann Windfield, messaging on her cell phone. Madison stared, silently willing the woman to look her in the eye. Leann had harassed her back in school, and Madison had never forgotten how cruel she'd been.

Leann didn't look up.

Madison continued to study the audience. She finally spotted Alice, her hood still up, sitting at the end of the front pew. The space next to her was one of the only open seats left. Hurt that too many people gave Alice a wide berth, Madison considered taking the seat, but it didn't offer access to her escape route.

Several rows behind Alice was Brett Steele, Emily's ex-husband.

Leaving that ass was the smartest thing Emily had ever done.

He'd tried to control Emily, expecting her to account for every minute of her day.

And he'd seemed to think the third Mills sister should be his next conquest.

How sick is it to work your way through all the sisters in one family?

Brett had hit on her in bars several times, and she had shot him down. He seemed to take it as a challenge, so he'd come to the diner and attempted to engage Madison in conversation. She'd made it clear that he was wasting his time, but he disregarded that fact, convinced he could connect with her.

Clueless.

As if he felt Madison's stare on his neck, Brett turned and looked directly at her. His eyes went to her cap, and he gave a half smile, telling her she had failed in her desire to be overlooked. She yanked away her focus, agitated that he'd caught her.

He'd take their eye contact as a reason to keep up his pursuit.

Movement caught her attention. Emily entered and took a position against the back wall, a mulish expression on her face, clearly not wanting to be at the meeting. A dark-haired woman had followed and now stood beside her, leaning to whisper something in Emily's ear.

Special Agent Ava McLane.

Madison wondered if the agent had encouraged Emily to come.

"Folks? Can we quiet it down?" Harlan Trapp's voice echoed over the loudspeaker. Vina had stepped down, and she took the seat beside Alice and exchanged a few words, making Madison's heart warm. The low buzz of conversations stopped, and the room grew silent.

"That's better." Sorrow flooded Harlan's round face. "I know everyone's heard about the horrible murders of Lindsay and Sean Fitch, and I'm sure you have lots of questions."

"I thought it was a murder-suicide," one female voice called out from the crowd.

Harlan rubbed the back of his neck. "Well, now . . . I think they said that at first, but last I heard it was a double murder, right?" He looked out over the room. "Where's the sheriff?"

Quiet murmurs spread as people looked right and left, seeking the sheriff.

"He's working," announced a man in a plaid shirt leaning against the wall opposite Madison. She didn't know his name but recognized him as a county deputy.

"What's the point of this meeting if he's not here to give us accurate information?" asked an indignant female voice.

"I thought he was coming," Harlan said in a mildly panicked tone. "Who was supposed to tell the sheriff about the meeting?" No one answered as he frantically scoured the crowd.

"Well, darn it." His countenance sagged.

Madison sighed. Organization wasn't Harlan's strong suit.

"I don't think we need the sheriff here to remind us to lock our doors and look out for our neighbors," Vina said in a strong voice to reach all ears. "It's up to us to help our community stay safe, and we do that by keeping our eyes open."

A man spoke up from the back. "And what do we do if we see the murderer?"

"You know what he looks like?" shot back another man, sarcasm heavy in his tone.

"Yeah. He's a skinhead."

Opinions erupted in reaction to the description, creating a din that echoed through the sanctuary.

Harlan ran a hand over his bald head. "Okay! Everyone settle down!" His voice quivered slightly. "Josh, that kind of comment isn't helpful. We don't judge people by their looks around here."

"Bullshit." Leann Windfield spoke clearly, still leaning against her wall. "Looks are exactly what got Sean Fitch killed. If you can't see that, you're part of the problem."

Madison's mouth fell open. *His skin color got him killed?*

Dozens of voices rose in anger, and Harlan struggled to take control of the room. A woman in the center stood up, and a hush finally came over the crowd. Madison recognized her as a retired schoolteacher. "We don't have racism in this town," she announced. "I've lived here all my life, and I've never seen anything that even hints at it."

Madison wanted to nod in agreement, but something prickled at her subconscious. Leann's statement was echoing in her brain, stirring up a faint memory of similar statements.

She couldn't put it together.

"Just because you've never experienced it doesn't mean it doesn't exist," Leann told her. "Take a look around this room. It's ninety-nine percent white. No wonder you feel it doesn't exist." Leann looked to Harlan. "If Sean's murder isn't racially motivated, why is the FBI here and working with the sheriff on this case?"

The room was silent as all eyes turned to Harlan.

"The FBI?" Sweat glistened at Harlan's temples, his voice high.

A few moans and mutters sounded. Her uncle snorted, and a small laugh erupted from his throat. Madison briefly closed her eyes. *Pull it together, Harlan.* Watching the mayor flounder was painful.

Harlan glanced about the room. "Anyone else heard the FBI is here?"

Several people nodded.

Madison glanced at Agent McLane. *Is she going to speak up?* The agent's lips pressed together as she took stock of the crowd. McLane had asked her if she'd heard of threats directed at Sean or Lindsay. She hadn't specified that the threats could have been motivated by race.

"You're trying to make this murder into a social issue, when it's not," announced a white-haired man Madison didn't recognize. "I've also never seen any racism in this town. What we've got is a psycho killer on the loose, and I'll be sleeping with Betsy on my nightstand until they catch him. Betsy will put a hole in anyone who tries to break into my house."

Several heads nodded in agreement.

Harlan grimaced.

"Did you know that Oregon was the only state that began as whites only?" Agent McLane's voice was low but clear and carried through the room. "The original state constitution excluded all nonwhites from living here." Heads swiveled in her direction, and questioning looks were exchanged as people tried to place her.

"That was over a hundred and fifty years ago," someone answered.

"It was," agreed Ava. "And just a few years ago, recruiting flyers were spread in southern Oregon asking people to join an organization that descended directly from the KKK. Its name is different now; its purpose is not."

"Flyers are free speech," argued a man a few feet from Ava. "That's protected."

"You're correct, they are," agreed Ava. "I'm not challenging the right to hand out flyers. The 1920s were a very active decade for the KKK in Oregon, but most residents would agree that it has fizzled out. No one has seen a white hood around here for decades, right?"

Nods answered her.

"The point I'm making is that hate never dies," Ava continued. "It can go dormant and seem to disappear when it's actually hiding and evolving, passed from generation to generation. Did you know the KKK was *very* active in Portland as recently as the 1980s? Someone even called Portland the skinhead capital of the US back then. We can't say racism doesn't exist because it's never personally touched us. It's here and it can be deadly."

The agent clearly knew what she was talking about and had presented it tactfully, but scowls on several faces indicated they didn't appreciate a lecture from an outsider. Many people in the pews studied the agent in confusion. Curious glances to neighbors were met by shrugs. No one knew who she was.

"Uh, thank you . . . Miss . . . ?" Harlan asked.

"Special Agent McLane," she said solemnly. "I'm part of the FBI presence looking at whether or not the Fitch murders are a hate crime."

The room erupted again.

Madison blinked. She'd assumed the FBI was present simply because the sheriff needed help investigating the two deaths. This was the first mention of a hate crime.

Am I dense?

"What the hell?" Her uncle shook his head, scowling.

The realization made her head swim. Sean and Lindsay might have been killed because of the color of Sean's skin. The FBI's presence indicated Leann Windfield's theory could be right.

A long-forgotten memory poked at Madison's brain again, wanting to come out.

"Is it true Nate Copeland was also murdered this morning?" someone shouted. "Was he murdered because he was the first deputy that saw the Fitch murder scene? He's not black."

Shock hit Madison, and she saw Leann straighten, surprise on her face.

Someone else has been killed?

"Holy shit," her uncle said under his breath. "Another murder?"

All eyes went to Agent McLane. She said nothing but held up a hand until the loud conversations stopped. "I can't comment on Deputy Copeland's death, but the Clatsop County sheriff has the full support of the FBI in their investigation."

In other words, they're paying attention because it's related to the Fitch murders.

Agent McLane set a hand on Emily's shoulder and spoke rapidly to her. Madison's gaze locked on her sister's face. Emily was completely pale, her eyes wide, clearly alarmed by the news of Copeland's death.

The reason for Emily's fear struck Madison, and her heart skipped a beat.

Emily was there too.

Did Copeland see something at that murder scene that got him killed?

"Who's the guy with the sheriff?" Rod mumbled beside her.

Sheriff Greer had stepped through the sanctuary door with Agent Zander Wells right behind him. Greer raised a hand in greeting to the townspeople while Wells swiftly took in the crowd, his gaze darting from face to face. He stopped when his eyes landed on Emily, ten feet to his right.

Relief and something else flashed on his face, and a ripple went through Madison's female instincts.

The agent is attracted to Emily.

She set aside the observation to mull over later.

Emily and Agent McLane hadn't seen the two men enter. Sheriff Greer worked his way around the pews toward the front of the room, stopping to shake an occasional hand or slap someone on the back. Ava finally noticed him and immediately turned to check the door. Spotting Agent Wells, she gestured for him to join them.

He took a place on Emily's other side and joined their conversation.

Now that's a conversation I'd like to hear.

She watched her sister listen intently to the agents. *She's upset and trying not to show it.*

Madison was suddenly swamped by an image of a handful of odd coins. The fascination and curiosity she'd felt about them as a child swirled in her mind. She felt them in her hands, the cool, round surfaces, and she wondered what had triggered the memory.

What coins?

16

"Any updates on Nate Copeland's death?" Ava asked softly as Zander joined them in the crowded sanctuary.

Surprised she'd asked in front of Emily Mills, Zander simply shook his head. "We'll know more tomorrow."

"Like whether he was murdered or not?" Emily's question was delivered with her usual bluntness, but Zander noted her pallor. Her pupils were large in the bright light of the church, and her hands were clasped tightly together—to the point of white knuckles.

Ava caught his eye. "The autopsy will give us answers," she said, her low voice quieter than usual.

"Do you need to tell the other deputies that were at the Fitch house to watch their backs?" Emily asked. She didn't look at either one of them, her focus straight ahead. Still candid, but lacking her usual spirit.

Zander exchanged another glance with Ava. "We're not at that point."

"I see."

"Can I have everybody's attention?" Sheriff Greer had made it to the microphone. A sweating bald man darted away from the podium, relief apparent on his face.

Another man stood up near the front of the sanctuary. "What's going on, Sheriff? How come no one's giving us any answers?" Many heads nodded.

"I just got here," Greer said. "Can I talk before you accuse me of not talking?"

The questioner folded his arms across his chest. "We're listening."

"Thank you." The sheriff cleared his throat. "I know you're all concerned about the deaths of the Fitches."

"Damn right!" came a shout.

"Be quiet!"

"Let the man talk!"

"What we're concerned about is our safety," said the first man. "We all hate what happened, but the natural reaction is to worry about our own families. *Are we safe?*"

The air grew still as the audience waited for the sheriff's answer.

Zander didn't envy Greer.

The sheriff studied the audience, many of whom were leaning forward in anticipation, hoping to hear him say everything was okay.

Greer took a deep breath. "I'm not going to pretend everything will be fine. We don't know who killed the Fitches, and we don't know why." His face softened. "I can't stand here and honestly tell you nothing else is going to happen. I can't predict the future."

The brief stunned silence was disrupted by voices. Just about everyone's voices. Some people stood and worked their way past the others in the pews, their children's hands clenched in their own. Several streamed past Zander, fear and anger in their eyes, bits of their conversations reaching his ears.

"—going to Grandma's in Portland."

"—out of my gun safe tonight."

"—dogs go bonkers if they hear someone outside."

Beside him Emily tensed as people passed, many of them stopping to pat her hand or say a brief word about Lindsay.

"Folks!" The sheriff knew he'd lost the crowd. "Any more questions?" He was ignored as more people stood and left. A few gathered at the podium, peppering Greer with questions. Others met in small groups, their heads together as they spoke, occasionally casting suspicious looks at him and Ava or the sheriff.

"Fuck." Ava was succinct. "This accomplished nothing except to rile up everyone."

"What do you expect when they've been told that they could be the next murder victim?" snapped Emily.

"That's not what—"

"I know that's not what the sheriff said," Emily stated. "But that's what they heard."

Zander couldn't argue with Emily's logic. Her color was better. Anger had replaced the earlier anxiety.

He liked her better this way.

She turned to him. "When will you have a motive?" Her dark-blue eyes probed him, expecting an answer.

"I don't know." He couldn't lie.

"You've figured out nothing."

"I wouldn't say that."

"Am I in danger because I was there at the same time as Nate Copeland?"

Zander held her gaze. "We can't rule it out yet."

She swore under her breath. "Now what?"

Madison stepped quietly through the mansion's front door and slowly closed it, the knob tight in her grip, attempting to be as silent as possible. Her aunts were home from the meeting at the church, and Madison didn't want to listen to a discussion in which they rehashed every word. Emily's car wasn't parked in its usual spot out front—which was fine with Madison. She didn't believe her sister had seen her at the meeting; Emily had been focused on the FBI agents.

Emily probably wonders why I didn't attend.

Her sister was always looking over Madison's shoulder, checking up on her, being a mother hen. It made her feel like a teenager with a chaperone.

The staircase creaked as she lightly jogged up the treads, keeping one ear open for her aunts. She passed the open door of Emily's room. And then stopped. The coins from her earlier memories reappeared in her mind and drew her inside Emily's room.

Is this where I saw them?

It couldn't be. The memory felt very, very old.

She flipped on the light switch and studied her sister's things. Madison had nosed through Emily's things in the past simply out of curiosity and because she had the opportunity. She assumed her sister had done the same with Madison's belongings. The three sisters—and then two—had constantly gone through each other's things for as long as Madison could remember.

All sisters snooped. Right?

Madison slid on her stomach, the hardwood cold against her bare knees. The space under Tara's bed was tight, and Madison kept a cheek to the floor to stay low enough without banging her head. Tara's bed was pushed into the far corner of her room, and Madison had spotted a large box underneath in that corner. She wanted to know what was in it. She pushed shoes and games and smaller boxes out of her way. She'd already rooted through those little boxes and found nothing of interest. But that large box by itself was like a beacon to her nine-year-old brain.

Emily shared a room with Madison, but at seventeen, Tara had her own. Jealousy ran rampant in Madison's heart. Tara got to do everything. Dates, movies, driving. She got to work in the diner and earn money to buy all the clothes she wanted.

Madison couldn't wait to be a teenager.

Her fingers reached the cardboard box, its brown surface rough to the touch. It was too tall to open under the bed. She backed up the way she'd come, sliding with one hand awkwardly grasping a corner of the box. It was heavy and kept slipping from her grip. Excitement curled in her chest.

What would it be?

She emerged from under the bed. Dust from the floor left odd pale patterns on her navy T-shirt, and she tasted it on her tongue. Kneeling, she flipped open the box's flaps. And exhaled in disappointment.

Books. The box was full of books. She dug to the bottom, searching for hidden treasure. Nothing but books. She picked one up, wrinkling her nose at the embracing man and woman on the cover. Flipping it open, she noticed someone had used a pen to underline sentences.

Mom would be furious if Tara had marked in books.

"Madison!" Tara stood in the doorway, fury shining in her eyes.

Dropping the book back in the box, Madison felt her stomach swirl and churn, ready to vomit.

Madison trembled, experiencing the same guilty nausea as she searched Emily's room. But somehow the nausea was different. Now more regret and disgrace affected it since she was an adult but committing the sins of a child.

This time I know what I'm searching for.

That excuse didn't settle her stomach the way she'd hoped.

She listened, still hearing only the far-off murmurs of her aunts. Emily's room was a mirror image of hers. Every room in the mansion had high ceilings, and the bedrooms each had a wide bay window or two. Everyone complained about the stupidly tiny closets, but no one did anything about it. People had owned less clothing when the mansion was built. Remodeling the bedrooms to have the spacious closets that reflected the current day's excess would cost a fortune that they didn't have.

Emily's room had a queen bed, a dresser, two nightstands, the minuscule closet, and a desk. Any of which could hide what Madison was searching for.

Why do I think I'll find them here?

The sensation of holding the cold metal disks tingled through her nerves. She'd never encountered anything like the coins in her previous searches of Emily's room. She considered starting under the bed and then chose the closet. Grabbing a footstool, she opened the door. The closet was crammed. She stood on the stool and scanned the shelf above the clothing. A dozen shoeboxes. Most of which, Madison knew, contained shoes. She didn't have the patience to search each one again. Stepping down, she closed the door and replaced the stool, feeling the urge to get out before Emily came home.

Maybe she was no longer the horrible snoop she'd believed herself to be.

Deciding to leave soon, she slid open a drawer in the closest nightstand and caught her breath.

Not coins. A pocket watch.

She picked it up in awe, the watch familiar to her fingertips. She recognized its weight, its polished surface, and its tiny clasp.

This is Dad's.

She pressed the stem, and it sprang open. Her gaze halted on his initials inside the little door. The hands showed an incorrect time. Lifting it to her ear, she heard nothing. She closed her eyes and saw him.

He sat on the back porch of their home, grinning as he shouted for her and Emily to beat Tara in the impromptu tug-of-war they'd started with the hose. It was hot. She wore the turquoise bathing suit—the one with the unicorn. Tara and Emily had matching orange suits. Their mother had tried to buy a third one for Madison, but she hated orange and had fallen in love with the unicorn.

The water made the hose cool in her hands. It gushed out near Emily, making the grass squish between their toes. On their father's loud count, she and Emily yanked with all their strength, giggling with delight as their oldest sister tripped and fell face-first into the grass. In a flash he was beside Tara, lifting her up and exclaiming at the blood gushing from her nose. It dripped down the orange suit, leaving dark, crooked trails. Mesmerized,

Madison watched as they grew longer. Her father dug in his pockets and pulled out the watch and a tissue. He dropped the watch in the wet grass and pressed the tissue to Tara's nose.

Madison looked at the watch in her hand, remembering how shocked she'd been that he had let his precious watch fall to the ground, risking water damage and breakage. To her it had shown how much he loved Tara—all of them—to endanger his most prized possession. A wave of loss and love slammed into her, and she leaned on the nightstand for support, tears blurring her vision.

She'd lost so much.

Breathing deep, she waited for her eyes to clear and pushed the emotions behind a locked door in her brain, where they belonged.

The watch had been a gift from her dad's grandfather, who'd had the same initials. Her father had allowed the girls to examine it whenever they asked, as long as he stayed close by. It was precious to him, and the sisters regarded it with awe. Below the engraved initials in a fancy script was a phrase in a foreign language. *Latin maybe?* She remembered her father telling them it meant to care for others.

The case door closed with a snap, and Madison clenched the antique, her mind racing.

It was always in her father's pocket. He'd kept his keys and spare change in one front pocket and the pocket watch in the other.

After he'd died, the pocket watch was nowhere to be found. Her mother had been furious, convinced his killer had taken the watch, or possibly one of the investigators. When the police had suggested it was lost in the house fire—since *all* their belongings had burned—her mother had brushed off their theory. Her father had worked late that night and still had on his jeans when he was killed; the watch would have been in his pocket.

How? How did the watch end up here?

Did one of the aunts have it and give it to Emily? Without telling Madison?

Her mother had pointed out that her father's wallet was still in his pocket. Why would anyone take an old watch and leave the leather wallet with thirty-two dollars?

No one had an answer, and the watch was forgotten, presumably never to be seen again.

How long has Emily had it?

Hearing the front door open and shut, Madison slipped the watch in her pocket and darted out of the bedroom. She silently jogged to her own room, where she listened as Emily came up the stairs. The light switch in Emily's room clicked, and Madison held her breath, hoping she'd left everything the way Emily'd had it. Madison yanked off her *Goonies* cap, ran a hand through her hair, and shed her coat. After a long moment, she went back to Emily's room.

Her sister sat at her desk, leafing through a stack of papers.

"Hey, Em."

Emily didn't turn and continued sorting her papers. "Hi, Madison. Did you know there was a meeting at the church tonight about the Fitch murders?"

Her sister's casual tone was like nails on a chalkboard.

"I was there," Madison replied in the same tone.

That made Emily swing around, her eyes narrowing, a slight frown on her face. "I didn't see you."

"I was standing by Uncle Rod. I saw you at the back with the two FBI agents."

"I didn't notice Rod either. I bumped into Agent McLane in the parking lot." Emily's gaze dropped to the floor. "Agent Wells showed up later."

Madison cocked her head at the subtle change in her sister's tone as she mentioned Agent Wells.

She's attracted to him too.

Her mouth twitched as she studied Emily. How long would it take them to realize it was mutual? Madison wasn't jealous; Agent Wells was attractive but not her type; he kept himself restrained behind his cool exterior.

The agent's and her sister's mutual attraction was a moot point. Any professional would know better than to become involved with a witness in a murder investigation.

"It got pretty heated in there," Madison said, just to keep the conversation going. "Sounds like no one knows what's going on."

"Two days haven't even passed since they died," Emily snapped as she glared at her sister. "This is real life, not TV. Murders aren't solved in an episode."

Madison lifted her chin. "I'm well aware of how long Lindsay's been dead." The words were spoken to dig at her sister, but they pierced her own heart. Her breath seized at the sharp pain, and she looked away.

She felt Emily's perceptive gaze on her and fought to get her mourning under control.

"It's like losing another sister," Emily said.

Sister . . .

"Tara's not dead." Madison refused to believe it. Anger emboldened her. She brushed her hair off her shoulder and met Emily's stare. "Why does no one care or talk about Tara? Why did we let her push us out of her life?"

Her sister's face went blank. "Her life, her decision. If she doesn't want anything to do with us, so be it."

Madison glared. "I can't believe you're still that cold."

"I simply said what everyone else is thinking."

"This is our *sister* we're talking about. Don't you care?"

"Tara left; she had that right. Something made her decide to put a lot of space between us and herself, and until she wants to talk about it, it's none of our business."

"But what on earth would make her *never* contact any of us? Don't you ever wonder?"

"No." Emily spun around to her papers. "Let it go, Madison."

Madison stared at her back. This wasn't the Emily she knew. Emily released spiders outdoors instead of killing them. She let senior citizens talk her ear off for an hour at the diner without interrupting once. She was blunt, but Emily proved over and over that she was a caring human being. Except when it came to Tara.

"What did Tara do to you?" Madison whispered as the hair rose on her arms. Something wasn't being said.

"Go to bed, Madison."

"You're not a fucking post without feelings. Why will no one talk about this? Why am I the only person who's bothered to search for *our* sister?"

Emily said nothing.

Suddenly light-headed, Madison took a half step back, understanding that secrets were being kept and it was possible that lies had been told about Tara for decades. She touched the bulge of the watch in her pocket. More lies.

What is going on?

17

Madison guzzled an energy drink for breakfast as she quickly handled the mess in the mansion's kitchen and kept an eye on the time. She needed to be out the door in five minutes to get to the diner by six thirty. Her aunts had left dishes on the counter from what appeared to be apple pie and vanilla ice cream. Dessert must have been needed after last night's meeting.

"Morning, dear. Is there coffee yet?" Dory yawned. Her white hair was flat against her head on one side, and mismatched slippers peeked from below her faded chenille robe. Thea and Vina had the same robe.

"I'll get it started for you." Madison snatched the carafe and held it under the faucet. "I don't make coffee the mornings I work. I get mine at the diner."

"Oh. I guess Thea makes it on those days. It's always ready when I come down." Dory peered at the clock on the microwave. "My goodness. I didn't realize it was so early." She rubbed her backside. "My sciatica bothered me all night. Nothing I take seems to touch the pain. It's been good for months, so I don't know why it's suddenly acting up."

Madison knew all about Dory's sciatica woes. The doctor had assured Madison that her great-aunt had the healthy spine of a fifteen-year-old and suggested the lower pain was from something else. Madison measured coffee grounds into the filter. "Maybe it flared up from those hard pews last night. They always make me sore."

Her aunt's mouth opened in a large O. "I bet you're right. It was impossible to get comfortable during that meeting. Thea threatened to sit elsewhere if I didn't hold still. You're a smart girl." She chuckled and patted Madison's arm. "You look very nice today."

Dory always gave her a compliment when Madison wore the wide-legged swishy jumpsuit. It felt like weightless silk against her skin, and she knew few people could pull off the thick black and white vertical stripes the way she could. Emily hated the jumpsuit. Which might have been part of the reason Madison had put it on that morning. A slicked-back high pony along with nude makeup—except for her favorite fire engine–red lipstick—completed her look du jour.

"Is Emily up?" Dory asked.

"No. She doesn't work until later."

Madison closed the top of the coffee maker and hit the START button, wondering if Dory knew anything about her father's pocket watch. Like how in the hell something that was missing for about twenty years had suddenly turned up in Emily's drawer.

"Dory . . . do you remember that pocket watch that Dad always carried around?"

"Of course." She tilted her head, sympathy in her eyes. "Have you been thinking about your father?"

"Sometimes. I remember how upset Mom was about its disappearance."

A wistful expression crossed her aunt's face. "She was crushed, the poor thing. I think it was the one thing that she truly missed of your father's. It would have been a good keepsake."

"It never turned up?"

Confusion wrinkled the soft skin of Dory's forehead. "Not that I know of. I think I'd remember that."

The conversation wasn't revealing the information Madison wanted.

"It was horrible what was done to your father, leaving you girls with nothing. Even *he* didn't deserve that."

Even he?

"You think so?" Madison asked casually, watching the coffee start to stream into the pot.

"Oh yes. Even with the kind of man he was, that sort of cruelty shouldn't happen to anyone."

Chills lifted the hair on Madison's forearms. No one had ever spoken of her father in those terms.

"What did people say?"

Dory yawned again. "Is the coffee almost done?"

"It's barely started. Give it a few minutes. You were going to tell me what people said about Dad."

"Oh, you know. Just talk. It meant nothing." She gazed longingly at the coffee maker.

Has Dory never made coffee?

"I know people used to spread rumors." Madison knew nothing of the sort, but she hoped it would fuel the chatty moment Dory had started.

"Oh yes. People are cruel. Your poor mother. We all begged her not to marry him."

Madison's head spun. Again. She'd never heard such talk.

"Poor Mom. How did she handle it?"

Dory waved a dismissive hand. "Like she handled everything. She did whatever the hell she wanted. Look what it got her."

Is Dory drunk? Madison subtly leaned toward her aunt and sniffed the air. Nothing.

"I'm so sorry, dear. It was very unfair to you children. Tara most of all."

What was unfair?

Madison didn't want Dory to stop but knew the conversation was treading on thin ice. Either Madison would hear something she did not want to hear, or Dory would lose her train of thought and the moment would be over. "Why do you think it was the worst for Tara?"

"Well, she was older. People viewed and treated her as an adult." She shook her head sadly. "She was still a child. It was so wrong."

"It was wrong." Madison had no idea what she'd just agreed with.

"It was the money, you know. Everything was always about the money." Dory sighed. "But that had been gone for years. No one knew. Even today they still believe we're rich." She opened a cupboard and frowned. "Oh, my cows. Are there any Pop-Tarts left? The cinnamon ones are perfect with coffee."

Madison was lost, and she suspected Dory was too. She automatically opened the adjoining cupboard and handed Dory the Pop-Tarts box. "People like to gossip about the Barton money?" Madison already knew this was true. She'd heard the gossip all her life.

"Among other things, but it was your father they loved to gossip about the most."

She wanted to scream in frustration at the rambling. Dory struggled with the shiny foil package. Madison took it, ripped it open, and handed her a pastry. "They were wrong about him."

"Oh, no. The rumors were spot-on." Dory bit a corner of the frosted Pop-Tart and closed her eyes in satisfaction. "He married your mother because he thought we were rich. Up to the day he died, he thought we were still hiding money from him and was bitter about it."

Madison's energy drained out of her limbs in a rush. Her father had been loving and fun, not like this person Dory was describing. *Is Dory telling the truth?* Some conversations with her were like this. A scattered bunch of memories tied up in knots.

A memory surfaced.

Six-year-old Madison couldn't pull her gaze from the beautiful doll in the glass case. She, Emily, and their father had stopped at a neighbor's garage sale. As her dad looked through the tools, she stared at the doll, ignoring the books and videos that Emily was trying to show her.

"These are only a quarter each," Emily said. "Dad won't have a problem with that." She noticed Madison's fascination. "Ohhh. She's beautiful."

Emily walked around the table to check the back of the glass case. "Seventy-five dollars!"

Madison knew that was bad.

"That's a collector's item," said the owner as he approached. "Not a toy. But you like it, don't you?" he asked Madison.

Madison could only nod.

"Well, let's get your dad over here." The owner spotted her father. "Hey, Lincoln. Your little girl found something she likes."

Her father walked over, holding a hammer and saw, his smile wide for his girls. Madison crossed her fingers. He looked at the back of the glass case, and his smile faded. He eyed the owner. "Is that a joke?"

"Nope. She's actually worth more than that."

"Sorry, hon," her father said. "Find a new book, okay?"

Disappointment crushed her.

"Aw, come on, Lincoln. Everybody knows you've got Barton money."

Madison stumbled backward at the instant fury in her father's eyes as he turned to the owner. Emily saw it and grabbed Madison's hand, yanking her toward the driveway. She'd left the books and videos. "Let's wait out here," Emily said in a cheery voice.

Something was wrong.

Her father came out seconds later, no tools in hand, his smile back. "Nothing today, eh?" He took Madison's other hand, and the three of them walked to his car.

She must have imagined the anger in his eyes.

Madison stared at the coffee maker.

Had Emily been protecting her from her father's anger?

"I think there's enough for a cup." Dory greedily eyed the pot.

"Only if you like your coffee super strong and bitter."

"In that case, I'll wait. But please hurry up."

Is she talking to me or the pot?

"The rumors were that Dad married Mom for money?" Madison tried to steer her aunt back on track.

"That and those horrible things."

"What horrible things?" Madison's voice cracked.

"Those people." Dory's voice lowered. "Those awful people."

"Was Chet Carlson one of those people?" Madison's hate for her father's killer burned anew in her gut.

"Of course not." Dory was adamant.

"Who, then?" She forced the words out. Why would Dory defend Chet Carlson? The man sat in prison for her father's death.

"They're gone. Most weren't from around here to start with."

"That's good." Madison didn't know what else to say. The conversation had completely confused her as she analyzed every word out of her great-aunt's mouth from a dozen angles.

"It is." She squeezed Madison's upper arm and smiled. "One of these days, Tara will be back."

"Why do you think Tara hasn't returned?" Madison wondered if she should wake Dory up early more often. Yes, her conversation was a scattered stream of subjects, but Tara and her father had been mentioned more times this morning than in all of the past year.

Is it her medication? Madison wasn't sure how many drugs her aunt took. She had put complete trust in the pharmacist to notify her if Dory had been prescribed medications she shouldn't be taking at the same time. Dory saw dozens of doctors, but fortunately there was only one pharmacy in town. The pharmacist was well acquainted with Dory and her maladies, real and imagined. Madison made sure the pharmacist also had a list of the "natural" medications Dory used.

"Well, you know how Tara can be. More stubborn than you and Emily added together. She broke our hearts when she left."

Madison was well aware of her sister's disappearing act. It'd taken her years to convince herself that Tara hadn't left because Madison was a super snoop who couldn't stay out of Tara's room.

"She'll be back one of these days. When she's ready." Dory pointed emphatically at the pot. "I'll take a cup now."

Madison poured the coffee and checked the time. She would be late if she didn't leave now.

Leo can handle the diner if I'm a little late.

This conversation was too extraordinary to walk out on.

"Dory," she asked carefully, "do you know why Tara left so soon after Dad's death?"

Her aunt had sat down at the table in the kitchen and was alternating bites of Pop-Tart with sips of coffee. "I don't, dear," she said between bites. "Probably too much pressure. It was a hard time for all of us."

"It doesn't seem callous to you? I mean . . . she didn't even call when Mom died."

"She didn't call, did she? Tara has to live with that guilt. Your poor mother."

Dory had referred to Madison's mother as "poor" one too many times, and anger provoked Madison's next words. "You know Mom was manic-depressive, but you talk about her as if she was constantly miserable. I remember her laughing, taking us for hikes, and swimming in the river. She may have had down times, but she was *happy*."

Dory blinked in confusion. "I'm not saying she wasn't. She was a wonderful mother to you girls most of the time, but she put up with a lot from your father. He was older than her, you know. She was like a child in their relationship."

Dory checked the hallway behind her before leaning toward Madison. "He seduced her before they married," she whispered like a conspirator.

Many images of her mother and father sharing passionate embraces flashed through Madison's memories. She was positive it hadn't been a one-sided attraction.

"He was very possessive of that pocket watch," Dory told her cup of coffee.

Their conversation's backward leap startled Madison.

Is this what it's like to be inside Dory's head?

"I didn't know what that watch was until Vina explained it to me." The white head solemnly wagged back and forth. "She was glad it vanished."

"It was just a watch." *Right?*

Dory pinned her with a schoolteacher stare that pierced deep into Madison's brain. "It was a link to his past. His grandfather was that way, and he passed it to his grandson. We didn't need that type around here," she lectured.

Madison had no words.

Pity filled her aunt's features. "The hate and anger, Brenda. He's feeding it with those meetings and won't listen to reason from any of us. No good can come of it."

She thinks I'm Mom.

Dory looked at the clock again. "You're going to be late. That's not fair to Leo."

Madison grabbed her purse and stooped to kiss her aunt on the cheek. She lingered, full of questions but not knowing how to put them into words. "Love you, Dory."

She darted out the door into the cold dark, pulling her hood up against the light rain. Once in the car, she pulled the pocket watch out of her purse and opened it, seeing nothing but the initials and the foreign phrase. Flipping it over, she closely scanned the back and then the front again, seeking any bumps or cracks. Nothing. Wedging a fingernail into a groove on the side, she tried to lever the clock side apart. It didn't budge.

It was a watch. Nothing else.

She eyed the foreign words, remembering that she had accepted her father's translation as truth. Grabbing her phone, she typed the words into Google. *Non Silba Sed Anthar.*

"Not for oneself, but for others," she read aloud.

That sounds selfless and kind.

She scrolled further, scanning the results.

This can't be right.

Her heart in her throat, she opened web page after web page, finding multiple confirmations.

The lovely-sounding phrase was a common slogan of the KKK.

18

Zander had been working at the Clatsop County sheriff's office for an hour when Ava showed up. She walked in with a glare and a coffee holder with two cups. "Why didn't you tell me you were starting at the butt crack of dawn?"

"Didn't see the point of waking you." He'd woken at 4:00 a.m., unable to go back to sleep. After doing what work he could from his laptop, he'd gone to the sheriff's office and requested the murder book on Lincoln Mills, Emily's father. He also hadn't called Ava because he didn't want to explain why he was looking at an old solved case when they had three unsolved deaths.

He was curious about what made Emily Mills tick. Understanding what had happened to her father might give him some insight into what made her so intriguing to him. Besides the obvious physical attraction.

Ava handed him one of the coffees, and he nearly dropped it, the extreme heat radiating through the cup. "Careful. You need to toughen up your hands," she quipped. "Maybe do something else besides tap on a keyboard." She pulled a coffee sleeve out of her pocket and passed it to him with a grin.

"Funny."

"I bet someone would be willing to take you logging or fishing. That would help."

He removed his lid, and steam gushed. "No thanks. I'm happy with my keyboard. Why is this so hot?"

"Dunno." She tilted her head to see what he was reading. "Lincoln Mills?" The frown he'd fully expected appeared on her face. "Why are you—"

"Looking at a solved case when we have work to do," he finished, unable to maintain her scrutinizing eye contact.

"Exactly."

"You know why," he hedged. "Our witness's father was hanged. We agreed it was too big to be a coincidence." He risked a glance at her, but her blue eyes still stared. Into his guilty soul.

"Uh-huh. Yep. That's why," she said.

"It's a fascinating case," he added, grasping at straws. *And I'm curious about one of his daughters.*

"You can tell me about it later. We have *work* to do." She set her overflowing laptop bag on a chair and hauled out her computer.

Zander closed the thick three-ring binder and set it aside. "I called Dr. Rutledge this morning."

"You didn't mind waking *him* up?" She focused on her computer.

Zander understood he would pay for not calling her. "He told us yesterday that he starts early. I asked him to hold off on Nate Copeland's autopsy."

Her head snapped up. "Why?"

"I want to be there. I felt at least one of us should have observed the Fitch autopsies, but we were buried in the case. Copeland was law enforcement . . ."

Ava immediately got it. "We'll both go."

They shared a bond with the young deputy. All law enforcement did. As uncomfortable as it was to witness an autopsy, being present showed respect. It highlighted their commitment to finding the answers behind the man's death.

"But what about Billy Osburne?" Ava grimaced. "This morning I wanted to find out where he's hiding."

"The sheriff will be on it," said Zander. "He knows better than us which rocks to look under first. I think the autopsy is important. Rutledge has done the X-rays and photos on Copeland and sent his clothing to the lab. He'll hold off on the rest until we get there. We can ask Dr. Rutledge more about the Fitches too," Zander added. "I've been reviewing where we're at. We don't have any current leads on Billy Osburne. None of the employees at the auto parts store knew who he hung around with. Greer put a deputy on the Osburne house for a bit to see if he shows, and I've got watches on his credit cards and cell phone."

"There's nothing back from forensics on the Copeland scene," Ava added. "Forensics did check the Fitch cups and beverages for the presence of GHB. They didn't find any. They're checking the food next."

"Rutledge said it was probably in a liquid."

"*Probably* is the key word there."

"If it's not found," Zander said slowly, "that means someone walked away with the method of delivery."

"Possibly someone they knew—"

"Someone they trusted to share a beverage with," Zander finished. "Shit. I can see that scenario working with Copeland too."

"We don't know if he had GHB in his system yet."

Zander's gut told him the toxicology report would show he had.

"Now." Ava cleared her throat and turned her laptop so he could see the screen. "Yesterday I got a warrant for Emily Mills's cell phone records." She aimed her gaze at her computer.

Coffee cooled in Zander's mouth. She hadn't told him of the request.

"Why didn't you just ask to see her phone?" he asked, knowing the suggestion was weak the moment he said it.

She looked up, faint condescension shining in her eyes.

"I know, I know. What did you find?" Coffee acid churned in Zander's stomach. Had he put too much trust in their primary witness?

"Twenty minutes are missing."

He couldn't speak.

"Emily's phone records show she got a call at 6:47 from the diner. That would be her cook calling to tell her he couldn't reach Lindsay." Ava pointed at the entry with her pen. "She told you she left immediately for the diner. When I talked with Madison yesterday, she told me she heard Emily's phone ring and stated she left within minutes."

"She must have already been up and dressed," Zander said numbly. "Seems reasonable."

"I think so. The records show a call to Lindsay's house at 6:50 that lasted two seconds."

"She must have reached her voice mail and hung up."

"And either she called right before she left, or she called while driving. Either way, I drove from the Barton mansion to Lindsay's home. It took me eight minutes in the middle of the day. At that time of morning I imagine the roads are even quieter."

"They're always quiet here," Zander said.

"There's another brief call to Lindsay's phone at 7:02. Your interview notes said she knocked and then tried to call again. That's when she heard the phone ringing inside and tried the door, finding it was open."

Zander remembered Emily's description exactly.

"According to 911, Emily's call came in at 7:29."

"Jesus." Ice flooded his veins. "What did she do for all that time? I can understand it might take a few minutes to find Lindsay and then Sean. But going twenty minutes before calling it in?" He ran a hand through his hair. "I don't get it."

Ava's lips were tight, her face grim. "That makes two of us. She didn't make any other calls during the time."

"I need to interview her again."

"*We* need to interview her again."

Her emphasis made him pause. "Why do you say it like that?"

She sighed and gave him a look that reminded him of his mother when she was disappointed in him. "You're too nice."

"Nice? I'm not nice. We're working a murder case."

"You're nice around her." Ava raised both brows and held his gaze.

He got it. "You think I'm attracted to her."

"I know you are. She's a very attractive woman, and I know exactly what you look like in that scenario." Her lips twisted in a wry smile.

Ava would recognize that.

He rubbed his forehead, analyzing everything he'd said or done in Emily's presence. "I don't think I've treated her any different than, say . . . her sister or aunts."

"Just be more aware. Okay?" Ava's tone said she was done with the subject. "When should we talk to Emily about this? She might have a reasonable explanation—maybe she spent time vomiting in the bushes . . . or . . . I don't know."

"What could she have done indoors for twenty minutes?" Zander was stumped.

"Or outside."

"The bodies didn't appear moved. Copeland admitted he was the one who'd cut down Sean. We wouldn't know if anything else had been changed."

"They took her fingerprints to check against any found inside," Ava said. "Maybe they'll turn up somewhere."

"I'll email forensics and tell them we want the locations where her prints turn up ASAP," Zander said, opening his laptop. The churning in his stomach had subsided, but now he felt numb and determined to get to the bottom of Emily's movements.

Is she involved somehow?

As hard as he tried, he couldn't see her participating in murder. But Emily might have done something to compromise the scene, purposefully or not.

"You're in android mode now," Ava commented.

He glanced up. "Android?"

"All business."

"Make up your mind how you want me to act." He refocused on his email. Ava's scrutiny was making him surly.

"We can discuss it on the way to the medical examiner's office in Portland."

"I can't wait," he groused, risking a glance at her.

She was grinning, her eyes warm with humor, and for the briefest second, he regretted what he'd lost because he'd kept his feelings to himself in the past.

The regrets occurred less and less, but he'd be happier once they completely vanished. Frowning, he sent his email, knowing Ava was right that Emily had caught his notice. But this was no time for feelings. She was a witness, and he had a murderer or two to catch.

19

"Where'd Isaac vanish to?" Madison asked Leo as he flipped hash browns on the griddle.

"Dunno. He was here a minute ago."

"What do you think about holding a memorial for Lindsay and Sean?" she asked.

The gruff man frowned. "Isn't that something their families will do?" The shredded potatoes sizzled as he pressed them with his spatula.

"I don't know, but if they do, I doubt it will be here in Bartonville. They'll probably hold something in their hometowns. I feel like we need something too."

"It makes sense. Memorials are for the living, not the dead," Leo stated with a knowing glance.

He read her perfectly, understanding that she needed closure. Many of the people in town could use the same. They were silent, walking grievers, seeking a place to ease their pain.

Isaac appeared and headed toward the supply room with a box of huge tomato-sauce cans. As he passed, Madison touched his arm, and he flinched away, nearly dropping the box.

"Sorry, Isaac."

Fear flashed in his wide eyes as he stopped and turned toward her.

He looks scared of me. Why?

"I wanted your opinion on a memorial service for the Fitches," she said, forcing a small smile to put him at ease. His brief terror had rattled her.

Isaac looked from her to Leo. "Yeah. That's a good idea." He continued around the corner to their storage area. Isaac had always been skittish, but he'd been so much better over the last six months. It hurt her to see him looking like a kicked puppy again.

Leo shrugged as she sent him a questioning look. "People process things in different ways. I'm sure it's about Lindsay. Don't take it personally."

She didn't.

Leo had asked Emily to give Isaac a job a year ago, claiming he was a nephew from out of state who needed a fresh start, and Emily had immediately hired him. Several weeks later Leo had confessed he'd found Isaac hiding in a shed on his property and had lied about the nephew story. The bruises, burns, and scars on the boy's back had kept Leo from sending him home. Leo had done some investigating a few hours south in Isaac's hometown of Lincoln City. He'd shared with the sisters that he'd learned Isaac's father was a drunk, and that two of his old girlfriends had brought charges against him for assault. He'd been in and out of jail most of his life.

Isaac had simply left home instead of going to the police.

Emily had promised that Isaac had a job for as long as he wanted.

Three months into Isaac's employment, Madison had found him reading an article on Leo's tablet in the break room. When she'd asked what was so interesting, he'd replied, "Nothing," and then closed the browser and left. Madison had sat in his chair, opened the browser, and clicked on the first page in the history. Her skin had tingled as she read about an assault in Lincoln City. A forty-year-old resident had been attacked with a baseball bat outside a bar. He'd suffered severe head trauma and two crushed ankles. Madison had not recognized the name, but the police were searching for the attacker they'd briefly caught on camera. A grainy image accompanied the story.

The man in the picture wore Leo's coat. He also wore a hat, so his bald head was covered, but Madison had *known* the coat. Two years ago, she'd sewn on new buttons after she noticed he'd lost more than half of them. Since then he'd worn it nearly every day. There was nothing identifiable about the coat to anyone else; hundreds of men on the coast wore similar tan canvas coats.

I could be wrong.

She'd closed the story, erased the history, and sat thinking for a long moment. The victim's last name wasn't Smith like Isaac's.

Smith. Could there be a more common name?

Spinning around in her chair, she'd checked the employee coat hooks. Leo had worn a denim jacket with fleece lining that morning.

She never saw the canvas coat again, but she followed the story. The victim would never walk without a heavy limp, and no leads were ever found on his attacker.

Madison had asked no questions and exercised more patience and sympathy around the teenager.

But this morning, Isaac's flighty behavior was another oddity that tipped her day off-balance. Dory's weird rambling had been the first, and the slogan from the pocket watch consistently beat a fierce tempo in her brain as she worked, making her mess up orders and nearly spill coffee. Twice. Usually her shift ran like a well-oiled machine. Today her mental gears were grinding and sticking.

The watch and Dory's words sucked up her concentration.

Why would Dad have a watch with that slogan? Maybe he didn't know what the words meant . . . it had been his grandfather's, after all.

But Dory said, "Even with the kind of man he was."

Was there something we didn't know?

The thoughts warred in her brain. She had memories of her loving father. But if she thought hard, there were also glimpses of anger. Glimpses she'd pushed away, not wanting to remember.

"Dammit!" her father roared from the driver's seat. Madison and Emily went silent in the back seat and craned their necks to see what had made their father yell and pound on the steering wheel.

"Damned bitch." He threw open his door and strode to a car that had just pulled into a parking place.

"I think Dad was waiting for that spot," said Emily.

"Why doesn't he just find another?" asked Madison. She could see empty spots a few rows over.

She gasped as she saw him kick the rear tire of the other car. Putting both hands on the glass, she pressed her face close to see. The other driver was frantically rolling up her window, her wide eyes terrified in her black face.

Madison's stomach clenched.

Who can I ask about Dory's comments about Mom and Dad? And about Tara?

She didn't want to go to her other great-aunts. Past conversations had proved the aunts stuck to a script when it came to discussing her parents. Dory had gone off script, and Madison was certain her other aunts wouldn't approve. She had to think of someone else who'd been around during her parents' early years. And would be willing to talk.

Remembering she'd entered the kitchen to grab extra butter for a customer, she scooped a generous ball into a tiny dish and darted back to the floor. The customer said nothing as Madison set it near her pancakes.

You're welcome.

She sighed and checked the restaurant front for new customers. A single male waited, his back to her. She grabbed a menu for him, feeling tension crawl up her spine. He turned as she approached.

Brett Steele.

She tossed the menu onto the hostess stand and met his gaze. "Why are you here?"

"To eat of course."

"Emily's not here yet."

"I didn't come to see her." He looked pointedly at the menu she'd cast aside. "Can I get a table?"

She reluctantly picked it up and led him to the closest booth.

"You look good today, Madison," he said as he slid in. "I'm liking the lipstick."

An urge to wipe it off consumed her, and she hid a tremor.

"Coffee?" she asked instead.

"Yep. And a short stack with a side of bacon." He smiled.

Out of the corner of her eye, she saw Emily walk through the kitchen door, clearly headed to her office. Brett's sudden attention shift indicated he'd also spotted her. Madison rolled her eyes at his flash of longing.

Get over her.

His comment about her lipstick curdled in her brain. The man had issues when it came to the Mills sisters. All three of them.

"I'll get your coffee in a minute." Madison dashed away in pursuit of Emily, catching her as she unlocked her office. "Can you watch the floor? It's quieted down from breakfast, and I have an appointment."

"Seriously, Madison? Why would you schedule it during your work hours?"

"I just made it this morning. I've got a tooth that throbbed half the night. They said they could get me in now."

"Oh." Emily's gaze sharpened. "Yeah, I'll cover it." She wrinkled her nose. "Did I see Brett out there?"

"Yes. He wants the usual, but I didn't put in his order yet. And keep an eye on table eight. They're needy." Madison pulled her apron strap over her head, wadded the fabric up in a ball, and squeezed past

Emily into the office to grab her purse. "Gotta go." She darted out and down the hall.

"I hope your tooth feels better," Emily called after her.

Madison had already forgotten the lie. "Thanks."

She'd thought of someone who would answer her questions.

Madison rapped on the window, spotting Anita at a desk inside her beauty parlor. The front door was locked because the shop didn't open for another twenty minutes. Anita waved at her and headed toward the door.

Anita was Madison's choice for answers for several reasons.

First, she'd lived in Bartonville all her life and knew every person in Madison's family, including her parents. Anita had been a few years older than Madison's mother, Brenda.

Second, the Anita Haircut shop was a gold mine of gossip—or cesspool, depending on one's personal preferences.

Third, Madison knew that Anita and her aunts had quarreled off and on over the years. Anita wasn't afraid to stand up to her aunts. They were still friends, but that didn't mean Anita toed their line like some people in town. She spoke freely.

Anita smiled as she opened the door. "Madison, so good to see you." She ushered her in. The shop smelled like hair spray and nail polish. Anita had remodeled two years before, and the beauty parlor of Madison's childhood had vanished. No more pink vinyl chairs or black-and-white-checkered floors. Now it was "soothing and modern," with its clean lines of quartz counters, succulents, and whitewashed shiplap on the walls.

But the smell was the same. The scent of promises and expectations from beauty products.

Anita was in her sixties and impossibly thin. She always wore black from head to toe, and her hairstyle hadn't changed in several decades, but she was perpetually chic. She'd mastered the secret of appearing timeless through classic styles. Her platinum hair was bobbed at her jawline but had a perfect lift at the roots and a subtle curl at one temple.

She'd abandoned cigarettes years ago but still had a faint smoker's rasp. Everyone passed through her shop—even the teenagers who pursued the latest cuts, because Anita was on top of current trends. But she would still do a wash and set for her older clients. With a flick of a wrist, she gestured for Madison to sit in one of the stylists' chairs as Anita settled into another and spun to face her, gentle curiosity in her eyes.

How does she know I need to sit for this conversation?

"What's going on with you, child?"

Everyone was "child" or "darling" to Anita. Even the men.

When Madison had decided to visit the shop, her questions had been clear in her mind. Now they were a jumbled mess of ridiculous elements. Doubt tied her tongue.

Anita picked up on her hesitation. "Let me get you a cappuccino." Anita hopped out of the chair and fussed at the huge professional espresso machine. She'd served her clients espresso and cappuccino before anyone had ever heard of Starbucks.

"Anita . . . what do people in this town think of my family?" The question was vague, but it was a start.

The shop owner didn't look up from her task. "The Bartons or the Millses?"

Madison frowned. *People distinguish between the two?* "Bartons."

The milk frother made conversation impossible for a long moment. "The Bartons are the foundation and backbone of Bartonville," she finally answered.

"That sounds like a statement from the chamber of commerce." Hollow and rehearsed.

"I'm sure it's in a pamphlet somewhere." Anita added the milk to the espresso and brought the cup to Madison. "These days when people say the Barton name, they're referring to your great-aunts or your great-great-grandfather. Your uncle Rod has moved far away enough that people generally forget he's of George Barton's direct line."

"Emily and I haven't."

"As it should be. You two are 'the Mills girls.' And Tara too, of course."

"What do they say about Tara?"

Anita tilted her head as she held Madison's gaze and handed her the cup. "Do you mean now or back when she left? And why are you asking?"

"Both time periods." Madison didn't know how to answer the second question. "I heard some things."

"Mmm." Anita returned to her chair and swung one leg over the other, all her attention on Madison. "I'm sure it was all bull, but many people thought she left because she was pregnant."

"I've heard that one."

"Others said your aunts drove her away. They were rather autocratic back then. All three of them."

"They've mellowed, but Aunt Vina will still go head-to-head with anyone."

Taking a sip of her cappuccino, Madison doubted the wisdom of her decision to ask questions. The old rumors hurt. "Dory made some odd statements this morning."

"I see."

"She kept implying that my mother was miserable and that people felt sorry for her."

"How old were you when she died? Nine?"

"Ten. I knew she would get tired and stay in bed sometimes. It wasn't until I was an adult that I learned she was manic-depressive."

"A child's view is much different from an adult's. And your mother was so doting and affectionate, I know she showered a lot of love on you girls. We all saw it."

"What else did you see?"

"A sad, confused wife."

Mild shock ran through Madison's fingers, making her cup quiver. *As Dory implied.* Anita had spoken carefully, her expression calm, her eyes sharp, watching for Madison's reaction. There was a ring of truth in her words.

"So they had marriage problems. Everyone does."

"No marriage is perfect, and your father deeply loved you girls. It was unmistakable."

"Did people say Dad married Mom for her money?"

"Yes."

"But the Bartons weren't rich. Vina says the logging business tanked, and some bad investments wiped out nearly everything in the eighties."

"That is what I understand too, but people believe what they want. They see your home and the restaurant and make assumptions." She paused. "If you still want to hear old rumors, there was one that said your father's death was a message to the Bartons for leaving working families in the lurch when the mill closed."

"That makes no sense at all."

"I agree. I don't think people put much stock in that one. A lot still think you're hiding money, though."

"That's ridiculous. The mansion is crippling us with its upkeep, and the restaurant does okay, but it's not making us rich. It's how we get by."

Anita shrugged. "That's what I tell people. But you know how rumors are."

"Dad was a gold digger. What else was said about him?" Madison's muscles tensed as she braced for the answer. *I know he loved my mother; I saw it many times.*

The shop owner sighed and looked out the window. "He was a good ol' boy. Thought he was funny and had no qualms about telling ugly jokes. He was a racist."

The room went very still, the phrase from the watch ringing in Madison's brain, and the female driver's scared face flashed again. "Because of how he was raised."

It wasn't a question, but Anita nodded.

"He didn't teach us to be like that."

"I doubt your mother would have put up with it."

"But he had similar-thinking friends?" She recalled Dory's words about awful people—but she'd said they were gone now.

"People always seek out others like themselves."

Madison wasn't satisfied with that answer. "He hung around with other racists is what you're saying."

Anita gave a half smile with no warmth. "Bingo."

The word sliced Madison's heart wide open. She blinked rapidly.

Regret colored Anita's expression, and she leaned forward to set a hand on Madison's knee. "He *loved* you, and you have every right to love him back. There is good in everyone, and he showed you girls everything that was positive about himself. It was the outsiders—and some family—who saw the rest. With most people, what you see is what you get." She focused hard on Madison's eyes. "But others present themselves in ways that don't reflect their true selves. It's like protection for their tender souls."

She sees me.

Her defenses leaped into place, her hands tight on her cup, and disappointment shone in Anita's eyes.

"What did people say after he was murdered?"

Anita looked away, her mouth clamped tight. "No one wanted him murdered. They just wanted him to take his racism and white supremacist views elsewhere."

"Who killed him?" she whispered.

Anita started. "Why, Chet Carlson, of course." Her brows came together as she studied Madison. "That's an odd question."

"Chet Carlson didn't even know him." Madison's brain spun in a million directions. "He wasn't from around here. He knew nothing about how *the town* felt about my father. And he went through all the trouble to *hang* him?"

"Your father's bloody jacket was found in his hotel room. He was convicted on the evidence."

"Of course he was." Madison closed her eyes, seeing her mother running in the woods and Emily standing in the backyard of their home, staring into the distance as smoke crept into the home.

What did Emily see that night? Why didn't she tell anyone she'd gone outside?

"Now, Madison," came the lecturing tone, "you're letting this new information affect everything you've ever known about your father. *It doesn't matter.* Nothing about your time with him has changed."

Who would thirteen-year-old Emily want to protect?

Madison opened her eyes, her gaze heavy with the weight of her new knowledge. "Everything has changed. He was horrible."

"That doesn't change that he was your father and he cherished you girls. You are still the same person who walked in my door five minutes ago. So is he."

Madison wasn't listening. *Emily must have a reason to carry a secret for this long.*

She'd probably done it for the same reason Madison had told no one she'd seen Emily outside that night or her mother in the woods.

The reason was to protect them.

Love for my mother and sister kept me quiet all these years.

Who would Emily stay quiet for?

20

Zander slipped on the clear face shield and checked out his partner in her shield. Ava's eyes crinkled at the corners, indicating she was grinning behind the blue mask over her mouth.

"That's a good look for you, Zander."

He looked down at his gown and booties, feeling slightly claustrophobic in the protective gear. Part of him wanted to rip them off and head into the hallway for fresh air.

Fresher air, he corrected himself. As soon as they'd entered the medical examiner's building, they'd encountered its unique smell. It wasn't like a hospital smell or a funeral-home smell—both of which he'd experienced too many times.

It was a combination of professional-strength cleanser, refrigerated meat, and an underlying hint of decomposition. His nose had already grown used to it, noting that the odor didn't bother him as it had at first. He'd learned early in this job that he could handle most odors—death, excrement, rot—if he toughed out the first ten minutes or so. He also knew to shower afterward as soon as possible and immediately dump every scrap of clothing in the laundry. Today he'd left his coat in the car, not wanting it to soak up any odors.

He and Ava stood in the autopsy suite. There were four stainless-steel tables, each with a sink at one end. A large hose and nozzle hung over each table, along with strong lights and a scale. Two assistants went about the suite, setting out instruments and getting things organized for the examiner.

On the closest table, Nate Copeland's corpse silently waited for Dr. Rutledge.

Zander felt like a voyeur; he didn't want to see the dead man, but it was his duty. The medical examiner had already done the Y incision from chest to groin but hadn't removed the ribs. Ava fidgeted, and she lifted her shield to wipe her eyes. Usually she had no problem with autopsies, but she'd warned Zander that this one would be tough for her, given that she'd talked to the man the day before. At the Copeland house she'd held it together, but here the explicit details of the young man's horrible end were laid out under the harsh lights.

A stark contrast to the very alive young deputy she'd interviewed—actually she'd grilled and guilt-tripped—about the Fitch crime scene.

Zander had told her not to feel sorry for doing her job.

"I'd convinced myself that the person he'd been is gone. This body is an empty shell," Ava whispered. "But then I see that." She pointed at a tattoo on Copeland's deltoid. "He's suddenly very human again."

Zander understood. The tattoo represented something everlasting that Copeland had selected to carry with him. It symbolized a decision, a love, a permanence.

The tattoo remained, but the person was gone.

Copeland's skin was pale, but along the edges of his lower back and legs, a dark bruised shade indicated he'd died faceup. Blood followed gravity after the heart stopped, and the livor mortis was in the right places for a man tipped back in a recliner. The dark color would also cover his backside.

The suite door swung open, and Dr. Seth Rutledge walked in, slipping his arms into a gown. An assistant tied the strings at the back as he shook Zander's and Ava's hands.

"Good to see the two of you. It's been a while—I know, I know—that's a good thing, in your opinion." Seth focused on Ava. "Victoria said you're getting married at a winery this summer?"

"Yes." Her voice shook the littlest bit, and she didn't expand on wedding descriptions as she usually did when asked about her plans.

Seth paused, but realized he wasn't going to hear more. Sympathy filled his eyes. "That sounds great."

"You and Victoria are on the list." She sounded stronger.

"We better be." He pulled on a pair of gloves. "Let's get started." He shifted into work mode as he neared the table.

Zander spotted something new. "I don't remember seeing that sign before." He pointed at a large, elegant plaque high along one wall.

THIS IS THE PLACE WHERE DEATH DELIGHTS IN HELPING THE LIVING.

A bit morbid. *Delights* as death's verb felt wrong, but Zander figured it was medical examiner humor.

"Yes. Victoria gave me that for Christmas."

Zander exchanged a glance with Ava, whose eyes had crinkled again, agreeing it made for an odd gift too, but Seth's wife was his forensic anthropologist. The two of them worked in grim professions.

"The two of you are a match made in heaven, Seth," Ava told him.

Seth's eyes lit up above his mask. "I agree. Now, I'd already done a few things before you called this morning to ask me to wait. The external exam is finished, and you can see I stopped after the Y incision, but I sent fluids to toxicology and had his X-rays done."

"Which fluids?" asked Ava.

"Blood, bile, urine, and vitreous humor."

Zander was glad he hadn't been present to watch Seth stick a needle in Copeland's eye to draw the fluid. "You can get quick toxicology results?"

"We can for the basic tests since we run them here. Anything outside the norm, I send to another lab."

"What's the norm?"

"Alcohol, marijuana, opiates, barbiturates, psychostimulants. We also test for arsenic and heavy metals." He paused. "We found Nate had the same GHB as in the Fitches."

Zander and Ava looked at each other. "So this investigation has taken a new turn," Zander said.

"There's more than that," said Seth. "The GSR test on his hand came back very high. Well over a two-thousand-particle count. He definitely fired the weapon, *but* it was an odd pattern. Part of his hand had virtually no GSR, as if something had been covering it—like another hand."

Not suicide.

Zander was satisfied to hear that the young deputy hadn't taken his own life, but the fact that he had been murdered wasn't an improvement.

"I don't know if one is better than the other," muttered Ava, echoing Zander's thoughts.

"It appears the same person who murdered the Fitches may have murdered Nate."

"May have," repeated Ava. "Even with this new evidence, it's not definite. We need to remember that."

Zander agreed. "Anything else from the external exam?"

"No abrasions or injuries," the doctor went on. "Livor mortis matches the photos I saw of his position when he was found in the recliner. He has a tribal-style tattoo on his deltoid and one on his calf. A few scars. The X-rays don't indicate any past broken bones, which I've found to be unusual in males. Usually *something* has been broken."

"Females are better at seeing consequences," Ava muttered. "Even as kids. You men do stupid, risky things."

Zander couldn't argue with that.

Seth peeled back the flaps of skin and muscles at the Y incision, exposing the rib cage. He took the large pruning shears from his assistant and started cutting ribs far under the flaps. The first sounds rattled Zander; they always did. But by the fourth cut, he was inured to the loud cracks. When Seth finished, he lifted out the front half of the rib cage.

Ava sucked in a breath.

"You good?" he whispered.

"Good as I can be."

Next Seth systematically removed each organ, scrutinized it, weighed it, sliced it open for further scrutiny, and cut samples for testing and preservation. A recorder hung above Seth's head to catch his observations, but an assistant also took notes.

Zander watched closely as Seth cut open the stomach. "I can smell alcohol. Smells like beer," the examiner said. "There's no solids in here, but there is some fluid. I suspect most had already passed to the small intestine."

"Dr. Ruiz put his time of death at midmorning," Ava said.

"This isn't the first person I've opened who had beer for breakfast. It's more common than you think."

Even with a mask covering it, Zander saw Ava wrinkle her nose. "A mimosa for breakfast I can understand, but not beer," she said.

"Why not? Who decided champagne was acceptable in the mornings but not beer?" Seth shrugged as he set the stomach on the scale. "They're both alcohol. I've gained a different perspective on a lot of things in this job."

"Do you have beer for breakfast?" Ava asked the examiner.

"Nope. Sounds disgusting."

Ava snorted. "So there's a good chance the GHB was in the beer."

"I'll have the fluids from his stomach tested," said Seth.

"I don't think any open beer bottles were found at the Copeland scene," said Ava. "I'll check with the team."

Zander wanted the autopsy to be over, ready to follow up on what they'd just learned.

The doctor quickly sped through the rest of the organs and turned his attention to the head. He leaned close and palpated the skull with gentle hands. Zander wondered how he'd cut a cranial cap under the scalp when a large portion of the skull was missing. The primary concern was the presentation for an open-casket viewing.

"His parents have agreed to a closed-casket funeral," Seth said softly. "But I'll do what I can for their personal viewing. It shouldn't be too bad with a deep pillow."

Zander stepped in for a closer look. Typically the medical examiner cut through the scalp around the back of the head from ear to ear, then peeled the scalp forward over the face, leaving it attached to the forehead. Next they would cut out a large piece of the skull to gain access to and remove the brain. After removing the brain, the examiner would replace the cranial cap like a puzzle piece and return the scalp to its former position, stitching it in place under the hair, making it acceptable for an open casket.

The issue with Copeland was the damage at the back from the exit wound. The skull could break into several pieces as Dr. Rutledge worked and never look quite right for his parents' final viewing.

"Let's see how the bone looks and figure it out from there," Seth said to himself. His assistant lifted the head, and Seth used his scalpel to make a cut around the back of the head and then worked the scalp forward. Seth's gloved fingers showed through the hole in the scalp left by the bullet.

Once exposed, the bullet's damage to the skull was brutally clear. "Big one," Seth said under his breath.

"He carried a G 21," Zander told him. "A .45 round."

The bullet's impact had created a star pattern of cracks that led away from the large exit wound. "If I cut the cap a little lower than usual, I can avoid crossing the cracks, and I believe the cranial cap will stay in one piece." Seth nodded firmly, confident in his decision, and picked up the Stryker saw.

The saw wasn't much larger than Zander's drill at home, but the Stryker's sound reminded him of a dentist's drill cutting into his tooth and reverberating through his head. He stepped away as a cloud of fine bone dust bloomed.

Beer. Zander found that odd. Nate Copeland had beer early in the day when he was already planning to go drink more with his friend? Was he getting an early start, or had he been entertaining someone else?

Ava tugged his sleeve. "You're glaring. What are you thinking about?" she said loudly to be heard over the saw.

"I want to know who drank beer with Nate Copeland in the morning."

"You're not the only one." She watched the doctor move to the other side of Copeland's head for a new angle. "Where was Billy Osburne yesterday morning?"

"His shift at the auto parts store didn't start until noon."

"So he was available. Is he someone Nate would have a beer with? Did he have motive?" Ava questioned.

"The Osburnes are about ten years older than Nate," Zander said. "But I don't know if that means they wouldn't hang out together. We can find out if they knew each other enough to have a morning beer."

"But why Nate?"

The saw stopped, and the silence was a balm to Zander's hearing. Seth lifted the cranial cap as if it were the most delicate glass. In a way, it was. The doctor had managed to contain the cracks in the cap, but a few puzzle pieces of the skull had been dislocated adjacent to the exit hole. Fierce concentration shone in his eyes as he gently set the large piece aside.

Zander held his breath for several long seconds as he followed the doctor's movements, Ava's question buzzing in his brain. "Nate must have seen something he shouldn't have at the Fitch murders—even if he wasn't aware of it," he replied. "Or *Nate* was seen at the murders. Did anyone go farther into the woods behind the Fitch house? Maybe someone was watching when Nate arrived."

"I think I read that the woods were checked a bit. I doubt they looked very hard."

Based on the sloppy work Zander had seen that morning, he agreed. "Okay. We need to take another look at the property. What else?"

"Do we need to go over the Fitch autopsy reports with Seth?" Ava asked. "I saw his final report in my in-box, but I haven't opened it yet. He talked to you about preliminary findings. Have you discussed anything else?"

"No. But he was going to check to see if Sean fathered Lindsay's baby. We can ask if that is done." Zander glanced back as Seth weighed the brain. "He's almost finished."

After the brain had been examined and the samples removed, all the organs were typically placed in a plastic bag and returned to the empty chest cavity. Then the ribs were replaced and the Y incision stitched closed.

Seth returned to the cranial cap and lifted it with precision gentleness. There were two notches on the edges, sawed by the doctor to line the cap back up in position on the skull and keep it in place. With skill and caution, he set it in, and his eyes crinkled in pleasure.

"That will do," he said with satisfaction to the assistant, who'd watched the process with concern. The two of them efficiently stretched the scalp back over the cap. "You got it from here?" Seth asked. She nodded and picked up a curved needle to stitch the scalp back together.

The doctor took a few seconds to study Copeland's face. With the jaw closed, there was no visible sign of the bullet hole in the palate. Seth rested a gloved hand on the officer's shoulder and took a deep breath.

After a long moment, he turned to Zander and Ava, and gestured for them to follow him to the other side of the room, away from Nate Copeland. Seth's expression was all business. "You had wanted to know if Sean had fathered his wife's baby. I got the lab results back, and he is the father."

Something relaxed in Zander's chest. It didn't mean Lindsay wasn't having an affair with Billy Osburne, but it eliminated a possible minor motivation.

"But Lindsay and Sean wouldn't know that was a fact if she *was* sleeping with Billy Osburne," said Ava.

Shit. She's right. The motivation couldn't be crossed off the list.

"We need to find Osburne," Zander said.

"I want to look at the property behind the Fitch home first. Billy Osburne second."

Zander agreed.

21

It was well past lunchtime by the time Zander and Ava returned to the coast from their visit to the medical examiner's office. They had hit a Dairy Queen drive-through on their route back, and the SUV still smelled of french fries.

It was a better scent than in the medical examiner's building.

"Straight to the Fitch house?" Zander asked.

"No time like the present."

The sheriff hadn't found Billy Osburne and was getting frustrated. Even over the phone, Zander heard it in his voice.

He took the narrow winding road to the Fitch location, feeling a sense of déjà vu. A lot had happened over the two and a half days since he had been there last. The road turned to gravel, and the homes grew farther apart. He spotted the Fitch house and parked on the road's shoulder. The two of them studied the small white ranch in silence. Behind the house, tall firs swayed, shedding needles and small branches.

"Windy," Ava commented.

"I wouldn't live with trees of that size near my house."

"Hell no." She leaned forward and pointed at low bushes a dozen yards from their vehicle. "Look."

Several bikes lay on their sides, partly hidden by the greenery.

"Kids." Annoyance had Zander immediately opening his door. Kids would be curious and snoop around a crime scene; that was a natural instinct at that age. But he'd have to be the bad guy and chase them off. He counted four bikes, each in a different stage of wear and tear.

Nostalgia enveloped him. A bike and a deep inquisitiveness had sent him and his childhood friends on many adventures. They were fearless, convinced that their world was open to exploration. The more prohibited the location, the more exciting. The fenced-off electrical station behind the middle school. The barn with the caved-in roof on the neighboring property. The row of rotten-smelling dumpsters behind the strip mall.

Three locations that would distress their parents—which made them powerful kid magnets.

"At least they're outside and not playing video games."

Zander snorted. "I'll grab a couple of flashlights from the back." He popped the rear hatch and grabbed two small LED units. It wasn't dark, but the gray clouds cast a pall. It would be hard to see in the shadows of the forest.

She took a flashlight, and they headed around the left side of the home.

"Think the kids would go inside?" Ava murmured.

"I trust the county locked it up tight, but I can guarantee you the kids tried every door and window."

"Guarantee?"

"I was a nosy kid once," Zander admitted. He would have been fascinated, oblivious to the disrespect, if this had occurred in his childhood neighborhood.

"I was too, but I wouldn't try to enter a home where people had been murdered."

"You can add this to your list of differences between the sexes."

"Not all boys," she added.

"Not all boys," he agreed with a grin. He held up a hand as he heard young voices behind the home.

Ava sighed. "Crap. They must be at *the tree*."

The two of them turned the corner and saw three boys who appeared to be eleven or twelve circling the trunk of the tree. A fourth was up the tree, several branches above where Sean Fitch had been hanged. The branch used in the hanging had been removed to process for evidence. Crime scene tape still circled a large portion of the backyard.

Zander fought back the instinct to yell at the boys. *They don't understand.*

"A teaching moment," Ava said quietly. She raised her voice. "Hey, kids? Can you get away from the tree and come over here for a minute?"

Four startled faces spun their way. *"It's the cops!"* The boys froze and then scrambled, each darting in a different direction. The boy in the tree shot down the trunk quicker than an angry bear and took off, the red hood of his jacket flapping behind him.

Zander took a few rapid steps after one and halted, glancing back at Ava. Her hands were on her hips, acceptance in her expression.

There was no point.

"We could wait by the bikes," he suggested.

"What for? I suspect we scared them enough to stay away, and I doubt they would listen to the lecture I was ready to give."

"How'd they know we were law enforcement?"

She gave him a droll look. "You ooze law and order in your stance alone. Even if you weren't FBI, they'd struggle to look you in the eye."

"'Ooze'? Is that a compliment?"

"I think so."

Zander wasn't so sure. "They probably saw us here the other day. No doubt spying from a distance."

"Possibly." Ava exhaled, scanned the backyard clearing, and eyed the dense forest that started beyond the police tape. "How do you want to do this?"

"We should have more people."

"In a perfect world. But it's you and me." She spread out her arms, stepping away from Zander. "Fingertip-to-fingertip distance. We'll start by that big fir and pace a grid. Keep an eye out for anything that a watcher could have left behind . . . trash . . . footprints."

They spent the next half hour attempting to walk in straight lines while stepping around thick trunks and underbrush, sweeping every inch of the ground with their lights. Every few feet Zander looked up, tracing his beam up the bark and branches of the firs and trying to avoid being poked in the eye by falling pine needles. The gigantic trees creaked and slowly swayed in the wind.

"The ground's fucking moving," Ava said.

Zander had noticed it too. "The dirt is so wet and saturated, the wind is making the roots lift."

She looked up. "If one starts to fall, it will probably hit ten others before crashing down. We should have time to get out of the way."

"They won't fall. Aren't roots supposed to keep the trees in place?"

"You ever seen the roots of a fir?" she asked. "They make a ball. Totally out of proportion to the weight and height of the rest of the tree."

They searched in silence for several more minutes, methodically moving flashlights right and left and kicking leaves out of the way. He was glad he'd grabbed the lights; a thorough search would have been impossible without them. He swung his beam of light forward and choked.

"Jesus."

He gaped at the older woman in front of him and sought to catch his breath. She stood fifteen feet away, her empty hands at her sides and her happy smile on display. His brain registered that she posed no immediate threat, but he slowly unzipped his heavy jacket.

"Can we help you?" Ava asked. She'd gasped when Zander swore and moved so her left hip was toward the woman, her weapon hand free and her light on the woman's face.

"Oh, no, I'm just watching." Her young voice didn't match the gray hair and lined face. Her long coat was a blotchy dark tan that was possibly a result of its having never been washed, and her rubber boots were muddy.

He wondered if she was homeless.

"What have you been watching?" Ava asked. Zander stayed silent. Ava had an unusual low, mellow voice that could calm anyone—including him—but his heart was still trying to beat its way out of his chest.

"You two looking around. Saw those boys." The woman frowned, deep grooves forming between her brows. "They shouldn't be here," she added in a serious tone.

"Why not?"

Her chin came up and her eyes flashed. "They just shouldn't. This isn't a place for kids."

Zander didn't disagree.

"What's your name? I'm Ava. This is Zander."

"Alice. I know who you are."

Ava tilted her head to one side. "You were at the meeting last night, weren't you?"

Zander searched the instant image of the people at the meeting that popped up in his memory. It was mostly the backs of heads.

"I was. I know you're with the FBI. You're trying to help that young couple."

"The Fitches, yes." Ava paused. "Do you know what happened to them?"

"Everyone knows what happened to them."

Zander started. *Everyone knows?*

"I mean, do you know who hurt them?" Ava clarified.

Disappointment rocked through him. Alice had taken Ava's question literally. The woman's eyes seemed very alert, intelligence in their depths, but clearly something wasn't quite right about her.

Alice shoved her hands in her pockets, and Zander tensed, hyperaware of his weapon at his ribs.

"Can you keep your hands out of your pockets?" Ava asked. "I'm more comfortable when I can see them."

Confusion flashed on Alice's face, but she did as asked, and Zander's spine relaxed. "I didn't hurt Sean or Lindsay."

"I'm glad to hear that. Do you know who did?"

"No."

It was worth a try.

"Do you live nearby?" Zander asked. Alice focused on him and blinked several times.

"No. I'm just visiting a friend."

"Where does your friend live?"

She frowned, turning her head a bit as if she hadn't heard him quite right. "I don't know."

He repeated the question in a louder voice.

That earned him a scowl. "I said I didn't know."

"Can we take you home?" Ava asked, her voice infused with kindness. Zander's lips twitched. Ava's fiancé claimed no one could refuse Ava when she used her smoky voice.

"I haven't visited my friend yet."

Apparently Alice could refuse.

"How about we go with you to make sure you get there all right," Ava suggested. "This wind is getting worse."

Zander agreed. The wind had penetrated their work space below the trees, making his jacket flap. Alice had demonstrated some confusion, and they couldn't abandon her in the woods.

"Fine." Alice turned and headed south.

Ava raised a brow at Zander, who raised his hands. *Might as well.*

Zander took a mental picture of where they had stopped their grid search and followed in Alice's wake. She was slow, her steps shuffling on the forest floor.

After a few minutes, he leaned close to Ava's ear. "I'm concerned she doesn't know where she's going."

Alice humphed. "I know where I'm going."

Mirth shone in Ava's eyes, and she pressed her lips together. Zander decided to keep his mouth shut. Several yards later they came across a fallen tree. Ava was right. The roots were a ball, disproportionate to the grandeur and length of the trunk.

Their guide stepped over a few of the fallen tree's roots, grabbing another for balance. Zander lunged forward and took her arm, helping her navigate the rough ground. She thanked him politely. They rounded the roots and started to walk along the toppled tree.

Alice stopped. "Here we go."

Zander glanced around. "Where—"

"Right here." Alice pulled her arm from Zander's hand and squatted, gazing under the trunk. She brushed aside a heavy layer of pine needles, stirring up the scent of damp musty dirt. "She's safe here, you know."

The empty eye sockets of a skull gaped at him.

22

Zander and Ava were rattled by the discovery of the skull and several other bones of Alice's "friend."

"I don't like how close the remains are to the Fitch scene," he quietly told her.

"But they're completely skeletal—this body has been here a long time. It can't have anything to do with the Fitches."

"I know." But he couldn't shake the feeling that it did. "I want the best person out here to remove them. Not some county deputy or local crime scene tech."

"Dr. Victoria Peres is your person," Ava immediately replied. "I'll call Seth to see if she's available."

The medical examiner agreed to send the state's forensic anthropologist—his wife.

Zander called Sheriff Greer to report the remains and then waited for him in the cold woods with Alice and Ava.

Alice turned out to be quite chatty. Her side of the conversation had a tendency to ramble in odd directions, and her eyes had moments of clarity that ebbed and flowed.

"What's her name?" Ava asked with a gesture toward the skull.

The older woman leaned her weight against the fallen trunk, willing to wait now that Zander had explained they were getting help for her friend. "I don't know," Alice said thoughtfully. "But I call her Cindy."

"Do you know how long she's been here?" asked Zander.

Alice frowned. "A very long time, I believe."

He had gone with Alice's assertion that the remains were female because he had no idea how to tell the difference. When he looked at the skull, his gut told him it was a woman, but that could be Alice's influence.

"Did you know her before?"

"Before what?"

I can't be vague. "Did you know her before she was . . . a skeleton?" He grimaced at the word.

"No."

"How did you meet her?"

"I saw them bring her here."

Adrenaline rocketed through his muscles. "Who brought her here?"

Alice's hands fluttered and picked at her coat. "I don't remember." She no longer met their eyes. He glanced at Ava, who made a subtle *slow down* motion with her hands.

He wanted to press but knew Alice would close off more.

The arrival of two deputies and Sheriff Greer interrupted their discussion. Their response had been quick—within ten minutes.

"Good evening, Alice," Greer said kindly as his sharp gaze took in the sight of the bones by the tree. "Getting cold this evening, isn't it?"

Alice muttered something and refused to meet the sheriff's eyes. She'd tensed as the three law enforcement officers arrived and shuffled closer to Ava. Zander suspected she'd had previous run-ins with the sheriff's department.

A quick conversation with Greer confirmed that suspicion. "She gets confused," Greer told them as they stepped away from the scene, leaving a deputy to keep an eye on Alice. "She means well, but several times she's wandered onto other people's property and even looked in their windows. We just take her back home. She's been evaluated, but every time we get the same reply: she's capable of taking care of herself and doesn't present a danger to herself or others."

"She's thin," Ava pointed out.

"She's been thin as long as I can remember," answered Greer. "But even I've run into her at the grocery store. She's quite competent . . . most of the time."

"Then why is she wandering around in the forest? She could get lost."

The sheriff was emphatic. "No one knows these woods or the coastline like Alice. She's been wandering both for the last fifty years." He gestured for one of the deputies to come closer and asked him to drive her home. "We can question her tomorrow," he told the agents. "She's sharper in the mornings."

By the time Alice left, Zander noted she looked exhausted.

"Who are your missing persons in the area?" Ava asked the sheriff, all business now. "We might need to go back decades. Clearly the remains have been here awhile."

"Well, now . . . I've heard of bodies reduced to skeletons in less than a year," the sheriff said, tapping his chin, deep in thought. "Depends on the environment and how exposed they are." He tipped his head at the skull. "Doesn't look like anybody buried the body. Could have died naturally. Maybe got lost in the woods or had a heart attack."

"Yes," Ava said impatiently. "Any of those could have happened, but they'd still be reported missing, right?"

"True. Let me think . . . We had a woman go missing from a trail along the cliffs south of here. Her husband was found guilty of her murder even though they never found the body. He claimed she slipped while taking a photo and went over the edge. State police handled that one."

Zander eyed the skull. "Could her husband have dumped her body here and claimed she went over the cliffs in an accident?"

"Possible," said Greer. "Either way, he's already locked up."

"What about Hank West?" asked the remaining deputy as he strung crime scene tape and listened to their conversation.

The sheriff's face cleared. "That's right. How long's that been? Five years?" He looked from Zander to Ava. "Old Hank had dementia. Wandered off from his home in Warrenton. Never did find him."

All three of them turned their attention to the skull.

"Maybe we should do a database search for missing persons instead of relying on memory," Ava suggested tactfully.

"Not that many people go missing around here," Greer said. "But that would be more efficient. I'll get someone started on it. My deputy can bring up some lights and watch the scene if you want to grab dinner. It'll take a few hours for that anthropologist to get here from Portland."

Zander scanned the darkening woods. It was cold, but an inner voice wouldn't let him leave. "I'll stay. I can help with the lights."

"I'll pick up some takeout," Ava told him. "And lots of coffee. It'll be a late night."

Dr. Victoria Peres arrived two hours later, and the forensic anthropologist immediately took charge of the scene. Peres was tall, with librarian glasses and long, dark hair. Zander had heard her referred to as the Ice Queen but had never seen anyone say it to her face.

The forensic anthropologist was intimidating.

She shook Zander's hand and gave him a once-over even though they'd met a few times. Ava knew her quite well. As they worked, the women exchanged small talk about mutual friends and Ava's upcoming wedding.

Zander watched Peres in admiration. The doctor moved with an economy of motion as she gave orders to her assistants and set up the station for removal of the skeletal remains. Everyone jumped to do her bidding. Even the wind had stopped after she glared at the swaying trees. She had lighting, tarps, buckets, sifters, and bins ready to start her excavation. As she waited for her assistants to set a grid and finish taking photos, she lifted the skull.

He observed with fascination. The doctor's hands were gentle with reverence—reminding him of her husband's hands at the autopsy—as she raised the skull for a closer look. The mandible still lay on the dirt, and Zander's stomach twisted, jarred by the sight of the jawbone outside of its rightful position on the skull.

Dr. Peres softly hummed as she studied the skull and turned it in her hands, holding it closer to one of her bright lights, peering inside, and then studying the face again. "Hello, pretty girl," she said in a quiet voice.

"It is female?" Ava asked.

"Oh yes, definitely. Young, too."

Zander scratched Hank West, the missing man with dementia, off his mental list. "How young?"

The doctor turned the head upside down, ran a finger across the teeth and then along a few of the seams in the skull. "Teenager. Early twenties at the latest."

She glanced down at some of the half-buried bones. "I need to examine everything to give a definite answer, but you can take that with ninety-five percent certainty."

"Got some coins of some sort here, Doc," said one of the techs as she pushed a small grid stake into the dirt. Zander squatted beside her, not surprised they hadn't noticed the small disks. They were caked with dirt and blended perfectly into the ground. The tech poked at a few with a tool. "I don't think they're money . . . at least not US money."

Zander agreed. They were larger than quarters but smaller than half dollars. The faint pattern under the dirt was unrecognizable, and he stopped himself before picking one up to wipe it off. "Maybe a foreign tourist?" he suggested to the tech, who shrugged.

"You can't tell us how long she's been here, can you?" Ava asked.

"No. I'll need to do some testing," said the doctor. "But she has a few composite posterior fillings. No alloy. That tells me she's probably not from the 1970s or earlier. Dentists were doing composite fillings pretty regularly from the 1980s on, but primarily on anterior teeth. These posterior fillings indicate she's from a more recent decade or else had an ahead-of-his-time dentist. Sorry . . . I know that's vague."

"It helps," said Zander. "Tightens the window of when to search."

"She's African American."

Zander went still.

"You're sure?" Ava asked in a flat voice.

The doctor's lips rose. "Yes." She raised an are-you-questioning-me brow at Ava.

"I didn't mean it like that," Ava began, dismay in her eyes.

"See the rectangular shape of her orbits?" The doctor traced the edges of the bones around where her eyes should be. "Caucasians have angular orbits. Asians, round. But that's not all I see. At the top of the skull there's a slight depression where it'd be flat on Asians and Caucasians, and the nasal aperture is broad and rounded—"

"We trust your judgment, Victoria," Ava said quickly.

"How was she killed?" Zander cut in, his heartbeat pounding in his ears.

Dr. Peres eyed him over the top of her glasses and made a deliberate show of examining the skull. "She wasn't shot in the head." She gave him a side-eye.

He knew he had asked too early. "Forget I asked that," he said in apology. "It was unfair." He met Ava's eyes. "Did Greer mention any missing African American teens when you went for food?"

She pointed. "No. But you can ask him."

Zander turned and saw the sheriff returning to the scene. The deputy who'd taken Alice home was with him. Both men had their jacket collars turned up against the cold, and the deputy wiped his nose continually with a tissue.

Ava introduced the sheriff to Dr. Peres. "The doctor says this is an African American female in her teens or early twenties," she announced. "Does that match any missing person records?"

The sheriff looked grim and exchanged a glance with his deputy. "Yep. Cynthia Green."

Cindy? "Alice called her Cindy."

Surprise crossed the sheriff's face. "Well, why in the hell didn't Alice tell us this missing girl was up here?"

"Because she's Alice," said the deputy.

"True." Resignation flashed in Greer's eyes.

"Missing from when? What happened?" Ava crossed her arms, her tone one of heavily tested patience.

The sheriff pulled out his phone and tapped on the screen. "Cynthia Green's parents reported her missing a couple of decades ago." His eyes darted back and forth as he read. "They're from Seattle and were vacationing along the Oregon coast during spring break. Their nineteen-year-old went for a walk along the beach south of here near Gearhart and never returned."

"She vanished on their vacation," Ava repeated, her eyes wide. "But we're miles from Gearhart."

"I remembered the case once I saw her name come up in our search," Greer said. "I was a deputy, and all of us spent many hours combing the beach and surrounding hillside, even though the state police were in charge of the investigation. I remember they'd speculated that she'd been picked up by a car or knocked into the ocean by a sneaker wave. She had two younger sisters, and her parents were out of their minds. It was heartbreaking."

"Alice said she saw the people who brought Cindy here," Zander stated. "We pressed her for a little more info, but she shut down."

Greer didn't look surprised. "Gotta know how to handle Alice. She's skittish." He shook his head ruefully. "Don't know how good her memory will be."

"Alice said, 'She is safe here' when she showed us the skull," Ava added. "Maybe she didn't tell anyone because she was worried for the girl's safety."

"Even though she was already dead?" asked Dr. Peres.

"It might have made sense in Alice's mind," Zander said, remembering the protective look on the woman's face as she brushed the debris from the skull.

"How long will it take you to remove the remains?" Greer asked Dr. Peres.

"A few hours, maybe less. It appears nothing was deliberately buried. We'll get the bulk of it tonight and then come back tomorrow to widen the search area."

"Widen?" asked Ava.

"Yes, tiny animals will have dragged off the smaller bones of the hands and feet. Frequently we find them nearby."

"Will you be able to tell how she died?" Greer asked.

Greer asked the question in a much better way than Zander had.

"Sadly, with skeletal remains, what I can find is very limited. Bones can show stab marks, blunt force trauma, strangulation if the hyoid is present—which I don't hold a lot of hope for since it's a tiny bone and the body might have been here for twenty years. We're lucky we have as many bones as we do." She gave a curt nod, determination in her gaze. "I'll do my best."

The skull in her hands held Zander's attention.

Are you related to the Fitch case?

The race of two of the victims and their adjacent locations were the only connections.

Only connections so far. The length of time between the deaths—

"Sheriff, what's the exact date of Cynthia Green's disappearance?" he asked.

Greer checked his phone and told him.

Ava's wide eyes met Zander's.

Cynthia had vanished two weeks before Emily Mills's father had been hanged.

23

Zander had barely slept.

The skeletal face of Cynthia Green haunted him as he followed Ava into the county sheriff's department the next morning, his coffee in hand. He saw Cynthia when he closed his eyes and when they were open. He and Ava had spent an hour last night discussing every direction they needed to investigate in their ever-expanding case. The hate crime of the Fitch deaths was spiraling larger and larger.

A missing black girl found a few hundred yards from the Fitch residence.

She'd disappeared two weeks before Emily's father was hanged.

A hanging also happened at the Fitch home.

The same homemade GHB that was in the Fitches had been found in Nate Copeland.

The facts were tenuously connected, as in a spiderweb, and many pieces were missing.

"This won't do." Ava put her hands on her hips as she considered the table and chairs in the small room. They had asked Emily Mills to meet them that morning for follow-up questions.

"What's wrong with it?" It was a bare-bones room that the sheriff's department used for interviews. Crumbs on the table and fast-food wrappers in the overflowing wastebasket told Zander it was frequently used for other things.

"I don't want a table between us and Emily."

Zander made a face, understanding what she meant. Ava had insisted on conducting this follow-up at the station because the location "felt official." Now she didn't want a table because it could give suspects a feeling of protection, as if they could hide behind the table. She wanted Emily to feel exposed.

A little anxiety could make people reveal deceptive behaviors—possible indicators of lying.

He handed his coffee to Ava, shoved the table out of the center of the room and up against a wall, and then arranged three chairs to face each other. "How's that?"

She grinned, pleased, and returned his coffee.

"Nothing from Dr. Peres yet?" he asked as he lowered himself into a chair and stretched out his legs.

"It's only nine a.m. Give her a chance to get to work at least."

"I figured if her husband started early, then maybe she did too."

The forensic anthropologist had driven back to Portland after midnight, promising to have her forensic odontologist take dental films of the skull and compare them to the X-rays from the state police who had originally handled the disappearance of Cynthia Green.

A silver stud earring and a beaded bracelet had been found with the odd coins near the remains. A few small shirt buttons had been scattered in the ground cover, but there were no shoes.

The sheriff had refused to notify the family until the dental records had been examined and confirmed. "No point in getting their hopes up twenty years after her disappearance when we aren't positive," he'd said. Everyone had agreed.

Even exhausted, Zander could barely sit still in the airless room, needing to know if they had found Cynthia Green. Questions bubbling in his head had kept him up half the night.

Emily appeared in the doorway, curiosity in her features, a cautious smile on her lips. She was dressed for the cold in tall boots, jeans, and a heavy wool coat.

Ava's allegation that Zander had a fondness for the witness had taken hold in his brain, popping up at odd moments and disrupting his focus. Now he purposefully detached to analyze his reaction to the woman in the door.

He felt a small prickle in his stomach. A pull toward her. And he felt suddenly awake.

Shit.

Knowing that Ava was about to expertly grill Emily over her previous interview bothered him. And it wasn't a worry that he hadn't been thorough in the first interview; it was a stupid caveman instinct to shield her from Ava's sharp and probing exam.

Ava is right about my feelings.

No wonder Ava had ordered him to say as little as possible to Emily today.

"Are we doing this here so you can easily lock me up afterward?" Emily joked as she stepped in the room. She slid off her coat, unwrapped the scarf, and pushed her long hair off her neck. Taking a seat, she looked at Ava and Zander expectantly, her gaze acute, her posture alert.

"Thanks for coming, Emily," Ava replied with a half grin. "I don't think we'll need a cell today."

"Maybe I need one for protection."

"What?" Zander sat up straight. "Have you been threatened? What happened?"

Emily held up her hands. "I was kidding . . . sort of. Nothing's happened, but I've had a hard time getting Nate's death out of my head, and I'm constantly looking over my shoulder. Has it been determined if it was suicide?"

Zander didn't miss the faint hopeful note in her tone.

"It wasn't suicide," Ava said. "The forensics lead us to believe he was murdered."

Emily went perfectly still. "How do you know for certain?" she finally asked.

"You'll have to trust us," Ava said. "We can't share that information right now."

Emily glanced at Zander. He gave a short nod to confirm Ava's statement.

She's scared. With good reason.

"What does that mean for me?" Emily bluntly asked. "Knowing that someone *might* want me dead has been on my brain for almost two days—I can't get it out of my head. Now it's confirmed." She gripped her coat tightly in her lap, her knuckles white. But her chin was up and her gaze steady.

"We don't know what it means for you," answered Ava.

"That's no help at all," Emily stated.

"It means be careful." Zander finally opened his mouth. "Watch your surroundings. Stay with other people. Don't take risks."

Annoyance flashed. "That's the everyday norm in a woman's life. And that didn't help Lindsay." Her voice cracked. "She was killed in her own *fucking bed* with her husband next to her."

Ava leaned in, catching Emily's attention. "Awareness is your best defense. I'm sorry how shitty that answer is, but short of locking you up until we catch our killers, it's the best I can tell you. This isn't a movie or TV—we don't have extra law enforcement to watch you twenty-four-seven, but we can ask county to frequently drive by your home and suggest they stop at the diner for meal breaks. Show a presence."

Rage simmered under Ava's words. She hated their powerlessness as much as Zander did.

"Stick around," Zander said. "Either stay at the diner where people are present, or you can hang out here at the station."

"You should have told me to bring a book." Emily looked from him to Ava, resignation heavy in her eyes. "Now. What did you want to talk to me about?"

Ava slipped a thin folder out of her bag and flipped it open. "I want to go over what you saw at the Fitch home again. These are Zander's notes from your interview that day."

"Go ahead."

"You said you called Lindsay three times before going to her home," Ava began.

"And Sean once," added Emily.

"And when you got to the house, you rang the doorbell and then called Lindsay's phone from the front porch because no one answered the door."

"Correct. Their cars were there, so I figured someone had to be home."

"That's when you opened the door because it was unlocked." Ava kept her attention lowered to Zander's notes.

"The unlocked door surprised me."

"You went right in?" Ava asked. "It didn't take a minute to work up your nerve to enter?"

Emily thought. "It took a few seconds. I didn't like the idea of walking right in, so I called their names a few times as I opened the door a bit."

"What happened next?"

"When I stepped in, I smelled the blood." She glanced at Zander, and he kept his face impassive as he watched and listened.

So far Emily's body language and replies had appeared normal to him. No jitters, no touching her hair, no rubbing her nose. No little tension movements. In his previous encounters with her, he'd learned she wasn't a mover. When she talked, she didn't shift her weight or gesture with her hands or frequently touch her face or hair. She generally held still, and this conversation was consistent. Zander had observed and heard more anxiety when they discussed how she could keep herself safe.

"I walked in and saw the blood trail that went from the bedroom to the kitchen and then out the back door. I checked the bedroom first—"

"Was the bedroom light on?" Ava cut in.

Emily paused. "It was."

"How long were you in the bedroom before you went into the backyard?"

"Only a few moments." Emily squeezed her eyes shut as if she could make her visual memories disappear. "I touched Lindsay's neck for a pulse even though I *knew* she was dead." She blew out a breath and opened her eyes. "I immediately followed the blood out back, hoping to find Sean still alive."

"Would you say you were in the bedroom less than a minute?"

"Easily."

Unease crawled up Zander's spine. Ava was systematically tracking the time between Emily's phone call on the front porch and her call to 911.

Where are the extra twenty minutes?

"What did you do when you saw Sean?" Ava asked.

"I went closer. I felt his wrist for a pulse." Emily had shifted to an empty monotone, struggling to keep her emotions in check.

"Did it take you a few minutes to work up the nerve to touch him?"

Emily vehemently shook her head. "No. I knew waiting could mean the difference between life and death. I checked immediately. No pulse."

"And then?"

"I called 911."

"Why didn't you call 911 right after finding Lindsay?"

Emily scratched near her temple. "I remember I had my phone out—I was about to, but I followed the blood instead." She swallowed audibly. "She was dead—there was no urgency for an ambulance. No one could bring her back," she whispered.

"Sean was dead too," Ava said in a kind voice. "But you called right after checking for a pulse?"

"I did. An ambulance wasn't needed, but the police were."

"From outside? Or did you go back in the house to call?"

"Outside."

Ava shuffled through the papers on her lap, and Zander watched Emily out of the corner of his eye. Her shoulders sagged, and anguish was evident in her downturned mouth.

He hoped to God Emily had a good explanation for the time inconsistencies. He shifted forward, leaning his elbows on his knees, wishing he could hide his tension behind a table. Ava was silent as she studied the next papers in her file, and the silence in the room grew heavy. Long periods of silence were meant to create unease for the interviewee, but Zander seemed to be the only uneasy one. He studied Ava, noting the lines on her forehead and the slight tightening of her lower lip. She was frustrated.

Ava hopes for a good explanation too.

And she had alleged that Zander's emotions were affecting his work.

Ava was also rooting for Emily.

"Emily. I have a copy of your phone records for that day." She handed a page to Emily, who accepted it with a stunned look.

"Why didn't you ask to see my phone if you had questions?"

"This is more official."

"You mean it has calls that can't be deleted," Emily snapped. She angrily scanned the sheet, running a finger down the entries. "One, two, three calls to Lindsay, my call to Sean, and then one more to Lindsay's phone. Exactly as I told you. What's the issue here?"

"The issue is the twenty minutes between your last call from the porch to Lindsay and the call to 911."

Emily froze and stared at the paper. She finally looked up, determination in her gaze. "I can explain."

"Please do."

Zander held his breath as he watched a war of guilt and frustration play out on Emily's face.

"After I found Sean, I sat on the back porch before calling—I didn't realize I had sat for that long, though." Emily rubbed at an eye. "Jeez—I must have really been out of it."

"What do you mean?" asked Ava.

"Shock. Disbelief. Confusion. It took me a while to get myself together."

Ava cocked her head. "That doesn't sound like you . . . I can see you're levelheaded. You were the one who stopped the deputies from making a bigger mess at the scene and reported the mark on Sean's forehead."

"Trust me. After finding Lindsay and Sean, I was anything but levelheaded." Emily closed her eyes. "But I was also shook up from something else I saw."

Zander's breath caught. "Something else? What?"

"I'm sorry I didn't tell you. I should have, but . . ." She buried her face in her hands. "I didn't understand. *It didn't make any sense.* It still doesn't!"

"Emily—" Ava started.

"Give me a minute," she said. Her chest moved as she took several deep breaths, her gaze scanning every corner of the room, avoiding Zander and Ava. "I found my father's pocket watch in Lindsay's backyard," she said quietly.

Now I don't understand.

Zander lifted a brow at Ava, who gave a minuscule shake of her head. "Emily," he asked. "what does finding that watch mean to you? I don't see the significance."

Other than that you shouldn't have removed possible evidence from the scene.

"I don't know," she whispered. Her eyes were haunted. "It disappeared the night he was killed. He had always kept it in his pocket, but it vanished when . . . And its loss added to my mother's upset—it was a prized possession of his."

Zander's mind spun. "How did it end up in the Fitches' backyard?"

Her hands lifted and fell to her lap, her eyes shiny with tears.

"Zander." Ava moved closer to him, her blue eyes warning. "She took evidence from a murder scene."

He no longer cared that Ava wanted to handle the interview.

"I was completely shocked," Emily added. "I'd stepped on it as I backed away from Sean. When I looked down, I *knew* what it was."

"Then what?" he asked as Ava frowned at him.

"I picked it up and opened it, convinced I was seeing things. But it had his initials inside." She blew out a breath. "I sat on the porch steps and just stared at it. I couldn't think . . ."

"You sat for nearly twenty minutes in a murder scene?" Ava's vocal pitch rose. Emily gave no sign she noticed.

"Until you said it, I had no idea I sat so long. I would have said a minute or two." Emily pressed her eyes with her fingers. "It doesn't make sense. How—"

Ava opened her mouth, but Zander held up a finger. "Emily, what scenarios ran through your head to answer how the pocket watch got there?"

She wouldn't look at them. "I don't know."

"Who could have left it there?"

"I don't know!"

Frustrated, Zander sat back. Ava slowly shook her head as they stared at each other.

Emily cleared her throat. "My aunts, I guess, my sister . . . my father's killer . . . ," she whispered, looking lost.

"Madison could have left it?" Ava asked.

"No. I meant Tara when I said 'sister'—although I guess Madison could have found it somewhere."

"Why do you say Tara over Madison? Madison's a good friend of Lindsay. It makes sense that she could have left something behind in Lindsay's house, and you said Tara hasn't been around in years."

"She was there." Emily's hands trembled.

Zander kept his questions calm and steady, but inside he wanted to drag the answers out of her. "Who was where?"

This watch could indicate who killed the Fitches.

Emily finally met his gaze. "Tara was there the night my father was killed," she whispered. "She told everyone—even the police—that she had spent the night at a friend's. But I saw her with someone else just beyond the yard in the woods." Her shoulders slumped. "Oh God. That's the second thing I've hidden from the police."

He tried to pull her back to the present. "You think Tara has something to do with the pocket watch being at the Fitch home?"

"I don't know." Emily stood and threw up her hands, pacing the small room. "I don't know anything! Everything is a mess!"

"Where is the pocket watch now?" Ava asked.

"At the mansion."

"How about you and I go get it?"

Zander started to say he'd come along, but a look from Ava stopped him.

Am I still being too nice?

"I'll stay here and talk to the sheriff," he said instead, not knowing if Greer was even in the building. It didn't matter. He wanted to review everything that Emily had just told them and figure out the implication of the appearance of a watch that had been missing for decades.

"Let's go," said Ava.

24

Outside, Emily drew deep breaths. Her nerves still quaked from the session, but there was a small sense of relief that she'd told someone she'd seen Tara at her father's murder scene. Even if it made no sense to the FBI agents, it was good to have off her chest.

The pocket watch.

That was also a weight off her shoulders and conscience. She didn't know why she hadn't told the police about the watch. All she'd known was that she had been confused and afraid when she picked it up in the Fitch backyard. *What was I afraid of?*

Afraid of suggesting one of her relatives had been involved in a double murder?

The very idea that one of her family had been involved was ridiculous.

Finding the watch that morning had opened a door to painful memories, overwhelming her. According to Ava's cell phone report, she'd been overwhelmed for nearly twenty minutes.

"I'll drive," Ava said as they strode through the county lot.

"Actually, I'd like to."

Ava wrinkled her nose. "Do you think that's a good idea?"

"I'm feeling better, and I'd welcome the distraction of concentrating on the road," Emily admitted. Anything to get her present thoughts out of her head.

"Fine by me. I'll make some calls while you drive."

Emily guided her Honda down the narrow two-lane road. Ava was on her phone, making calls and frowning at various emails. Emily's earlier stress started to drain away. But the pocket watch kept pulling her attention.

"I'm going to take Emily with me," her father told her mother. "You're too sick to look after her, and I don't want her to catch anything from Madison."

Ten-year-old Emily hid behind the door, crossing her fingers. Her mother was in bed, and Madison was sound asleep beside her. Her sister's cheeks were flushed, and sweat plastered her hair to her forehead as she clutched a big empty bowl in her sleep. She had thrown up twice.

"Emily will be fine here. She can watch TV," her mother suggested.

"No, she needs to get out of the house. She's been stuck here all week while you've been sick."

"That isn't a meeting for children."

"She'll be quiet and read her book. I'm not concerned."

He won, so Emily accompanied her father on the long drive to Portland, ecstatic over the one-on-one time with him. He stopped for ice cream and told stupid jokes. They played the game where one of them told a story for thirty seconds and then the other person picked up the thread and continued for another thirty seconds. Emily timed the segments with his pocket watch, proud to hold the heirloom. Both ridiculously twisted the story, giving the other person the most bizarre lead-ins possible.

The meeting was dull. Twenty men sat in a room and listened to a speaker drone on and on. Emily sat at the back and ignored them, her head buried in her book about a boy at a school for wizards. After it was over, her father spoke earnestly with a few other men.

Hoping he was ready to leave, Emily approached and tucked herself under his arm. He held her against his side but kept talking. The men listened. Some frowning, some nodding. Some looked like soldiers because their hair was so short she saw skin. Several crossed their arms as they listened, and she studied their tattoos, fascinated by the colors and shapes. Bored, she dug out his pocket watch and played with the little hinged door, loving the feel of the smooth glass.

She had felt the same smoothness that morning at the Fitches'.

She shook the memory away and turned on the car's music, seeking more diversions. The ocean appeared on Ava's side of the car, its gray water blending seamlessly with the misty gray of the sky. On a blue summer day, it would take her breath away. Today it was bleak and dismal, but she let it hold her attention, still needing a distraction, any distraction.

"Who runs in this rain?" she muttered out loud, spotting a jogger ahead on the shoulder of the road. There wasn't enough chocolate in Oregon to tempt her to do that.

She listened to Ava's phone conversation with her husband-to-be. Their dog had brought a squirrel into the house, and it had promptly disappeared. Ava's choking laughter only added to his frustration, judging by the curses coming out of the phone.

Emily stole quick glances to her right, absorbed by the glimpse into the agent's real life.

As they started to pass, Emily saw the jogger stop and raise his arm toward her car.

Does he want a ride?

A flash. A deafening crack. Ava's window shattered and she shrieked.

Bits of glass and warm blood hit Emily as she wrenched the steering wheel to the left and stomped on the brake. The car spun across the wet road, and Emily's side of the vehicle slammed into two huge firs.

Her head hit the door as white filled her vision.

And then black.

25

"Mason?" Zander answered his cell, wondering why Ava's fiancé would call him.

"Where is Ava?" Mason yelled in his ear.

"She left a few minutes ago. What hap—"

"Call 911! Tell them she's been in a car accident. I was on the phone with her when it happened, but I don't know where she is! She's not answering me, and I can't pinpoint her phone's location!"

"Hang on." Zander gestured at Sheriff Greer, who'd joined him a minute ago. "Call 911. There's been a car accident somewhere between here and Bartonville. Emily just left five minutes ago. They can't have driven far."

"I heard gunfire and then a crash!" Mason panted as if he were running.

"Gunfire?" Zander repeated. Adrenaline raced through his veins as he looked at Greer, who was already on the phone. The sheriff's eyebrows shot up, and he spoke rapidly into his phone. Zander darted out the door and jogged down the hallway.

Someone shot at their car? Are they injured?

"What is going on out there?" Mason hollered at him.

A car door slammed in the background of the call. "We're on a case—"

"I fucking know that! Who would shoot at Ava?"

Zander shoved open the department's doors, running as he spoke. "I think—"

"I'm headed your way." An engine started on Mason's end. "Go find her! Call me back."

The call ended with a beep in his ear.

"I'm on it." Zander yanked open his SUV door.

It was twenty minutes before Zander found the wreck, and he'd pushed his temper to its limits during the wasted time. He'd followed what he believed was the most direct route, but Emily had taken a back road used primarily by locals. A call to Sheriff Greer got him on the right road. The only thing the sheriff knew about the accident from the first responders was that two people were severely injured. No deaths. Yet.

Please be all right.

Zander caught his breath when he finally spotted the flashing lights of two fire trucks, an ambulance, and three county patrol cars clustered together.

It's bad.

Mason had called two more times, demanding details, and furious that Zander had been on the wrong road. Zander relayed the sheriff's update, and told Mason he'd call *him* when he saw Ava.

With his heart in his throat, he pulled onto the shoulder and jumped out into the rain. Emily's Honda had gone down the embankment on the wrong side of the road and stopped against two firs. A deputy recognized Zander and waved him down to the accident.

He couldn't breathe.

The passenger door of the green Honda was open, the front seat empty, the door's window nearly gone. Rescue and law enforcement were working on the driver's side. As he drew closer, he saw the driver's door was open and the workers were strapping Emily onto a board to carry her up the slope. Blood covered the left side of her face and hair.

But she was talking.

Relief swamped him and his knees went weak.

He searched for Ava and panic blossomed. He grabbed the closest deputy. "Where's the passenger?"

"On her way to the hospital."

"Which one?"

"Columbia Memorial in Astoria."

"What's her condition?"

"Not sure. I wasn't here when she left."

Zander let him go and joined the rescuers to help lift Emily's board from the ground. A deputy awkwardly held an umbrella over her head, keeping most of the rain away.

"Hey," he said as he caught her gaze.

"Zander." Her hand reached for him but couldn't touch him because of the board's straps. "Ava was shot." Tears mixed with the blood on her face. "I don't know how bad it is. She was unconscious."

A brick formed in Zander's gut, and he took her hand.

How will I tell Mason?

"Anyone know about the passenger?" He directed his question to the others carrying Emily's board.

"Gunshot to her shoulder and neck. Possible head injury. She was stable when they left."

A neck wound could be fatal.

"What happened?" he asked Emily, who had his hand in a death grip. Holding the board with his other hand, he helped the others start up the slope.

"Someone shot at us. I thought he was a jogger on the shoulder. I swerved and hit the brakes, but we went off the road." She closed her eyes, her voice cracking. "I shouldn't have yanked on the wheel. This wouldn't have happened."

"It sounds like Ava would have still been hit, and you might have been in a position to be shot at again."

Her eyes had opened, but she didn't believe him. "I screwed up."

"Stop it," he ordered. "Someone shot at your car. Even I would have done the same thing."

The others holding her board muttered in agreement.

"Can you describe the shooter?" asked Zander.

"Not really. It was raining. He wore dark clothing. I'd wondered why he wasn't wearing something brighter to be seen alongside the road."

"I assume you didn't see the weapon."

"It was a handgun, not a rifle."

"Are you hurt anywhere else?" Zander asked, scanning the rest of her. She had blood on her shirt and jeans, but it appeared to have dripped from her head wound. He brushed at a faint spray of reddish-brown dots on her right cheek. It was dry.

Mist from Ava's injury?

Bile rose in his throat.

"I think I'm okay."

"We'll let the hospital decide that," he said firmly.

"I really don't need to go—"

"You're going."

Feeling numb, he watched as they loaded her in the ambulance and closed the doors. Emily didn't look too bad, but would Ava be okay?

His phone rang, but he ignored it. He'd call Mason from his vehicle on his way to the hospital.

That call would suck.

Zander sat in a chair in Emily's emergency-room bay, waiting for her to return. After cleaning up the cut on Emily's head and checking her thoroughly, the impossibly young-looking ER doctor had sent her off for an MRI. That had been almost an hour ago. Ava had gone directly to surgery, and there had been no updates on her condition.

Right now, no news was good news about Ava.

His phone call with Mason on the way to the hospital had gone as expected. The Portland police detective had been irate and worried over Ava's condition and frustrated that he wasn't at her side. Zander easily imagined how fast the detective was driving and hoped he wouldn't get in an accident.

Zander's phone rang. "This is Wells."

"Agent Wells, this is Tim Jordon at RCFL."

Zander's interest was piqued. He'd sent Sean Fitch's laptop to the Regional Computer Forensics Laboratory in Portland. "Is this about the Fitch case?" Zander had been a software engineer for ten years before he joined the FBI. He'd spent some time in cybercrimes because of his background, but his skills were nothing compared to what the techs at the lab could do.

"It is," said Tim. "I started on it yesterday, and I'm not done, but my boss said you wanted an update as early as possible."

"Were you able to get into his email?"

"That's where I started. He had two accounts. One for the school district and one personal. I've gone through both."

"Anything threatening? Any indication he was arguing with someone?"

"Not that I've come across. Even the purged emails don't point to any problems. His search history is primarily historical research websites."

"That makes sense since he was a history teacher."

"There's a lot of well-organized documents on here. He seems to be rather anal about classifying his files and folders. I see a lot of classroom-related stuff, mostly American history, but he's got loads of other files on old records that I don't think were for school. They appear to be for a history book he's writing. He has a few chapters and an outline in here."

Zander wasn't surprised.

"The rest of his online searches don't raise any flags for me. Amazon, Home Depot—maybe they mean something to you."

"Can you get me a list of his browser history and what he's purchased online in the last three months?"

"No problem."

"Does he have a calendar?"

"Yeah. Want that too?"

"Please."

"You got it." Tim paused. "Lotta photos of him and his wife. Wedding stuff too. Looks like they were real happy. Pictures of him with teenage football players—I can tell they liked their coach. What happened to this couple is horrible."

The tech's personal observation caught Zander off guard.

"Computer forensics can be pretty dry," Tim said hastily, as if he realized he'd stepped over a line. "I try to stay detached, but sometimes it's next to impossible . . . This is one of those cases."

"I get it. I can see that with these deaths," said Zander. The investigation had made the couple come alive for him as well. He believed the small emotional connection was a good thing—more motivation to catch the assholes who had killed them.

"I hope you find who did this."

"We will."

"I'll email you that stuff within the hour."

Zander ended the call.

He couldn't analyze the information from Sean's laptop until he received the reports, so he refocused on the shooting that had caused Emily's car accident. His mind was a jumble of questions and scenarios.

Emily's description of the shooter's actions indicated he'd deliberately shot at them. But who had been his target? Emily or Ava?

If Emily had been his target, was it the same person who had shot Nate Copeland?

If Ava had been the target, was it someone trying to interfere in the investigation? Or could it be someone from a previous investigation of hers?

Or neither? It could have been random.

The fact that the women had been in Emily's car gave more weight to the theory that Emily was the target.

But how could the shooter have known the women would be on that road?

Their destination had been decided moments before they left. Had they been followed? After which a second person had informed the shooter of their direction?

The road is a locals' route.

Their shooter was most likely local.

If Emily had been the target, what did the shooter believe she knew or had seen? Something at the Fitch murder site?

Zander ran a hand over his head. It was all speculation; he needed facts.

What if Ava doesn't make it?

The intrusive thought pushed him over an edge. He jumped to his feet and frantically paced, both hands in his hair as ugly memories broke loose.

Faith. Fiona.

He hated hospitals. His wife, Faith, had spent her last weeks in a hospital, growing sicker and more unrecognizable as the cancer rapidly spread through her body. She'd felt ill for a few months but had blamed it on her pregnancy. When she was finally diagnosed, the cancer was stage four. She refused to abort their twelve-week-old daughter, Fiona, and then refused any cancer treatments that could affect the baby, convinced she could make it through the pregnancy on willpower alone. Every doctor told Zander she wouldn't make it.

A no-win situation.

They'd been right.

Eight years ago Zander had lost the two most important people in his life.

Am I about to lose another?

Ava knew his history—the vile agony of his wife's and never-seen daughter's deaths. Was he about to lose one of the few people left who truly knew him? Abandonment and loneliness pushed him back into his chair, swamping him, and he lowered his head to his hands, willing the horrific images of his dying wife out of his head.

Alone in the curtained bay, he silently fell apart, broken by the wash of agony and heartbreak.

It engulfed him, the pain as fresh and raw as long ago. Sucking in deep, wet breaths, he fought for solace, relief from the pain. Minutes later it finally came, leaving him battered and drained. He grabbed two paper towels from a wall dispenser, appreciating their roughness as he wiped his eyes and nose.

This was why he allowed himself one day a year to mourn his wife. To avoid moments like this.

Fiona and Faith had died on October 30, and the date was now his annual day of hell. He would lock himself away, wallow in alcohol, and revisit old pictures and dreams that had never come true. It was twenty-four hours of misery and torture, but knowing the date would come each year helped him keep it together the rest of the days.

Ava had witnessed him at his absolute lowest on October 30 of last year.

"Oh my God! What happened? *Is it Ava?*" Emily's voice rose, startling him as he turned toward the curtained opening. She sat in a wheelchair, a nurse behind her, both of them staring wide-eyed at Zander.

Clearly he looked like shit.

"I haven't heard anything about Ava yet," he forced out, wiping his eyes again.

Emily visibly relaxed. "Are you all right?" she whispered, concern in her tone.

Zander glanced at the nurse, who eyed him as if he would fall apart. "Yeah, I'll tell you later." He moved his lips into a wooden smile. "What's the word on your head?"

"The MRI was fine," Emily told him. "The radiologist is here, so he reviewed it immediately, and outside of the gash in my scalp, I'm okay. They want me watched for the next twenty-four hours, but I can do that at home. I'll need stitches before I can leave." She cautiously touched the bandage above her ear as the nurse helped her out of the wheelchair and onto the exam table. Emily moved with ease and seemed to be her confident self again.

"I'll tell the doctor you're ready for stitches," the nurse said, and she handed Emily some blue fabric. "When she's done, you can change out of the gown and wear these scrubs home." Tactfully avoiding direct mention of Emily's bloody clothing.

"But what about Ava?" Emily asked. "I'm not going anywhere until I know what's happened."

"I'll see what I can find out," the nurse said with a noncommittal smile as she vanished.

"I'm surprised your family isn't here," Zander said.

"I didn't let anyone call them. I knew I was fine. My aunts don't need the stress."

"They should know what happened."

"I'll tell them when I get home." She openly studied him. "Are you going to tell me what was wrong when I came in?"

He held her gaze, a debate raging in his mind.

She's just a witness. I don't need to tell her about my life.

Am I fooling myself? I want to tell her.

His desire to open up to her about his past and his reaction to her accident had made his feelings about Emily Mills pretty darn clear to him. Feelings he should keep to himself. An invisible ethical line was in front of him, warning him not to step over it.

Fuck it.

"I have a history with hospitals." He clenched his teeth together as his memories amassed for another emotional attack. "Their antiseptic smell alone can push me over an edge."

She said nothing, her gaze strong yet empathetic.

"I don't want—"

"Tell me."

He told her.

By the end of his story she was holding one of the rough paper towels to her eyes. "I'm so sorry, Zander." Her breathing hitched. "I can't imagine what you went through. I'm sorry this happened to you today. You must be worried sick about Ava."

"She's like a sister." A superficial description of what Ava was to him.

Loud voices carried into their bay, distracting them. Several people were having an argument, and Zander recognized the loudest voice. He pushed the curtain aside, looking past the nurses' station in the center of the emergency room.

"I'll be back," he told Emily.

"I'll be here. Hopefully having a needle stuck in my scalp."

He strode through the emergency room and into a short hallway where Ava's fiancé, Mason Callahan, argued vehemently with several people in scrubs.

"Mason!" Zander caught his attention.

"Get these people to tell me what's going on with Ava." Mason's eyes were livid, and stress rolled off him as he clenched the brim of his cowboy hat. Zander had never seen him this close to losing his temper.

"There's no news yet," Zander told him, assuming it was true.

"She's still in surgery," Emily's ER doctor informed him, her eyes snapping. The young woman was also close to losing her temper. "We'll tell you when we know something."

"Why is it taking so long?" Mason lowered his volume.

"It's hard to say," the doctor said. "I'll have someone take you to the surgical waiting room." She indicated an orderly, who asked Mason to follow him.

"Zander?" Mason glanced back as he took a few steps after the orderly.

"I need to talk to the witness. I'll check in soon."

Mason nodded and left, his cowboy boots loud on the tile floor.

Zander watched him go, fully understanding the man's turmoil. Not knowing was hell.

26

Madison listened to Emily on her cell, shock rocketing through her nerves.

Who shot at Emily's car?

"Hey, Madison? Is this done?" Isaac tentatively poked at a pancake with the metal spatula. "How can I tell that the other side is browned enough?"

She tipped the phone away from her mouth. "Peek under the edge. It doesn't take long to cook."

Isaac squatted almost to the floor to get at eye level with the grill and lifted the tiniest edge of the pancake, his focus intense. "A little longer." He straightened and stood guard over the grill, staring at the three round cakes.

"Ava just came out of surgery," Emily continued. "Her shoulder and collarbone were damaged, but they're very optimistic about her recovery." Her sister's voice lowered. "Everyone thought the bullet had hit her neck, but it was actually embedded with glass from the window."

"You must have been terrified."

"You have no idea." Her sister exhaled loudly. "Don't tell the aunties what happened yet. I'll talk to them when I get home."

"Okay."

Dory bustled into the kitchen, an empty coffee carafe in her hand, delight on her face. She set it on the big coffee machine and punched the right series of buttons. Madison was pleased. She'd finally taped a cheat sheet to the machine because Dory forgot how to run it every time.

"Can you ask Uncle Ron to find something to do at the mansion?" Emily asked. "I'd feel better knowing he was there. He's talked about fixing the outside railing. Maybe this would be a good time."

"Why?" A small alarm started in Madison's brain. "Why do you want him there?" Isaac checked the pancakes again, awkwardly slid them onto a plate, and set it up. He lifted a brow to Madison, and she gave him a thumbs-up. A wide grin filled his face.

She couldn't believe he'd never cooked a pancake.

Emily was quiet for a moment. "There's some concern that I'm being targeted."

Madison remembered Emily's white face at the community meeting. "Because of Nate Copeland's death?"

"And this shooting today. They could be wrong," she added quickly. "It could have been random, or maybe Ava was their target."

"What did you see at Lindsay's house that morning, Emily? Why is this happening?" Madison whispered as she stepped away from the grill and stoves, out of Isaac's hearing.

"I didn't see anything that indicated who killed them." Emily's voice wavered, shocking Madison. Emily was the rock of the household—after Vina, of course. She never let a weakness show. "They're being cautious. Can you talk to Ron?"

"Yes, I'll call him, but it's raining, and the wind is horrible. I doubt he'll want to repair the outside rail."

"I don't care what he works on. I just want him at the house when our aunts are there."

"Is this my short stack?" Dory asked, grabbing the plate Isaac had just filled.

"Yep." Pride radiated from the teenager.

"Was that Dory?" Emily asked.

"Yes. I've got all three aunts working the floor. I'm covering the grill, but I'm giving Isaac some lessons."

"Where's Leo?"

"I sent him home before we even opened today. He had a sore throat and was barely functioning. The aunts were glad to pitch in."

"It takes all three of them to cover your job," Emily stated.

Was that a compliment?

"They're doing it well," Madison said automatically, still off-balance from Emily's observation. "When can you go home? Do you need a ride?"

"I'm almost done, and I don't need a ride. Agent Wells says he'll drive me home."

"He must be relieved that his partner is okay," Madison said. She liked Ava McLane—she was the type of woman Madison wanted to be.

"You have no idea."

They ended the conversation, and Madison slid the phone into her apron pocket.

Her sister could have died. A chill washed over her, and an old memory of terror rose from the marrow of her bones.

"Your turn!" Madison shouted at ten-year-old Emily.

Madison checked on her parents. They sat several yards away on a big rock that looked out over the ocean. The park was a favorite of the girls, but it took intense begging, chores, and promises to get their parents to bring them.

It was a blue day at the coast. The ocean reflected the deep, vivid color of the sky. It was the first warm day of spring, and the three girls pretended it was summer, wearing shorts and sandals for the first time since last fall. Emily had started a cartwheel contest in a patch of green grass. Tara had turned her nose up at the game and wandered off with some girls from the high school. Madison had seen one of them flash a pack of cigarettes.

Gross.

Madison had completed four cartwheels without stopping, and Emily needed to beat that. Emily lifted her hands and flung herself into the first cartwheel. As she finished the fourth, her left foot landed wrong, and she slipped. Twisting, she lost her balance and staggered, trying not to fall. The ground caved away at Emily's feet, and she vanished.

Madison screamed and lunged to the edge on her stomach.

They'd been playing a safe distance away from the edge. It was the same place they always played, but the rains had dug out part of the slope and left a false top.

She saw Emily ten feet down, hugging the slope with her entire body as the ocean crashed into giant rocks a hundred feet below.

Madison shuddered. Her father had carefully inched down the rough slope and rescued his daughter as his wife and Madison shrieked. Emily had nearly slid to her death.

That sensation of utter helplessness as her sister clung to the earth returned like a slap in the face.

The fence at the overlook had been ten yards behind them. Everyone hopped over the fence to get a closer view despite the warning signs.

Her father had been a hero.

Does that make up for his racist views? Could he have been both?

Madison pulled herself out of the past and found Isaac watching her.

"Is something wrong with Emily?"

Madison had never seen his brown eyes so serious. Maybe it was because of the hairnet keeping his hair out of his eyes for once. He'd been thrilled when Madison offered him some cooking lessons, making her wonder why Leo had never bothered. The teen was like a son to him.

"She was in a car accident—she's fine. A little banged up, but nothing broken." An idea occurred to her. "Would you mind stopping by the mansion this evening? I have some odds and ends that need doing, and I'll pay your usual wage." *I'll figure out what those odds and ends are later.*

His eyes narrowed. "What's wrong?"

She hesitated. "There's been some extra focus on the family since Emily found Lindsay and Sean."

"What do you mean, 'extra focus'?"

"It'd be good to have some more people around the house for a bit. Keep an eye out for things." Her reason was lame.

Isaac studied her a little longer. "Yeah, I'll come over."

Madison forced a smile. "Thank you." She pointed. "You've got another order."

The way his face lit up warmed her inside. He grabbed the ticket and studied it carefully.

Her conversation with Emily played in her head.

What is Emily involved in?

◆◆◆

As he drove Emily home from the hospital, Zander mentally regrouped.

He was down a partner. Ava would be in the hospital for at least a night or two as she recovered. He put his money on one night; as soon as she was coherent, he knew she'd argue to be released. Mason would have to talk some sense into her.

Zander had left a very relieved fiancé at the hospital.

"Her upper arm and shoulder are more metal than bone now," Mason told him. "She already had four screws in that humerus from getting shot about a year ago."

Zander remembered.

Sheriff Greer had interviewed Emily about the shooter and received the same story Zander had heard. The sheriff had confided to him that they couldn't find any sign that someone had been along the road. Understandable with the pouring rain, but no one had seen another vehicle either. He was still looking and asking questions.

Zander's boss had agreed to send him another agent, but she wouldn't arrive until tomorrow evening at the earliest. For now, Zander was on his own and needed to decide what to do next.

Alice Penn. He wanted to interview Alice about when she had seen Cynthia Green's body dumped in the woods. He was pessimistic about the results since Alice was flighty and the death had happened twenty years ago. But the Fitch murders were his priority. Cynthia Green—assuming her identity was confirmed—would have to wait.

Billy Osburne. Still missing. Sheriff Greer had taken the lead on finding the man, but nothing concrete yet.

Tim Jordon's email with Sean Fitch's purchases and calendar from his laptop had landed in Zander's in-box an hour ago. He had studied them as he waited for Emily to be discharged.

"Do you know a Simon Rhoads?" he asked Emily, breaking the silence in the vehicle.

She turned toward him, and he continued to focus on the road, looking beyond the rapid movements of the windshield wipers. The interior of the vehicle was warm and comfortable, a contrast to the growing storm outside.

"I do. He has a thing for Aunt Dory."

Zander's lips quirked. "A thing?"

"He's asked her to marry him at least a dozen times, but she always says no. They're good friends, but she doesn't want to live with him. She likes the mansion and her 'girls.'"

"Are you considered one of her girls?"

"Yep. She loves having her sisters and the two of us around. In her mind it's a nonstop slumber party. Why do you ask?"

How much can I tell her?

"I got Sean's calendar. He had an appointment with Simon two days before his death."

"That makes sense. Simon is the unofficial town historian. As a history teacher, I'm not surprised Sean knew Simon."

"Unofficial?"

"The city council pays for an office for his records and allots him a small budget. They can't afford to pay a salary, but Simon doesn't mind. He'd do it without the location and the budget. He's a bit obsessed."

"Aren't all historians obsessed? I found out Sean Fitch was writing a book. Maybe Simon helped him."

"I recall Lindsay mentioned Sean was writing a book."

"Where is Simon's office?"

"Downtown. It's in a tiny house owned by the city." She checked the time. "We'll need to hurry. He won't see anyone after three o'clock, and there are no exceptions."

"I'll take you home first and then stop by."

"Do you have an appointment?" she asked.

"I need one?" The question surprised him.

"You better believe it. Simon is a stickler for routine. He may be obsessed with his records, but he's also obsessed with procedure. You can't do anything to alter his schedule—especially since you're a stranger. It flusters him."

"Then why did you say *we* need to hurry to get there before his day is done?"

She grinned. "He'll make an exception for me. Anything or anybody that has to do with Aunt Dory gets special treatment."

Zander eyed the bandages that peeked through her long, dark hair. "How do you feel?"

She considered. "In light of what's happened, not too bad."

"Probably the pain pills."

"I admit I'm enjoying some pleasant side effects." Her eyes danced.

"Most people fall asleep."

"Not me. They've always given me some get-up-and-go. Which typically doesn't help whatever injury I've had to take them for." She felt her bandage. "I'm fine to go with you to Simon's, if I take it easy and don't stand for long."

"If I think you're in pain or discomfort, we're leaving."

She snorted. "Fine. But let me do the talking. You'll know when it's safe to speak up."

Safe?

27

As they went up the cracked walkway to the front door of the tiny home, Emily reminded Zander to let her lead the conversation. She'd known Simon Rhoads all her life, and he'd always been kind to her and her sisters, but he was definitely odd and sometimes struggled with outsiders in his personal space. Under everything he was good-hearted—and very excited about local history.

She knocked.

Her head started to throb, and she tightened the tie on her scrubs again to keep the baggy pants from falling to her feet. She was determined to see this through for Zander and the Fitches.

The door opened a few inches, stopped by a chain, and a bespectacled gaze peered out. "Emily!" He closed the door, unhooked the chain, and yanked it open. His grin faltered as he spotted Zander behind her.

"Hi, Simon," Emily quickly said to pull his stare away from Zander. "I need your help with something. It just came up today, so I'm sorry I didn't set up an appointment." She schooled her features into a contrite look.

Simon was shorter than Emily—most people were shorter than Emily—and consistently wore slacks that bagged at his ankles. His striped button-down collared shirt had yellowed and grown thin, and several holes had been worn through the collar. His hair was nearly solid gray, the same as his beard, and both needed the attention of a barber.

She also felt he could use the help of an organized woman.

Dory wouldn't be much help. Her great-aunt wasn't one for detail . . . but maybe that would make her the perfect match for Simon.

Simon looked from her to Zander and back. "I'm always available for you, Emily." He shot a look at Zander that emphasized the words weren't for him.

"I appreciate it." She put a hand on Zander's arm. "This is Zander Wells. He's with the FBI and is investigating the murders of Sean and Lindsay."

Bushy brows narrowed as he scrutinized Zander. "You were at the meeting the other night," he said.

"I was."

Simon's attention went back to Emily. "How is your aunt?" His gaze was full of hope.

She didn't need to ask which one. "Very good, thank you. You should come over for dinner soon."

His entire demeanor perked up. "Fabulous! I'll take you up on that. Come in, come in." He stepped back, waving them in. Emily silently exhaled; he'd accepted Zander's presence.

The city had bought the tiny house several decades ago after the owner died, intending to fix it up and sell it at a profit. But the city budget had virtually no money for repairs, and no buyer was ever interested. For years the poorly planned purchase had caused local tongues to wag. The grandson of the woman who'd died had been on the city council and had convinced the council to buy her house. One day he abruptly stepped down from his position and moved to Florida.

The city never bought another piece of property.

Simon Rhoads had finally come along and offered to do some basic repairs if they'd let him store his historical records there. The council acquiesced, and eventually Simon's treasure trove of history earned a tiny permanent spot in the city budget. Now he was available by appointment two days a week.

Emily knew those appointments were rarely filled.

The scuffed wood floor creaked as Emily and Zander entered. The home smelled of old, brittle paper and leather. An ancient damask couch, a battered coffee table, and a faded rug desperately in need of a good vacuuming filled the living room. Filing cabinets lined every wall of the attached dining room, with file boxes stacked three deep on top of each one.

Standing out in the shabby office was a beautiful, wide cabinet with a dozen shallow drawers. A controversy in the city council had played out in the local paper as the city considered purchasing the expensive cabinet. Her aunt Vina had firmly pointed out that Simon Rhoads did Bartonville a valuable service, never asked for *anything*, and needed a proper place to store his vintage maps.

Simon got his cabinet.

"You two sit on the sofa. I'm sorry it's a bit lumpy, but you know I take what I can get and appreciate it all. Beggars can't be choosers." He scurried around the coffee table and sat in a wooden chair. "What can I help you with?" he asked Emily, eagerly leaning forward. Simon always exuded energy; all her aunts except Dory found it exhausting.

"I would like Agent Wells to explain it," Emily said.

The historian blinked and nodded reluctantly, reining in his enthusiasm.

"Mr. Rhoads, did Sean Fitch have an appointment with you a week ago?"

Simon cocked his head, his gaze curious. "He did."

"What was it for?"

"Well now." The historian pinched his bottom lip and averted his focus to the coffee table. "I'd say that's confidential between Sean and me."

Zander started to reply, but Emily touched his thigh. "Sean was murdered, you know," she said gently, willing Simon to look at her. "The FBI is tracing his last movements."

The man jerked upright. "Do you think *I killed him*?" One knee started to rapidly bounce.

"Of course not," Emily said.

She felt Zander stiffen at Simon's outburst but stayed quiet.

"We're hoping you can illuminate what he was doing in the days before he was killed." Attempting to use gentle language, Emily felt as if she were balanced on a fence. The wrong words could make Simon lock down and refuse to help.

He scowled, thinking hard, and then took a deep breath. "Sean and I spoke on the phone several times over the last month or two. His appointment was the first time he'd come in, and it was a pleasure to speak with someone who has a deep knowledge of history. Most people are only interested in research for their family trees. Sean and I talked for three hours. Much longer than I had scheduled him for. He was a knowledgeable and intelligent man."

"What was Sean researching?" Zander asked.

"Several things. Shanghaiing was one of his main interests. In this little corner of the state, we have a dark history of the practice and other crimes against people. Sean was fascinated. You know he was writing a book, right?" Simon jumped to his feet and darted to the file cabinets in the dining room behind the sofa. "There were so many interesting events in this often-ignored area of the US, it's a pleasure when someone wants to discuss them. I was more than happy to show him what I had." He sorted through a drawer and yanked out a thick file, his eyes lit with delight.

Simon came alive as he talked about what he loved best.

"There's tons of information, but these are some of the items I scanned for him." He paused and looked over at the two of them. "Scanning is the most *wonderful* invention. So much better than making paper copies." He hummed under his breath as he went back to his file. "Makes my life so much easier. Email. Thumb drives. Wireless scanning. We live in an amazing world."

"I admit I don't know much about shanghaiing," Zander said. "Just what I've seen in movies, which I doubt is accurate."

"Astoria was Oregon's shanghai capital," Simon said. "In the late nineteenth century, ships from all over the world came to the port in Astoria. Timber and salmon were two of our biggest exports, and all these ships needed labor. Shanghaiing was called crimping at first. The ship's captains would make contracts with crimps—another name for men who would provide the labor by whatever means possible. The crimps would sometimes use alcohol to trick men onto the boats, or force them at gunpoint. It didn't matter who the victims were . . . loggers, farmers." His eyes sparkled. "Astoria even had a female crimper. Her husband had drowned, and she needed to support herself, so she sold unsuspecting labor to the captains."

Emily and Zander moved to look over Simon's shoulder.

The historian tapped on a photo of a solemn older woman surrounded by family wearing early-1900s fashions. "She doesn't look like a criminal, does she? New laws around the turn of the century finally made shanghaiing a federal crime, and it mostly disappeared."

"What else did you and Sean talk about?" asked Zander, a hint of impatience in the tightening around his mouth. Emily understood. She didn't see how shanghaiers in the nineteenth century could have anything to do with the Fitch murders of today.

"Let's see . . ." Simon pinched his lip again. "He was researching crime on the northern Oregon coast, so information on Fort Stevens, crimes against the Clatsop Indians and other races . . . A lot of these crimes took root in Portland and spread over here. I also gave him research on founding city families, Columbia River bar pilots—"

"I've never heard of a bar pilot," said Zander.

"All those big ships I mentioned? They needed a local pilot to board and safely navigate the shallow passage of the Columbia River. Where the river meets the Pacific Ocean is one of the most treacherous navigated waters in the world, so they'd boat out an experienced local to guide the ships in safely. Local pilots are still required by law for every ship engaging in foreign trade. These days they board the ships via helicopter or boat about fifteen miles from the mouth of the river."

"Sounds dangerous," said Zander.

"Very dangerous. Boarding the ships in the rough ocean was a huge risk for bar pilots in the past. Still can be."

"Did Sean contact you after the meeting at all?" Zander asked.

"He came back for a short visit a day or two later. I'd sent him to Harlan for more information."

"The mayor," Emily clarified for Zander. "He had an ancestor who owned a tavern in Astoria that was a very active shanghai location. Everyone knows he has a ton of research on the topic. It's one of his hobbies."

"Harlan isn't the only one in town with a relative accused of shanghaiing," Simon said with a wink at Emily.

"True, but no one in my family is fascinated the way Harlan is. We prefer to let the stories about our lawbreaking ancestors fade away."

"No, no, no." Simon vehemently shook his head. "I've had many discussions with Dory about this. You don't let history die." He opened another file cabinet, and his fingers danced across the tabs. "Here it is." He slid out a narrow file. "I've been working on this as a surprise for your aunt, but I think you should spend some time with it." He thrust it at Emily, and she instinctively took it. The printed label on the tab read BARTON.

"What is this?" she whispered.

"Your homework. You need to learn to appreciate the stories of your past. I've made copies of everything I come across that relates to Dory's family—which includes you. One of these days, I'll put it in a nice big binder as a gift for her—so don't let her see it."

Emily stared at the file, stunned. "This is so thoughtful."

The historian blushed. "Just put in a good word with Dory for me."

"I will."

◆◆◆

"I'm sorry Simon wasn't much help," Emily said as Zander drove her home. "It was a waste of your time. I can't see a connection between Sean's research of hundred-year-old shanghaiing crimes and his murder." The agent didn't appear that disappointed, but Emily suspected he hid it well.

"It was interesting," Zander said. "I think hanging and shanghaiing have a tenuous correlation—weren't men hanged back then for abandoning their ship's duties?"

"I don't know. Could be. But the relationship seems to be a stretch."

"Agreed."

She studied his profile in the pale light. He was preoccupied, his mind hard at work on the case, no doubt. "I feel like I've distracted you from your primary investigation."

He glanced her way in surprise. "Not at all."

"First my accident and now Simon—"

"Stop right there. Nate Copeland's shooting requires me to take a closer look at your shooting. Yes, I'm juggling a few things. The Fitches. Nate Copeland. The skeleton we found—who I hope is confirmed as Cynthia Green with dental records soon. It's all important. Interviewing Simon Rhoads had to be done. Just because it didn't pan out doesn't mean it was a waste of time."

"But your manpower has been reduced."

"The sheriff is helping, and I've got another agent coming tomorrow." He stopped at the curb in front of the mansion. "Someone shot at you. I don't take that lightly. Especially since you were at the Fitch deaths." He turned off the engine and faced her, determination rolling off him.

He meant every word.

His gaze went past her, and he frowned. "Who is that?"

Turning, she spotted Isaac loading an armful of small fir branches into a wheelbarrow. A hood covered his head, and rain ran down his coat. "It's Isaac. I asked Madison to get our uncle over here to hang around—a male presence at the house, you know? But it looks like she recruited Isaac instead and gave him some outdoor busywork. There's no point in picking up those branches until this storm is over."

"He's scrawny."

Her mouth twitched. "He's stronger than he looks."

"Your safety is a concern."

"So is the safety of my sister and the aunts," she said pointedly. "We take what we can get. If deputies driving by the home is a deterrent, then I think seeing a man working around the house can help too. Hopefully my uncle is also here somewhere."

"True." He continued to stare past her, following Isaac's movements.

She wanted to know what he was thinking. He often wore a perfect poker face, probably necessary in his line of work. But at the hospital, she'd caught a glimpse behind it. Zander Wells had very strong emotions; the FBI-agent attitude was a front.

"Thank you for telling me about your wife and daughter today," she said softly, watching his eyes in the fading light of the evening.

He met her gaze, and the agent mask lifted a bit. "I'm sorry that I—"

"I was married too."

His gaze intensified. "What happened?"

"Nothing at all like what you went through." She felt a little embarrassed for bringing it up. "It ended five years ago. He was . . . controlling."

Anger flickered. "He hurt you?"

"No. He never laid a hand on me." She gave a shaky laugh. "He slowly tore me down inside. It was emotional and mental. His words, his actions, some gaslighting . . . I was no longer myself. He's a narcissist.

Everything is about him, and he wanted everything about me to be about him."

"You mentioned him in the present tense."

"He's still around." Emily snorted. "In fact, I saw him yesterday morning. Would you believe he has the gall to think we could get back together? The narcissist in him still doesn't understand why I filed for divorce."

"Sounds like a prince."

"He's a cop in Astoria."

"Emily." Zander leaned closer. "Could he have shot at you?"

She sat very still. "No—I would have known it was him." But her brain raced through a million possibilities.

"He's a cop, so I assume he's a decent shot. Could he still be bitter? If you saw him yesterday, you'd be on his mind."

Emily couldn't speak. Her limbs were frozen. *Would Brett . . .*

"No," she whispered. "I would have recognized his stance, his shape. Even though I didn't see a face, every part of me says the man I saw wasn't him. I *know* Brett."

Zander didn't look convinced. He pressed his lips into a tight line, and his gaze softened, making her face warm.

He cleared his throat. "This is inappropriate and poor timing, but when this case is over . . ."

Emily instantly understood. "I have a lot of baggage," she murmured, unable to pull her gaze away from him.

The way he's looking at me . . .

I could get lost in his eyes.

His smile was wistful. "Then that makes two of us." He took her hand, holding it and running his thumb over her palm.

Her heart rate quickened. *He feels it too.* She'd been immediately attracted to him but had shut the feelings away. Until now.

"One time I made a mistake by keeping my feelings to myself," he said. "I swore I'd never do that again. I know now is not the time . . . but I had to say something in case time slipped away from me again."

"I understand. And I'm glad you said something." Happiness bubbled deep inside her chest.

Damn, I wish this investigation was behind us.

He moved closer and kissed her, the sensation warming her everywhere. She melted into the kiss, frustrated by the vehicle console between them.

Too soon, he pulled back and rested his forehead against hers, his chest rising with deep breaths. "When this is over."

"When it's over," she promised.

28

A few hours later, Zander was alone in his hotel room and working on his laptop, but his mind kept wandering.

I shouldn't have kissed her.

Like he could have stopped. He'd felt a subtle pull toward her the first time he saw her. Now that he'd voiced it out loud, he wanted more. But anything between them had to wait. He had a killer or two to find, and Emily was waist-deep in this case.

Be a fucking professional.

The thought made him grouchy. His phone and laptop rang, and he answered through the laptop.

"Wells."

"Good evening, Agent Wells. I'm Dr. Lacey Harper from the medical examiner's office, and I did the dental comparison on a case of yours."

Zander immediately sat up straighter. "Is the skull Cynthia Green?"

"It is."

He pumped a fist. Finally something was going his way. "Thank you. You have no idea how much I appreciate this."

"Not a problem. It's rewarding when I can definitively identify someone. It helps answer questions for family members left behind."

"You're positive about this, correct?" Zander asked tentatively, afraid he was insulting her.

She laughed. "I am. Would you feel better if I showed you how?"

"I'm not questioning your work," he added rapidly, relieved that she hadn't taken offense. "But I would like to see how it's done. Teeth look alike to me."

"Can you FaceTime?"

"Yep. Switching over now." A few moments later he was looking at a very attractive blonde woman with a broad smile. "You work with Dr. Peres?" he asked.

"I do. She's a close friend, and I've met Ava a few times, and I know her fiancé very well. I'm glad to hear she'll be okay."

"Me too. What can you show me?"

She switched to the other camera on her phone, and a computer screen of dental X-rays was in front of him. The screen had two large films, the type that show the entire jaw and the lower half of the cranium. They were grim skeletal smiles, creepily stretched wide to convert the three-dimensional objects into two. The images were a mishmash of shades of gray. He could identify teeth and jaw joints but not much else.

"I received Cynthia's dental records from the state police, who'd collected them after she went missing twenty years ago. I'm glad they still had them, because the dentist whose name is on the films closed up his practice over a decade ago, and he was legally required to only keep records for seven years. They might have been tough to hunt down."

She touched the top image. "This is from the state police and was taken seventeen months before Cynthia disappeared. It's a copy of the dentist's original panoramic image, which is why it seems dark. Copies are good, but not as clear as original films. Below is an X-ray I took today on the skull. We don't have a panoramic X-ray machine here, so I took it at a friend's dental practice. It was a bit awkward to shoot."

Zander had experienced the dental X-ray machine that rotated around his head as he stood in a booth.

"I had to crouch while holding the skull above my head with one hand. I'm just glad they kept their patients from walking by at that moment."

The mental image made him snort. He looked from one image to the other. "They look different, though. The top one is grainier and seems to . . . uh . . . smile a little more?"

"It's the angle that makes it smile. I tried to match it the best I could, but it always takes trial and error. The graininess is because mine is digital. The top one is real film that they had to run through a developer. They're always sharper." Her fingertip stopped on the last tooth on one side of the lower jaw and then touched the same tooth on the opposite side. "Wisdom teeth. As you can see, they're both angled differently than the rest of the teeth. They tip in quite a bit instead of being straight up and down."

"Right."

"And up here." She touched the corresponding teeth in the top row. "These wisdom teeth are still high in her maxilla. You wouldn't see them if you looked in her mouth."

"But you'd see the bottom ones?"

"Partially. The partial exposure shows better on the next set of films. But my point is that the wisdom teeth are in identical positions in the old film and the one I took today." She moved her phone closer and shifted between the films a few times.

"Okay." He took her word for it. They were blobs to him.

"She's nineteen, right? The length of the roots and the position of the wisdom teeth don't contradict that age."

She indicated the bottom film. "She has two white fillings. Here and here."

He squinted. More shades of gray.

"I can't make them out."

She clicked something, and the panoramic images vanished, replaced by eight little rectangular films. The type taken frequently at the dentist.

"Four copied original films at the top, and the four I took at the bottom. Film images versus digital images again, so mine will be grainy." She picked up a pencil and pointed at a tooth on a lower X-ray, outlining a small shape. "Can you see the filling here?"

He could. It was whiter than the rest of the tooth. Automatically he checked the coordinating film above it. The same exact shape appeared in that tooth.

"It's the same as the film from the state police."

"Yes. And here is the other one." Her pencil tapped the odd shape of another, whiter filling.

He compared it to the film above it. "But it doesn't match the original X-ray."

"Correct."

"Why not?"

"She had the filling placed after the dentist took the films."

"But you can't know for certain. Doesn't this bring everything into doubt?"

"It doesn't." She touched the state police's film with a pencil and moved her phone in close to the film. "You probably can't see this, but she has a cavity in this tooth. The dentist would have filled the cavity after diagnosing it on the films he took.

"A virgin tooth can acquire a filling. But you can't return a tooth to its virgin state or make a filling disappear—there will always be something in that tooth once it has been worked on. It can be a bigger filling or a crown, or the tooth might have been removed.

"There are many other things that match up in the films. Bone levels, root shapes, sinuses. But the fillings and wisdom teeth confirm it for me. Teeth shape and positions are unique. You won't find the same dentition in two people."

"What if they've had braces?"

"The tooth positions and angles will be different, but the fillings and tooth shapes will be the same."

He mulled it over.

Lacey appeared on his screen again. "Trust me. I can't explain everything I learned in four years of dental school and ten years of practice in this call."

She was right.

"I believe you. The missing filling made me doubt for a moment."

"Good. I'm glad we identified her. Her family has been waiting a long time."

"Did Dr. Peres find a cause of death?"

Lacey looked grim. "No. That's common when the remains are completely skeletal. I'm sure you'll have a report from her tomorrow. I'll email my findings later tonight."

Zander thanked her again and ended the call.

Cynthia Green. Nineteen-year-old African American woman. Missing twenty years.

What happened to you?

Vanished two weeks before Emily's father was hanged.

She'd disappeared from the coast and turned up miles away in the forest. How?

It bothered him. In his short time on the northern coast of Oregon, he'd learned there usually wasn't a lot of violent crime. Two incidents so close together made his senses tingle.

Zander checked the time. It was late, but he suspected he could reach his contact at the prison.

He needed a favor.

29

Zander studied his computer monitor early the next morning, waiting for the start of the video interview with Chet Carlson, the convicted killer of Emily's father, from the state prison.

Chet shuffled into the frame and sat down.

He looked like a murderer.

If Chet had been cast in a movie, the audience would know he was the killer the moment he appeared on-screen.

He was big, intimidatingly big, with hands that appeared to be twice the size of Zander's. The shaved head and neatly trimmed goatee enhanced the stereotype.

Chet studied Zander on his screen as a guard chained his hands to the bar in the table. His weight was on his forearms as he leaned on the table, curiosity on his face.

According to Zander's research, Chet Carlson had lived at a dozen addresses before he was arrested in Astoria for Lincoln Mills's murder. He was a wanderer, never in one place for very long, with a lengthy record of arrests for vagrancy, theft, and DUI. He'd been using a suspended driver's license when he was arrested.

Zander introduced himself. "I have some questions about Lincoln Mills."

"That was a long time ago."

"It was."

"What is the point of revisiting it now?" Chet spread his hands as far as the chains would let him, the restraints clinking. "I'm here. Lincoln's dead. End of story."

Zander had expected a low, rough voice to emerge from the large man, but instead Chet spoke in mellow tones. Not feminine, but serene and calming, as if he were settling a wild animal. Or an overstimulated toddler.

"Everything I read says you claim you didn't kill him."

"That is correct."

"But you pled guilty to murder."

"Also correct." Indifference came through Zander's monitor.

Zander considered the man. "Explain."

Chet shrugged and averted his gaze.

"Did you kill Lincoln Mills?"

Chet picked at a notch in the tabletop. "It doesn't matter now."

"Why not?"

"I don't have proof I didn't do it."

"Lincoln's bloody jacket was found in your motel room."

Chet said nothing.

"You'd lived in a dozen different cities in five states over four years before landing in Astoria. Why were you in Astoria?"

"Why are you asking questions that you already know the answer to?"

"I want to hear you say it, so I can judge for myself."

"A real judge already took care of that. Who are you to pass judgment on me again?"

"Touché," said Zander. "Humor me. Do you have somewhere else you need to be? My contact told me you rarely get visitors."

Chet's chin lifted, his eyes flat. "I got nothin' going on right now."

"So . . . why Astoria?"

He tipped his head and worked his lips, appearing to weigh a decision. "The ocean."

"What about the ocean?"

"I wanted to work on a fishing boat. I like the ocean. I'd already tried in a few towns south of there with no luck." He attempted to cross his arms, his biceps flexing. The chain stopped him.

Zander could easily imagine him pulling ropes and throwing lines or doing whatever physical work was needed on a commercial fishing boat.

"It smells good." The prisoner's nostrils flared slightly.

"Fish don't smell good."

"No. But the ocean does. And I like being outdoors."

Prison is not the place for an outdoor lover.

"I don't understand why you confessed to a murder that you now say you didn't do."

"I'm pretty sure I didn't do it," Chet clarified.

That makes no sense. "Then why did you plead guilty?"

His mouth twitched, and he went back to picking at the notch. "When they brought me in, the officers told me I had done it."

Zander frowned.

"I believed, because of my drinking, that it was impossible for me to remember."

"You were an alcoholic." Zander had wondered if that was the case because of all the alcohol-related arrests in Chet's record.

"Still am. But back then I would drink until I was fall-down, black-out drunk. Don't get to do much of that anymore," he joked.

"You were too drunk to remember hanging someone from a tree." Zander struggled to believe it.

"Yep. But in my sleep, I could see myself do it. I figured I had some weird subconscious block about the hanging and that what the police told me was truth."

"You confessed because you assumed you killed him?"

"Something like that. Did you see I took a polygraph? I knew it couldn't be legally used, but I took it because I hoped the test would tell me if I did it."

"That doesn't make sense."

"The results of the polygraph said there was something going on in my head at the subconscious level, so I figured what the cops had told me was true. I'd had a lot of drunk blackouts before that—and people had always told me about shit I'd done that I had no memory of doing. This didn't seem very far-fetched."

Zander was incredulous. "But you had never killed anyone while you were drunk before."

"No, but I got in plenty of fights and banged up a lot of people that I don't remember."

"What made you change your mind and start saying you were innocent?"

Chet wrapped his fingers around the table's metal attached to his chain. Even via the video, Zander could see his knuckles were huge and dark hair sprouted from the backs of his hands. "I decided I didn't do it."

"A complete reversal."

"I didn't wake up one day and decide I was innocent. It took time. I got in a couple of brawls here—even when I thought I was going to die in one, I never had the instinct or desire to kill the person who was fighting with me. Never. I just wanted to live."

Zander listened, and a slow chill started at the base of his spine.

"Lincoln and I got in a bar fight that evening. That's the first time I'd met the guy. I remember bloodying his nose—which is another reason I thought I mighta killed him—but nothing happened beyond me ripping off his jacket. That's why they found his jacket in my hotel room."

Chet's gaze was steady. He wasn't trying to sell Zander on his innocence. He was simply telling his side.

Dammit, I believe him.

"Does the name *Cynthia Green* mean anything to you?"

Chet thought. "No. Should it?"

"She disappeared two weeks before Lincoln Mills was hanged. We recently found her remains near Bartonville."

Annoyance wrinkled his features. "Do you know how many times cops have been in here to ask if I committed another crime simply because of the Lincoln Mills case?"

"A lot?"

"Yeah. It's ridiculous. They come from all over the US. Talk about desperate."

"She was a teenage African American girl who disappeared from a beach near Gearhart."

"Telling me what she looks like doesn't prod my memory because *I've never done shit like that.*"

He seemed insulted.

"Did you know there was another hanging in Bartonville a few days ago?"

The surprise on Chet's face seemed genuine and then faded into contempt. "Hadn't heard. At least they can't convict me for that one." He scowled. "Who'd they hang?"

"A young man in town. Schoolteacher."

"That sucks."

"You don't know anything about it?"

His brows shot up. "Seriously? Didn't we just cover this? Fuck off." He snorted, derision in his eyes.

Zander considered asking more questions about the hanging, but Chet's reactions felt natural. He wondered if the man had had any recent visitors who might have talked about the Fitch hanging—before or after it happened.

Zander wrapped up the video session and again called his buddy at the state prison, requesting the name of anyone who had visited Chet

Carlson in the last five years. He specified a long period, hoping to get an idea of whom the man associated with. The prison employee promised an email within a few minutes.

He idly tapped his fingers on the desk in his hotel room, craving an omelet from the Barton Diner. His stomach made him fully aware he hadn't eaten breakfast yet. He refreshed his email for the third time, spotted one from the state prison, and immediately clicked.

Over the last five years, Chet had had a single visitor. But she had come twice.

Both visits had been within the last twelve months.

Terri Yancey.

Zander stared at the name for a long moment. *Who is she to Chet Carlson?*

She hadn't visited enough times to be family.

A suspicion formed, and he accessed the state DMV records, immediately finding a driver's license for Terri Yancey. She was thirty-nine, brunette, and lived in Beaverton, a few miles west of Portland.

He caught his breath at the photo. *Madison.*

Terri Yancey looked like Madison. Emily and Madison shared family similarities, but if Madison had been run through an age-progression app and been given dark hair, she would look exactly like Terri Yancey.

Terri. Tara.

Could this be Tara?

The resemblance was there.

Why did she visit Chet Carlson?

The bigger question was why she had never contacted her family.

Plugging Terri's address into his phone, he saw he could be at her front door in less than two hours.

Do I tell Emily?

Emily's stomach convulsed. "Are you sure?" she whispered to Zander as they stood on the mansion's porch.

Zander pulled up an image on his phone.

Emily clutched the phone, staring at the picture. Tara looked back at her. She was older, her hair was dark. But it was Tara.

"How?" She forced out the word.

"I had a video interview with Chet Carlson this morning."

Her gut twisted and spun again. "Jesus, Zander. Any other shocks for me?"

He paused. "No."

Emily wasn't sure she believed him. She focused on Tara's face again, her heart trying to beat its way up her throat.

"After I talked to him, I checked his visitor records. Your sister has been to see him twice in the last year."

She blinked hard, trying to keep Tara's face in focus. "Maybe you don't consider that to be another shock, but I do. Why did she do that?"

"I don't know. I thought I'd go ask her."

Emily's head jerked up, her pulse pounding. "You're going to see Tara?"

"She goes by Terri now. Terri Yancey. She lives in Beaverton."

Emily sat in one of the heavy metal chairs on the porch. Her brain was spinning; Tara was close by.

"Would you like to come?" He crouched beside her, his gaze even with hers. Substantial concern radiating from him.

"I don't know." She couldn't process his request. Her mind was locked on the fact that Tara lived two hours away. And had never called. *Why?*

"Chet Carlson still claims he didn't kill your father."

"Yes," she said woodenly. "He's said that for several years. Did he try to explain why it wasn't him?"

"A little. He doesn't have any proof."

"What did he say about Tara?"

"I didn't find out about Tara until after the interview." He had a hopeful look in his eyes.

He wants me to go with him.

She could think of worse things than to spend a few hours with Zander.

In her heart she was dying to see her sister, but her emotions were all over the place.

Am I ready to find out why Tara abandoned us? Will she talk to me? What if she refuses?

She had to decide *now*.

"I'll go."

30

It was nearly noon when Emily and Zander stopped in front of a beautiful house.

A tiny bit of envy sprouted in Emily's heart—an unusual sensation—as she bit back a gasp. Tara's home was in a well-to-do neighborhood where the lawns were perfectly manicured, and a German luxury vehicle sat in her driveway.

Emily compared her totaled Honda to the Mercedes. She could barely afford to keep her car in tires. Soon she'd find out how little money her insurance company would pay for her now-totaled old car. It wasn't going to be pretty.

She felt Zander study her.

"I can't believe Tara lives here," she muttered. "The mansion is falling to pieces around our ears."

"You don't have to come in."

Surprise made her choke. "I came all this way. You bet I'm coming in. Especially now that I see Tara's been living here while I struggle to take care of three elderly aunts, my sister, the mansion, and the diner."

Emily yanked on the car door handle and stepped out, embarrassed at how bitter she had sounded. She waited for Zander, and they walked the brick-lined path to the front door, where he rang the bell.

A young girl opened it, and Emily caught her breath.

She looks exactly like Tara as a child.

The girl appeared to be nine or ten. Emily hadn't thought to wonder if Tara had children. Or a husband. It had been shortsighted of her.

"Can we speak to your mom?" she finally managed to ask.

"Moooom!" the girl yelled over her shoulder. Her long, blonde hair was in a single braid, and she wore black jeans with ripped knees.

I have a niece.

The thought hit her like a semitruck, making her lungs seize, the oxygen gone.

Behind the girl the house had high ceilings and white wainscoting. An elegant staircase curved to the second level. The wood floors gleamed.

Footsteps sounded.

The woman who arrived was not Tara, but she looked at Zander and Emily expectantly.

"We're looking for Terri Yancey," Zander said. "Is she home?"

The woman's face shut down. "She's not feeling well." Her manner was guarded, and suspicion hovered in her tone. She was twenty years too old to be Tara. "Can I give her a message?"

Emily and Zander exchanged a long look, and he nodded encouragingly. The decision was in her hands.

Should I?

I have a niece.

"Tell Tara her sister Emily is here," she stated calmly, defying the drumbeat in her chest.

The woman took a half step back, her hand rising to her chest, her mouth in an O.

She knows.

The girl tilted her head, studying Emily with intelligent eyes. "Who?" She looked to the older woman. "Who is she?"

Emily said nothing, and the woman visibly pulled herself together. "Why don't you come in?" With one hand on the girl's shoulder, she stepped back and opened the door wider.

Emily caught Zander's surprised expression. She shrugged at him. They'd come this far, she wasn't about to stop now.

The woman led them to a formal living room and indicated for them to take a seat. "I'll get her." She vanished through the glass double doors, and her footsteps tapped up the arced staircase.

Tara's daughter—Emily assumed—stayed, her expression watchful. She'd picked up on the unease among the adults.

"I'm Emily. This is Zander." When the girl didn't reply, Emily continued. "And you are . . ."

"Bella."

Was Tara a *Twilight* fan?

Emily used to be.

"How old are you, Bella?" Zander asked.

"Why are you here?" Bella asked bluntly. "Why is Grandma upset?"

Zander leaned closer to Emily. "She's definitely related to you," he whispered.

"You're being rude." Bella tossed her braid over her shoulder and raised her chin.

"You're right, and I'm sorry," Zander said. "You remind me of someone."

"Who?"

"You don't know her—but you will soon."

Bella wrinkled her nose and rolled her eyes at his nonanswer.

Emily lost her breath. The movement was like looking into a mirror. She'd trained herself not to use the eyeroll except around family, but the wrinkling of the nose was too hard a habit to break.

Female voices sounded. People were coming down the staircase. Bella left the room, but her question was audible. "Mom, who are they?"

Then Tara was in the doorway, one hand gripping the jamb for balance, shock opening her mouth. "Emily." The name was faint.

Tara's appearance jolted Emily. Her sister was now a brunette with chin-length hair. Emily had seen the brown hair in her license photo, but seeing the dark—and short—hair in person was a shock. As a teen Tara had always made a big deal over her long, blonde hair. Her sister was now bone thin and had deep circles under her eyes. She looked on edge, nervous.

That's my sister.

All her confusion and questions evaporated. After twenty years they were in the same room. *Nothing else matters.* Emily stood and rushed across the room, enveloping her sister in her arms, her heart breaking at the sensation of the bones just under her skin. She pulled back to look Tara in the eye and struggled to see through tears. Emily wiped one eye, and Tara did the same.

"I'm sorry," Tara cried. "I'm so sorry," she repeated over and over.

◆◆◆

Zander watched the reunion, glad Emily had come with him. Once the sisters had gotten past tears, both talked nonstop. Madison. The aunts. Bartonville.

He'd noticed Tara had a slender face on her driver's license, but in person the woman's thinness looked unhealthy. She was unsteady on her feet, but that could be from the roller coaster of emotions the women were experiencing. The two finally moved to the couch and continued to talk over each other's sentences.

"Wendy," Tara said to the older woman, "can you take Bella in the other room so we can have a bit of privacy?"

"I want to know what's going on," the child stated firmly.

"I promise I'll tell you later."

"She said she's your sister. You've said you don't have any family."

Tara paused and briefly closed her eyes. "It's a long story. I'll get to it, I promise."

The girl shot Emily and Zander suspicious glares but reluctantly left with Wendy. Emily watched her departure, a hungry look in her eye.

The room went silent. Tara's and Emily's emotions had crested and fallen, and the awkward moment stretched. Unanswered questions wove between them. Why had Tara left? Why no contact?

They faced each other on the couch, and Tara knotted her hands, twisting and clenching. Emily saw them and separated her own clenched hands.

Zander took pity on the quiet women. "How old is Bella?" he asked. A neutral question.

"She's nine."

"She looks like you," he told Tara, noticing she didn't wear a wedding ring. "Is her father still around?"

Tara paled. "No. He died in an automobile accident five years ago. Wendy is my mother-in-law, and she took us in after that." Her voice wavered.

"Tara, I'm so sorry." Emily touched her sister's arm. "How horrible for you and Bella."

"Everyone around me dies." The statement was flat and lifeless; the emotional woman had vanished.

Zander flinched. "Are you all right?" he asked cautiously. He didn't know exactly what he referred to . . . her health, her current emotions, her living situation, her dead husband.

She simply looked at him and then turned to Emily. "What happened to your head?" Tara asked, eyeing the bandage under her hair.

"It's nothing. I whacked it pretty good, and they had to stitch it up. I'm okay."

Zander wasn't surprised Emily didn't go into detail. Especially after Tara had just said everyone around her died.

He decided to outright question Tara. "Why did you visit Chet Carlson?"

Tara blanched. "That's how you found me." The whisper high and reedy.

"Why are you hiding?" Emily cut in sharply. "How could you go for twenty years without contacting us? *Your family?* I lost three members of my family within a week back then!" She waved her hands as she spoke, scaling another emotional peak.

Tara's face crumpled. "I can't talk about it."

A theory percolated, and Zander studied the woman, wondering how to phrase his suspicion.

"Why?" Emily begged. "What is so horrible that you can't tell us?" She pointed at Zander. "He's an FBI agent, Tara. He can help with whatever it is."

Zander wasn't so sure about that, but Tara was listening, impulses warring on her face, the line of her back tense. She regarded him warily.

"I have a niece," Emily said softly. "I never knew—Madison never knew. We missed her birth, her chubby baby cheeks, losing her first tooth . . ."

"She's not yours." Tara grew fierce. "That is my daughter, and I do everything I can to keep her safe. You are to tell no one that you saw me or her."

A mama bear had replaced Tara on the sofa.

Emily snapped her mouth shut.

"What did you see that night, Tara?" Zander questioned.

"Nothing. I wasn't there." She didn't ask which night.

Emily started to speak and stopped, pressing her lips into a thin line.

"I was at a friend's. We were drinking. I don't know anything about what happened to Dad. You already knew this." She looked Emily in the eye.

"You didn't answer Zander's question about Carlson," Emily said.

"What happened that night has haunted me all my life. I wanted to see that man's face."

"Do you believe he killed your father?" asked Zander.

"Of course," she said quickly. "Even though he claims he didn't do it."

She's lying.

"My life has been hell for twenty years," Tara said. "First Dad's murder and then Mom's after I left. The only way I could put it out of my head was with booze. Now I have constant insomnia and can never relax."

Zander exchanged a sharp look with Emily.

"Tara, Mom committed suicide." Confusion laced Emily's words.

Tara blinked several times. "No, she was murdered."

Emily shook her head. "Where did you hear that? It was ruled suicide from the start."

Her sister sat very still, focused intently on Emily, and a hesitant fear crept into her eyes. "You're wrong."

"I swear. It's true." Emily swallowed hard, shadows crossing her face.

Zander's throat constricted as he watched the painful conversation.

"No." Tara rose to her feet, her hands in fists. "*You're lying.* The people who killed her are the same that killed Dad."

"No. I know—"

"Who do you believe killed your father, Tara?" Zander jumped in. "A moment ago you said Chet Carlson did it. Now you just said *people* did it. Who was it?"

Her frantic gaze bounced between Emily and Zander. "Chet Carlson did it. I meant that he killed Mom too."

She's lying again.

"I need to lie down." Tara turned to leave, and Emily leaped up, grabbing her arm and making her sister face her.

"I don't know what's happened to you, but it's okay, Tara. I just want you back in my life, no matter what. I don't care what you did."

Zander went still. *Emily believes Tara was involved.*

"Go to hell." Tara shook off Emily's grip. "Remember what I said. You didn't see me or Bella." She strode out of the room.

◆◆◆

"What is she hiding?" Emily asked.

Zander was hesitant to voice the theory that had festered in his thoughts since they'd left Beaverton. They were nearly back to the coast. "I think she believes someone else killed your father."

Emily was silent.

"And she believes this same person killed your mother. Whether or not she is correct, she believes it's true."

"I don't know how reliable she is," Emily said. "I smelled alcohol on her, and she admitted she has a drinking problem. She's a tightly wound person, and I don't remember her being that way. Thank God she has Wendy to help care for Bella."

"Her mother-in-law reminds me of a warden. I wasn't surprised when she refused to let us speak to Tara again and then pushed us out the door."

He watched Emily with his peripheral vision as he drove. She was thoughtful, quiet. Not her usual outspoken self. "You told me Tara was there the night your father died, but she told the police she wasn't there."

"Correct. I saw her there with another person."

"Was your father already hanged when you saw Tara?"

Her shoulders quaked ever so briefly. "Yes."

"And she repeated her story again today that she wasn't there." He paused, trying to frame his next question. "Is it possible your memory is wrong?"

Her lips worked, and she turned to look out the window. "I've asked myself that a million times over twenty years. Part of what kept me from telling the police what I saw was the thought that I was wrong and also that I didn't want Tara in trouble. But even if my memory is wrong, there's something Tara is hiding about Dad's death."

"Your mother committed suicide a few days after Tara left, right?"

"Yes. I've always wondered if Tara even knew that Mom had died."

"Who handled your mother's investigation?" asked Zander.

Emily faced straight ahead, her mouth in a frown. "I assume the Clatsop County sheriff. They were already working Dad's murder. I've never asked." She exhaled. "I didn't want to ask," she added softly.

Zander understood. Digging up the past was painful. He avoided it as much as possible.

Emily's back stiffened. "The traffic lights are out." They'd just turned onto the main road through Bartonville.

"Not surprised," said Zander as he watched small branches and debris blow across the road. It'd been a windy drive all the way across the Coast Ranges, but once they'd neared Bartonville, he'd noticed that the tops of the fir trees waved in a frenzy. "At least the rain has stopped." The gray clouds were high, not threatening to dump more water.

"The church's power is out, and so is the post office's," Emily said as they passed through town. "Take me to the diner instead of the mansion. If anyone still has power, it's the diner."

"How come?"

"We didn't ever spend money on cameras, but a decade ago Vina invested in an excellent power backup system. She said people will always need to eat, especially if they can't cook in their own homes. The system has paid for itself a few times over."

Zander turned into the parking lot and saw Emily was right. The lights were on in the diner, and the lot had more cars than he'd ever seen there. "I guess I'll get a cup of coffee and sandwich to go," he told her. "Hopefully they still have power at the county sheriff's office."

"It's busy. The diner will need my help."

"How are you feeling?" He scanned her from head to toe.

"Pretty darn good. I took more medication when we left Tara's house."

He was skeptical but didn't argue.

He parked and followed her inside. Most of the seats were full as Thea and Vina worked the floor, scuttling from table to table. Dory was nowhere in sight. He didn't see many people eating, but everyone had coffee and appeared settled in to wait out the storm. The mood inside was chipper, the storm now a social event.

Emily pointed at the kitchen door. "Go tell Leo I said to make you something to go. I need to get to work."

"Stick close to other people."

She gave him a blank look that was immediately replaced with one of understanding—and apprehension. An abrupt nod followed, and she headed toward her office.

She already forgot that someone shot at her yesterday?

Zander crossed the floor and hesitantly pushed open the swinging door, feeling like an intruder.

From behind the grill, Leo spotted him immediately. "Hey, Zander," said the bald cook.

"I dropped Emily off. She said you'd make me something to go?"

"You bet. A BLT okay?"

"Perfect."

A sizzle sounded as Leo lay bacon on the flat top. Zander's mouth watered.

"There's some to-go cups next to the coffee maker," Leo told him.

Zander grabbed a cup and poured a huge cup of coffee. He was pressing on the lid when Isaac touched his arm. He jerked, nearly spilling the cup. The teenager had approached as silently as a cat.

"Sorry." Isaac stared at his shoes. His hair was windblown, and he wore a heavy coat. He smelled of the outdoors.

"It's no problem. You just coming to work?" Zander asked, wondering what the quiet kid wanted.

"Returning. I already worked this morning. They called me back in since the power went out and half the town showed up. Happens every time." He continued to stare at his shoes.

Zander waited but finally spoke. "Did you want to ask me something?"

Isaac finally made eye contact. "Are you still looking for Billy Osburne?"

Every cell in Zander's body went on alert. "Absolutely. You've seen him?"

"Yeah. I think he's staying with a girl."

Zander controlled his impatience. "Can you be more specific?"

Isaac grimaced. "I swear I saw him in this girl's car. She lives three houses down from us. Before I came to work just now, I walked over there to check, and he was outside clearing some branches out of her driveway."

"That's pretty cocky on his part."

"It's a long driveway, and this was right in front of the garage. All the houses there are set way back in the trees with a lot of space between them. You can't see your neighbors. I didn't get too close."

"What if he saw you?"

"He didn't." Isaac was confident.

"How long ago was this?"

"Fifteen minutes."

"Here's your BLT, Zander." Leo slid over a white box.

"Thanks." Zander grabbed the box and turned back to Isaac. "Why didn't you call the police when you saw him?"

"I'm telling you." Isaac flushed, and his gaze went back to his shoes.

"You didn't know I'd be here."

The teenager squirmed. "I didn't want to talk to the police."

Zander let it go. Whatever the kid's reason for avoiding the police didn't matter now. He tucked his sandwich box under an arm, picked up his coffee, and walked out of the kitchen, dialing the sheriff with one hand as he left.

31

Madison found Emily in the diner's office. She'd seen her sister come in with Zander Wells and then head down the side hall.

She watched Emily dig through files for a moment from the doorway. A wide white bandage was visible on the side of her head, under her hair.

She could have died.

She's the heart of our unusual family.

Madison had never appreciated the many things Emily did to keep all their lives on track. Until now. "Are you okay?"

Emily started, jerking her head up from her work. "I'm fine. It's nothing."

"It's not nothing. I talked to Janet at the hospital. Your injury could have been very serious."

"You need to inform your nurse friend about HIPAA regulations."

"I'm sure she knows."

Emily humphed. "Everything running smoothly?"

"Yep. Vina and Thea are keeping everyone company and filling their coffee cups. Dory is on her way in. It sounds like three-quarters of the town doesn't have power—including the mansion."

"I figured. Seems like we're always the first to lose it."

"What's that?" Madison pointed at a thick file on the office desk.

Emily's face brightened. "Simon gave me that yesterday. He put together pictures and documents that relate to the Bartons." She sat at the desk and flipped it open.

Curiosity and some glossy black-and-white photos drew Madison closer. The first photo was labeled *Barton Lumber Mill* in crooked writing across the bottom. She touched a familiar man in the image. "That's our great-great-grandfather." He stood with a dozen other men, looking rugged and proud as they posed. "This has to be in the early 1900s."

"Yep. That's George."

Madison scanned the other men, wondering who they were and if some of their descendants still lived in Bartonville. Heck, maybe some were eating in the diner right that minute.

"I haven't seen this picture before, have you?"

"No," said Emily. "It's not among any of the photos I've seen at the mansion."

Madison flipped through a few more logging photos. George Barton leaning against a felled fir that had a trunk wider than he was tall. A log truck with the Barton name on the door and a single humongous log on its trailer.

"It's all gone," Madison said under her breath, feeling a small pang for the family business that she'd never known. At the end the mill had cut wood only for other companies, its own supply of lumber gone. The mill was sold in the 1980s, and the new owners shut it down, intending to use the property for something else that never came to fruition. Now it was a small, rusting ghost town of buildings. Madison quickly flipped through more black-and-white photos, stacking them neatly, wanting to see the color ones deeper in the file.

The first color photo was a formal picture of the mansion. Emily sighed, and Madison understood. The mansion shone. It was a summer day, and the landscaping was immaculate. The paint perfect and the rails on the porch intact. Someone had set glasses and a large pitcher of lemonade on a table on the porch, waiting for the owners to sit and relax.

Madison placed it facedown on the viewed stack.

"Ohhh!" Emily picked up the next photo.

Four young women stood on the steps of the mansion, their arms hooked together, laughter on their faces. The simple dresses had wide knee-length skirts, the waists were tiny, and the women wore short white gloves. A holiday, perhaps Easter, judging by the daffodils and tulips.

Eagerly studying the faces, Madison recognized each of her great-aunts and her grandmother.

So young.

"She's pregnant." Emily indicated their grandmother.

Sure enough, one of the waists wasn't that tiny. "Do you think she was pregnant with Mom or Uncle Rod?"

"This looks like the late 1950s. I'll guess Uncle Rod."

Madison held the photo closer, searching her grandmother's face for a hint of herself but not finding it. Her grandmother had died when her mother was young. Madison had never known her.

"All girls," Emily commented.

"The Barton curse," Madison joked sadly. Male children had been few and far between in a century of the Barton line. Their ancestors typically had many girls and a single boy.

"Look at what's on Grandmother's wrist." Emily pointed. "Do you remember that bracelet?"

Madison did. "The button bracelet. I didn't realize it was that old."

All three girls had played with the bracelet in the photo. It was wide, made of a diverse assortment of dozens of brass buttons with a few colored ones mixed in. "Grandmother must have given it to Mom. Remember how we fought over who got to wear it?"

"I'd spend hours looking at each button." A dreamy expression covered Emily's face. "I really loved it."

Madison had too. One more thing lost in the fire.

"All four of the sisters are so beautiful," Emily said. "Why did only Grandmother marry?"

Madison didn't know the answer. Each of her great-aunts had brushed off the question in the past. She moved on to the next photo and immediately spotted her father, a big grin on his face.

"Where is this?"

Emily studied the photo of seven men with their fishing gear in front of a small tavern. "Isn't that the bead store now? But why is this picture in the Barton file? Dad was a Mills."

"Uncle Rod is in it." He stood next to their father, an arm slung around his neck.

"I didn't recognize him." Emily squinted. "Look . . . isn't that Sheriff Greer?" She giggled. "And Harlan Trapp—with hair."

"Simon Rhoads too." They looked like a rowdy group, ready to cause havoc for some fish.

"I think we could use this picture to blackmail Harlan or the sheriff," Madison said. "I don't think this is the image they're currently trying to project." She sifted through two more pictures of the same group of men in juvenile muscle poses. "Idiots."

Emily elbowed her, fighting back laughter. "They were young. And probably drunk."

A photo of a couple on a lookout high above the ocean made her stop. "Mom and Dad," she breathed. "I've never seen this one." Their mother was in profile, looking up at her husband, bliss on her face as he laughed at the camera. This was the loving couple her aunts had always described to Madison and her sisters.

A sad, confused wife.

Anita's sentence echoed in her mind. Aunt Dory had said something similar two days ago. The words didn't describe the woman in the picture.

Did Anita and Dory not tell me the truth?

"That's the spot I nearly died at. Jeez, I was a stupid kid," Emily said.

"Yes, you were."

"You could have just as easily gone over the edge."

Her father's pocket watch popped into Madison's thoughts—the shooting had wiped it from her mind. She glanced at Emily, her nose close to the photo of their parents, a hungry look in her eyes. *Now or never.*

"Em . . . I found Dad's pocket watch in your room."

Emily set down the photo and turned to Madison, dismay on her face. "You were in my room?"

"Yes. And I'm sorry, but why did you have it? Have you hidden it all these years?" Her sister's expression was blank, but Madison knew anger simmered under the surface. "Mom searched high and low for that watch."

"I know."

Madison crossed her arms and tipped her head, waiting.

"I found it at Lindsay's . . . that morning."

Her heart stumbled. *"What?"*

"It was in the backyard. I stepped on it."

"How . . ." Madison's brain shut down. "Why . . ."

"I don't know." A shadow passed across Emily's eyes. "Trust me, I'm still as confused as you are now. I told the FBI agents, and Agent McLane and I were driving to get it when . . . the accident happened." Her throat moved as she swallowed hard.

"What d-does it mean?" Madison's tongue stuttered over the words.

"I wish I knew."

The memory of Emily picking up something in the yard the night their father was murdered suddenly rushed over her. "I saw you outside the night that Dad—I saw you pick up something from the grass. When I found the watch, I assumed that's what you picked up."

Emily paled. "You never said anything back then."

"*You* never said anything. The investigators believed you were in the house. *I saw you outside.*" Her heartbeat accelerated, and a lightheadedness made her sit in the other office chair.

Her sister's mouth opened and closed, her eyes wide.

"Why didn't you tell anyone?" Madison caught her breath. "What are you hiding?" she whispered, her voice pleading for truth.

Tendons stood out on Emily's neck, her pulse visible.

"Emily."

Her sister ran a hand over her forehead and pressed at her temple. "What if I'm wrong?"

"Wrong about what?" Madison tensed, every muscle like rock.

Emily turned her attention back to the photo of their parents. "Wrong that I saw Tara out there that night."

Her head reeled, and Madison clutched the arms of the chair. "Tara? No—she wasn't there. She was at a friend's. She said so." Nausea swamped her. "I thought I saw Mom in the backyard moving in the trees." Madison covered her face. "What is going on?"

"It wasn't Mom," Emily said. "I understand how you thought it was her because of the hair, but it was Tara."

"Are you sure?"

"I'm positive. I saw Tara." Emily's voice was hollow. "In the woods, running."

"Why didn't you tell anyone?"

"Why didn't you tell anyone *you saw me*?" Emily shot back.

"Because I wanted to protect you!"

"I was doing the same for Tara!"

The sisters stared at each other, both of their chests heaving, the air in the tiny office heavy with guilt and secrets.

Emily believed she was protecting Tara by staying silent.

"What did Tara do?" Madison whispered.

"I don't know—I don't want to know."

Realization struck Madison like a hammer, stealing her breath. "That's why you never searched for her."

"I didn't want to know what she had done." Emily's eyes were wet. "It had to be bad—why else would she leave?" She set down the photo as a struggle played out across her face.

"What is it?" Madison's heart sank at her sister's expression. "Tell me."

"Zander found Tara this morning. I talked to her just hours ago."

Madison's mouth dried up, and her core turned to ice.

"Girls?" Dory stepped in the office, worry on her soft features, her hands in knots.

"What is it, Auntie?" Emily asked as calmly as if she and Madison had been discussing the weather. Madison was still speechless, Emily's revelations ricocheting like a Super Ball in her skull.

Dory frowned, the lines around her mouth deepening. "I believe I just saw Tara."

Emily rose out of her chair. "Where?" she gasped.

"Well, I think it was her. You know I've thought I've seen her a few times in the past." Her gaze was uncertain.

True. Dory had directed them on a few wrong expeditions, startling confused young women.

"She looked right at me," Dory continued. "She was older, of course, and her hair was short and brown, but I'm sure it was her."

Disappointment filled Madison. Dory was confused.

"Brown hair?" Emily grasped Dory's arm. "Are you sure?"

"Yes. It was about this long." Dory lifted a hand to her chin.

"Madison. That's her." Excitement filled Emily's face. "She's come back."

"Wait." Madison struggled to catch up. "You mean that's how her hair looks *now*?"

"Yes. Is she in the diner, Dory?"

"No. I saw her in a car—well, one of those SUV things."

"Where?" Impatience rolled off Emily.

"She passed me as I drove to town. When I looked in the rearview mirror, I saw her turn onto Seabound Road."

"That road only goes to one place," Emily said. She picked up one of the pictures, holding it for Madison to see. "This one."

Their parents posed on the overlook.

32

Zander met Sheriff Greer in front of Leo's home.

According to Isaac, Billy was hiding out three houses down from where he lived with Leo. A deputy had done a drive-by, but the house sat too far back in the tall trees to be seen from the road.

"How confident are you in your witness?" Greer asked Zander, holding his hat against the wind. Two deputies had joined them, forming a huddle in Leo's driveway, out of sight of any cars that would pass.

Zander doubted anyone would drive down the road. The area felt deserted. Isaac had been right when he described it as isolated. Only the presence of gravel driveways that fed into the road hinted that homes even existed.

It was a good place to disappear.

He thought about how Isaac had struggled to tell him the news. As nervous as he was, Zander had seen certainty in his eyes. "He got pretty close. He was positive it was Billy."

"The house is a rental. The owner says a young woman named Rachel Wolfe is the current renter."

"That backs up Kyle Osburne's suggestion that his brother might be with a girl."

"Fifty-fifty chance that the renter was female," Greer pointed out.

"But a young female?"

The sheriff grunted. "Wish I knew if he was armed."

"There's a good chance he is since he's a suspect in Nate Copeland's murder," Zander said.

The two deputies muttered and shuffled their feet, shooting angry looks at the mention of their murdered coworker. The two men were young, probably in their midtwenties, and Zander hoped their emotions wouldn't affect this outcome. The one named Daigle seemed familiar, and Zander realized he was the deputy who was to go to the beach with Nate the day he died.

"I've activated our SERT team," the sheriff said. "I want them here if we confirm Billy is in that house, but it'll take at least an hour for them to arrive. The team is made up of some of my deputies, a few Astoria officers, and Seaside officers."

"Understood." Impatience swamped Zander. Calling in the specialty team was the right thing to do. They knew how to handle a possible standoff or hostage situation.

"But I don't want to wait around for them to find out the house is empty," said Greer. "I'm always in favor of an old-fashioned knock on the door. Ninety-nine percent of the time it solves the situation."

Zander eyed the two deputies in their heavy vests, belts, and coats. A door knock was simple, but it could turn deadly in a split second. The men looked confident, a hint of adrenaline in their eyes. Zander felt it himself. "I'll grab my vest." He popped the trunk on his vehicle, stripped off his coat, and strapped on the vest. He grabbed his jacket with *FBI* emblazoned across the back and put it on over the vest. The evening was approaching, and he didn't want anyone to arrive at the scene and mistake him for a suspect.

"Daigle and I will do the door knock. I'll park in his driveway," Greer said. "You and Edwards cover the back in case we flush him out." Greer keyed the mic at his shoulder and relayed their plan to dispatch.

Zander and Edwards jogged down the road to get in place behind the rental home before Greer pulled in the driveway. Before they reached the third driveway, they darted off the road and into the firs that filled most of the large lot. The tree branches whistled and swished high over their heads, and the air smelled of wet dirt, that subtle odor of earthy decomposition. They silently hustled between the trunks until they sighted the back door of the home. The door opened onto a small wood deck with three stairs that led to a cleared space behind the home.

"I'll move to the other side and let Greer know we're in position," Edwards said. He jogged off, and Zander stayed in position behind a fir, the door in sight. A sporadic rain of pine needles peppered him, and small branches clattered as they landed on the home's roof. Somehow this small stretch of homes still had power. He doubted it would last long.

Lights swept over the house and trees as Greer drove up the driveway. Two car doors slammed.

Zander waited, alternating between watching the back door and watching a window on his side of the home. He listened hard, wishing he could hear voices from the front to indicate whether the operation was going smoothly or not. Edwards wasn't visible, and Zander assumed he was covering the windows on the far side of the home as well as the back door.

Only the wind in the firs and the plinking sounds on the roof were audible.

The back door opened, and Billy Osburne took two running steps across the deck, leaped over the stairs, and made a break for the woods.

"Runner! We've got a runner!" Zander sprinted after him.

The ground was rough, and visibility was limited. His chest heaved as he raced as quickly as he could without tripping. He hadn't seen a weapon in Billy's hand, but that didn't mean he wasn't armed. He kept Billy in his sights, his white T-shirt a blessing in the dim woods. Ahead and to his left, he saw Edwards barreling between tree trunks. The deputy was closer.

Edwards would have notified Greer he was running. They're probably somewhere behind us.

"Stop! Police!" Edwards shouted.

Billy paid no attention and continued his mad scramble. Zander turned up his momentum, choosing speed over safety, praying he didn't fall.

Edwards shouted another warning.

Then Zander lost sight of Billy. He pushed forward, not slowing his pace. Ten yards ahead, Edwards rapidly covered ground in the direction where Billy had vanished.

Zander's toe caught, and he slammed to the ground and tasted dirt. He was instantly back on his feet and scrambled to make up lost time, his hip and ribs aching where they'd landed on a rock or root. He spotted Edwards and accelerated, his breaths loud in his head.

A white blur knocked Edwards out of Zander's view.

Billy.

He spotted Edwards on his back, Billy on top of him, his fists slamming the deputy in the face. Edwards wheezed and moaned, making no effort to stop the blows.

Got the wind knocked out of him.

Billy yanked on the officer's weapon, and Zander dived at the man, knocking him off Edwards. Zander landed on top of Billy, slamming his stomach and head to the ground. The air in Billy's lungs escaped with a deep *woof*, and he struggled to force Zander off his back.

Zander grabbed his wrist, swung his arm back until it was straight up, and twisted. Billy froze.

"Holy shit! Don't break my arm!"

"Don't move." Zander kept his knee in the center of Billy's back, and Edwards, who'd recovered, cuffed the other wrist and then the one Zander was holding. Zander got to his feet, adrenaline still pumping and breathing hard. "You okay?" he asked Edwards.

"Yeah." The officer was sheepish. "Haven't had the wind knocked out of me since I fell off a swing set in grade school."

"Worst feeling ever."

"You can't take me in, man! You've got to let me *go*!"

"You're joking, right?" Zander asked Billy. "We have questions about some deaths in town that I suspect only you can answer."

"No! No, you need to let me go. He's going to kill me." His voice was frantic, his head whipping from side to side as he lay on the ground.

Zander made a show of scanning the woods. "Who? Edwards here? He's a little pissed you knocked the wind out of him, but I don't think he'll kill you over it."

"*Not him.* I'm supposed to be gone!"

"Dead gone? Or just gone gone?"

"I'll be dead gone if he knows you've got me." Billy dug his forehead into the dirt. "Dammit. This can't be happening!"

The hairs rose on Zander's neck. The man was scared. *Who is he worried about?*

"You talking about Kyle?"

"Oh shit. He's going to kill Kyle first if he finds out I'm still around." Billy squirmed and pulled at his wrists.

Zander exchanged a look with Edwards, who shrugged.

Greer and Daigle arrived, both blowing hard. Greer slapped Edwards on the back. "Nice job."

"He popped out and tackled me," Edwards admitted. "Lost my breath, and he had his hand on my weapon until Zander took him down."

"Important part is that we have him." Now that Billy wasn't sprinting, Zander noticed the white T-shirt was yellowed and grimy, and his jeans were filthy. And this wasn't from his roll on the forest floor.

"Doesn't your girlfriend have a washing machine, Billy?"

"Fuck off."

"Let's go." Greer grabbed Billy under one arm and Daigle took the other, and they hauled him to his feet.

Billy stared wild-eyed at Greer. "You've got to let me go, Sheriff," he begged.

Zander started. *Are those tears?*

"Knock it off," answered Greer. "We've got a nice clean cell just waiting for you."

"He's gonna kill Kyle and Rachel if he knows I'm still here!"

"Wait." Zander stepped in front of Billy. "Rachel's the woman at the house here, right? Who's gonna kill her and your brother?"

He hung his head. "I can't tell you."

"Dammit," said Greer. "I don't have time for this." He tugged on Billy's arm.

The man started to shake, panic in his eyes, and he abruptly thrashed, breaking Greer's hold. He took one lunging step, and Daigle neatly tripped him. Billy landed on his side and curled into a ball, still shaking.

The three men exchanged curious glances.

Is he petrified or bullshitting us?

Zander nudged him with a foot. "We can't help Kyle if you don't tell us what's going on."

Billy moaned and coiled tighter, muttering under his breath.

"What?" Zander squatted again. His legs still ached from his sprint.

"You've got to promise me you'll protect Kyle and Rachel."

"Promised."

Billy sucked in a deep breath, and words sped out of his mouth. "I was paid to help someone with Sean, and then I was supposed to get out of town."

Zander struggled to speak coherently. "You helped someone kill Sean. Is that what you're saying? But not Lindsay?"

"Yeah." Billy seemed to deflate, sinking into the dirt.

"How much were you paid to take someone's life?" Zander spit out.

Billy turned his face into the dirt. "Two thousand dollars," he mumbled.

Reeling, Zander stepped away, his hands going through his hair. *He's lying. He's got to be lying. But why?* "Who was it, Billy? Who paid you?"

Billy wouldn't look up. "I'm a dead man."

"I'll kill you myself if you don't tell me what happened." Zander's temper hung by a thread. *He sold his soul for two thousand dollars.* "You've got two seconds."

"Harlan Trapp."

No one breathed.

"Bullshit," said Greer. "You're accusing the mayor of murder?"

Zander pictured the tall, bald man. The one who couldn't control a community meeting.

He is our killer?

Zander struggled to wrap his mind around it.

Billy turned to look Greer in the eye. "He's fucking evil. It was just supposed to be Sean, but then Harlan took down Lindsay too. *He brutalized her.*"

Greer jerked away and snarled in disgust.

"What about Nate?" asked Daigle. "*Did you shoot Nate?*"

Billy said nothing and curled tighter.

"You fucker!" Daigle hauled back and kicked him.

Greer and Edwards grabbed Daigle and yanked him back. Greer pushed him away with a rough shove. "*Go cool off.* If I see or hear of you doing that again, you're out of a job." Daigle lurched toward a fir, slammed a hand against it, bent over, and vomited.

The other three men turned away.

"I'm not lying about Harlan," Billy said in a broken voice from the ground. "He's psychotic. He threatened to kill Kyle if I also didn't take care of Nate. He thinks Nate saw us at Sean's."

"What about Emily Mills? Does he want Emily dead too?" Zander could barely breathe. "Did you shoot at Emily and Ava McLane yesterday?"

"He didn't say anything to me about Emily. And I don't know the other person you said."

"Why did Harlan want Sean killed?" Zander asked Billy, wincing as Daigle retched again.

"Dunno."

"You helped him kill a man and don't know why?" said Greer.

"He said Sean knew about him."

"Knew what about him?"

"Dunno."

Zander wanted to kick Billy himself.

33

Sheriff Greer insisted they knock on the door again at Harlan Trapp's home. Zander was hesitant. It had worked well with Billy, but trying it twice was pushing their luck.

"He knows me," Greer stated. "And the sheriff showing up on a night when most of the town is out of power won't surprise him one bit. He'll let me in."

"Power's out over there," Edwards said.

"Then he'll be happy I have a flashlight."

Zander had pulled the sheriff aside after a deputy arrived to take Billy Osburne to jail. "Billy pointed his finger at the mayor. How do you feel about that?"

The sheriff looked thoughtful. "What I feel doesn't matter. It's a serious accusation and needs to be followed up."

"But can you see him doing what Billy says?"

"Fuck no. I've known Harlan most of my life. Nicest guy imaginable. I expect we'll find out that Billy is full of shit, and I look forward to my next discussion with Billy. Hopefully he'll be more inclined to tell us the truth. Either way, he's admitted to murdering Nate and Sean Fitch." Fury colored the sheriff's tone.

"Think his brother was involved?" asked Zander.

"Next on my list."

Even with the sheriff's confidence, the four of them took the same positions as for the door knock at Billy's. Harlan Trapp's home wasn't deep in trees. It was part of a small subdivision with close neighbors. Luckily, no one had fenced yards. Zander and Edwards were close to each other near Harlan's back door. It was pitch-dark. No lighting at all. The mayor's little neighborhood looked like a town that'd been lost to zombies.

The sheriff parked in Harlan's driveway, and Zander waited.

Edwards's mic crackled. "No one's answering," said the sheriff. "And his car isn't in the garage."

"Knocking on the back door," answered Edwards.

Zander exhaled, and they both closed in on the sliding glass door to Harlan's patio. Edwards rapped on the glass with his flashlight. "Mr. Trapp! You home? Clatsop County Sheriff's Department."

A dog barked a few homes away, but no noise came from the house. Edwards repeated the knock and announcement.

"Seems like no one's here," said Zander as he finally looked through the door and gave the handle a small tug. Locked. He could make out furniture shapes inside but nothing else.

"Checking windows," said the sheriff over Edwards's mic. "Coming around the south side, Daigle's on the north."

A few moments later the four of them convened in the backyard.

"I checked the front door," Daigle said. "It was locked."

"Same with the back door."

"I'll head back to the station and see if Billy will talk a little more," said the sheriff. "You two get out the word with Harlan's license plate number and vehicle description," Greer said to his deputies. "If anyone spots it, they're to let me know first."

"I'll see if he's at the diner," said Zander. "That seems to be a meeting place when the power is out."

"Keep me updated," answered the sheriff.

◆◆◆

Zander scanned the diner but didn't see the bald head of Harlan Trapp. He took the small hallway to the office and found Dory sitting in a chair, happily flipping through photos. He recognized the folder that Simon Rhoads had given Emily. Zander liked the woman he thought of as Aunt #3. She was a little spacey but good-hearted and kind. She wore the same pale-yellow, thick sweater he'd seen earlier on her sisters.

"Evening, Dory, where's Emily at?"

Her face lit up as she saw him. "Special Agent Zander! How lovely to see you again. We need to have you back to the mansion for tea soon—well, as soon as we get power back. One time we lost power for five days. It was horrible." She held up a picture. "Can you tell which is me?"

The photo of the four elegant women made him smile. "You're the third. You looked a lot like Madison at that age."

"So you're saying I was a hottie?" She winked.

"Definitely. Did Emily—"

"I don't know where Emily got this file of photos, but it's brought back so many memories of when we were young. Now we get the senile-citizen rate," she said with laugh.

He winced, remembering that Simon had specifically asked Emily to not show it to Dory. "I imagine it has." He glanced at the photos spread across the desk, and one caught his attention, bringing a grin. "Is that the sheriff?" The men in the picture portrayed a group camaraderie that Zander had never experienced. He estimated that most were in their thirties or late twenties, fishing poles and tackle boxes at their feet. The sheriff was easy to pick out; he was as gaunt as he was today.

"Oh yes. That is Merrill. Can you guess who this is?" She pointed at a man.

Considering he'd been in town only five days, Zander wasn't surprised he couldn't place him. He shook his head.

She shuffled the photos. "Here's a better one."

It had been taken at the same time with the same men, but the face of the man she'd indicated was clearer. He struggled to place it.

"That's Lincoln. The girls' dad."

Now Zander recognized the man. He looked closer, recognizing that Emily had his eyes. Lincoln's hand caught his attention, and Zander tensed, ice filling his limbs. He immediately checked the hands of the rest of the men.

"Fuck," he whispered. He slid around the photos on the desk, finding two others that had been taken at the same time and comparing them.

"Dory, who is this?"

She studied the man. "Why that's our mayor, Harlan Trapp. I forgot he used to have hair." She giggled. "And there is Simon—he was a looker back then. Too bad he wasn't interested in me then. I might have said yes."

"Who are the other people?"

"Well, there's Rod Barton—he's Brenda's brother. Merrill Greer. I don't know the others."

Harlan Trapp stood next to Sheriff Greer, his right hand in front of his stomach, pointing at the sheriff with two fingers and his thumb. Lincoln Mills and the two men Dory didn't know were making the same gesture.

A KKK hand sign.

Harlan Trapp was a white supremacist. Along with Emily's father.

It added a little weight to Billy's assertion that Harlan had killed Sean Fitch.

Dammit. He wished Ava weren't out of commission. Zander needed to discuss this with someone. Now.

His gaze locked on Sheriff Greer, clearly buddies with the other men. No hand sign.

Was he part of it?

Do I tell him what I just discovered about the mayor?

The photos were twenty-five years old. They could mean nothing.

"Dory, where is Emily?"

"She and Madison are running an errand in this cockamamie weather. Picking up a fabulous surprise for my sisters."

"Madison went with her?"

"Yes."

At least she had taken her sister.

Who can I trust? He felt ill that he now had doubts about Sheriff Greer.

Did the sheriff warn Harlan Trapp that we were going to his home?

Vina.

Emily's aunt knew everything about everybody. But would she talk to him? Without holding back? "Thanks, Dory."

He left the office and hunted down Vina. She was on the floor, chatting at a table with a large family. Five kids. "Vina, can I talk to you in the kitchen?" She excused herself and followed him. Thea noticed and tagged along. The two women had curious looks as he led them to a quiet corner and showed them the photos of the group of men. "Can you identify these men?"

The two women exclaimed over the photos, stating they'd never seen them before. They confirmed all of Dory's identifications, and, like Dory, couldn't name two of the men. "I think those guys were from the coast guard," suggested Thea.

"No. I'm pretty sure they're friends of Lincoln's from Portland," countered Vina. "I remember this person. He upset Brenda about something."

Thea moved her nose nearly to the picture and then agreed with Vina. "Portland folks." Her nose wrinkled as she said it.

"I'm Portland folks," Zander said, curious as to the distaste in Thea's tone.

"But you're a nice guy," Thea said earnestly. "You treat our Emily well."

He nearly coughed.

Vina nodded. "We've seen it."

"And these guys weren't nice?"

"I wish Lincoln hadn't hung around with them," added Thea. "Things might have been different."

"You need to explain."

The women looked at each other and shrugged. "You know," added Vina, as if that answered everything.

They know what he was.

"Look here." Zander pointed at Lincoln's hands. "See anything odd?"

The women studied the photo. "No."

"What if I told you he's making a white supremacist hand signal?"

Neither woman flinched.

That tells me more than anything they've said.

"If that's so, then three others are doing the same," said Thea.

"Correct." Zander waited a long moment. "You once told me this town had an ugly underbelly, Vina. I took it as there was some racism, but did you know these men were associated with that sort of hate?"

The women were quiet.

He took that as a yes. "Your mayor, Harlan Trapp. What do you know about him?" He studied the women as he waited for an answer. Vina was better at hiding her thoughts, her appearance calm and serene. Thea was twitchy, her gaze unable to settle anywhere.

"There were rumors," Vina finally said. "There are always rumors . . . about everybody."

"I suspect you know which rumors to ignore and which to give a little more credence to."

Thea licked her lips, her right leg bouncing. "Harlan attended those meetings."

"What meetings?"

"In Portland. Lincoln went to them too. But he'd been raised by parents who believed the same. When he moved here from North Carolina, I think he felt like a fish out of water. He found what he needed with this group in Portland. And as long as he kept it to himself, we tolerated him with Brenda—we primarily had issues with the way he manipulated her. She wouldn't stand up for herself. But every now and then, his group would come to the coast and be obnoxious—no hoods and white robes, of course. They didn't do that sort of thing, but they'd drink and cause havoc in town—just blowing off steam like men do."

Zander bit his tongue. He'd never blown off steam that way. But apparently the women had tolerated Lincoln Mills as long as he kept his active racism behind closed doors.

It was a different generation.

"Did this Portland group have a name?" asked Zander.

The women considered. "Not that I remember," said Thea. Vina agreed.

"Did all the men in the picture belong to Lincoln's Portland group?" he asked.

"Oh, no. I'm sure Lincoln and Harlan were just hamming it up," said Vina. "Probably showing off. They liked to talk the big talk, you know."

Boys will be boys.

"What about Sheriff Greer? What was his reputation?"

Vina tipped her head and looked at Thea thoughtfully. "Merrill was always a quiet one. Not the brightest man, but dependable." Thea nodded in agreement.

"So you don't know if he was a member of this Portland group."

"Correct."

"Thank you," said Zander. The women went back to socialize with their guests, and Zander studied the pictures. *Am I jumping to conclusions about Harlan?*

He still couldn't decide if he should talk to the sheriff.

I'm getting worked up about a twenty-five-year-old photo that shows a few jerks.

He took the photos back to the office, where Dory was looking frustrated.

"Agent Zander? The girls are taking way too long. I've tried to call them, but neither are answering their phones." Her soft face was lined with worry.

Yesterday's car accident flashed in his head. "Where did they go?"

"Well . . . it's a surprise."

"Dory, you can tell me. The surprise is for your sisters." Tension ratcheted up his spine. "You're clearly concerned. I can't help unless I know where they are."

"They went to get Tara. Vina and Thea will be so excited!" She clasped her hands, glee on her face.

Emily told them about Tara?

"Madison and Emily are driving to Beaverton?"

"Of course not, Tara is here."

Is Dory confused?

"Tara is in town, Dory?"

"Well, we assume she's gone here." Dory touched a photo of a young couple on a ridge above the ocean.

Lincoln and Brenda Mills.

"I saw Tara turn onto Seabound Road. There's only one place to go on that road." Dory triumphantly picked up the picture of the parents. "This park."

She saw Tara?

"That's where Madison and Emily are? This park? Right now?"

She looked at him over the top of her glasses. "Didn't I just say that?"

"And they know Tara is there?" He struggled to believe that Tara had come to Bartonville.

"It's the only logical place."

"Tell me how to get there."

34

Emily held her breath, her mind reeling as Madison peered over the steering wheel in the dark. Why had Tara come to town when she'd clearly stated she wanted nothing to do with the family? Had Dory mistaken someone else for Tara again?

Emily's phone vibrated with a text.

Did you mean it when you said you wanted me back in your life no matter what I'd done?

Emily's lungs seized. She'd shoved her cell number into Tara's mother-in-law's hand, begging her to give it to Tara, as Wendy had showed her and Zander the door.

Apparently Wendy had listened.

Yes

What if someone is dead because of me?

It doesn't matter

Emily waited, holding her breath.

Madison shot her several glances. "Who is it?"

"It's Tara."

The vehicle jerked as Madison gasped.

"It's not what you think," Emily said quickly. "I started to tell you earlier that Zander found her. He took me to her house in Beaverton today, and I left her my phone number—I've had absolutely no contact with her since she left us."

"Emily . . ." Madison seemed speechless.

"She has a daughter, Madison. Her name's Bella, and she looks exactly like Tara."

"Oh my God." Madison stomped on the brakes just in time to avoid driving through a stop sign. "*Why didn't you tell me?*" Fury filled her sister's voice.

"It *just* happened. I'm still trying to process the visit."

Her phone vibrated again.

What if that person who died because of me is Mom?

Emily's lungs fought for air.

"What is it? What'd she say?" Madison tried to see the screen, and the car veered.

"Watch the road!" Emily snapped.

"You had no right to hide this from me!"

"I hid nothing. I was going to tell you as soon as . . ." She honestly didn't know if she would have told Madison. "Tara didn't want anything to do with us today. She made Zander and me leave." Her voice cracked, the pain still fresh. "She was a wreck—her mental health is poor, and I think she's an alcoholic." The last word was a whisper. "She denies she was there that night."

Emily stared at Tara's last text about their mother. *How do I reply?*

We love you

Her screen blurred.

Please come home

"But you told me you saw Tara there the night Dad was killed."

"Maybe I was wrong." Had she lived with a false memory all these years?

"Why is she here? Why didn't she come to the diner?" Madison asked, rejection ringing in her words.

"I don't know." The fear she'd seen on Tara's face was fresh in Emily's mind.

"Fucking ask!"

Where are you?

Emily waited, her fingers strangling her phone. Madison took the turn onto Seabound Road, and the road sloped upward. Seabound was a twisting, nausea-creating drive that climbed several hundred feet, winding through a crowded forest and ending at a small park with the overlook where her parents had posed.

"I can't see," Madison muttered. Her headlights aimed away from the road as they came upon hairpin curves, making her steer through blind turns. "Shit!" She stopped, and Emily looked up from her phone.

The park gate was closed, the road blocked. Two vehicles were parked on their side of the gate. One looked like the little Mercedes SUV that Emily had seen in Tara's driveway. "She's here."

Dory was right.

"But why?" asked Madison. "Why would she come here?" She gulped, and her voice choked. "You said Tara was a mess. Did she come here to *kill herself?*"

She's going to jump from the overlook.

"She just asked if I cared that it's her fault that Mom is dead." Emily opened her door, her heart in her throat. "We've got to stop her. Call 911."

Don't do anything! Madison and I are coming to the overlook. Please wait!

Why am I texting? Emily hit the CALL button, ignoring Madison as her sister spoke to a dispatcher.

Tara didn't answer her phone.

"Let's go!" She and Madison ducked between the metal bars of the gate and started to jog, her phone at her ear as she dialed Tara again.

"The police are sending someone. I told them the gate is locked," Madison panted as they ran.

"The overlook is nearly a half mile from here," Emily said. "And mostly uphill." The last painkiller had exited her system, and her head throbbed, her legs already weak. *Can I do this?*

"I don't understand what's going on," Madison breathed.

"That makes two of us," Emily replied, sucking in air. "But I know she's deathly scared of something. Something happened after—or during—Dad's death that made her leave and stay away all this time." She switched on her phone's flashlight, and Madison did the same. There was nothing but trees along the road between the gate and the park, making her suspect that Tara wouldn't do whatever she planned to do before she got to the overlook.

The ground rushed up at Emily, and she stumbled. Her phone flew and her palms grated along the blacktop. Agony shot up her nerves and exploded in her brain.

"Emily!" Madison grabbed her arm and hauled her to her feet. She shone her phone's flashlight in her sister's eyes, and Emily batted it away. "I forgot about your head injury. Are you okay?"

"I'm fine," Emily wheezed, her palms and knees stinging. She closed her eyes against the pain as bile rose in the back of her throat.

"I'll go ahead. You take it easy."

"No!" Emily pulled her arm out of Madison's grip and went after her phone, a small beacon of light on the shoulder of the road. "Shit." The screen was a spiderweb of cracks under her screen protector. She pressed the button several times. Nothing happened. She couldn't even turn off the flashlight.

I don't need this right now.

"We can't stop." Emily took off at a slow jog, her head pounding in time to her strides.

"You're nuts," Madison muttered, but she didn't try to stop her.

They ran in silence for several minutes, Emily believing every step would be her last.

"Dad's pocket watch," Madison finally said. "You know the quote inside?"

"Yes." Emily didn't have the breath to say anything else.

"It's associated with the KKK." Madison was silent for three steps. "I think Dad had been a member—or belonged to a similar group."

Emily processed her words. *That meeting long ago . . .*

"I think I may have subconsciously known that," Emily panted, "but ignored it."

"You knew?"

"Sorta. I can see it in hindsight. I was clueless to a lot of things as a kid. You asked what I picked up in the yard the night Dad died."

"Yes."

Emily struggled for breath to speak, the pain in her lungs matching her head. "I found some coinlike things in the grass that night, but they weren't money. I'd seen them before in one of his drawers." She stopped and rested her hands on her thighs, gasping for air. "I took them and hid them. We lost *everything* in the fire, and I thought of them as mine afterward. Something of his that was just for me, and I didn't want to share. If Mom saw them, I knew she would take them back."

"I found them in your things a long time ago."

Emily wasn't surprised. "I researched them online a few years back. They're not coins, they're tokens. A lot of groups make personalized tokens—the Masons or branches of the military. These were from a white supremacist group in Portland, and I didn't understand why he would have them."

Madison was silent.

"But I put them away after I learned that," Emily whispered. "I didn't know what to think about the coins and Dad. I remembered . . ." Memories flared.

"Remembered what?"

"I think Dad took me to some of *those* meetings. I didn't know what they were."

The wind in the trees was the only sound.

"I think everyone knew but us," Madison said softly. "It doesn't matter now. Come on." She took Emily's arm again. "We're almost there."

The cracks of two gunshots echoed through the forest.

35

Zander's headlights lit up three vehicles at the park gate, including Madison's car and a Mercedes that he recognized from Tara's home.

She is here.

He didn't know the third car. He called Sheriff Greer.

"Greer."

"It's Wells. Can you run a plate for me? I'm on the road."

The sheriff grunted. "Give me a minute."

"Has Billy said more?" Zander asked.

"Sticking to the same story. I had two deputies go pick up his brother, who is just fine, by the way, and thinks Billy is full of shit. Okay. Give me the plate."

Zander rattled off the plate.

"That's Harlan Trapp's vehicle. Where are you?"

A million questions burst in Zander's head.

Did Harlan follow Emily?

Nate Copeland's dead body filled his vision, quickly followed by Harlan Trapp and the sheriff in the old photo of men.

Who can I trust?

From a distance two shots were fired, and he flinched, his throat going dry. *Emily?*

"Where are you? Who's shooting?" the sheriff roared.

Zander made a decision about trust as he grabbed his tactical vest for the second time that day. "I'm on Seabound Road at the gate. It's locked. Emily and Madison are inside somewhere, and I assume Harlan is too. I don't know who fired the shots."

"I'll be there in ten minutes. Sending deputies now."

"Tell them I'm heading inside."

The sheriff paused. "I will."

Zander glanced at the Mercedes as he fastened his vest.

Why is Tara here?

He bent, stepped between the gate's bars, and silently ran up the road, listening hard, expecting more gunshots. The wind and the smell of the ocean grew stronger as he covered some distance. He didn't know exactly where he was going, but he figured he'd know it when he got there.

There were no turnoffs or footpaths leading from the road—that much he could see in the dark. He didn't use a flashlight, preferring not to draw attention or gunfire toward himself.

The roar of another shot made him drop to the ground, his heart hammering.

A man was yelling, but Zander couldn't make out the words.

He jumped to his feet and continued his trek.

"She didn't jump, she shot herself!" Emily gasped as the sound of the two shots faded away.

"Maybe whoever parked the second car at the gate fired the shot—maybe it's kids fooling around," Madison said in an uncertain tone. "It could have nothing to do with her."

That explanation wasn't good enough for Emily. She broke into a run, and Madison followed.

"You thought I would trust you?"

Emily slammed to a stop as Madison grabbed her arm. There was no mistaking the fury in the male voice up ahead.

"Who is that?" Madison whispered.

"You thought you could lure me to this place and shoot me?" A roar of laughter followed.

Emily knew the laugh and voice but couldn't connect them with a face.

"I've been searching for you for years, you fucking bitch!"

"That's Harlan Trapp," Madison whispered, her nails digging into Emily's arm.

"I don't understand." Emily's brain spun.

"He's yelling at Tara."

His words sank in.

Harlan has been looking for Tara for years. Tara was scared of someone hurting her . . .

Pieces snapped together in her mind.

"Could Tara have left because someone threatened her life? The only thing worth hurting someone over is if they witnessed . . ."

Tara running through the woods the night Dad was killed.

"Maybe she saw who killed Dad . . . Could it be *Harlan*?" Emily's instincts fought against her conclusion. She'd known Harlan Trapp all her life.

"Come out, come out, come out, little girl!"

He was hunting Tara, his words echoing through the forest. "She must still be alive," Emily said in hushed words.

"And hiding," finished Madison. "We should do the same before he spots us." She turned off her phone's flashlight, and Emily powered hers down, the screen buttons unusable.

The two of them moved off the narrow road and into the trees. Emily's eyes finally adjusted, and she could see the hazy shape of Madison's face.

"You thought you could pull a gun on me? Me? I'm the fucking mayor!"

The women slowly crept through the trees, keeping the road in sight and watching for Harlan or Tara. The road widened and fed into a small parking lot. Emily had visited only two or three times since she nearly slid off the cliff as a child. Each time she'd stayed far from the overlook fence, nausea heavy in her stomach. The big metal swing sets, tetherball poles, and slides from her childhood were still present, the swings swaying with the wind, the chains of the tetherballs clanking against their poles.

Harlan paced at the far end as he yelled, a faint silhouette against the dark sky.

"You're a whore!"

"I think he's between us and Tara," Emily whispered. "Now what?"

"Wait for the police."

"What if she's hurt? I don't even hear sirens yet!" Stress built in Emily's shoulders.

"Maybe they thought sirens would spook someone who might be considering suicide," Madison whispered.

"Who the fuck knew two sisters could cause me such problems?"

"Two sisters? Who else? Me?" gasped Emily.

"You were shot at yesterday," Madison hissed. "I bet he was trying to clean up his mess. First Nate Copeland and then you."

"But why would he kill Sean and Lindsay?"

"I don't know, but right now all I care about is that my sisters are on his list. We need to get out of here."

"I'm *not* leaving Tara."

"We can't help!" Madison said in a low voice.

A faint siren finally sounded. Help was coming.

"That took long enough." But it didn't give Emily the relief she needed.

Harlan heard it too and let out a string of profanities. *"Your family is the rot in this town! Your father was the worst of all!"*

"Look!" A black shape crawled along the ocean side of the parking lot. Emily dropped to her knees to see the person's form against the dark sky. She yanked Madison down beside her.

Tara.

"She's dragging. She's hurt," she whispered as she watched Tara lower herself flat to the ground and roll under the overlook's fence at the edge of the park. Harlan continued to pace and shout a dozen yards from where she'd seen Tara vanish. "She went under the fence."

Madison swallowed audibly. "There are some places to hide safely on the other side."

"One loose rock and she's gone." Emily shuddered, remembering the terror of clinging to the cliffside rocks.

The place where Emily had nearly lost her life.

"If we backtrack a bit and cross the road, we can follow the fence on its other side until we reach Tara," she told Madison. "He probably won't see us."

"No! There's a reason for that fence. We both know how unstable that ridge can be."

"But we can get her out. We can crawl back."

"Wait for the police!"

"But what if she's hurt?" Tara's dragging movements hadn't left Emily's thoughts. "Minutes could mean the difference between life and death if she needs a tourniquet or something."

"You're crazy," Madison hissed.

"I'm going."

"Dammit! *Fine.* I'll go meet the police," said Madison. "They should know what they're walking into. *Be careful.*"

Emily jogged back through the woods until she couldn't see the parking lot and then crossed the road to the trees on the other side. She wound through them until she spotted the fence. She estimated it was nearly fifty yards to reach the spot in the fence where her sister had vanished. Her head threatening to split with pain, Emily went under the fence and started to crawl, the surface treacherous with roots and loose rocks. The slope had several deadly steep areas, but if she stuck close to the fence, it was flat enough.

Sweat formed along her spine at the thought of being spotted by Harlan, but he was focused on searching the other side of the park.

Her hair blew around her face, and the poor light along with the crash of the waves far below made her wobble.

Harlan continued to rant. His shouts would get closer and then move away as he changed direction, his voice often hard to hear over the roar of the ocean.

Anxiety and strain fueled his words; the police had to be close. The sirens had stopped, making Emily assume they'd reached the gate. *They'll walk up the road, right?* The park hadn't opened for the spring yet, and she doubted the police had contacted the parks department for a key.

Madison would meet them.

Emily's level area near the fence suddenly narrowed, and she clung to the bottom rail to keep moving. Terror swamped her, and she pushed away the memory of clinging to rocks and weeds, screaming for her father. She moved on, one knee in front of the other. The ledge widened, and she paused to catch her breath, her heart pounding.

Keep going.

She glanced behind her, distressed at how short a distance she'd come.

Keep going.

She continued to move, feeling as if an hour had passed. Then she saw Tara.

Her sister was on the ocean side of a giant rock, where the land broadened sufficiently. It was the same rock where their parents had posed for the photo. The space between Tara and the drop-off was narrow. In that spot it was less likely Harlan would see her if he came to the fence.

But not a perfect hiding spot.

Her sister lay as close as possible to the rock. She was very still. Emily scooted closer, "Tara," she whispered.

Tara's head lifted. "Emily?" Her voice was weak.

As she reached Tara, Emily took her hand. It was wet and sticky. Shocked, Emily nearly dropped it, and the odor reached her nose. Blood.

In the poor light, she saw that Tara's pants were glossy with blood. "Where are you hurt?"

"My side." Tara's right hand was clamped against it. "I'm okay."

"No, you're not," Emily said. She slipped off her coat, lifted Tara's hand, and pressed it against the wound. Her sister gasped but replaced her hand to hold it.

"I want you to help Wendy with Bella," Tara whispered.

"Not now, Tara." Emily arranged the coat, her throat tightening.

"Wendy can do it, but I want you and Madison in Bella's life."

"Cut it out! You're not going to die." Emily gritted her teeth, terrified she was lying.

"Harlan threatened to kill all of you unless I left town."

"I figured," Emily whispered, her heart cracking in half.

"When I heard Mom died, I thought he was carrying out his promise. I've been terrified ever since—looking over my shoulder nonstop. When my husband died, I believed for months that Harlan had caused the accident."

"*Oh, Tara.* Why didn't you go to the police?"

"I couldn't trust anyone. Harlan told me there were several people involved."

Who?

"He'll never stop hunting me," said Tara. "He met me here because I said I wanted to talk. I brought a gun—I planned to kill him," she whispered harshly. "I just wanted a life where I wasn't petrified every day and didn't worry that he might hurt my daughter." Tara's words grew slower and slower. "I chickened out when I had the chance to shoot him first. He shot me, and I shot back." She laughed almost silently. "Then I dropped the fucking gun but managed to get to the woods. He never planned to talk; he came here to kill me too."

"Where did you drop the gun?"

"No. You can't do that!"

"Where did you drop the gun?"

Tara exhaled. "By the swing set. You'll never make it. He'll see you."

"I have to try."

36

"Zander!"

The female voice came from the trees to his right, and he halted his dash up the road. A light shone in his eyes. He raised a hand to block it. "Madison?"

"Where are the police?" She lowered her light.

"They're coming. Where's Emily?"

"She stayed with Tara. We think she was shot—"

"By Harlan?" Zander continued up the road, Madison following.

"Yes! How did you know?"

"His car is at the gate. I think he's the one who fired at Emily yesterday."

"He's going to kill Tara if someone doesn't stop him."

"How much farther is it?"

"The parking lot is just around the next bend. He was at the far end, and Emily was headed to find Tara on the ocean side of the fence."

"Where?"

"Beyond the fence there is a big drop-off, but there's a little room in some spots. People aren't supposed to cross the fence—the land's unstable."

Fuck.

Emily and Tara are on that side of the fence.

"Go down the road. Tell the deputies coming up that he's armed, and that me and two other women are here."

"What are you going to do?"

"Stop him." He took off at a dead run.

"Stick to the woods!" she yelled after him.

Emily crawled around the swing set, wishing Tara had been more specific about where she dropped the gun. Harlan was now searching in the woods at the far end of the parking lot, cursing and yelling for Tara. Emily frantically brushed her hands over the wood chips, feeling very exposed and silently pleading for the gun to appear. Tara's hiding place wasn't too bad, but if he checked along the fence, he'd probably spot her.

Emily would defend her sister until the police arrived. And to do that she needed the gun. Dust from the decomposing wood chips blew in her eyes, and they watered, making her limited vision worse. She crawled back to a place she'd already searched, convinced she'd missed the weapon. Hurriedly, she checked again. No gun.

The pain in her head throbbed. *What if Harlan picked it up?*

She could be wasting her time.

A figure moved out of the woods, and she dropped to her stomach, holding her breath, her gaze glued to the shape. Harlan strode determinedly to the fence.

He gave up on the woods.

Panic made her stomach churn.

How can I stop him?

Searching around, she spotted the chain that intermittently clanked against a tetherball pole, its ball missing. She checked Harlan. His back was to her. She rose and dashed to the pole, her back hunched, praying he didn't turn around.

Gripping the cold metal pole, she stretched, straining her arms, rising on tiptoe and reaching for the junction of the chain and pole, hoping it wasn't a fused attachment. Her fingers found the end, and she blindly explored the final link. One side moved and she pressed it, opening the link, and then she unhooked it from the pole. Relief made her knees weak.

She clutched the chilled chain; it was no match for a gun.

But it was something.

Harlan reached the fence and followed it. He'd find Tara's hiding spot in a few seconds.

Emily ran silently to the parking lot, her heart in her throat.

◆◆◆

Zander took Madison's advice and veered down the shoulder of the road and into the trees. It slowed him down. He could barely see where to put his feet and tripped a dozen times. The parking lot came into view and he stopped, searching for Harlan.

He must have heard the sirens. Where would he go?

Harlan had to know he was cornered. Dory had told Zander there was only one way in and out of the park.

Unless you went into the ocean.

Would Harlan react like a cornered animal with nothing to lose?

He had been dangerous to start with. Now he might be worse.

No one was in the parking lot. Dory had described green spaces with playground equipment along the wooded side of the lot and then steep ocean cliffs on the other side. He aimed for the ocean side, straining his vision to make out the fence Madison had mentioned.

Emily's mind was blank, her gaze locked on Harlan's silhouette as she ran. The cold chain tight in her hands. She had no plan, just determination. And fear.

Harlan stopped and leaned over the fence, his back to Emily.

He spotted Tara.

He said something, but he was facing the ocean, and the wind blew his words away.

Emily drew closer, her racing footsteps silent, and spotted the shape of a gun in his hand.

He stepped on the lower rail of the fence and swung one leg over, his weapon trained on the large boulder coming into Emily's view. Tara's rock.

He'll see me when he lifts his other leg over the fence.

She was sprinting across the parking lot; there was nowhere to hide.

Instead of turning to face her, Harlan sat on the top rail, kept his gun aimed toward the rock, and awkwardly brought his second leg over. He jumped down, his focus on Tara.

His caution was Emily's advantage.

She leaped to the middle rail, took one step to the top, and launched herself at Harlan's back. The impact sent him forward, landing on his knees and falling to his chest. Tuning out his shouts, Emily scrambled and got her weight on a knee in the center of his back and wrapped the chain around his neck. Once and then twice.

His hand caught inside the loop at his neck, allowing some breathing room. He flailed his other arm, and his weapon fired twice. Emily's ears rang, but she ignored the shots, focused on gathering a length of chain in each hand to increase the pressure around his neck. He thrashed, yanking on the chain at his neck and trying to throw her off his back. She pulled, leaning back, the chain too long between his neck and her hands. It was like riding a bucking horse.

Her knee slipped to one side, losing her point of pressure on his back, and he scrambled out from under her, one hand still stuck at his neck. On his hands and knees, he tried to turn to face her.

Noooo!

She hauled back on the chain, and he hacked and choked but swung his weapon backward and fired. A piercing pain bolted up her calf. She leaned back farther, practically on her back to keep the chain taut.

Tara scooted over and, from her position on the ground, kicked and shoved his legs and hips, screaming and effectively pushing his body toward the edge of the cliff.

She'll hang him.

If I let go, he'll fall to the rocks and ocean below. If I don't let go, he'll hang.

Hot fire burned in her lower leg. She couldn't think.

One of Tara's kicks knocked the gun from his hand, but not out of reach. Her foot hit the weapon again, causing it to skid away, and then she continued her barrage to push him off the edge.

"Tara! Stop!"

Harlan made horrible, angry choking sounds, yet Emily held strong to the chains.

Do I let go?

If she let go now, he could grab his weapon.

Tara shrieked and kicked with both her feet at once. Harlan thrashed to push away from the edge, and the ground under his legs crumbled and vanished. His fall yanked Emily forward, and she dug in her heels. He faced her now, most of his body dangling off the edge, held from falling by the chain around his neck. His loose hand grabbed desperately at dirt, seeking a purchase. Emily couldn't see the terror in his eyes, but she felt it.

Her damaged leg collapsed, and her foot slipped. His body dropped another six inches.

"Tara! Grab him!"

Her sister sat still, her chest heaving, one hand still clamped to her side where she bled. With a soft moan, Tara lay on her back, her energy drained. Harlan's weight pulled Emily closer to the edge, a slow but steady slide. She saw herself clinging to the cliff as a child, screaming for her father. The old terror sent ice through her veins.

Emily's vision narrowed, and dizziness swamped her. A pool of blood glistened in the dirt under her leg.

I have to let go.

I'm sorry.

Hands grabbed the chain near hers. *Madison.* "I've got him," she told Emily. Suddenly Zander was there, stretched out on his stomach, dispersing his weight, and reaching over the edge.

He yanked Harlan up by his belt, and Emily fell back, her muscles powerless. Zander pulled Harlan to a safe distance and unwrapped the chain. The man wheezed and swore. Rolling Harlan to his stomach, Zander fastened his wrists with a zip tie.

He finally turned to Emily, his face close to hers. His mouth moved. "Are you all right?" She barely heard his words as consciousness slipped away.

"I don't think so."

37

Two days later

A scabbing red band circled Harlan's neck.

Sitting across from the man in a small room at the county jail, Zander didn't feel sorry for him. The band was a glaring reminder of Emily's and Tara's fight to live.

Harlan Trapp had aged ten years in two days. Fury and anger burned in Zander. Harlan had left a path of death and destruction behind him for twenty years . . . maybe more. What kind of ego had made him run for mayor in a town that he'd haunted and torn apart?

"Start with Cynthia Green," Zander ordered. "She was nineteen."

He shrugged, and Zander ached to punch him.

"Don't know who you're talking about."

"What if I told you we were led to that girl by someone who watched your group leave her body by a downed tree? They were too scared to come forward until now." *A stretch of the truth.*

Alice Penn would never be a credible witness. She'd known Harlan for years and never said anything. *Did she even know it was him?*

Harlan mulled it over, chewing on one lip.

"Cynthia Green's body wasn't found by accident. This witness is ready to talk after twenty years." *Another stretch.*

Harlan sat back in his chair, a decision on his face. "It was an opportunity. There were a lot of talkers in our group—"

"Your race-hating white supremacist group in Portland."

"Your words."

"You bet they're my words, and they'll be your prosecuting attorney's words too."

"I had a bunch of guys out for the weekend—some new initiates—and we spotted the girl."

"Membership in your exclusive club required killing someone?"

"No." He leaned on his forearms, holding Zander's gaze. "But people were ready to prove themselves. Who was I to stand in their way?"

Zander closed his eyes as he controlled his rage, a bitter taste in his mouth.

"Everyone participated but Lincoln Mills," Harlan said with disgust. "It's always the biggest braggers, right? They boast and swagger to fit in when they *know* they're not made of the right stuff. He was all talk, and when it came time to man up, he failed. Tried to stop us from taking the girl."

"Lincoln's punishment was his death?"

Harlan looked away. "There were rumors that he would go to the police about the black girl."

"You cleaned house before that could happen."

"Something like that."

"Who were the other men?"

"I gave Sheriff Greer a list of names."

"What about Greer? He hung around with some of you guys back then."

Harlan scoffed. "Seriously? He has no backbone."

Zander disagreed. He'd had issues with the sheriff when he first walked the scene of the Fitch murders, but the sheriff had earned his respect. He truly cared about the people who lived in his county.

"Were there any other victims besides Cynthia Green?" Zander had checked closely for missing persons and unsolved crimes in the area involving people of color but hadn't found any.

Harlan looked away. "I heard there was some activity in Portland. I wasn't there. Can't really help you. All I heard were rumors . . . no names."

Right.

"How did Sean Fitch get involved?"

Harlan shifted in his seat, discomfort on his face. "Simon Rhoads sent him my way. Said he had questions about the history of the area."

Zander waited.

Licking his lips, Harlan went on. "He had a bunch of questions about shanghaiing around here. One of my ancestors ran a tavern that was infamous for it. Along with the information I had on my relative's operation, I showed him some old trinkets that I had. Some scrimshaw, some rings and bracelets, a diary." He scowled. "A pocket watch."

Aha.

"He flipped the watch open, looked at it, and then set it back with the other stuff. He asked if he could come back again if he had more questions, and I agreed. He was back two days later. He brought a few historic pictures of Bartonville from Simon. Some weren't that old. He'd told me Simon had identified most of the men in one of the pictures, and he asked if I knew the rest since I was in one of the photos."

"I think I know the photo you're talking about. Are Lincoln Mills and the sheriff in it?"

"Yeah. I didn't know it was still around. Simon keeps everything. I said I couldn't remember the two unidentified men, and Sean didn't believe me. He was fired up and angry. Got in my face. Said his research told him Lincoln was involved with some nationalist groups and shoved the pocket watch in my face like it was some sort of proof. I told him he was full of shit, but he was raging." Harlan glowered. "Then he asked about Cynthia Green's disappearance."

Surprise struck Zander. "He figured out you were involved in that?"

"Not exactly. I think he was grasping at straws, but he caught me off guard, and my reaction convinced him he was onto something. He kept pushing—wouldn't shut up. He jumped to Lincoln's death and asked me if I'd specifically chosen a hanging to make a point."

Zander tried to imagine what it had taken for the young man—who everyone swore was the nicest guy around—to accuse the town mayor of murder. Twice. Sean's dead face flashed in Zander's mind, and admiration for the high school teacher flared.

Why do people like that get punished while the slime before me still lives?

"Sounds like Sean had your number."

"When he left that night, I saw the pocket watch was gone. The watch has Mills's initials in it along with—"

"A Klan saying. I've seen the watch. It was found at the Fitch murders. Sean saw it in your possession, saw you in a photo with other white supremacists, probably did a little research into the Mills hanging and discovered a mention of a missing pocket watch—"

"Yes, there's an article where Brenda Mills is quoted begging for the watch's return, saying her husband always carried it with him."

Zander enjoyed the sullen expression on Harlan's face as he acknowledged that his own actions had tripped him up.

"I searched for the watch at the Fitches'," said Harlan. "Didn't find it."

Sean must have had it on him when he was dragged outside.

"You decided Sean had to die before he went to the police and suggested that they look at you for Lincoln Mills's hanging."

Harlan was silent.

"How'd you get Billy to help you?"

"A little money goes a long way with Billy. And a threat to turn in evidence that he was dealing GHB."

"Who drugged the Fitches?"

"Billy. He and his brother deal a little GHB on the side. It's not hard to make. He added it to a bottle of wine and told Lindsay to share it with Sean that night. She and Billy had a thing going, you know." Harlan's leer turned Zander's stomach. "Well, maybe not a *thing*. She was a little drunk one night at the bar a few weeks ago and hooked up with him. After that he blackmailed her by threatening to tell her husband about that night. Claims he had pictures."

"I can't see Lindsay having anything to do with an ass like Billy, no matter how much she had to drink." Both Emily and Madison had adored the woman.

"Well . . . I suspect Billy mighta put something in her drink that first night."

Zander wasn't shocked; Billy Osburne's actions no longer surprised him. "Why Lindsay?" he asked. "You didn't have to kill her too."

"She's a race traitor."

Chills locked Zander's limbs at the ugly words. Harlan Trapp was pure hate. The medical examiner's description of the huge number of stab wounds in both bodies echoed in his head. Zander had suspected a high level of anger was involved.

He had been right.

"I had more issues with her actions than Sean's. She married the piece of shit and then cheated on him with Billy. Cheap whore."

"I assume he drugged Nate Copeland's beer before killing him. Did Nate see you at the Fitches'?"

"I wasn't sure. Billy and I were in the woods behind the home when Emily and then Nate arrived. We stayed too late trying to get the fire to take hold . . . shoulda left as soon as we saw Emily, but I wanted as much evidence destroyed as possible."

"You decided to play it safe and eliminate any possible witnesses." Zander held very still. "You shot at Emily."

Harlan scratched his arm. "Was just trying to scare her."

"Bullshit. You were starting to panic and getting sloppy. You don't scare people, you kill them. You nearly killed an FBI agent *and* Emily that day."

The man simply looked at him. No regret.

"Who dumped dead animals at the Barton Mansion?"

Harlan snorted. "That's all Billy's doing, stupid fuck. He did some tire slashing too. He holds a long-standing grudge against the Bartons that goes back to the mill closing and his father losing his job. Idiot. As if those three old hens had anything to do with it closing."

Standards à la Harlan.

"The fire you set at Lincoln Mills's death could have killed his entire family."

A muscle twitched in Harlan's cheek.

"Why in the hell did this town elect you mayor? From what I've heard, your name's been connected to racism rumors for years."

Harlan looked confused. "Do you really think people care? They were just rumors. And besides, I've done a lot of good for this town."

Zander didn't agree. "How do you feel about Chet Carlson spending twenty years in prison?"

"He shouldn't have been so stupid and pled guilty." Harlan wrinkled his brow in puzzlement. "Who admits to a murder they didn't do?"

Harlan Trapp would spend the rest of his life in prison. Zander should feel elated that Harlan wasn't fighting the charges, but instead he felt drained and empty from the exposure to how Harlan's brain worked. It was narcissistic. Indifferent. Twisted.

Zander was done asking him questions.

But he had questions for Tara.

38

After leaving the county jail, Zander drove to the mansion. The weather had cleared, showing cloudless skies for the first time since Zander had arrived at the coast. The ocean and sky were rich blues, but the temperature was a chilly forty-five.

Tara and Emily had been treated and released from the hospital that morning. Both of their gunshot injuries had caused muscle damage and heavy bleeding. Zander had checked in with both of them several times. The doctors were optimistic about their recovery, but neither woman would be up and about very soon.

Vina let him into the mansion and directed him upstairs when he asked for Tara. He knocked on the open door to a bedroom where Tara sat in a rocking chair, staring out a window.

She jumped at the knock and then winced, a hand going to her side. "Agent Wells."

"Call me Zander."

Her brown gaze eyed him skeptically, but she agreed. "What can I do for you?"

"I have a few questions."

"You and everybody else. I've already talked to detectives from the county and state police departments. I hoped you would give me a break." A small twitch at the corner of her lips told him she was teasing.

In that second she reminded him of Emily. Her smile and the shape of her face were like Madison's, but the attitude and intensity in her eyes at the moment were all Emily.

"Did I thank you for the other night?" she asked. Then she scowled. "Maybe I shouldn't thank you. He's still alive because of you."

"You didn't want him to go over the cliff."

"Wanna bet?" she asked softly.

"What happened the night your dad died?" he asked abruptly, slightly disturbed by the truth he'd heard in her words.

She looked back out the window. "I'm not sure."

She's lying. He waited.

"We were high," she finally said. "I wanted to believe it was a dream."

"You and who?"

Fierce eyes met his. "My friend doesn't remember anything. And Harlan never saw her, so he doesn't know she was there. I didn't bring her into it back then, and I won't now." She swallowed hard. "From what I can put together, my friend and I had returned to my house in the middle of the night. I'm not sure why. Somehow she drove us there and back, both of us high as kites."

"You're lucky you didn't kill anyone."

Guilt flashed.

"*You* didn't kill anyone," Zander told her, understanding she felt partially responsible for her parents' deaths in some twisted way.

She didn't appear convinced. "I think we'd come to the house to sneak in and get some more pot from my room."

"You kept pot in your bedroom?" *Emily was right. Tara was there that night.*

"I was a teenager." She frowned. "With very snoopy sisters, I knew how to hide things. I don't think either one ever found it."

"What did you see outside?"

Tara took a deep breath. "I don't remember seeing my father, but I think I remember several men outside the house and having an overwhelming need to hide from them. I don't know why—it was just a feeling. Something evil hovered. I remember telling my friend to run and that we needed to leave. I can still feel my hands pushing branches out of the way and smell the smoke." A haunted look entered her eyes. "I didn't see a fire. I don't remember leaving or riding back to my friend's home. The next morning I convinced myself it was just a dream. Then the police came before I asked my friend about it. Her reaction to the police was pure shock, so I knew she didn't remember."

"Was your mother outside that night?"

Tara frowned. "I never saw her. I heard she was asleep until Emily woke everyone."

"But Harlan saw you that night."

"He did. I didn't know until he came to me two days later. By then I'd convinced myself I hadn't been there, and I had a hard time believing his accusation."

"You're lucky you're alive. He has a habit of killing the people he believes can cause trouble for him."

Her face reddened, and she dropped her gaze.

Oh shit.

"You were involved with him," he said flatly, his stomach churning at the thought. "He's got to be twenty years older than you—and you were a kid."

"I was eighteen," she snapped. "People looked at me as an adult—especially men. Do you know how many men had propositioned me by the time I was sixteen? Married men. Men old enough to be my grandfather."

"I'm sorry—"

"Not your fault. But it made me view myself differently, you know? I believed they wanted me because I was special. The attention felt good. After a while I sought it out. At least Harlan wasn't married."

"Harlan told you he saw you in the woods the night of your father's death. Then what?"

"He told me to leave town and never return, or he'd kill my sisters and mother." Her gaze was steady, her voice monotone.

That sounds like the Harlan I know.

"You got a free pass because of your relationship."

"My life has not been a *free pass*." Fire shone in her eyes. "Do you know what it's like to believe the man you slept with murdered your father? And I fully believed he killed my mother until Emily told me otherwise—it still hasn't sunk in that she committed suicide. Back then her death was the proof that he was serious. My sisters would be his next targets. As I got older, I knew my husband and my daughter could be targets."

"I find it hard to believe you simply packed up and left Bartonville."

One eyebrow rose. "That's exactly what I did. When I told people I was leaving, no one seemed too surprised." She forced a laugh. "I had a reputation as a wild child. A slut. My parents were at their wits' end with me. People were happy to see me go."

"Your sisters weren't happy. Neither were your aunts."

"Doesn't matter now." Her voice cracked and pain flashed.

"Are you going to leave again?"

"No," she said firmly. "For the first time in twenty years, I feel like I can breathe. I no longer have to look over my shoulder or fear that my daughter will be killed." She tipped her head, wonder in her eyes. "You have no idea how different the world looks to me today. I don't know what to do with myself because I'm not focused on hiding. Two decades of ingrained thought patterns suddenly have no purpose. On one hand I feel free . . . on the other I've lost the impetus that drove my every action for years."

"You will find new things to strive for. Your sisters, your aunts, a new world for your daughter."

"I will, but it will take some getting used to. Bella deserves to know her family and vice versa, so we'll spend lots of time here on the coast in the future. I've missed it." Her face softened. "There's nothing like the smell of the ocean. I've avoided the entire coast since I left."

"Your family will be glad to have you back."

"Emily and I have talked, and we have a lot of catching up to do. I've missed so much. When I thought Harlan was about to kill me on that overlook, I was angry. Angry that he'd made me lose my mother and father and then twenty years with the family I had left."

"Did Emily tell you she refused to search for you all that time?"

"No." Surprise registered in her eyes.

"She was worried you were involved with your father's death. She saw you outside that night, and then you left town. She was afraid to discover the truth of why you left."

Tara was silent.

"Madison looked for you when she got older. She'd argue with Emily because she refused to help, but Emily never told Madison of her suspicions about your involvement."

"That's a heavy burden to carry for two decades," Tara whispered.

"In a twisted bit of logic, she was trying to protect you."

Tara sniffed and wiped her eyes.

"Both Madison and Emily are overjoyed to have you in their lives again. Bella too."

"They're good sisters," Tara said. Her gaze turned curious. "And what about you? Will you be around too?"

He blinked. "I work in Portland."

She shot him a withering glance. "I'm asking about Emily. The air crackles whenever you two are in the same room."

He grinned. Apparently Tara spoke her mind like Emily did. “That’s up to her.”

“Maybe you should persuade her.”

“I’m working on it.”

“Are you staying for tea?”

“I wouldn’t miss it.”

39

"I hired two waitresses. I think they'll work out," Madison told Emily as they waited at the table for the aunts to finish up whatever surprise they were making in the kitchen for tea. Emily looked almost back to normal. She had crutches to keep the weight off her injured calf, and the bandage in her hair was gone. They'd shaved part of her scalp when they stitched up the cut from her accident, but her hair covered almost all of it.

Madison had almost lost another sister. Twice.

By the grace of God, she now had both.

With Emily out of commission for the last two days, Madison had stepped up at the diner. She knew how to manage the restaurant, but this was the first time she'd relished the responsibility.

An odd feeling.

"The aunties said I only should hire one—a girl to take Lindsay's shifts—because they'd cover the floor until you were back." Madison smirked as she rolled her eyes, and Emily laughed.

"Absolutely not," agreed Emily. "They're fine to fill in for a few hours here and there, but if they did it full-time, we'd be broke. They give away too much free food."

It was true. The aunts didn't like to charge families for all the kids' meals or collect payment from friends they knew were struggling financially. "It's just a little food. We can spare it," they'd guiltily tell Madison when she caught them. The restaurant could spare food but not half of the day's receipts.

Madison relaxed in her chair and realized this was the first time in forever that a cloud of tension no longer hung between her and Emily. "You know, Em," Madison began, but she stopped. Her throat had constricted as long-forgotten emotions started to flow. She licked her lips and pushed on. "I was scared to death when I saw you struggling on the edge with Harlan and Tara. It felt like the time I'd seen you slide down it when we were kids. All I could do that day was scream. I was helpless."

Emily listened, her full attention on Madison.

"But this time I could do something, and I didn't hesitate. Zander had told me to go meet the deputies coming up the road, but something told me to follow him instead. I'm glad I did."

"I was a split second from letting him fall," admitted Emily. "I'm glad you were there."

The sisters studied each other, uncertain how to handle the fresh emotion between the two of them.

Madison took a deep breath. "I was always so jealous of you." Madison hadn't realized she had something to say. Her words had come from nowhere.

"Me?"

"You were always so perfect. You looked out for everybody, especially me." Now that she'd started, Madison couldn't stop the eruption. "I pushed everyone away."

Emily dropped her gaze. "It hurts that you didn't notice how your indifference affected me or the aunts," she said softly. "It felt as if we weren't worth caring about."

A wave of regret hit Madison. By protecting her heart, she'd hurt the people in her life. "I didn't want my heart to be destroyed again," she whispered. "First Dad, then Mom, and then Tara. It ripped me up inside. I thought it would be better if I wasn't close to anyone again.

Especially family. That way I'd never feel like my world was being devastated again."

Emily's eyes were wet. "You were so young when they died. I can see why you felt that way."

"You were only three years older . . . but you handled it like an adult. I didn't know how to do that."

"I had no choice but to stand up," Emily said. "Everyone was gone. I had to protect you."

The women were silent for a long moment, holding each other's gazes.

The enormity of the years she'd lost hit Madison. *Tara isn't the only one who sacrificed her family.*

She hated the thought of being vulnerable. But to regain what she'd lost with her sisters, she would have to do just that and take the risk.

I've got nothing to lose. And everything to gain.

Madison smiled. "I've enjoyed being the boss at the diner. You should let me do it more often."

Indecision flashed in Emily's eyes, and Madison bit her tongue to hold in her laughter. Her sister had always struggled to relinquish control. "Let me prove it."

Emily hesitated. "I can agree to that. Let's see how it goes until I'm back on my feet."

"Did Tara say how long she was staying?" Madison asked, changing the subject before Emily could change her mind.

"A few more days. It's been nice to get to know Bella. And Wendy."

"Bella loves the mansion," Madison told her. "She made me show her every inch."

"It's like a castle to a little girl. But their home in Beaverton is very nice." Emily gave a small frown. "Tara has been nagging me to spend a few weeks with them. Has she done that to you?"

"She did," Madison lied. "I can't wait." Tara had extended an open invitation to visit, but Madison noticed Tara had focused her energy on getting Emily to commit.

Madison suspected she knew why.

Emily looked past Madison, her face lighting up. Madison turned in her chair and saw Zander helping Tara into the room. She smirked.

He is the reason Tara is striving to get Emily closer to Portland.

The aunts swarmed the dining room at the same time, talking nonstop, their hands full with the tea things and plates of colorful cookies.

"Macarons!" Madison's mouth watered at the sight of the delicate French cookies. "Where did you get them?"

"Simon," Dory announced, her smile nearly as wide as her face.

Zander helped Tara into a chair by Madison and then took the seat by Emily. They exchanged a pleased glance, and he leaned closer to ask a question, frustrating Madison as the aunts' chatter kept her from eavesdropping.

She started to shoot an annoyed look at her aunts but froze at the sight of the happy women's smiles. *I'm lucky to have aunts who chatter.*

She looked from Tara to Emily, her pride growing. *And two sisters.*

There would be no more keeping everyone at arm's length.

They are worth it.

"How are you feeling?" Zander asked Emily. Her blood warmed at the sound of his voice as his gaze held hers.

"Better every day."

"We need to talk."

Her heart stuttered. *Has he changed his mind?* But there was no regret or concern on his face. He looked more relaxed than she'd ever seen him, his gray eyes serene and patient.

Did my toes just curl?

"Are you saying that the Fitch case is over?" she asked, curving her lips, remembering his promise to her in his SUV.

"I am." Satisfaction colored his words.

"So now what?" Worry sparked. She had thought long and hard about whether she wanted a long-distance relationship, and the answer had eluded her. Driving back and forth for hours would wear on both of them.

Is it worth trying?

Tara.

Emily's gaze shot to her sister in conversation with Aunt Thea, a suspicion forming. "Tara wants me to spend a few weeks with her. Or more. She's been very persistent about it."

Zander tipped his head. "You don't say."

"Faking innocence doesn't suit you."

"Getting you closer to Portland for a while was her idea. You'll get to know her and Bella, and we can spend time together without me being on the clock." He studied her face. "Will you do it?"

"Yes." *Absolutely.* She couldn't stop her smile.

"Good . . . and I found something you might be interested in." He handed her a small, narrow box. "Madison told me how much it meant to you and your sisters. And Simon Rhoads helped me find it. You're right . . . he'll do anything for Dory—or you."

Emily took the box in apprehension. "You didn't need to—"

"It's nothing."

His gaze was on the box, avoiding her eyes. *It's something.*

"I know the original was lost in the fire, but this one is close," he said.

She barely knew Zander Wells. She didn't know where he had grown up, how he liked his steak, or what kind of music he enjoyed. But she *knew* him. She knew his character; he had integrity and honor and intelligence.

He was a good man.

She lifted the lid off the small white box and lost her breath. "Where did you find it?"

"Like I said, Simon did most of the work. I asked him about it, and it became a mission for him." He leaned closer.

The bracelet of buttons in the box started to blur. She picked it up, examining each button. Someone had invested a lot of time and effort to make a very special bracelet.

Damn, how I loved the original.

This bracelet was so similar. But that wasn't the important aspect. What was important was that Zander had listened and cared.

She blinked away tears and studied him. A fresh vulnerability shone in his eyes.

How did this happen so fast?

"I need a date for a wedding this summer," he finally said, holding her gaze.

"Ava's?" Emily had hoped to see the agent again.

"Will you go with me? She'd be thrilled to see you."

"Is that what you want?" she asked, an undertone in her question, her heart in her throat.

"Absolutely."

ACKNOWLEDGMENTS

Thank you to Colleen Lindsay and Anh Schluep, who helped me brainstorm the skeleton of this story, and to Charlotte Herscher, who supervised the addition of the flesh.

My readers have begged for a book for Zander Wells since his first appearance in my Callahan & McLane series, and I'm excited that I found a way to make that happen.

Thank you to all the usual suspects on my Montlake team. I count my blessings every day that I work with the most innovative publishing house in the world.

Thank you *so* much to my partner in crime Melinda Leigh, who patiently listens to me moan and groan when the words won't come and always suggests I blow something up when my plot gets stuck.

WANT TO LEARN HOW ZANDER, MASON, AND AVA MET? READ THE FIRST CHAPTER OF *VANISHED*, THE FIRST BOOK IN THE CALLAHAN & MCLANE SERIES

Mason Callahan hadn't seen Josie in three months.

The leanness of her face and the indentations above her collarbones told him she'd lost weight. In a bad way.

Time hadn't been kind to her, and the scabbed sores on her cheeks hinted that meth was probably the new love of her life.

There'd been a time when he'd fought a bit of an attraction to the woman.

She'd been sweet and eager to please, a pretty woman in a wholesome-country-song sort of way.

She and Mason shared a rural background and a similar taste in music that'd made her more enjoyable than his other confidential informants.

But now she'd never work with him again.

His fingers tightened on the brim of the cowboy hat in his hand, and he swallowed hard at the sight of her contorted body on the floor of the bathroom in her cramped apartment.

Anger abruptly blurred his vision. Someone had taken a baseball bat to her skull. The murder weapon was dumped in the shower, blood and hair sticking to the bat.

"Holy mother of God," muttered his partner, Ray Lusco.

The two detectives had spent several years responding to brutal crimes as part of the Oregon State Police's Major Crimes Unit. But this was the first time they'd both known the victim. Josie's murder wouldn't be their case.

Their sergeant had assigned it to another pair of detectives, knowing that Mason had worked with Josie several times for information during a prostitute murder case. Detectives Duff Morales and Steve Hunsinger were the team chosen to find justice for Josie. Mason would look over their shoulders and ride their asses the entire time.

"You got your look. Now get out of my crime scene," Morales said from the hallway.

Mason glanced back at the man but didn't move. He and Ray were still studying the scene. Josie had broken fingers. She'd tried to protect herself against the bat, perhaps even tried to grab it from her attacker. Once she was on the bathroom floor, the attacker had continued to beat her. Arcs of blood trailed up the walls to the ceiling, where the weapon had flung blood as it was whipped up for another swing at her head.

"What are the bits of broken green metal by her head?" Lusco asked.

"Earrings. Christmas balls," answered Morales.

Mason silently swore. Did Josie's family expect her for Christmas next week? Did she have family? He'd seen the decorated plastic tree in her living room. A few presents were stashed below, waiting for eager hands to rip them open.

Mason closed his eyes, remembering the last time he'd met Josie at the Starbucks four blocks away. She'd ordered the biggest, most sugary Frappuccino on the menu and talked a mile a minute. Had she already been using meth? He'd assumed she'd been overcaffeinated and lonely. Even prostitutes get lonely for conversation. They'd been an odd pair. The perky prostitute and the cowboy detective.

He'd followed her back to her tiny apartment because she had some twenties from a john who was part of a recent big drug bust. Mason wanted to tell her the bills probably wouldn't have prints or aid the investigation, but he went along because she wanted to help and seemed to need some company.

Being in her home had been a bit awkward. He'd been hyperaware of the intimacy of simply standing in her feminine space. She'd offered him a soda, which he'd declined, but he'd accepted her suggestion that he grab a bottled water from the fridge for the road. Her fridge held water, soda, and milk. Nothing else. What did she eat? He should have known then that she was using drugs instead of calories to function. He'd exchanged her bills for some out of his own pocket and offered her sixty dollars extra. She'd politely turned it down, but he'd tucked the money under the saltshaker on her kitchen counter, and she'd pretended not to notice.

Mason had seen enough of Josie's blood. He turned and pushed past Lusco and the other pair of detectives, avoiding eye contact. He strode into her tiny kitchen. The kitchen was a nasty-smelling pit of dirty dishes and take-out containers. On his previous visit it'd been immaculate.

The saltshaker was still there—part of a set of silver cats—but the money was gone. He scanned the sad room. It wasn't even a room, more like a large closet with a sink and small microwave. He wanted to open the fridge to see if she'd finally added food, but he knew he couldn't touch anything until the crime scene unit had processed the apartment. The kitchen showed cracks in the counters from age and heavy use. Sort of how Josie had always looked. Her cracks had shown in the stress lines around her eyes and mouth. Lines that shouldn't have been present on a woman younger than thirty.

Who slipped through your cracks, Josie?

She'd told Mason she never brought johns back to her apartment.

She'd kept a careful line between her work and where she lived. Had she broken her own rule? Or had someone followed her?

"Just another dead hooker," said a voice behind Mason.

He whirled around to find an unfamiliar Portland police officer studying him with sharp eyes.

"Show a little respect," snapped Mason.

The officer smirked, and Mason wanted to use the bloody bat on his head.

"She's been picked up three times in the last month. Twice for public intoxication and once for a catfight with some other hookers. I have a hard time feeling sorry for her," the officer stated.

Mason was taken aback. That didn't sound like the Josie he knew. Why hadn't she reached out to him if she was having problems? He'd smoothed her way out of small jams before. Had she gotten into something she didn't want him to know about?

"Let's get out of here," said Ray. Mason's partner had silently moved to the doorway of the closet-size kitchen and had probably witnessed the anger on Mason's face.

Mason shoved his hat on his head and moved past the uniform.

The officer barely turned to give him room to get by.

"Nice hat," the officer muttered at Mason's retreating back.

Mason ignored him. He didn't mind the occasional jabs about his hat. Or his cowboy boots. He was comfortable with his clothes. Cowboy hats were rare on the west side of the Cascade mountain range, but when he headed back to his hometown of Pendleton on the east side of the state, they popped up everywhere.

Right now he was upset that he hadn't checked up on Josie.

Usually he heard from her about once a month with information she wanted to sell. He hadn't heard a peep from her in three months, and she hadn't crossed his mind.

Guilt.

He followed Ray out the apartment door and down the dark stairwell. They avoided the elevator in the old apartment building. The stairwells might stink of piss, but it beat getting trapped for a few hours in an old creaking elevator. It'd happened twice to other detectives in other buildings. Mason didn't care to share the experience.

He pushed through the outer door into the bright sunshine and sucked in a breath of icy air. It was one of those rare clear winter weeks in the Pacific Northwest when residents dug out their sunglasses and pretended not to need heavy coats. Mason's skin soaked in the sun that'd been hiding behind dark-gray rain clouds for months. He'd nearly forgotten that the sky could be such an intense blue.

A few groups of people clustered on the sidewalk, squinting in the sun and speculating as they studied the four double-parked police cars. The Portland neighborhood was made up of dozens of short apartment buildings and old houses on narrow streets. It was a neighborhood known for its population of college kids and transient adults. No one stayed very long. Ray glanced at his watch.

"Almost noon. Want to grab a bite?"

Mason muttered that he wasn't hungry as he pulled out his silenced cell phone. He had five missed calls from his ex-wife. *Shit. Jake.*

His heart sped up, and he returned the calls with abruptly icy fingers. "Something's up with Jake," he said to Ray. "Robin has called five times in the last half hour."

"Is he home from college for winter break?" Ray asked.

"Robin picked him up from the airport two days ago. I haven't heard a word from the kid except for a reply to my text asking if he'd landed safely." His son lived with his ex-wife, her new husband, and their joint young daughters. Mason had planned to reach out to his son this weekend to see if he wanted to go to the next Trail Blazers basketball game.

Just as he expected Robin's cell phone to go to voice mail, she finally answered. "Mason?" she asked.

Almost ten years had passed since their divorce, but he knew from the tone of her voice that she was terrified.

"What happened? Is Jake okay?" he barked into the phone.

"Jake's fine." Robin's voice cracked. "It's Henley. She's missing."

She burst into sobs.

Mason's mind went blank. *Henley? Who—*

"Lucas is a mess," Robin wept.

Aha. Henley was Robin's stepdaughter. Mason couldn't remember the girl's age. Early teens? Jake rarely mentioned her, and Mason had met the girl only once or twice. She lived with her mother most of the time.

"When was she seen last? Did you call the police? How long's she been missing?" Mason rapid-fired the questions at his ex.

"Of course we called the police. Clackamas County sheriff. She's been missing since this morning. She left for school, but they say she never made it." Robin's voice was steadier.

"School's not out for vacation yet?"

"Today's the last day."

"Okay. I'll call Clackamas County and see what's going on. How old is she?"

"Eleven," Robin whispered.

Crap. Mason closed his eyes. "We'll find her."

Mason shifted his weight from boot to boot as he waited for Lucas Fairbanks to usher him into his home. The entryway of the accountant's suburban house was huge, with a heavy wood-and-iron door that belonged in a castle. And the home looked exactly like the other fifty homes in the suburban upper-middle-class subdivision. Mason had never been a fan of Lucas, but he respected the man for doing a decent job of helping raise Jake. Robin had always seemed happy once she'd married the accountant.

Lucas had succeeded where Mason had failed. Robin had known she was marrying a cop when she married Mason, but she hadn't understood how hard it would be to always come in second place to the job. Mason had tried to get home at a reasonable time each night, but it was rare. Crime didn't work nine to five, and neither did he. During the divorce Robin admitted she'd spent years thinking of herself as a single parent to save her sanity. It was the only way she could mentally cope with his absences. Otherwise she was always waiting and waiting. In her head it made more sense for her to never expect him; that way she was never disappointed. When he managed to walk in the door in time for dinner, it was a nice surprise.

Mason followed Lucas into his formal dining room and tried not to gawk at the flashy chandelier. The room was packed with adults. Outside there'd been three cars from the Lake Oswego Police Department, two Clackamas County vehicles, an unmarked police car, and three generic American sedans that indicated the FBI had arrived. Mason scanned the room, searching for familiar faces. He didn't know any of the officers. Robin sat at the table, gripping the hand of another woman, who spoke with two men in suits. Both women had a well-used pile of tissues in front of them. Mason figured the other woman to be Henley's mother, Lilian.

Mason had never seen a slump in Lucas's shoulders. His usual chipper greeting had been severely muted, and he looked like he'd been sick for weeks. "The FBI is sending more people," Lucas said quietly. "I guess they have some sort of specialized team they pull from the other West Coast offices to respond to kidnappings."

“The CARD team,” Mason answered. “Child Abduction Rapid Deployment. They take this shit seriously. We all do.” He swallowed hard and thanked heaven again that it wasn’t his kid who was missing.

He glanced at Lucas and felt instantly guilty. The man was staring at his ex-wife as she sobbed on Robin’s shoulder. Mason didn’t know how their marriage had broken up. He’d never asked and now it didn’t matter. They had a little girl to find.

The Oregon State Police would offer resources, but Mason couldn’t be one of them. As a family member, he couldn’t be an official part of the investigation. But he’d set a plan in motion to get around that rule. He’d already requested some time off. And God protect anyone who tried to tell him his help wasn’t needed.

“Tell me what happened,” he said in a low voice to Lucas.

Lucas glanced at the two women and then jerked his head for Mason to follow him into the breezeway between the kitchen and dining room.

“Henley has been staying with us this week. Usually I get her one of the two weeks of winter vacation, but her mom asked me to add this extra week while she got some work done. Henley left for the bus stop like normal at about seven thirty this morning. Robin watched her walk out the door. A few hours later, her mom called, asking if Henley had stayed home sick from school, because she was getting automated calls and emails that Henley wasn’t at school.”

“The school will contact you if your kid doesn’t show up?” Mason asked.

Lucas nodded. “You’re supposed to call in on a special line if your kid will be missing any part of school that day. I know we forgot once or twice with Jake when he stayed home sick, and so we got a bunch of notifications. It’s a good system.”

“But it still takes a few hours to process.”

“Well, they have to compare the attendance to the sick calls. That’s entered by hand. Discrepancies trigger the calls and emails.”

"What happened when Lilian called here?"

"Robin assured her Henley had gone to school and immediately called the school to confirm that she was there. I think Lilian called them too. Henley's homeroom teacher said she hadn't shown up."

"What about the school bus driver? What about the other kids on the bus? Anyone talk to Henley's friends?" Mason rattled off question after question.

Lucas seemed to deflate more. "They're working on all that."

"Wait. How does Henley ride the bus if she doesn't usually live with you?"

"We live in the same school district and have the same elementary school boundaries."

"I didn't know you lived so close to your ex. Has it always been like that?"

"Yes, Lilian has a place about five minutes from here. It's really convenient for Henley. Lilian and I get along pretty well."

"Is she remarried? Do they have more kids?"

Lucas shook his head, and his gaze went over Mason's shoulder as the volume rose in the dining room. Mason turned around to see more people joining the group—judging by the dull suits, FBI agents.

Good. No one knew more about child abductions, and the unique skills the FBI could offer to the local police were gold. Depending on its size, a police department might deal with one major child abduction over a decade. The FBI dealt with them monthly. Mason had never seen the CARD team in action, but he'd heard good things.

Mason turned back to Lucas. "Officially I can't join whatever task force they set up, but I can help as a family member. I'll be the family voice for the media and the liaison to the police and FBI. Let me do this for you guys. I've already told work I'm taking some time off. However long it takes to bring Henley home."

Lucas started to refuse, and Mason put a hand on his shoulder, giving the man a little shake. "Listen to me. Your wife and ex-wife are gonna need you for support. You don't have time to deal with the politics of the situation. I know how these guys work. Let me handle that. Everything I find out, I'll immediately pass on to you. Robin, Lilian, and you are going to want to be in the center of the investigation, and that's not going to help."

Lucas's eyes looked bleak. "Will they let you do that?"

"If you back me up. Make it clear you'll step back a bit, and they might be more accepting."

Desperation lurked in Lucas's gaze as he looked into one of Mason's eyes and then the other. "I don't know what to do," he whispered. "I have to help. I have to know what's going on. She's my *daughter*, for God's sake. I can't just step back and do nothing."

"You won't be idle. They're going to interview the heck out of all of you. Over and over. Everything you can tell them will help, but they're not going to let you look over shoulders in the command center. I'll do that and report back to you."

"Command center?" Lucas's voice cracked. "You think they'll need—"

"They'll set up something within the hour, I'm sure. You need to let them do their job. That's going to be your hardest role." Mason frowned as he glanced back at the growing crowd. He'd originally hated Lucas with a passion, ever since he'd first heard Jake excitedly talk about the man. Lucas was everything Mason wasn't. He'd coached every boy sport in existence, and Mason had never heard a foul word from the man's mouth. Lucas always had a big smile. Until today. Mason had fought the urge to wipe the smile off Lucas's face the first few times he'd met him, believing the man was gloating. But it had turned out he was one of those rare always-happy guys. Lucas wasn't a faker. It'd taken years for Mason to accept that the man was the real thing. He couldn't have asked for a better man to help raise his son.

Didn't mean they had to be best friends.

Guilt swept through him again as he remembered all the resentment he'd held against the man. Part of Mason had been jealous that he hadn't created the type of picket-fence family with Robin that she had with Lucas. Now he wouldn't want to be in this man's shoes for anything.

"Where's Jake?" Mason asked. His son hadn't made an appearance.

"In his room. He was down here for a while but said he couldn't handle seeing his mom fall apart. I don't blame him," Lucas said with a glance at his wife. She and Lilian were still clutching hands but paying close attention to the man speaking quietly with them.

A dizzying need to see his son swamped Mason. "I'll be right back." He left Lucas behind as he headed for the stairs.